THE
JACK MCCLURE
SERIES

ALSO BY
ERIC VAN LUSTBADER

ERIC VAN LUSTBADER

BELOVED ENEMY

HEAD
ZEUS

First published in the USA in 2013 by Forge Books,
an imprint of Tom Doherty Associates.

This paperback edition first published in the UK in 2014 by
Head of Zeus Ltd.

9 7 5 3 1 2 4 6 8

A catalogue record for this book is available from the British Library.

Paperback ISBN 9781781856208
Ebook ISBN 9781781856178

Printed and bound by CPI Group (

Head of Zeus Ltd
Clerkenwell House
45-47 Clerkenwell Green
London EC1R 0HT

WWW.HEADOFZEUS.COM

What Came Before

Four years ago, while on assignment in Moscow with the late president, Jack McClure was introduced to Annika Dementieva through a violent incident set up by her grandfather, Dyadya Gourdjiev, a man of great charisma with a Machiavellian mind. Gourdjiev needed Jack to solve a vexing puzzle for him that ran all the way from Ukraine to the highest levels of American government. During this time, Annika was forced to lie to Jack again and again. Nevertheless, the two were gripped by a powerful attraction, and fell in love—a love that was to be tested time and again in the ensuing years. Jack learned that Annika had been abducted by her father, causing her mother's death. Gourdjiev bent all his will to getting her back. It took years, during which time Annika's politically powerful father subjected her to unspeakable abuse. But it wasn't only Annika who loved Jack—her grandfather saw qualities in him that caused him to subtly alter his plan, so that when he died Jack was drawn more tightly into Annika's orbit. Jack discovered that the old man had formed an alliance with Iraj Namazi—known to the world as the Syrian—a terrorist more interested in money and power than ideology. What the two men were planning was a mystery, but Gourdjiev's death brought Annika to the Syrian's side, parting her once again from Jack.

To gain, you must yield;
to grasp, let go;
to win, lose.

–Chinese proverb

God has given you one face,
and you make yourself another.

–Hamlet to Ophelia, Act III, Scene 1

BELOVED ENEMY

PROLOGUE

APRIL 21

Méribel, Switzerland

Jack McClure, squeezing through a tapering tube of icy metal, had run out of options. There was no way back; he had to go forward, farther into this curved tube—a massive decorative talon, one of four built at the corners of the chalet's roof.

He inched forward, his breath coming in steaming clouds. In front of him, sunlight slid into the open end of the talon. It seemed to inch toward him with a terrible slowness. Placing one hand in front of the other, one knee sliding forward, then the other, he continued on, while the tube shrank around him. Ahead of him, the brightness of sunlight quickened. Just a few feet more.

And then he stopped. He was stuck. He tried to push forward, but there was no room. A kind of panic welled up in him—the same feeling he'd had as a child when the letters on the pages of books he tried to read swam in front of his eyes like schools of frightened fish.

He closed his eyes, emptied his mind of panic, then of fear. His mind's eye looked around, found the place outside himself of perfect calm. He projected himself there. The place fit over him like a familiar glove, giving to his particular contours. Here he felt safe.

Here he could accomplish anything—even interpret two-dimensional objects.

Relaxing his body, he breathed out, emptying his lungs. And moved forward, out of the icy talon, into the brilliant sunlight, the landscape dominated by sparkling Alps. For a moment, he clung to the outside of the talon, then he made his careful way along its curved length, to alight at last on the chalet's roof.

He crouched down, fired the Airweight three times.

Then the Syrian appeared in the helo's open doorway, a gun aimed at him.

"You poor fool!" Namazi shouted over the rotors' din. "Do you know what you've done?"

Jack kept on coming. Now he was within two or three yards of the rising helo.

The Syrian stared fixedly at Jack. His gun hand was perfectly steady. "Annika will never forgive you for this. Never," he said, and fired.

PART ONE

TERMINAL

Ten Days Ago

ONE

"I caught him on the rooftop, diagonally across from the club. It was twilight, the best time, in my opinion, for sniper work, so I was lucky. I admit that. I was also pretty pissed off: a fucking sniper at my rdv. A leak somewhere, that was what I was thinking when I came at him . . ."

"This was in Bangkok," Jack McClure said.

Dennis Paull, the head of homeland security, nodded. "That's right."

The two men were sitting in Paull's study, secreted within his red brick, Federal-era townhouse in Georgetown. Outside, a velvet night had descended, along with a rain that pattered softly, misting the windowpanes.

Jack shifted in the leather club chair. "How long ago?"

"Legere's rendezvous or his debriefing?"

"Both."

Paull opened a dossier on the desk in front of him. It was buff-colored, with a black stripe down the left side, denoting Eyes Only status. He looked sallow and worn, his pale gray eyes lying sunken within dark circles. "The encounter occurred eight days ago. The debriefing, which was conducted by myself, a day later."

Jack sat forward. "You conducted the debriefing alone?"

"Legere is my asset."

"I didn't know about him."

Paull's eyes flicked up to encounter Jack's steady gaze.

"Nor did I know why you had gone to Bangkok. Why didn't you tell me?"

"I'm telling you now."

"Now," Jack said, taking a sip of his Bulleit rye, "that there's a problem."

Paull sat back in his swivel chair. "And you're my problem solver." He cocked his head. "What is it, Jack?"

"Nothing."

"Don't give me that."

Jack sighed, placed the old-fashioned glass on his boss's desk. "Ever since I got back from Sharm el-Sheikh I've been under the impression there's a glass wall between us."

"You're wrong." Paull took up his three fingers of bourbon, sipped it thoughtfully, then placed the glass precisely three inches to the right of the open dossier. "It wasn't Sharm el-Sheikh; Sharm el-Sheikh is where all the debts were settled, where Alli's past was finally healed. How is she, by the way? Adjusting to Interpol's procedures?"

"She's based out of Paris, but currently she's on assignment; a back of beyond where she's unreachable."

"Good for her. But, Fearington being an FBI feeder academy, I had assumed she'd apply there."

"I don't think that was ever her intention. In any case, she needed to gain some distance from recent events." Jack waved away the diversion. "Let's get back to the problem at hand."

"We are faced with several problems," Paull interjected. "Let's start with Rome. It's what happened in Rome that concerns me."

"Specifically Annika."

"Specifically the Syrian, or should I say Iraj Namazi, the Iranian, so you have informed me." His gaze fell heavily on Jack. "Annika is now with Namazi, in what capacity . . ." He paused, thinking out the route he would take. "Now that her grandfather is dead, she's allied herself with Namazi, isn't that right?"

Jack nodded. He didn't trust himself to speak. His breath was hot in his throat, and his heart contracted at the reminder of Annika's latest betrayal.

"This woman," Paull said, "is perhaps the most dangerous female on the planet." He reached for his bourbon, then seemed to change his mind. "This is the woman you love."

"Loved," Jack said, finding his voice. "Past tense."

"Is that so?" Paull steepled his fingers, tapping the tips together ruminatively.

"It is, Dennis."

"You can turn it on and off at will." His tone made his skepticism clear. "You'd tell me if it were otherwise, wouldn't you, Jack?"

"I would." Jack nodded to the tape recorder on Paull's desk. "Let's get on with it."

"We're talking now of allegiance." Paull turned his glass around and around on the desktop. "Speaking bluntly, my fear is that you'll try to find her."

"I'm your problem solver, Dennis. That's why you hired me; that's why I'm here." But Jack now knew that Paull had a second agenda. In addition to being a fine administrator, he was an astute judge of human nature. Possibly the two facilities were intertwined. He knew full well how deep Jack's love affair with Annika went. In addition, though he and Jack had never spoken of it, he suspected there was depth to Jack's friendship with Annika's grandfather, Dyadya Gourdjiev, murdered a year ago in Rome.

As if to prove Jack right, Paull said, "It's not just Annika. Now that she's shown her true colors, your relationship with her is, I think, complicated enough without members of her family further gumming up the works."

"What works?" Jack said, a bit too sharply.

"Your thought processes." Paull leaned forward suddenly, elbows on the desk. "Your intense loyalty is one of your strengths, Jack. But, in this case, I wonder if it might become a liability."

"I haven't thought about it," Jack lied.

Under Paull's penetrating gaze, he reached out and depressed the "play" button. Legere's plummy voice rolled out across the wood-paneled study:

"He must have heard me because he swung the M82A3 Special Application scoped rifle right into my face—"

Jack stiffened. "That's a U.S. Marine weapon."

Paull nodded, silent.

"Beneath this thick bandage the wound is horrendous."

"Legere was pointing to his cheek," Paull said.

"I'll need plastic surgery. I can't go back into the field with this on my face. How would I ever melt into a crowd? It's like a neon sign."

Paull's voice on the tape said, *"The sniper,"* guiding Legere back on track.

Legere: "Yes, well, I hope he was a better sniper than he was a hand-to-hand fighter."

Paull: "And yet you killed him."

Legere: "An accident. I hit him, his knees buckled, and he fell against the concrete parapet. The back of his head split open."

Paull: "Pity he couldn't tell you who he worked for."

Legere: "I know who he worked for: the Syrian."

Paull: "Have you brought me proof?"

Legere: "The sniper's rifle. Who else but the Syrian would have access to a U.S. Marine rifle?"

Paull: "Please continue."

Legere: "I found the sniper after twenty minutes of recon of the rdv's immediate area. It was now one hundred hours. I went into the club."

Paull: "Name."

Legere: "WTF. It's at Thonglor Soi 10. Very *farang* friendly, so I felt right at home. Lots of girls in shorts cut so high you can see the lower hemis of their ass cheeks. They're all dancing in super high heels, though God alone knows how. Snotty kids, anyway."

Paull: "Your contact, Legere."

Legere: "Right. I bellied up at the far end of the neon-lit bar, just as planned. He came in several minutes later, ordered a drink, then, after checking out the nightlife, sauntered over to where I stood. We exchanged the proper parole and got right down to it."

Paull: "What did he say?"

Legere: "You're right. There's a worm in the casket. The Syrian has a mole high up in the U.S. government. *Very* high up."

Paull: "Which branch?"

Legere: "Well, I . . ."

Paull: "Out with it, damnit!"

Legere: [sighs deeply] "That's just it. The contact's head exploded, and I turned tail and ran."

Paull: "You ran."

Legere: "The place was a fucking madhouse—blood all over the bar, people screaming, vomiting at the sight of the contact's brains and fragments of his skull bobbing in their gin blossom specials. I'd never have found the shooter, and the cops, who keep an eagle eye on these places after midnight, were already infiltrating the club floor. I did the only thing I could do: I got the hell out of there."

Paull: "Without the name of the Syrian's mole or where he works."

Legere: "I fucked up. In retrospect, the sniper was a feint. The real assassin was waiting in the club. The Syrian's as clever as a demon."

Paull: "The question to answer now, Legere, is how your rdv was compromised. It wasn't from this end. You and I were the only ones who knew about your assignment."

Legere: "That means someone on the ground in Bangkok."

Paull: "Someone you met or spoke to."

Legere: "Boss, no one knew why I was in Bangkok. No one."

Paull: "Clearly not true. Go back over it in your mind."

[A pause.]

Legere: "I'm clean, I swear. Maybe my contact said something inadvertently."

Paull: "You were shadowing him that day. Where was he before the rdv?"

Legere: "At a massage parlor he frequents, off Phaholyothin Road, in Soi Aree."

Paull: "That's clear across town."

Legere: "Which gave me the time to do my reconnoiter of the rdv site."

Paull: "All right. What was the name of your contact?"

Legere: "Connaston. Leroy Connaston."

Paull: "Whose idea was it to meet in Bangkok?"

Legere: "His."

Paull: "And WTF?"

Legere: "Also. He said he felt secure there, amid all the young people, all the frantic energy."

Paull: "Maybe he had a death wish."

Legere: "There's another possibility."

Paull: "Out with it."

Legere: "The Syrian turned Connaston, promised him the world if he led him to me."

Paull: "But it was Connaston the Syrian killed, not you."

Legere: "The Syrian is a notorious paranoid. Would you trust a man who could be turned? Besides, he has now ID'd me. If he killed me, another agent he wouldn't know would just follow in my foot-steps."

Paull: "The devil you know."

Legere: "Right."

[Another pause.]

Paull: "Okay, Legere, hang tight and don't leave Bangkok. I'm going to need you again."

Paull, reaching out, stopped the tape. He looked up at Jack. "That was the last time I—or anyone else, for that matter—had contact with Pyotr Legere. His mobile number is dead. The safe house he had been using has been cleaned out. None of my agents-in-place have been able to find him. He's fallen off the face of the earth." He sat back. "Which is where you come in."

"You want me to follow in his footsteps," Jack said.

Paull nodded. "It is imperative that we find the Syrian's mole, Jack. Do you understand my concerns now?"

"Iraj Namazi had Dyadya Gourdjiev killed."

"Interpol sent on the official police reports from Rome. Gourdjiev was a victim of a hit-and-run."

"Why would you believe an Italian police report?" Jack said curtly. "Namazi killed him or ordered him killed. I want to find him, too."

"Have you proof that the report is false?"

"I know what I know."

"No, for you this is all emotion." Paull's eyes glittered in the lamplight. "This is what I'm talking about, Jack. Gourdjiev—"

"I knew Gourdjiev."

"You *thought* you knew him. The man was a snake in human form. He lacked both morals and scruples." Paull worried his lower lip with his finger. "You want to find Iraj Namazi. I'm ordering you to find Pyotr Legere and, with his help, run down Namazi's mole."

"I can do both."

"God alone knows how much damage the mole has done or how much of our intentions abroad, our secret intel, Namazi possesses."

"I understand."

"I wonder if you do, Jack. There is an obsessive streak in you."

"Dennis—"

"Don't try to fool me. The Dementieva woman has gotten

under your skin. I'll be honest. If I could find her, I'd terminate her with extreme prejudice."

Jack sat very still, scarcely breathing.

Paull rose and, coming around from behind his desk, perched on the corner closest to where Jack sat. "I'm afraid that your obsession has blinded you as to just how dangerous Annika Dementieva is."

Jack was silent.

Paull leaned forward, his hands clasped as if he were a priest. "If push comes to shove, Jack, would you be able to kill her, or would she kill you?"

Jack remained silent, his gaze unwavering.

Turning, Paull grabbed his drink and slowly sipped what was left of it. "You're biting off more . . . you're in danger of choking to death."

"It's my life, Dennis. My funeral." He stood and held out his hand, and Paull, keeping the dossier open on his desk, handed Jack a micro SD card.

"This material is all I have, Jack. Take it in to the living room and memorize it before you leave." He, too, stood up. "Take as long as you need."

Jack nodded.

As he was about to enter the open doorway, Paull said, "I hope to God you're ready for this, Jack."

Jack turned back. "I think we both are."

He took his drink and, slipping the SD card into his phone, went out of the study, down the darkened hallway, and stepped into the townhouse's burnished-wood living room. The comfortable furniture was a vivid reminder of Louise, Paull's deceased wife, who had supervised the decor. Photos and mementos of Paull's college and service life, as well as family photos, lined the narrow shelves.

Jack chose a spot at the end of one of the plush sofas and, setting his drink down on a round end table, settled himself against the cushions and keyed on his phone, scrolling to the electronic copy of the dossier on Pyotr Legere. Apart from the written transcript of the debriefing Paull had played for him, there was some brief background on Paull's secret contact.

At first the paragraphs looked like a school of frightened fish, swimming in all directions. This was Jack's dyslexia at work. He took a deep breath. When he let it out, he emptied his mind of all thought, projecting himself to a spot of absolute calm just to the right of where he sat. From this place of utter peace, he looked again at the paragraphs, which now began to form into recognizable letters, chunks of letters—words—then sentences, lined up, one by one, in, neat, orderly progression.

He began to read:

Pyotr Legere grew up in Moscow, the only child of Galina Yemchevya, chief translator for the Kremlin, and Giles Legere, a trade legate for a prestigious Parisian and New York art gallery, in permanent residence in Moscow. An attached client list included everyone from the president, select Kremlin ministers, and FSB top-tier officers, to the oligarch overlords, who, in league with the Kremlin, ran the major businesses in Russia.

Jack came to a photo of Pyotr. Though black-and-white and slightly blurred, the photo revealed a darkly handsome man in his late twenties, with a long face. A distinctly Gallic nose and deep-set eyes leant him the curiously anachronistic demeanor of an eighteenth-century swashbuckler.

Pyotr owned a bookstore in central Moscow, a shop specializing in technical manuals, but occasionally he also sold paintings, doubtless left over from his father's personal collection, though he had been seen purchasing the odd painting at auction. In addition, he operated a Web site, connected with the store, which offered specialized technical apps for mobile phones and tablets. Very cutting edge.

Jack now turned to the transcript of the debriefing. He went through it slowly and painstakingly, contrasting the words to what he had heard coming from the tape, so that he could almost taste them. He added to this the memory of Pyotr's photo contained on the micro SD card. This image was most helpful when he came to sections he hadn't heard. Paull had only played him the relevant parts; he absorbed the complete debriefing as it scrolled slowly across his mobile's screen.

It was after two a.m. when he finished. Rising, he crossed the living room and went down the short hall, but when he stepped into Paull's study his boss was nowhere to be seen and neither was the dossier, though Jack performed a thorough search. Probably Paull had gone up to bed. Shrugging, Jack went silently back through the house, letting himself out the back door. He spoke briefly with Lenny, one of the men on guard duty that night. Lenny told him a dirty joke and both men laughed, then Jack got into his car and drove home. Twenty minutes after he turned the key in his front door he was fast asleep, having only partially undressed.

He dreamt of walking down a seemingly endless corridor, dank and so poorly lit he could not make out any significant details. His rhythmic footsteps echoed off the bare walls. At some point he became aware of another set of footsteps, but whether they were behind or in front of him he could not tell, though he peered in both directions. His heart rate increased with his anxiety, until . . .

He awoke with a start, the sound of the other set of footsteps still in his ears. Then, as the last vestiges of sleep cleared, he sat up. There were the footsteps—they were in his house, moving stealthily about. Reaching out, he drew open the drawer of his night table, but his gun wasn't there. Where had he last left it? He passed a hand across his forehead, came away with a slick of sweat. He couldn't recall. He grasped the LED flashlight in the drawer instead.

Rolling off the bed, he crossed to his closet. Reaching inside, he grasped the baseball bat Gus had given him years ago and, turning, stepped out into the darkened hallway, moving to the head of the staircase to the ground floor. The house was pitch-black. It stood at the end of Westmoreland Ave, just over the Maryland border. There was no moon, and the nearest lights were streets away.

He stood stock still, listening to the movements. At first, he thought they were random, but soon enough he discovered that whoever was in his house was performing a formal grid search. Not a burglar or a street punk high on crack cocaine, then; a professional.

He slipped down the staircase, placing his bare feet carefully to avoid the old, dried-out wooden treads he knew creaked. It was an old house, one he had lived in from the time he had run away from home and been taken in by the former owner, a huge black man named Gus. Gus had owned a hockshop where Jack had worked until Gus had been murdered and Jack had set out to find his killer.

Jack felt Gus's presence in every room of the house, a kindly, ghostly presence that he often fancied looked out for him. Jack stopped in the kitchen. The intruder was in the next room. He could feel the tiny electrical pulses coming through the open doorway to the dining room. Listening again, Jack deduced two things: whoever had broken in did not know the layout of the house's interior, and the intruder was searching for his bedroom, which meant he or she was after him.

Silence.

Pressing his back against the kitchen wall, he turned toward the opening, listening as the small, furtive sounds rose again. The intruder was heading toward him. He raised the flashlight and, as the shadowed figure appeared, switched it on, bringing the beam to bear on the intruder's face.

At once, he saw the flash of a service pistol, and he swung the light away, palmed the kitchen light on. A dark-skinned hand over his plunged them both back into darkness.

"No lights, Jack." Nona Heroe's voice was both hushed and urgent. "No one must know that you're home."

Jack's heart leapt. "Is someone watching the house?"

"Let's hope not."

Nona, a Metro police detective in charge of the violent crimes unit Jack had worked with last year, had recently been promoted to chief of detectives by the new commissioner, after her boss, Alan Fraine, had been killed. She was a fine detective, serious-minded, with a keen brain and an acute sense of danger. That, combined with her tone of voice, brought Jack up short.

"Nona, what's going on?"

"Grab your coat." As she followed Jack back through the darkened house to the entryway, she added, in her soft, round New Orleans–inflected tones, "Do you have your passport on you?"

"Always."

"Get rid of it," she said. "Leave it here."

"What? Why?"

At that moment, twin beams of a vehicle's headlights swung across the front windows.

"Another egress," Nona snapped. "Quick!"

Now was not the time to question her, Jack knew. He heard car doors slamming, and he led her down to the basement. Gus, whose business had sometimes crossed the letter of the law, had made certain he had a way of exiting the house, should the need ever arise.

A dusty crawl space led to a large metal grate affixed to the concrete-block wall. Jack pulled it off, revealing a tunnel large enough for a grown man to comfortably crawl through on hands and knees. Gesturing Nona through, he followed her, turning in the cramped space, replacing the grate and locking it in place from the tunnel's side.

He touched her back to gain her attention, gestured her forward. The tunnel ran for perhaps three hundred yards, before making a dogleg to the right. This section sloped upward. At its terminus was a short vertical metal ladder.

Squeezing past Nona, Jack led the way up, pausing long enough to unscrew a heavy metal grate. When it was free, he pushed it aside. The sounds of speeding traffic came to them as they emerged in a section of filthy trees and underbrush on the far side of an expressway.

Nona looked around for a moment, getting her bearings. Then she nodded. "This way."

Risking a glance behind him, Jack saw light from his house streaming through the trees. People were inside. A siren wailed, approaching.

"Come on," Nona urged, pulling him along.

He saw her on her mobile, speaking tersely, before pocketing it. Her service pistol was in her right hand, and this alarmed him all the more. More sirens, more lights—some red now—behind them, until they turned down a side street.

An enormous black SUV without any ID idled, waiting for them. Nona bundled him into the passenger's seat, climbed in behind the wheel, and took off.

"Nona," Jack said, "what the hell is going on?"

She turned to him, her beautiful chocolate-brown face shining with the sweat of effort of their narrow escape. "Secretary Paull is dead," she said. "And the feds are convinced you killed him."

TWO

"This is a tragedy of the highest order." President Arlen Crawford looked at each of the five grim-faced men seated around the table in his bunker-like situation room. He was a big, rangy, sun-scarred Texan, a veteran of political wars on both the state and national levels. He had been vice president during the previous short-lived administration, had survived a Senate debate, and had now been elected president in his own right. "The secretary of homeland security is shot in the middle of the nation's capital."

"In his own home, no less," said Kinkaid Marshall, the director of the newly minted DCS, as he stared directly at Henry Dickinson, the acting director of homeland security. The Defense Clandestine Services was formed from the old DIA. Its mission was to beef up the U.S. intelligence presence in Africa, parts of Asia, and other Al Qaeda hotspots.

"Maybe I misheard you; I certainly hope I misheard you," Dickinson said. "Are you insinuating this is my fault?" He was quite naturally on edge; though Paull had named him to director, the president had yet to sign off on the promotion.

"I'm saying Dennis Paull was your boss. I'm saying that it was your duty to protect him. I'm saying you failed."

The antipathy between the two men was well known, stemming from Marshall's objection to Dennis Paull promoting Dickinson when Paull was bumped up to HS secretary by President Crawford. Marshall was a battle-hardened Army general of no little merit, the kind of ex-military officer who saw life as a constant battle between the public and the private sectors, in other words, between those who "knew how things worked," as he was wont to say, and those who didn't. To him, those outside the military command structure were basically dumb and uninformed. Overlords, such as he, were needed to save the private sector from its own stupidity. He was blind to the irony of his mission—how the very act of keeping secrets kept civilians uninformed.

"Dennis had adequate protection," Dickinson protested. "No one could have known, let alone guessed, that he and his security detail would be shot to death by his own man, Jack McClure."

"You should have known, Dicky." The nasty edge to Marshall's voice became razor-sharp. "It was your job to know these things."

Tim Malone, director of the FBI, stirred uneasily as he turned to address G. Robert Krofft, director of the CIA. "Speaking of 'should have known,' I can't for the life of me fathom what your boys were doing at Dennis Paull's house," he said.

"When the director of DHS gets shot by one of his own men," Krofft said frostily, "it's bound to be a matter of national security. And if the killer was directed by forces outside the United States—"

"That's a mighty big 'if,'" the president said.

"And in the meantime, you're getting your shit all over my jurisdiction," Malone said, his tone frosty. "Back off. If and when you're needed—"

"By that time, every trail is bound to be cold."

"Well, it's a good thing my men got there first because they found *this*."

He spun a dossier across the table. Everyone stared at it as if he had loosed a viper into their midst. Krofft shot him a venomous look.

William Rogers, the national security advisor, spoke up. "What the hell is that, Tim?"

Leaning forward, Malone flipped open the dossier. "It's one of Paull's personal files. We found it hidden under one of the locked drawers." Malone paused to take a breath, but also, one supposed, to underscore the importance of his find. "Gentlemen, there's a mole high up inside our government. Paull believed—and here we have his documented proof—that vital intel is being leaked to the Syrian."

A terrible silence reigned in the room for some time. Faces pinched and ashen looked from one to the other.

Krofft cleared his throat. "Does the dossier point a finger at the mole?"

"Not in so many words," Malone said. "But Jack McClure's prints are all over Paull's office. He was there; surely the last one to see him alive."

"McClure's gun was found in a Dumpster," Dickinson said. "Five blocks west of Dennis's house."

"Fingerprints?" Rogers asked.

"His," Dickinson said. "His alone."

"And there we have it," Krofft said. "McClure was the one who murdered him. His boss was getting too close to the truth."

"It would seem that way." Rogers nodded. "McClure tried to find the incriminating dossier, but an alarm was sounded when Paull's detail didn't check in. He was forced to flee without it."

"We now have our man," Krofft said, "and our mission, which is urgent. Mr. President, if we don't get our act together pronto, we're all going to have egg on our faces." He was acutely aware of Crawford's obsessive desire to keep his name unsullied by even the most inconsequential controversy. If the murder of the secretary of homeland security by his own subordinate's hand became common knowledge, a firestorm of disastrous proportions would erupt, engulfing them all.

But the president said nothing. His gaze seemed to be fixed at a point just above and to the right of Krofft's head. The antipathy between the two men was well known. Krofft vehemently objected to the administration bringing troops home from hot spots overseas, arguing that the United States would be perceived as going soft, as ceding control to rising military stars like China.

Dickinson, uncomfortable with yet another silence, looked around the surprisingly small room, which lay three levels below the West Wing of the White House. "Have you a suggestion, Bill?" Rogers was a former diplomat and Rhodes scholar. Everyone listened to his suggestions, even the notoriously feisty Marshall.

"I agree with Krofft." Rogers spread his hands on the brushed steel tabletop. "The very first thing we need is containment. Not a word of the cause of Dennis's death is to be leaked to the press."

"We can hardly hide his sudden death," Crawford said truculently. "This isn't Moscow or Havana, for God's sake."

"Of course not, Mr. President. Nothing could be further from my mind," Rogers replied in his calm, even-toned voice. "However, I do think we would be best served by promoting the story that the secretary of homeland security died in his home of a massive myocardial infarction."

"Excellent suggestion." Malone nodded. "*Containment* is priority one; Bill is correct about that," Malone said. "But *job one* is finding McClure, interrogating him, and then dispensing with him as quickly and quietly as we can." He was a man who looked like a field hockey player—big and meaty, with quick eyes and quicker hands. Judging solely from his appearance, it was difficult to imagine him sitting behind a desk all day. Those quick eyes swept the room, gauging each man's willingness to listen and to agree.

"The sea must swallow McClure up without so much as a ripple," Krofft said, continuing the thought. "The matter of Secretary Paull's death must be put to rest as swiftly and efficaciously as possible. Any attempt at an investigation beyond what has already been conducted is sure to leak to the press, and that we cannot afford."

"A valid point," Rogers said, already turned to the president. "What's your take, sir?"

Rogers knew Crawford liked to have the last word in his briefings and did not take kindly to anyone trying to add to the agenda, or, as he thought of it, upstaging him.

"Makes sense to me, absolutely," the president said, addressing Rogers. "The sooner we get the shit on our doorstep cleaned, the better." He looked around the room. "If there aren't any more points anyone would like to make."

Yet another significant silence filled the room to overflowing, making it difficult to breathe. The president nodded in the most decisive manner, and picked up an internal phone. "Get Alix in here ASAP," he barked. Alix Ross was his press secretary. He listened for a moment to the voice on the other end of the line, then interrupted peremptorily, "I don't care how high a fever she has, get her the hell over here now!"

"Dennis is dead?" Jack looked lost and bewildered. "But I was in his house with him just hours ago."

"I know," Nona said. "Your fingerprints are all over a glass of whiskey in the living room." She hadn't taken her eyes off him since they had scrambled into the SUV, which was now speeding along the highway to Dulles International Airport. "They're also all over the Glock 9mm used to shoot Paull and the members of his security detail."

Jack opened his mouth to say something, but his mind was too jammed up.

"I have to know," Nona said. "Is your gun in your possession?"

Jack shook his head.

"Do you know where it is?"

Jack could feel the itch of sweat at his hairline. "It should have been in the night table drawer at my bedside."

"But it wasn't there."

"I went to get it when I heard you downstairs."

"Jack!"

He shook his head. "It's missing."

"Not anymore," Nona said. "Nine will get you ten it's the murder weapon."

"Now I know why . . ." He ducked his head briefly. "Thanks for coming to get me."

"I owe you, Jack. Plus my gut tells me you didn't kill Paull—you couldn't have. It's not in you. Sadly, what I think doesn't matter. At the moment, you're screwed six ways from Sunday. And with Dennis dead, you're out of powerful friends."

"Yeah, I was never very good at that."

"Whoever set you up has done a bang-up job of it. He's a real professional. Any idea who it might be?"

In fact, Jack had a strong suspicion it was the Syrian's mole. Being high up in the U.S. government would give him both the juice and the means to steal Jack's Glock and to get into Dennis's house. Maybe he had even presented himself to the security detail, which would account for them being killed, as well as Paull.

"Jack?"

He let out a long-held breath. "Nona, there's a mole inside the government."

"How high up?"

"Very high. Dennis asked me to the late-night meeting outside the office to tell me about his suspicions. He wanted me to find the mole."

"Well, that's going to be impossible now."

"Good for the mole; bad for me." The thought of other people—most notably the mole—being privy to Pyotr Legere, Dennis's contact, sent a chill through him. Legere might be the only person on earth who could save him. If Jack could obtain evidence of his treachery, he had a shot at clearing himself.

"By the time I got there," Nona said, "the place was crawling with feds."

"Homeland security?"

"They showed up later. FBI suits were the first on the scene, but there was also a CIA presence. I didn't see much more than I told you. They elbowed me out of the way, like feds always do with Metro. I wouldn't have been there at all but the commish has given me full leeway. He's part of the mayor's weekly poker game, so even the feds have to tread lightly with him."

"Did you get a look at Dennis's desk?"

"Sure. The whole crime scene."

"Wait a minute. Dennis was found in his study?"

"Shot there, yeah. Why?"

"When I left he wasn't there. I assumed he'd gone up to bed."

She frowned. "Well, he sure as hell was shot and died in the study. I saw the body. No way had he been killed elsewhere and dragged there."

"The desk?"

She nodded. "Yeah, I saw it—there was nothing on it—nothing at all."

Someone has the dossier, Jack thought, *and if he finds Legere first, I'm a dead man.*

At this moment, Nona drew up in front of a small detached house. "The first thing I have to do is find you a way out of here." She put the SUV in park and got out. "Hang tight. I'll be right back."

Ten minutes later, she had returned with a large square leather bag. She fished out a packet and she handed it to him. Upon opening it, he found a sizable amount of money in dollars and Euros, as short list of names, a passport in the name of Edward Griffiths, and an official photo ID.

"That money should hold you for a while," Nona said. "The names on that list are all reliable, all specialists. Call them if you need their expertise."

Jack flipped open the ID, then looked up at her, stunned. "Edward Griffiths is an Interpol agent? How did a Metro police officer get all this?"

She laughed. "You'd be surprised at who I know. Lots of people here and there, and they all owe me. This guy—let's call him Willie—got your photo off the Web and adapted it for the passport."

"He must be some kind of genius," Jack said, "what with all the antiforgery additions governments have layered on passport pages."

"He can do anything," Nona said. "Trust me, that document will hold up even under FBI scrutiny."

"The Interpol ID, as well?"

"You'll have to be careful with that."

He gave a wry smile. "Is there an actual Edward Griffiths?"

"Well, you're Edward Griffiths now," she pointed out. "He *used* to be a two-bit hustler."

"Drugs."

"Drugs, girls, firearms. Anything he could lay hands on and move at a profit."

"Charming."

She grinned, showing large white teeth.

"And Mr. Griffiths is where, now?"

"Probably in the C&O Canal, but no one really knows. Bottom line: he's ghosted."

Jack nodded. "You did a helluva lot of work in a short time, Nona."

She grinned again. "My specialty."

"Really? I never suspected."

"No one does."

Jack regarded her in this new and startling light. "You've put yourself and your people in harm's way."

"Nothing you wouldn't have done for me."

He ducked his head. "I owe you, big-time."

"You can pay me back by staying alive, Jack. I went to a lot of trouble for you. It would be a shame if it ended with you facedown in a puddle of your own blood."

"I'll make sure that doesn't happen." He stole a brief glance out the SUV's rear window. "Assuming, that is, I get out of D.C. in one piece."

"You need to get out of the country. You can buy an international ticket under the name of Edward Griffiths. Take the first flight out."

"No." Jack shook his head. "The passenger terminal is covered by CCTV cameras. I'll be spotted."

She frowned. "Do you have a better idea?"

He thought for a moment. "As a matter of fact I do."

When he pulled out his mobile, Nona plucked it out of his hand. "You don't want to use this," she said.

"I know." He stopped her as she was about to drop it into the bag at her feet. Taking it back, he popped out the micro SD card containing the Legere dossier Dennis had given him. Then he handed it back.

"I hope you're not going to give me a burner," he said, referring to the cheap mobiles sold in drug and convenience stores with pay-as-you-go plans that were the favorites of drug and arms dealers. "I need something that'll read this."

She smiled. "We aim to please," she said, dropping a new Samsung into his palm. "It's all set up. The GPS function has been disabled. Even I won't be able to track you."

He stared at her for a moment. "Are you sure you work for Metro and not some black ops agency?"

She laughed. "If I did, I couldn't tell you."

Jack grunted, inserted the SD card into the phone, then fired it up. He did not have his old phone's directory, of course, but his brain could not help memorizing every number in it. He punched in a local number, and when Ben King answered, he said: "It's Jack. I need to get out of the States."

"Right," King said. "I'll get the plane ready."

King was the pilot of Paull's government plane that Jack had used over the past three years. King had already gotten him out of several tight spots.

"No," Jack said. "I need a more clandestine type of ride. No one can know I'm leaving, or even that I'm at the airport."

There was a silent moment while Jack held his breath. Then he said, "Look, Ben, something's happened to the Skip. I need to set it right."

"Is he okay?"

"No," Jack said. "He's dead."

There was an elongated silence during which Jack's ears were filled with the trip-hammer beat of his own heart.

"Jack," Ben said at last, "is this the only way?"

"Yeah," Jack said heavily, "I'm afraid it is."

"Okay. Let me make some calls." Ben's voice was crisp and sharp now, a military man carrying out his orders. "I'll phone you—"

"No," Jack said firmly. "I'll call you."

"That bad, huh?"

"Worse. Ben, I don't have a lot of time."

"Fifteen minutes," Ben said, and disconnected.

Dickinson, filing out of the situation room with the others, paused at Tim Malone's side, and together the two men went slowly down the corridor. They watched President Crawford talking with Rogers and Alix Ross. The three stepped into the elevator by themselves, the bulletproof reinforced steel doors closed as the others milled about, waiting for it to return for them.

"This way."

Malone led Dickinson through a fire door on their left into the bare concrete stairwell, and they began their ascent up to the White House's ground level.

"I've sent out a BOLO and an all-points on McClure," Dickinson said. "With the help of the Metro police, I've deployed agents and detectives at all rail and bus stations and airports in the D.C. metro area. Everyone has his photo. Also, we're canvassing every rental car office."

"And if he chooses to steal a car?" Malone said.

"I've sent patrol cars rolling everywhere. We'll catch him, Tim. That's a promise. Dennis and I went way back. He was the one who recruited me out of Georgetown."

"I know."

Dickinson shook his head. "I'm not going to let this fucker get away with killing Dennis." He licked his lips. "I screwed the pooch. I won't make director if I don't make it right."

"I feel for you, Henry. But if you get this job done quickly and efficiently, you can turn sentiment in your favor."

After that charged exchange, the two men kept their own counsel, each seemingly plunged deep in thought, as they passed out of the White House, through the various security checks, and into Malone's waiting car. Dickinson signaled to his security team, which had been doubled the moment Dennis Paull's body had been identified, and they vanished into their vehicles to take up position behind their boss. Before he ducked into the FBI director's car, he saw Krofft watching him from the steps of the White House.

"This is turning out to be a helluva morning," Dickinson said morosely as he settled in beside the FBI director. "I can't fathom how this could happen. It's unthinkable. Dennis was McClure's mentor, scooped him up when President Carson died in Moscow four years ago, gave him carte blanche. Why in the world would McClure betray him?"

Malone considered a moment. "That's what a good mole does: burrows in, gets close, then goes about his business."

Dickinson's gaze dropped. "This dossier is the most damning bit of evidence."

"I did us all a favor, Henry. We're lucky Krofft's agents didn't get their paws on it. You know his rep for sharing nothing."

Dickinson laughed ruefully. "My boss seems to have been good at that, too. The dossier names Pyotr Legere. Who the hell is he? I've never heard of him."

"It appears that he was Dennis's private contact."

"Off the books of homeland security."

"Off the books of all the clandestine services."

"Which is why he didn't tell anyone—even me—about Legere."

Malone nodded. "He didn't know whom he could trust."

"I'll bet he told McClure. He told McClure everything. Every. Fucking. Thing."

Malone gave him a look, but Dickinson was too busy with his thoughts. "Truthfully, had Dennis come to me with his suspicion, I would have been inclined to disbelieve him. After all, this isn't the Cold War. It's far too difficult these days to turn high-level personnel."

Malone pointed to a section of the interview where Paull asked Legere the identity of the mole. "But now Dennis is dead—shot to death by one of his most trusted men. You ask why Jack McClure would turn on his mentor. This is why, Henry. McClure is the mole. The moment he learned what Dennis was up to, he killed him. In order to escape from the house, he had to kill the security guards, as well."

Dickinson tapped a forefinger against his pursed lips. "This is a transcript of the interview. My people didn't find a tape or CD. Did yours?"

Malone shook his head. "There was nothing of the kind. Dennis was too canny to leave the original lying around. My guess is it's someplace safe outside his house."

Dickinson had come to the end of the dossier. "How well do you know this man known as the Syrian?"

"Not well at all. No one knows who he is. We have no photos of him, we don't know his background. He's a ghost, or maybe a straw man Al Qaeda or another terrorist group has created for us to follow."

Dickinson tapped the dossier. "It says here that the mole is being run by the Syrian."

"That's what Legere believed—or what he told Dennis, at any rate."

"At the end of the day, it doesn't matter who's running the mole, the Syrian, Al Qaeda, or some other cadre," Dickinson said, "just that we shut the leak down."

Dickinson blew air out of his pursed lips. "Any idea where this Pyotr Legere is at the moment?"

Malone shook his head. "But we do know from his debriefing that he was last in Bangkok."

"That's where I should start looking for him."

"I don't see why. We need to concentrate on running McClure down."

Dickinson looked thoughtful. "You may be right, but knowing McClure as I do, it's likely to be a helluva lot easier finding Legere than—"

"With all due respect," Malone interrupted, "you don't know McClure at all. Let's focus on him." When no immediate response was forthcoming, he added, "Listen, Henry, you start sniffing around in Bangkok, Krofft's going to get wind of it. Then he'll want to know what you're doing and why you haven't briefed him on it."

"Because the minute he finds out, he'll take over. That's Krofft's way."

"Precisely. I mean, he had his boys at my crime scene. What the hell." The flat of Malone's hand cut through the air. "No, Henry, we leave this strictly domestic, we keep Krofft out of our hair."

Dickinson sighed, then, reluctantly, nodded. "Right you are, Tim." But he was already thinking of the best person to send to Bangkok in search of Dennis Paull's elusive contact.

THREE

"Dulles Cargo," Jack said to Nona the moment he ended his second call to Ben King.

Nona pulled over, drew a stained hoodie out of her bag. "Put this on," she said. Then she cuffed him. "Now just keep your face averted and we'll be okay."

When he was settled, she put the SUV in gear, changed direction, and headed off.

Jack said, "My sense is we'll only have one shot to get into the foreign trade zone, which will gain me access to the cargo runways without going through the terminal. An InterGlobal Logistics aircraft is due to take off in just under fifty minutes."

Nona nodded. "We're no more than eight minutes from the airport, so the time frame shouldn't present a problem. It's getting you there that's bound to be tricky. In light of the secretary's murder, a cordon has surely been deployed around the entire D.C. area by now."

As if to punctuate her words, she said, "We've got a problem."

"What is it?"

"Two state police cruisers parked in a chevron formation half across the highway. They're funneling traffic down to one slow-moving lane."

"Roadblock?"

The lights on the tops of the cruisers were flashing, and, as Nona steered the SUV to join the line waiting for clearance, she could see heavily armed officers interrogating the people in every car, checking identities of everyone in each vehicle before it was allowed to pass through.

"Uncuff me. I'd better get out of here."

Nona shook her head. "You get out now, you're a dead duck."

He looked into her dark eyes. "Does that mean you have a better suggestion?"

Bobby Brixton had applied three times to be a fed, and three times he had been turned down. He had no idea why and no one would tell him. Gradually his disappointment and rage had been subsumed into his work as a state police officer. So it was understandable that when he received orders to head out to Dulles International as part of a district-wide cordon to intercept a known murderer he was immediately psyched, even though his partner was less than enthused.

"Who'd we piss off this time?" his partner, Andy Hay, had said as Brixton switched on the top lights and floored their police cruiser. "These cordons, I've been on 'em before. The only thing more boring is a stakeout. At least, when you're part of a cordon you can pee without worrying that you'll miss the perp."

"This one's different." Brixton's eyes were alight with anticipation. "The flag came down from the feds."

"The feds!" Hay spat out his window. "Fuck, let state do their grunt work for them, sure, why not? Then if on the off chance something happens, they take the credit. Fucking feds. I don't know why the fuck you want to join their team, Brixy."

Brixton laughed. "I want to be able to break your balls, is why."

"Fuck, you do that already, you cocksucker."

"True that!"

They had arrived at their appointed coordinates to find another state cruiser already there. One of the uniforms in the other car had already stopped traffic on its way to the airport, and the two vehicles formed up into the standard chevron formation to better handle traffic flow. Brixton and Hay got out and started checking the IDs of the vehicle occupants. They pulled trucks to one side and inspected whatever was in the transport compartments.

After forty minutes of this, Hay said, "What'd I tell you? A whole lot of nothing." He gestured. "And look at this fucking lineup. Except for FedEx, mornings are the worst for cargo traffic."

Brixton, who'd had just about enough of his partner's bellyaching, said, "Go take a crap or something, maybe that'll lighten your mood."

Hay grunted. "The only thing that'll lighten my mood is getting the fuck outta here and back to some meaningful police work. This is like babysitting the fucking blacktop."

Brixton waved his partner away as yet another black SUV rolled to a stop beside him. "IDs," he said automatically.

Nona showed him her ID.

Brixton found himself admiring her heavy breasts before he tore his gaze away to check out her creds. "A bit far from your home turf, Chief Heroe, aren't we?" Then, craning his neck, he saw the SUV's second occupant and he felt the hair at the back of his neck stir.

The man was leaning forward, his manacled wrists crossed at the small of his back. A black hood obscured his head.

Brixton felt his mouth go dry. "Christ, is that a terrorist?"

Nona looked up at him, her expression maddeningly neutral.

"Sure," Brixton said, "I know you can't tell me. National security. No doubt. I'll bet you're taking him for interrogation, I'm right, aren't I?" He tried to force more of himself through the open window. "How about taking me along? I just want to observe. I've heard so much about . . . You guys still waterboarding? That's what I really want to see."

"Waterboarding is illegal," Nona said.

"Sure it is." Brixton winked. "I know that, but hell, you've got a terrorist there. It's a matter of national security to find out what's inside his head. Secrets, right?"

"I'm not at liberty to say—"

"Sure, sure. I understand."

Nona stared up at him. "We're on the clock. We need to pass."

"Yes, ma'am. Of course." Brixton stepped smartly back. "Sergeant Robert J. Brixton, ma'am." Maybe she'd remember him and put in a good word for him the next time he applied. But who was he kidding? He was never going to be a fed; he was doomed to remain a sergeant in the state police until the day he collected his pension.

Like an idiot, he saluted her as the SUV rolled majestically through the aperture between the two cruisers, picking up speed as it headed toward the airport perimeter.

"That was close," Jack said from beneath the hood, as Nona unlocked the manacles. "I owe you more than I can say."

Her eyes locked with his, and he saw the strength and determination there.

"Just don't make me look like a fool," she said.

"You have no worries there."

The SUV reached the chain-link fence surrounding the foreign trade zone. There were six warehouses, beyond which could be seen four runways outlined in blinking bluish-purple guide lights.

"This is where we part company," Nona said. "Metro has no jurisdiction out here. I have no believable excuse to enter the FTZ, and my presence will only call unwanted attention." She handed him a slim packet. "Keep this safe, will you."

"Nona—"

The form and quality of her smile stopped him. "I know what

it's like to lose a boss who was also your friend. The difference is I know who was responsible, and he's dead."

As Jack opened the door, she added, "Jack, if you need me for anything, my private number is in the phonebook of the mobile I gave you. And don't worry, the conversation will be encrypted. No one will eavesdrop; no one will know who you are or where you're calling from."

He stepped out onto the pavement.

"Godspeed, Jack," she said just before slamming the door shut.

He watched the SUV make its arc as it turned around, heading back to downtown D.C., then he turned and surveyed the immediate area, making his assessment. One of the advantages of being dyslexic was that he could assimilate an entire area with a single glance. Another, was that his brain worked a hundred times faster than those without his gift.

Within the space of several heartbeats, he had the plan of Dulles Cargo securely memorized. Had he been Nona, he would have accessed the plan on his mobile via Google. But he would have been looking at two dimensions—he was far better at seeing in three.

There was a great deal of activity on the other side of the fence, but none at all where he was. Five hundred yards to his left the gate into the FTZ was manned by an airport security officer, who this night was joined by a pair of suits, who were either FBI or CIA.

Vehicles—trucks and vans of every sort and description—were driving in and out through the gate. The manifest of each truck entering was scrutinized, its cargo inspected to ensure it matched up. Jack moved back, away from the airport lights, toward the road that led up to it. A large van with an unusually tall profile slowed as it turned off the road to join the line of vehicles awaiting entry. As it passed through a shadowed area, Jack swung onto its rear bumper, hoisted himself to its roof, and immediately flattened himself against it.

The van rumbled forward, a bit at a time, until it arrived at the gate. The inspection was made, the manifest read, the rear doors unlocked so the suits could make certain no one was hiding inside. The driver and the two suits were inside the van for several minutes. When he felt them emerge, Jack held his breath, but no one thought to check the roof. After a short exchange, the driver returned behind the wheel, put the van in gear, and passed through the gate.

Jack was inside the foreign trade zone.

The sun was just rising off a low pink, cotton-candy cloudbank in the east. The sky was filled with a pearly radiant light. Jack checked his watch: twenty minutes to takeoff. Plenty of time left. Now that he was in the FTZ, the worst was over. From the truck's roof, he had a clear look at three of the four runways. The Inter-Global Logistics aircraft was scheduled to use runway 1R/19L. In fact, he could see the plane. It was not yet moving, Ben King having notified the pilot of Jack's last-minute, clandestine boarding.

Jack waited until the truck slowed, then wormed his way down onto the ground. He made his way directly toward the aircraft, which was no more than a thousand yards away. He had made the decision that once inside the FTZ, the best way to proceed was to look like he belonged there, rather than skulking about in the shadows. Around him maintenance people were hurrying to and fro, calling to one another. Small trains of crates were being ferried back and forth between warehouses and the cargo holds of aircraft being serviced prior to takeoff.

Last-minute packages and crates were still being loaded into the InterGlobal aircraft; the open cockpit door, reached via a rolling aluminum ladder, shone in the morning sunlight, beckoning tantalizingly. A cargo vehicle finished loading up the next plane over and rumbled toward him, then stopped, turned, and slowly backed up to the rear of the warehouse along which Jack was striding, where a small crane was waiting.

As soon as the cargo vehicle was in place, the crane began loading enormous windowed crates onto its flatbed. Jack paralleled the warehouse wall in order to keep to the most direct route to the InterGlobal Logistics's aircraft and had just passed a side door when he felt a sudden presence behind him. Before he could turn, he felt the cold steel of a pistol muzzle press into the back of his neck.

"Don't move," a deep male voice said from just behind him. "Don't even fucking breathe."

FOUR

Redbird's hands were full of blood when the call came in. Amid the stench of death, he stripped off his latex gloves, and responded to his master's voice.

"Here." His voice was a low rasp.

"Commission status," Henry Dickinson said, half a world away in his D.C. office.

"Done and done." Redbird stared down at the two corpses, lying in dark pools of their own blood. Bare limbs entwined, they looked like lovers caught in an eternal embrace. Perhaps that was what death was, Redbird thought—an embrace by an unknown lover.

"That's a relief," Dickinson said.

Redbird frowned. "Did you have doubts?"

"Not at all. But I have a new commission for you that can't wait."

Redbird stepped carefully over the corpses and went to the window, stared out into the German early afternoon, dull as flint. "I'm—Hold on."

An American Air Force jet, taking off from Ramstein Air Base went screaming through the leaden sky, the sound of its engines rattling the small items inside the cheap hotel's ground-level room like an earthquake. There was an elevated risk in closing this commission so close to the U.S. military presence, but that very risk was what he lived for, sinking into the delicious shiver down his spine when he trod the dangerous precipice.

When the noise subsided sufficiently, Redbird's mind returned to the conversation. "I'm good to go," he said.

"Fine," Dickinson said. "I'm sending the dossier to your mobile. But I have to warn you, there isn't much."

"There rarely is." Redbird's lips were curled into a permanent smile he did not feel. The smile was a quirk of genetics, as was his white hair, which he wore in a clipped military brush. He was at once slim and powerful, his energy coming from his lower belly, the spot sensei had taught him where *ki*, the life-force energy, began.

"This commission is different. You are to find one man, but as you'll see, the commission could turn out to be a complex one."

There was a pale scar in the sky cut, moments before, by the stubby wings of the military plane. He turned away from the window, admiring as much as surveying the careful mayhem he had wrought. As always, there seemed to be a second heart beating deep inside him.

"All the better." Now Redbird did smile. It was a sight to chill the blood.

"Face the wall," the voice said from behind Jack, "hands and legs spread. Lean in."

Standard law enforcement officer procedure, Jack thought, as opposed to a fed. But what kind of a cop?

The leo began to pat Jack down, looking for concealed weapons. "Thought you were so clever lying on the top of that truck." One hand ran up the inside of Jack's left leg and down the right. "You'd have made it, too. Except for the fact that I was looking out my fourth floor window, taking a break from my monitors, and saw you spread-eagled atop that truck and thought what the fuck is that fuck up to?" The hand made a circuit of Jack's right and left sides, up into his armpits. "So I came down to have a look at the clever boy."

He grunted. "So you're clean. Turn around."

"Listen."

"Shut the fuck up!"

Jack had a momentary impression of a long, lean face atop a wiry body clad in the uniform of airport security just before his right hand lifted, drawing the leo's attention. Instantly, Jack's left arm swung up, his fist smashing into the leo's jaw. As the man staggered back, Jack immobilized his gun hand, wrapping the wrist in a fierce grip. But the leo jabbed out his left hand, grabbing Jack by the throat.

"You fucker!" the leo whispered. "You're not going to get away from me that easily."

"You're making a mistake that'll cost you your job," Jack said in a half-strangled voice.

The leo's eyes narrowed. "Let go of my hand or I'll rip out your throat."

Jack unwound his fingers from the leo's right wrist, and, released, the gun was pointed at Jack again.

"How's that?" the leo said.

"I'm Interpol."

The leo snickered. "Sure you are, pal."

"Check my ID," Jack said. "You'll see."

"When we get back to my office. Let's go."

"I don't have time; I'm following a lead," Jack persisted. "You want to check my creds, do it here."

The leo hesitated, then, relinquishing his grip on Jack's throat, said, "Stand the fuck back."

When Jack complied, he said, "Okay, hotshot. Hand 'em over—slowly."

Jack put his hand inside his jacket, drew out the folder, and dropped it open. The leo's eyes flicked to the Interpol ID, then back to Jack's face to check it against the photo. Then he put his gun up.

"Okay. Sorry. No hard feelings."

Jack slammed his fist into the point of the leo's chin with such force, the officer's head slammed back against the corrugated steel wall of the warehouse.

Turning away as the body slid down the wall, he was about to emerge from the shadow thrown by the corner of the warehouse when he saw two suits standing between him and the now fully loaded InterGlobal Logistics aircraft.

When his hands weren't steeped in blood, Redbird was a meditative and studious individual. He read assiduously, his knowledge both deep and wide-ranging. He loved Carlos Fuentes and Amitav Ghosh, but his heart and soul belonged to the Austrian poet Rainer Maria Rilke. Often, when he read Rilke, Redbird felt that they were spiritual twins, or, even, that he might be Rilke reincarnated. *"I want to be with those who know secret things or else alone,"* Rilke had written, just as if he had somehow time-traveled into the future to read Redbird's innermost thoughts.

Redbird, sitting in the first-class lounge at Flughafen Frankfurt, waiting for his flight to Bangkok, had his tattered, German-language copy of Rilke's *The Book of Images* open on his lap. Redbird was fluent in more than a dozen languages and always chose to read in the author's native language, not trusting translators to capture the masterly beauty of the original.

The soft buzz of hushed voices, the comings and goings of wealthy passengers, cradled him. A cup of black coffee and a plate with a hard roll and a pat of foil-wrapped butter sat on the low table by his right hand. Occasionally, he sipped his coffee while studying the made-up and well-oiled faces of those around him, but the roll remained untouched. Food was of little interest to him. It was people he found fascinating.

He looked like a professor, or a researcher, which, in a way, he was. Being a student of human behavior had served him well in his chosen profession. Though he seemed to be reading, he was actually absorbing all the intel Dickinson had provided from Dennis Paull's dossier on Pyotr Legere and the late Leroy Connaston. His mission ultimately was to find Jack McClure, who was believed to be following Legere's trail, and bring him back to D.C.

"As you'll see, the commission could turn out to be a complex one," Dickinson had said, and now Redbird knew why. Redbird was, by and large, an expert in dealing death. He could count on one hand the number of commissions that had involved something other than straightforward political murder.

But there was something about this commission that excited him. Maybe it was Legere's connections to the Kremlin's elite or his curious involvement in the clandestine world of espionage. But, on second thought, maybe Legere's involvement wasn't so curious. With his highly charged client base, Legere was in a unique position to trade secrets.

Redbird glanced up just as his flight was called. Rising, he grabbed his overnight suitcase and joined the small exodus out of the lounge.

Plunged into the maelstrom of the airport, he felt a surge of adrenaline, and thought of another line from Rilke: *"It is a tremendous act of violence to begin anything."*

Jack knew there was no point dressing in the leo's clothes or using his ID; the suits were sure to have his photo on their mobiles—he'd never get past them. There had to be another way, and time was fast running out. He had just over six minutes to get on the InterGlobal Logistics aircraft before it taxied out onto the runway. If it lifted off without him, he was trapped in D.C., and sooner rather than later, he'd be caught, with no chance to clear his name.

Then he remembered the cargo vehicle backed up to the warehouse. A quick glance confirmed that it was still there. He turned to the warehouse door, but it was locked. Crouching down beside the fallen leo, he went quickly through his pockets until he found a ring of keys. Checking the lock manufacturer, he found the matching key, inserted it into the lock and pushed open the door. Turning, he grabbed the leo by the back of his collar, dragging him into the interior. It wouldn't do to have anyone see him lying there, especially the suits.

From the moment he entered, he could tell this was no ordinary warehouse. For one thing it was overheated, for another, it stank of animals. Jack realized he was in one of Dulles Cargo's several specialized warehouses, equipped for all manner of exotic cargo, including live animals for Washington's National Zoo.

Moving through the interior toward the rear doors, which were open to the crane and the cargo vehicle, he saw that only one crate remained to be loaded. He sprinted the remaining distance. The crane's steel fingers moved downward to lock into the last crate as he came up on it. There was a locked door and several slit-like windows set with bars, but it was so dim inside, a hurried glance through them revealed nothing of the crate's contents, except a powerful stench. Something big was inside.

The crane's tines gripped the edges of the crate, beginning to dig into the sturdy wooden frame, and Jack began working on the lock. Unlike the one guarding the warehouse door, this one was a simple tumbler he was able to pick in a matter of seconds. Swinging the clasp away, he opened the door and stepped in.

He shut the door behind him, but not before he had caught a glimpse of the beast curled in one corner. Its eyes briefly glowed a brilliant emerald in the light, its tail switched back and forth as it stared at him.

Jack had seen tigers before, but this one was massive, a third again as large. Years ago, he had read about the gigantic Royal

Bengal tigers whose habitat was the tidal islands of the Sundarbans, on the edge of the Bay of Bengal in eastern India. If he remembered right, besides their size, what set these tigers apart from all others was that they were known man hunters as well as man-eaters.

He could hear the coughing of the great beast's breath, like a high wind soughing through tree branches. Its musky odor was overpowering. The tiger didn't move a muscle, not even when the crate began its ascent, but Jack was absolutely certain it was staring at him, sizing him up.

Slowly, he crouched down on his haunches, back to the door, and tried not to breathe.

FIVE

"How the hell could this have happened?"

Kinkaid Marshall and G. Robert Krofft sat across from each other in a Dunkin' Donuts on K Street NW, but neither of them cracked a smile at the thread-worn joke. It might seem odd for the directors of the DCS and the CIA to be taking their early breakfast at a fast-food shop, but they both knew that they would remain undetected and anonymous in the continuous foot traffic that headed in and out. Over coffee and powdered donuts, they discussed the president's emergency briefing.

"A rotten apple happened," Krofft said, with a dismissive air. "Dennis Paull and his security team were shot to death by that fucking snake Jack McClure."

"Could Dennis have been so blind?"

Krofft broke open two packets of sugar and added the contents to his coffee. "Who the hell cares? What's done is done."

Marshall, listening to the reassuring background hum of human voices, cut his donut into four precise pieces with a white plastic knife. Every movement he made appeared precise and considered.

"Well, we'll find out soon enough when we have McClure in custody. There are going to be a lot of people who want a piece of him."

"You've got it wrong, Kin. We don't want McClure in custody, we want him dead. Containment is priority one. The quicker this sorry incident is put to bed the better."

Marshall made a meditative sound in the back of his throat. The scent of warm sugar was as thick as the morning fog down by the water. "Maybe you're right."

"Of course I'm right."

The rest of the quarter vanished into Marshall's mouth. "But what if you aren't?"

Krofft, dunking his donut into his coffee, laughed harshly. "Don't be absurd. Come on, we both saw the evidence. The case against McClure is open-and-shut. Let's at least refrain from bullshitting each other." He eyed Marshall. "Unless you have another agenda."

"I'm simply trying to be thorough. I'd like to do some follow-up investigation on Dennis and McClure."

Krofft's eyes narrowed. "Why?"

"Because the two men were friends as well as colleagues." Marshall peered at him.

"McClure was a mole. That was part of his job."

"It would seem so." Marshall looked thoughtful. Absently, he ate two quarters of his donut before he spoke again. "But Dennis's murder has given me a weird feeling in my gut."

The shop was awash in early morning customers now, all of them bleary-eyed and rushing to get their morning fix of caffeine and sugar before they set foot in their offices. No one paid them the slightest attention. Nevertheless, Krofft produced a small oval with a plastic shell that gleamed like polished metal and was just as hard. It looked like a beetle. He thumbed a tiny switch and a red LED light popped on. He pushed the electronic jammer across the table so that it sat midway between him and Marshall, protecting them both from eavesdroppers.

"That the latest doohickey from DARPA?" Marshall was referring to the Defense Advanced Research Projects Agency.

"A prototype. I like to stay one step ahead of everyone else."

Marshall nodded. "So what's really on your mind?"

"First Malone, now you."

"What are you talking about?"

"I saw Dickinson getting into Malone's car and driving off. I don't know what those two fucks are planning, but you can make book that it doesn't include us."

"On these shores, G.R., your hands are tied. Mine, too, for that matter."

"I wish to God I had Malone's car bugged."

"You'd be the one to do it, too," Marshall laughed dryly.

Krofft hunched forward. "Are you serious about that feeling in your gut?"

"Lookit, Dennis's death set me to thinking. I mean, why now, at this particular moment? And then the answer came to me: Atlas." The word was voiced in no more than a whisper.

"We are about to begin the operational phase of Atlas. He was the fucking architect of Atlas. We all signed off on it, but it was his idea. He built it from scratch."

"And a brilliant plan it is," Krofft said. "Ever since Al Qaeda in the Arabian Peninsula arose in Yemen, we have kept an eye on the growing threat of domestic terrorism. But it wasn't until the AQAP started actively recruiting disaffected Westerners to their cause on the Shumukh and Al-Fidaa jihadist forums, among others, that Paull really began to take action."

Krofft unlocked his briefcase, pulled out a sheaf of papers, shuffling them until he found what he wanted. He cleared his throat, and read: " 'Corresponding with those who yearn for martyrdom operations and the brothers who are searching to execute an operation that would cause great damage to the enemies the goal now is to activate those brothers who reside in the land of the enemy . . . whether Jewish, Christian, or apostates as clearly individual jihad or the so-called lone wolf has become popular.'"

Krofft looked up. "The usual drivel, we thought, but Paull became alarmed."

"Hence Atlas."

Krofft nodded. "An operation to plant our own people, posing as disaffected Americans—Muslims or Christians wanting to convert—aligning themselves with AQAP's jihadist aims."

Marshall tapped a forefinger against his lower lip. "Do you think McClure knows about Atlas?"

Krofft frowned. "Atlas is a director-only operation. But because of their close friendship, I'd say it was probable."

Marshall passed a hand across his eyes. "Fuck me. Stealing the Atlas field personnel list would be a disaster of epic proportions."

"The list isn't even complete," Krofft said, "Just the first wave is about to be sent out."

"Even that would compromise over a hundred specially trained operatives," Marshall said.

"A perfect disaster." Krofft nodded. "Okay, Kin. Much as my own gut tells me this is a waste of time, I have an idea how we can satisfy it. You and I are going to cook up three pieces of red-hot intel. We're going to feed them, one each, to Malone, Rogers, and Dickinson, then sit back and see what happens. But I'm telling you nothing is going to happen. McClure was the leak. The faster we find him and air him out, the better."

The crate settled with a small crash onto the flatbed, jolting the door open slightly. The Royal Bengal was momentarily illuminated in the sliver of light—it was larger even than Jack had first thought. Its left forepaw was extended to brace it against the jolting movement and its head was low, bobbing between its enormous shoulders. Its tongue came out, licked around its dark muzzle. Then the light winked out as Jack pulled the door closed.

The vehicle and the animal began to move at the same moment. Jack felt the vibration of the vehicle as it rolled over the tarmac. He could feel the presence of the tiger looming over him. He was, quite literally, between a rock and a hard place. If he escaped now he'd be right in the line of sight of the suits, who were undoubtedly on the lookout for him; but if he stayed where he was, he might become the tiger's next meal. He knew that if the Royal Bengal decided to attack him he wouldn't stand a chance against its jaws and raking talons.

Jack risked opening the door enough to see what was going on. At that moment, he heard voices raised in challenge and the vehicle ground to a stop. He saw the flap of a suit jacket, and then clearly one of the feds asking the driver what was in the crates.

By cracking the door a bit wider, he could make out the nose section of the InterGlobal plane. He was turned away from the tiger, but he felt its hot, panting breath, and he knew it had come halfway across the crate. And still it came on, its head lowered, its eyes glowing green.

Then he heard one of the suits say, "I don't care about flight schedules, we need to check your cargo."

That was his cue to leave. They'd see the lock off the crate door and be instantly on alert. Opening the door wider, he was about to leap out when he was brushed aside by the tiger's immense body. He froze in shock to see its entire length stretched out as it bounded from its cage.

A frenzied shout from the driver brought Jack to his senses. Leaping from the flatbed, he sprinted around to the right of the vehicle. On the opposite side, the tiger was confronted by the two suits, one of whom had the presence of mind to pull his service pistol.

From behind him, Jack heard the driver screaming, "No, don't shoot him! Don't shoot!"

Jack, running full out, made the rolling ladder in seconds. Racing up it, he kicked it away with one leg as he stepped into the cockpit with the other. Then the navigator slammed the door shut behind him.

"We thought you weren't going to make it," the pilot said.

"What the hell was that?" the navigator said as he slid back into his seat.

"You don't want to know," Jack replied, as he buckled himself into the third seat.

The pilot was going through his last-minute checks. "We're done loading, yes?"

"We're good to go," the navigator nodded.

The engines revved up as the pilot spoke to the tower. "Runway clear."

Opening his window, the pilot had to yell at the member of the ground crew who was supposed to kick away the chocks but was mesmerized by the standoff between the men and the animal. Getting an all-clear wave, the pilot slammed his window shut and released the brakes.

The aircraft turned and began taxiing toward the head of the runway. The pilot brought them around until they were parallel, the plane came to a stop, then it commenced its run, its wheels propelling it faster and faster until it lifted off.

They were airborne.

Jack put his head back and closed his eyes, feeling the rush of adrenaline coursing through him. His heart was in his throat. The rank stench of the beast was still in his nostrils, the image of its lambent green eyes imprinted on the back of his eyelids, and he trembled with the sensation, both terrible and exhilarating, of the Royal Bengal brushing past him on its way to freedom—or death.

Dreaming, Jack fell through successive layers of deepening gloom, like a diver going deeper than ever before. As he fell into darkness, he saw below him glimmers of light. As he approached them, they became dazzling bursts, like flashbulbs going off.

And then he was within the winking galaxy of lights, illuminating shards of his recent past: the sudden death of his daughter, Emma; his acrimonious breakup with his wife; meeting Annika for the first time in a hotel bar in Moscow; saving her in a nearby alley as she was assaulted by two men; finding out that she was an agent, working for her grandfather; hooking up with her when their missions overlapped; meeting Dyadya Gourdjiev, her grandfather; discovering what a brilliant tactician he was . . .

The lights flashed, more scenes burst upon him in a conflagration that caused his heart to contract: Annika's note, telling him how she had lied about everything, that, at her grandfather's behest she had spent six months researching him before they had ever met, that the meeting had been planned, the assault in the Moscow back alley staged, that they could never see each other again. He was already in love with her by then, ready to shed his old life like a snake sheds its skin. But, despite what she had written, he had seen her again; they could not stay away from each other, and their love had burned ever brighter, fusing them together:

"*Why? Why are you with me?*" The tip of her tongue traced the outer whorls of his ear. "*I am a Russian, and a murderer.*"

"*We're all murderers.*" His voice was thick with desire.

Her palms pressed against his shoulders as he pinned her to the wall. "*You know that's not true.*"

"*But it is. For us, killing is as much a part of life as eating or breathing.*"

"*Or making love.*"

"*No. Making love is entirely different.*"

"*How is it different? Tell me.*"

"*When we're together, making love, we're different. We're better people.*"

"*Only for a time—the space of a breath.*" She took his hands, placed them on her buttocks. "*Or a sigh.*" She sighed deeply, an ecstatic sound.

"*Even that is enough.*" He pulled the fullness of her hips to him. *"My fear is that we'll become like those before us. Living in the shadows, at the edges of society, gives us certain privileges, privileges that feed our egos, inflate them, until we believe that we're beyond the law."*

"But, darling, we are beyond the law."

"I don't believe we are. These moments together, no matter how brief, prove to us that we can go on with this life we've chosen." His hands sought her bare breasts. *"Without them, there's only a descent into a perpetual dark from which we'll never return."*

She looked up at him. *"Do you think we're criminals, that we kill without remorse?"*

"I hope not."

"But you don't know. You can't because it's unknowable." She put her fingers across his lips. *"We do what we have to do. There is no choice."*

Then the last, blinding flash overtook him, and he relived another searing moment, from a year ago, in a lavish villa outside Rome:

"I can't go with you, Jack."

"What are you talking about? Come on, Annika, the Syrian is coming."

"I know he is, Jack. That's why I have to stay."

Anguish gripped him just as it had then. *"I don't—"*

"Get out of here." Annika shoved him toward the front door. *"Now!"*

"Annika—"

"Good-bye, Jack."

At that moment, he got it, his reality collapsed like a house of cards, and his heart shattered. She wasn't coming. She didn't love him. Like her mysterious grandfather, she had aligned herself with the enemy. She had gone beyond the law, above it. It seemed incredible, and yet he was confronted by the truth.

He had fought with the Syrian, but in the end, outnumbered and already in mourning, he ran and had only escaped the villa through the inexplicable intervention of Annika's half-brother, Radomil Batchuk.

The flashing ceased, the lights dimmed, and Jack's dream slid away from him, falling faster than even he was, into the inky blackness.

"A mole," Krofft stared across his desk as Jonatha Midwood.

"Seems like very old times," Jonatha said. "There hasn't been a spanner in the works since Robert Hanssen in 2000."

Krofft nodded. Jonatha Midwood was an analyst of his, one of a very special nature, who he had recruited himself. She was smart as a whip and twice as clever. She worked alone and apart. Almost no one within the Company knew of her existence, which was just the way Krofft wanted it.

"It used to be that ideology could motivate a mole," she said now. "But not these days."

Krofft pressed several buttons on his vast desk. Multiple LCD screens rose like ghosts from the tops of low cabinets placed along three walls. The fourth wall was entirely taken up by a complex electronic monitoring station, manned by four IT technicians.

"Ideology has gone the way of the corded phone and the fax machine," she continued. "A forgotten, shadowed relic, a curio, nothing more."

Krofft laced his fingers together as his hands lay in his lap. "So what are we left with?" His voice had assumed a professorial tone.

"Money."

"Money, perhaps." Krofft nodded. "But in Jack McClure's case, I doubt it."

Jonatha shrugged. "What else is there?"

"Love."

The LCD screens were showing footage from Syria and Afghanistan, all of it unrelentingly loud, brutal, and bloody.

Jonatha tore her gaze away from bodies strewn along a rubble-encrusted street. "Love? Surely you're joking!"

Krofft shook his head. "I'm deadly serious."

"Share, if you please."

Krofft smiled. He loved her occasional anachronistic phrases. "McClure is a formidable agent. He's proved that time and again over the last several years while he was building up his bona fides with Dennis Paull and with homeland security in general, but he has a fatal weakness."

Krofft swiveled around and signaled to one of the IT techs. At once, the war-torn images were wiped off the LCD screen directly in front of them, to be replaced by the face of a beautiful woman. Her thick, lustrous hair was pulled back in a ponytail, revealing a wide forehead and a widow's peak. Her large, slightly uptilted eyes were a light brown with a scattering of reddish pinpoints, her lush lips sensual even without meaning to be.

"This fatal weakness has a name: Annika Dementieva."

The image switched to a snowy scene in what was clearly Moscow. It showed Annika with Jack and an older man, who had the predatory eyes of a shark.

"She's the granddaughter of the late, unlamented Dyadya Gourdjiev, the old man shown here," Krofft continued. "A more devious, dangerous sonofabitch has never existed. It was a happy day for the United States when he was the victim of a hit-and-run in Rome last year."

Jonatha contemplated the photo, her gaze roving from one figure to the next. "So McClure's in love with the old man's granddaughter. So what?"

"So," Krofft said slowly, "it's my belief that Annika Dementieva has taken control of her grandfather's business interests."

"Which are?"

For the first time, Krofft's expression lost a semblance of its sharp edge. "Could be steel, oil, ore mining, arms trading, terrorist training. Might even be all of the above."

Jonatha laughed softly. "You mean you don't know what the

old fucker did." Not too many people could speak that way to the director of the CIA. She was one of the few.

"What we do know is that over the decades he was comrades with every powerful Russian official who occupied a Kremlin office," Krofft said. "And if he wasn't a friend of theirs, he was an enemy, which was too bad for them, because shortly thereafter, they disappeared, never to be heard from again. Suffice it to say that he dipped his beak into more pies than we can count, all of them stinking to high heaven."

"Meaning?"

"We think he was supplying some of the top terrorists."

"Jesus. And McClure is cozy with the granddaughter." Jonatha drummed her fingers on Krofft's desk. "That can't be good."

"No," Krofft acknowledged. "In fact, it's very, very bad."

Jonatha pointed. "Let me see the girl again." When the close-up of Annika returned to the screen, she said, "Is the rest of her as erotic?"

Krofft raised his hand and another shot of Annika appeared, this one shot from a distance. Though it was slightly grainy, her long, powerful legs were clearly visible.

Jonatha nodded. "If you know about the relationship, Paull must have as well."

"What I can't figure out is why he didn't put a stop to it."

Jonatha spread her hands. "Maybe he tried."

"And maybe he didn't. McClure was his golden boy. I think that's what cost him his life."

"But we know that the Syrian is running the mole."

"What if he was running McClure through the Dementieva woman?"

Jonatha nodded slowly. "That makes perfect sense, but as of now it's just speculation."

"Not all of it," Krofft said. "Everything fits."

"Neat as a pin." Jonatha considered a moment. "How d'you want to play the Dementieva angle?"

"It's clear Dickinson blew his chance to capture McClure. McClure's on the run. Where d'you think he's going to go?" He inclined his head toward the image on the screen. "We find the Dementieva woman, we find McClure."

"That presupposes she'll be easier to find than McClure."

A thin, predatory smile split Krofft's face. "I have a line on her. I know where she is, or, rather, where she was forty-eight hours ago."

"Who have you tasked with the mission?"

"Better for you not to know." Krofft's forefinger stabbed out and the screens went black.

PART TWO

TWO HEADS ARE BETTER THAN ONE

SIX

The Sümela Monastery, built into an immense ledge carved into a steep cliff of Melá mountain, in Turkey's Trabzon Province, reached its height in 1204. Legend had it that it was founded by two priests who discovered an icon of the Virgin Mary in a massive cave set into the ledge. A crumbling ruin now, the buildings were still the site of pilgrimages from the Greek and Russian Orthodox faithful.

As she looked out at the inner edge of the Altindere valley, Annika wondered about the origin of the legend. From the time she was a little girl, she had been fascinated by myths and legends, not the least this one, for she had been making her own private pilgrimages to this valley for years.

The Assumption of Mary Clinic, through whose gates the car that bore her was now proceeding, spread its wings on either side of the green-gravel driveway that swept through lush stands of towering pine trees. The clinic was situated just inside the southern perimeter of Altindere, which nowadays was a national park.

The city of Trabzon lay along the southern curve of the Black Sea. In centuries past, it had been a major port, where merchants from Greece, Italy, and Belgium met with their brethren from the east, buying and selling all manner of goods. The rise of the Ottoman Empire brought this brief, highly lucrative golden age to an abrupt close. From that time forward, the line between east and west had been indelibly drawn in the blood of Crusaders and Janissaries alike.

The late afternoon was cloudless. The sun struck the stone structure of the clinic at a sharp, raking angle, turning it a deep bronze color, as if it were made of metal. An odd, purplish tint stained the vault of the sky, below which the black crosses of vultures silently wheeled.

Iraj Namazi, the large-framed, charismatic man sitting beside Annika in the backseat, had been speaking about the philosophy of terrorism. "It's a matter of dislocation," he was saying now. "After the bomb goes off, the gas is released, the plane or train is blown up, what is your real and lasting accomplishment? Beyond the immediate carnage, you have cut off the survivors—the families and friends of the victims who die in the attack—from the security of the past, while at the same time showing them the absolute uncertainty of the future. You have effectively isolated them in a present they can no longer recognize. That is the essence of terror."

The car stopped at the portico, held up by six fluted Greek columns. Namazi said, "*Chérie*, you are unusually quiet. What are you thinking?"

Annika was considering that it was horribly dangerous letting the Syrian anywhere near here. This was, after all, her sacred space, and truth be told, her grandfather's, long before her, but she was bound to a wheel that only went forward. She had made a promise to her grandfather to keep moving closer and closer to Namazi. This particular form of intimacy was a vital part of his plan—never mind that she hated it. One did what one had to do—that was how her grandfather had raised her. Doing his bidding was ingrained in her, like the grit of dust in the boards of an old house sitting on the prairie. Long ago she had sacrificed her own life to be part of her grandfather's plan. And how could she not? He had saved her from a father who had abducted her, abused her both physically and emotionally. That was a debt she would never be able to fully repay, though every day she woke up into a nightmare, trying.

"I was thinking what a discussion between you and Friedrich Nietzsche would be like," she said in a perfectly neutral voice.

"Do you think me a nihilist, then?"

"All terrorists are, by definition, nihilists."

"But, *chérie*, I love living so much!" Namazi opened the door, but before he could step out, she put a hand on his forearm.

"No, Iraj."

His dark eyes searched her face, so that she felt scorched inside.

"You don't want me with you?"

She kissed him on the lips. "You're sweet," she said quietly.

"I don't know why you couldn't have phoned him."

"Dr. Karalian was a close friend of my grandfather's, his long-time chess opponent. Sometimes bad news must be delivered in person. Please wait for me here."

He took a deep breath, then nodded. "Very well."

She stepped over him and onto the gravel of the driveway. Before she could turn away, he took her hand.

"Take as much time as you need, *chérie*." He kissed the back of her hand and let it go.

She smiled at him, then faced the clinic's stone facade. A brisk wind brought the lemon-balsam aroma of frankincense as the pine branches dipped and swayed. She lifted her head to the cliff face, to the ancient monastery. There had been good times here, as well as evil.

For a moment, time froze, as she stood paralyzed on the wide, basalt steps, crushed by the irony. Then, sounds and colors returned to normal, and she went up the remainder of the steps, into the cool, dim interior, echoing with the footsteps of doctors and nurses. The interior was lush with tropical plants, spotlit with sunlamps.

The domed ceiling was encrusted with a mosaic of the luminous night sky and its constellations, depicted as the heroes and creatures of their names: Hercules; Draco, the dragon; Ursa Major and Minor, the bears; Lynx; Leo, the lion; Serpens Caput, the serpent. Overstuffed chairs in small groupings were placed on either side of the circular space, which was dominated by the receptionist's station made of Lebanese cedar, polished to a high gloss.

"Good afternoon, Ms. Dementieva," the receptionist said with a smile. "I'll ring Dr. Karalian and tell him you're here."

Several moments later, Dr. Karalian appeared, an olive-skinned man of Armenian lineage who, with his black, spade-like beard and thick, curving eyebrows, looked like a traditional depiction of the devil. However, the moment he opened his mouth and spoke, his innate intelligence and gentle charm dispelled this image completely.

He stepped forward, embracing her hand with both of his. "Annika, how good to see you again! I only wish we knew you were coming. I would have prepared."

The smile she returned was tinged with both fondness and regret.

"And how is Illyusha? I miss our chess matches."

"You're the only one who ever called my grandfather Illyusha."

Dr. Karalian's smile flickered uncertainly. "What do you mean 'called'?"

Annika pushed stray wisps of hair off the side of her face. "I'm sorry, doctor. My grandfather is dead."

The effect on Dr. Karalian was extraordinary. He rocked back on his heels, as if she had struck him a physical blow, and his face grew white. "Oh, but, my dear, I am so sorry." He stepped forward to embrace her. "Illyusha was such an extraordinary man. As you know, I considered him a good friend as well as an important benefactor to this clinic. What a loss. Truly incalculable."

Annika waited some moments for the doctor to gather himself. "Are you all right?"

Dr. Karalian cleared his throat of emotion. Even so, his voice was slow in returning to normal. "Would you be so kind as to accompany me to my office."

Without another word being exchanged, she followed him out of the lobby down the central corridor, smelling of antiseptic, then along a somewhat narrower corridor to their left, at the end of which was Dr. Karalian's office. It was the doctor's habit to invite her to tea at the end of her visits, when they would spend a companionable hour or so absorbing her take on the latest world events, which he obviously valued.

Dr. Karalian's office was warm, intimate, full of personal items and trinkets from patients he had treated, as well as mementoes from his childhood in Armenia and travels as a young man throughout North Africa. The space had the appearance of a study in his home. Only the daunting phalanx of thick tomes on psychiatric and physical medicine that filled the shelves on the wall behind his desk gave evidence that this was a professional rather than a private room.

At his sweeping gesture, Annika sat in an armchair upholstered in a Turkish-patterned fabric while he settled himself behind his desk. To her right, a window looked out on the sun-slashed preserve and the rugged base of the mountain. To her left was an elaborate chess set, resting on a small, round marquetry table.

"Tell me," he said. "How are you doing?"

"As well as can be expected."

"If I may ask, how did Illyusha pass?'

"A hit-and-run. In Rome."

"How awful, but . . ." Dr. Karalian rocked back in his chair, his fingertips steepled.

Annika's finely tuned antennae gave an internal shiver. "But what?"

Dr. Karalian sat forward abruptly. "Well, it's just that Illyusha was always such a careful man. It's difficult for me to believe that he'd be the victim of a hit-and-run."

Of course he was correct. Knowing she had to end this line of speculation, Annika said quickly, "Have you ever been to Rome, doctor?"

"I can't say I have, no."

"Then you have no idea of the traffic there, nor the speeds the drivers reach even in the center of the city."

Dr. Karalian's gaze turned inward. "So. All things must pass." He gestured to his right. "I will miss him. He was a formidable opponent. I've never encountered a mind like his. We're all the poorer for his passing." He sighed deeply. "You know, when he came here, we played chess, certainly, but we spoke of my wife and children. He was very fond of them."

Annika captured Karalian's doleful gaze, brought it back to the present. "Did he ever talk about Rolan?"

"Naturally. He loved that boy. He often said he had been the best thing to ever happen to you."

"And the worst."

Dr. Karalian gave a grave nod. "As fate would have it."

She nodded. "Would you like me to leave you alone?"

"Thank you, but no." He smiled in that wistful way people have when they recall happier times.

Out of respect, Annika waited some time before she continued. "How is Rolan? Has there been any change?"

"I'm afraid not." Dr. Karalian pursed his lips. "No change at all."

Annika felt a chill spear through her. "Then I think we must consider the other treatment."

Dr. Karalian peered at her dubiously. "It's a radical step, Annika. The danger . . ."

"Have you changed your recommendation?"

"Of course not. No."

"Well, then . . ."

Dr. Karalian's hands worked a paper clip back and forth until it broke in half, the fidgeting a sure sign of his inner distress. "If you've made up your mind . . ."

"I have."

Dr. Karalian produced a wan smile. "Very well. Of course. Rolan is your husband. I must be directed by your wishes."

Iraj Namazi had no intention of abiding by Annika's wish for him to remain in the car. Three minutes after she had disappeared inside, he stepped out of the car, trotted up onto the portico, and pushed open the front door. His curiosity had gotten the better of him. He was curious about everything related to Annika Dementieva, but he was also curious about this Dr. Karalian. Namazi had been allied with Dyadya Gourdjiev, an alliance that traced its circuitous route through two decades, starting when Namazi had become known to the outside world as the Syrian. In fact, it had been Gourdjiev, the chess player, who had seen Namazi's long-range potential; the Syrian identity had been Gourdjiev's brainchild. It had made so much sense to Namazi that he had adopted it at once.

After spending ten or so minutes sitting in the clinic's lobby after he announced himself, he was ushered into Dr. Karalian's office.

"Did Annika just leave?" Namazi asked.

When Dr. Karalian made no reply, Namazi added, "I brought her here today."

"Annika left just a few moments ago." Dr. Karalian, sitting behind his desk, looked up from reading a note which he now folded and slid back into a buff envelope. "How may I help you. Mr. . . . ."

"Cardozian," the Syrian said, using one of the many identities he carried with him. He set his card on the desk but noted the doctor scarcely glanced at it. "Dyadya Gourdjiev and I were business partners. I was curious why I'd never heard of you."

Dr. Karalian smiled thinly. His teeth shone like pearls. "He and I were friends. He never mentioned you, either."

Deciding to take another tack, Namazi said, "I was in Rome when he died."

"I'm sorry to hear that."

"I saw him just after the accident. It was a terrible blow for all of us."

Dr. Karalian's face was entirely expressionless. "I have no idea who 'all of us' refers to."

Namazi's hesitation was slight. "All of us who did business with him."

"I see." Dr. Karalian crossed his hands over his stomach. "His friends and family mourn him, as well."

Namazi was, for the moment, at a loss as to how to proceed. This man had been a friend of Gourdjiev's; he must know Annika well. Namazi was very careful with anyone who had a connection to Annika. Now that the old man was gone, she was his sole link to the ongoing enterprise he and Gourdjiev had created. He could do nothing to anger her, or even to cause her to suspect that he wasn't blindly besotted with her, as were most males she drew into her orbit. It wasn't that Namazi didn't find her sexually attractive, but he was in a phase of his life where he found males more alluring than females.

Namazi gestured. "Do you mind if I take a seat?"

"Not at all." Those teeth again. "Would you care for tea?"

"Thank you, no." Namazi suspected he wouldn't get tea even if he said yes. "What I was wondering was why Annika wanted to see you."

"What, precisely, is your relationship with Ms. Dementieva?"

"You could say I'm acting as her protector."

Dr. Karalian took a moment to digest this. "She told me about Ill—about Dyadya Gourdjiev's death. I was grateful that she told me in person. That was exceptionally kind of her."

"Annika is exceptionally kind." Namazi cleared his throat. "So there was no other reason?"

Dr. Karalian cocked his head. "No other reason for what?"

"Her visit."

"I can't imagine why else she would visit the clinic."

"Then where is she?"

"There is a small garden I tend. It was started by her grandfather many years ago. She often visits it, perhaps to meditate. She doesn't ask me to come with her and I don't ask."

"Where is it, this garden?"

"On the other side of the building. It's off limits to outsiders. I'm sure you under—"

"I have no interest in gardens." Namazi slapped his thighs and rose. "All right, doctor. I'll be off now."

Dr. Karalian was sunk deep in his chair. "Good day, Mr. Cardozian."

At the doorway, Namazi turned for a moment. "Until next time."

Dr. Karalian seemed to start out of his trance. "There will be a next time?" But his visitor had already vanished.

Annika found Rolan in the conservatory. He was seated in a steel wheelchair with a light cotton throw over his wrists and lap. He was quite still, seemingly staring through the large windows at the mountain. Blue shadows crept up his lower half as the sun crawled slowly toward the horizon.

Apart from the two of them, the conservatory, though large, was deserted, as was always the case when Rolan was brought there. Annika had to pass between two burly orderlies as she stepped into the room.

For a moment, she paused to stare out at the mountain, a great shelf of rock into which the Sümela Monastery had been carved and then built. It was here that Rolan had taken her on their honeymoon. At first, she had been somewhat taken aback, having in her mind Paris or Venice—or even Capri. Somewhere quintessentially romantic. But that was before she had been introduced to the lush valley and the magnificent ruins that overlooked it.

In her mind's eye, she saw them walking through the ruined structure, overarched by the monstrous cavern hewn out of the living rock. Standing in those ancient roofless rooms, they had looked out onto the sun-splashed valley, lush with pines, streams, and stony hillocks.

"Beautiful, isn't it?" Rolan had said, taking her hand.

And she had to admit that he was right. At that moment, it was the most romantic spot on earth.

Now he sat, immobile in his wheelchair. While she stared at their shared past, what was he looking at? What did he see when he looked at that mountain? Did he remember their time together? Would he remember her at all? Sometimes he did, and she was heartened, but then would come those visits when his stare passed right through her as if she didn't exist, as if she had never existed. Those were the moments when her heart seemed to freeze in her chest and hot tears sprang into her eyes, when her emotions, long held in check, bubbled up, forcing her out of herself. She became a spectator at the disaster of her own life, in this way telling herself that it was a dream, that soon enough she would fly away and never have to see him again.

But, of course, that never happened, and, at length, she returned to herself, to the crushing weight of her past and what it meant to her now and in the future.

"Rolan."

She pulled up a chair, sat next to him, laid her hand upon his wrist through the cotton throw. She felt it, and slowly, heart beating hard in her chest, she peeled back the throw, as if it were a layer of skin the clinic had sewn onto him. His wrists were manacled to the armrests of the wheelchair.

"Oh, Rolan."

He did not turn to her, gave no sign that he had heard her. She could see the furrow the ball bearing had made as it had scored along the side of his head, a scar that no amount of plastic surgery could hide. There were other wounds in his torso, long healed now, but compared to the one in his head they were of no consequence. No one—not even Dr. Karalian—knew precisely how much damage the head wound had caused, but it was an irrefutable fact that he was now given to unexpected bouts of manic anger. He had injured a patient and two orderlies before Dr. Karalian had started him on a new drug regimen. Even so, whenever he was wheeled out of his locked room, he was manacled to his wheelchair.

When she settled the throw back over him, Rolan said, "Don't."

Annika froze. His voice was thick and rough, as if his vocal cords had been damaged, too, in the assault in Syria that had almost killed him. Rolan had been caught up in a terrorist attack, an innocent bystander who became collateral damage.

"I'll fold it away," Annika said, a bit breathlessly. It wasn't often that Rolan spoke, even less often that he actually responded to word or action.

"My grandmother used to cover me when I was ill."

As Annika had been raised by her grandfather, Rolan had been raised by his grandmother, after his parents were killed on a flight back to St. Petersburg from Moscow. This similarity was one of the ties that had immediately bound them. Over time, there were others.

"I'm not ill," Rolan said.

"It's good to hear your voice," Annika said after a moment's hesitation.

"You think I'm ill." Rolan continued to stare out at the mountain. "You shouldn't believe everything Karalian tells you."

Annika's brows knitted. "Don't you like Dr. Karalian?"

"I don't like anyone," Rolan said. "Except you." When he said this, he turned his head, his sky-blue eyes impaling her.

"Rolan, I—"

"Get me out of here."

Annika stared at him.

"You have the power to do it, I know you do."

She could see him straining at his manacles.

"Don't. Rolan, you'll hurt yourself."

"I'm already hurt." His body began to shake, his face turning red with a sudden rush of blood. "The only way I'll get better is to GET. THE. FUCK. OUT. OF. HERE!"

"I don't think it's wise to—"

She let out a scream as Rolan lunged at her with such force that he overturned the wheelchair. The two orderlies, having been alerted by his shout, were already running toward her. Rolan's heels were beating a military tattoo against the floor. His yells had become unintelligible. Then one of the orderlies grabbed her, dragging her out of range, while the other produced a syringe, which he plunged into the side of Rolan's neck.

"NO NO NO!" Rolan shouted. "MERCY! HAVE MERCY!"

As his eyes rolled up in his head, Annika was hustled from the solarium. Out in the corridor, Dr. Karalian came at a run.

"I heard, Annika," he said, as he neared. "I'm so sorry."

Annika scarcely heard him. She was weeping so hard she was forced to gasp for breath.

"Let her go," Dr. Karalian said to the orderly, who nodded, turned, and returned to help his partner right the overturned wheelchair. Kicking the door to the solarium closed, Karalian held Annika gently by her shoulders, walking her slowly toward his office.

Annika's head was muzzy. That all too familiar feeling of unreality had returned, bringing with it a sticky gush of sorrow, guilt, and rage. Part of her was aware of the doctor talking softly to her, but her mind was resounding with Rolan's desperate, heartrending cry: *Mercy! Have mercy!*

SEVEN

The InterGlobal Logistics plane came down through a twilight sky blurred by steel-colored rain, landing in Berlin without incident. But by the time it had taxied to a stop and begun to unload, the rain had turned into sleet.

The captain, who was known as Tweet, said, "This is the last stop of our current run, Jack, but since you've told me you have another destination in mind, we'll fly you there as soon as we've unloaded, fueled up, and run all our checks."

"You don't have to do that."

"Hey, I can't tell you how many favors I owe Ben King." He swiveled to his navigator, "Right, Hitch?"

Hitch nodded. He was a rangy blond with an easy, open face, and a ready smile. "It sure is."

Tweet rose, stretched, and yawned hugely. In contrast to his navigator, he was dark-haired, with long arms, a bulge at his waist, and an avowed weakness for Dunkin' Donuts and Big Macs. "See?"

Jack rose as well, stretching his legs. "I meant I don't want to get you guys in trouble."

Tweet spread his hands. "How're we going to get in trouble? Nobody knows you're here, and nobody will, right, Hitch?"

"Fuckin' A," Hitch said, giving a thumbs-up. "I'd die first."

"No, really, guys, seriously."

"We *are* being serious," Hitch said.

Tweet laughed. "As serious as we ever get."

"Listen, Jack, these milk runs are as boring as shit." Hitch picked up a clipboard, began filling out the first of what looked like multiple forms. "And when they're not boring, they're fucking tedious." He brandished the clipboard. "Ferrying you to Bangkok is gonna make our week." He grunted. "Hell, it'll make our whole damn month."

"Settle back, pard," Tweet said. "An hour or so and we'll be airborne again."

"You'll have to make out a flight plan."

Hitch hooked a thumb in Jack's direction. "Listen to him. A pilot already."

"Leave the flight plan filing to us, okay, Jack?"

Tweet sat back down and began to talk rapidly into his headset, presumably to someone in the control tower. After a minute of trying to translate the jargon on the fly, Jack stopped listening and got himself some food from the small locker built into the side of the cockpit. In the past seven-plus hours, he'd had enough Dunkin' Donuts to last him several lifetimes.

"Flip over one of those roast beef sandwiches," Tweet said as Hitch rose and went out of the cockpit. "And a Coke."

Jack tossed him the wax-paper-wrapped sandwich, but handed him the Coke. He had noted during the flight that these flyboys stocked only bottles of Coke manufactured in Mexico, where they used sugar instead of high-fructose corn syrup as a sweetener. Much to his surprise, the flavor was completely different from the domestic version.

He chose a turkey and swiss, and the two men ate in companionable silence until Tweet said, "Pardon my mouth, but d'you know what the fuck you're doing?"

"To be honest," Jack said around a bite, "I don't know."

"Then why—?"

"I have no choice."

"We all have a—"

"A friend of mine was killed. I've got to find out who did it."

"Bad shit." Tweet shook his head. "Well, for Christ's sake, don't get lost in Bangkok."

Hitch locked himself in the tiny toilet, unzipped his trousers, and enjoyed a good, long pee, all the while whistling "Zip-A-Dee-Do-Dah" and imagining a parade of his favorite Disney cartoon characters. When he was finished, he slipped out his mobile and punched in a number. He whistled a different tune, as if by doing so he could conjure up the flying monkeys from *The Wizard of Oz.*

"Yes?" the female voice said in his ear.

"We're in Berlin."

"He's with you?"

"Safe and sound, like I said."

"Has he deplaned?"

"Uh-uh. We've volunteered to continue on."

"That won't be a problem for you?"

"Nah. We have the locals greased—have done for years, it was seen to. No worries there."

"Has he told you where he wants you to take him?"

"Bangkok."

"Then he knows about Legere."

"It would seem so." Hitch picked at a piece of lint on his trouser leg. "And that Connaston was killed."

"Good. Keep him safe until you arrive in Bangkok."

Hitch stared at himself in the mirror. "And then?"

"Then," the voice at the other end said, "he's on his own."

———

Stepping out of the airport terminal into the Bangkok morning, Redbird felt as if he had fallen into a vat of chicken soup. The air was so thick, so dense with petroleum particulates that he unconsciously leaned forward, as if he were moving along the bottom of the sea.

He saw Dandy right away and headed toward her silver BMW motorcycle. Her left hand was curled around the handlebar and she held her gleaming helmet crooked like a baby in her right arm. She had cut her impossibly thick ribbon of hair short, so that it now bobbed at the length of her sharp chin. Her long almond eyes, which always seemed to be laughing, tracked him across the apron until he climbed on right behind her. As he picked his helmet off the saddle behind her, she settled hers over her head.

"When are they gonna figure out how to air-condition these things?" he said.

She laughed, stamped the engine on, and, as he wrapped his arms around her diminutive waist, buzzed away from the busy curb, threading her way between two cabs, painted yellow and green like forest parrots.

As usual, the highway was a seven-lane parking lot, bright with pink and orange cars, red and blue buses, and cyclists weaving between lanes. The vehicles were indistinct, wavery, and the air stank of diesel fumes. The heat was unbearable.

Over eleven million people lived in Bangkok and almost seven million vehicles drove its limited streets every day. It was a wonder that anyone could get to their destination. On the other hand, there were natives like Dandy who knew how to negotiate even the most flagrant of traffic jams. Dandy had grown up on a motorcycle, driven first by her father, then her various older brothers. She was ten the first time she drove on her own. Twelve years later, she was an old hand, as expert as anyone in maneuvering around the city at skull-cracking speeds.

Twenty-five minutes after she had picked up Redbird, they arrived at his safe house, which she maintained when he was out of town. He had similar safe houses in many other cities; all of them proved useful and were often worth their weight in gold. The place was small but bright, a corner apartment on the top floor of a modern building overlooking the Chao Phraya, removed from the city's oppressive, never-ending traffic. On the river's far bank was an ancient temple, gongs sounding at all hours of the day and night. Such was life in Bangkok.

Redbird turned the air-conditioning to low, crossed the room, and opened the French doors. Stepping out onto the narrow terrace, he breathed in the thick soupy air. On the river below him, boats and sampans drifted by, past the glittering tiers of the temple. He returned inside.

Looking around the room, he took in the black-lacquered walls and ceiling, the mosaic tile floor, the long cane sofa, and two chairs.

"Bag?"

Dandy, who had stepped into the small kitchen and was already preparing tea, pointed underneath the sofa, where an old-fashioned doctor's satchel sat, waiting. Redbird nodded, went over, fetched it, and pulled it open. Inside were the tools of his trade: two different caliber handguns, noise suppressors, ammo, three kinds of knives, small packets of C-4, timing devices, and wires, as well as a skeletal assault rifle handmade to his specifications by a German technician, broken down into three convenient sections.

By the time he had checked all the weapons and ammo, Dandy appeared with a Chinese tea service on a lacquered tray, which she set on a low table lacquered in the Chinese style, at which they sat cross-legged, opposite each other.

Redbird watched her appreciatively as her long, delicate fingers went through the calming ritual of brewing and pouring the tea. He hadn't seen her in eight months. She looked the same to him, but he knew she couldn't be. Time stood still for him each time he returned here, but for her each day, each night had to be lived. She had experienced events, people, movies, and sex of which he had no idea. Her days and nights were a blank to him. It was no wonder he felt like a stranger every time he came back. And each time he saw her anew, a wave of tenderness washed over him that he'd never felt for anyone before or since. Her significance for him lay somewhere between that of a sister and a daughter. He would protect her with his own life, if need be. He had tried to protect her father once, to no avail. But together, he and Dandy had exacted her revenge, an act that had bonded them for life. There wasn't anything Dandy would not do for him, an obligation she had taken on willingly. And because he had not asked it of her, she drew both strength and confidence from it.

Not a word was spoken until they had savored their first sip. They smiled at each other. Her name wasn't Dandy, of course—that's what Redbird called her because her Thai name was so long and, even for him, unwieldy to pronounce. She didn't seem to mind.

"My contacts tell me that the target, Pyotr Legere, has not returned to Moscow. In fact, he's off the grid altogether."

"Gone to ground."

Redbird nodded, turned his mobile so Dandy could see the photo of Legere that Dickinson had provided. "Look familiar?"

She shook her head. "But Chati might know."

Chaat Pradchaphet was a minor underlord in Bangkok's criminal underbelly. Despite his relatively low status, he seemed to know everything and everyone of interest in and around the city. Therefore, unlike others in his profession, his principal work was selling information. The answer to why he didn't use this information for his own advancement was simple: he was lazy. Chati preferred to work less, rather than more. Stress did not suit his sybaritic lifestyle.

"All right. Dinner at Chati's then." Chaat ran his business out of a restaurant in the Sukhumvit Soi area. The place was very upscale, *hi-so* in Thai slang. That was good for Redbird; Chati was in residence, day and night, squeezed into a chair at his private table next to the open kitchen.

As was her wont, Dandy sat on the closed toilet seat in the bathroom while Redbird showered. There was nothing sexual in this, but another form of intimacy that both craved. Redbird had no family to speak of, and as for Dandy, being the black sheep of the family, breaking off and going her own way, her brothers and their respective families had become distant. Frankly, Redbird and Dandy preferred each other's company, even when they weren't talking.

Dandy smoked a clove cigarette, drawing the aromatic smoke into her lungs and slowly letting it drift out through her mouth and nostrils, her head tilted back to reveal her throat and long neck. Years ago, when this strange ritual began, Dandy had wanted to scrub him down, but Redbird soon put a stop to that. That the offer was cultural rather than sexual made no difference. She took this rebuff with her usual equanimity. Redbird had only seen her cry once, when she had killed the man who had murdered her father, and then, as he cradled her, it seemed as if she would never stop. Since that time, she had developed a terrible calm Redbird found both fascinating and admirable. It was that calm that drew them even closer.

"You come here at the worst times." Her voice wasn't loud, but rather strong, carrying over the sound of the running water.

"Worst?" Redbird said from behind the translucent shower curtain.

Dandy took another drag of her cigarette. "The weather."

"Except for the rains, the weather is always the same here."

Dandy laughed, smoking like an engine. "Hot, hotter, hottest."

"Well, that's true."

Having rinsed off, Redbird turned off the water and pulled back the curtain. Dandy had an enormous bath towel ready, spreading it as she rose, preparing to wrap it around his shoulders. Before she did, though, her fingertip ran lightly over the scars on the back of his right shoulder.

"Do they hurt?"

"Not for some time."

"I mean inside."

"Towel."

She wrapped him as securely as a mother swaddles her child. Their relationship ran both ways.

"I know you won't talk about it," Dandy said, "but sometimes I need to."

Redbird had been wounded severely during their joint mission of revenge. He had presented himself as a target so that Dandy could creep up from behind and blow the murderer's head to smithereens. She had done it, Redbird had swept her off her feet and, though he had been shot three times, had carried her away from the scene of their crime. Between the adrenaline and the endorphins thundering through him, his shoulder had remained numb until an hour later, after her crying jag, when she had taken him to her cousin, a surgeon of some renown. He had gone into shock and was laid on the surgeon's operating table. At her cousin's direction, Dandy had covered him with blankets, and then, a syringe sliding into his vein, he had lost consciousness.

When he came to, his right shoulder was heavily bandaged, the pain was a red pulse behind his eyes. Dandy held his hand; her cousin had handed him the three bullets he had pried out of the flesh of Redbird's right shoulder. Small caliber. Some minor muscle damage, that was all. Painkillers and a strong antibiotic. Lucky. Redbird had thrown the painkillers away. He'd be no good to anyone doped up, especially himself.

Redbird padded into the bedroom, the walls and ceiling a deep, glossy aubergine, the bed huge, a semicircle, like the moon. "What do you need to say?"

She was at his closet, pulling a shirt and trousers of Thai silk off hangers. She liked choosing his clothes. "I don't understand why."

He pulled on underpants. "Why what?"

"Why you did what you did." She began to button his shirt after he had shrugged it on.

"Why do you ask me this question when I've answered it so many times before?"

"Because."

He grunted. "That's a child's answer."

"I am a child," she said, "in some respects."

He eyed her as he took his trousers from her. "In others, you're older than I am."

"Bangkok does that to you."

He sat on the bed while he pulled on socks so thin his skin shone through the close-knit mesh. Midway through, he stopped, elbows on knees. When he patted the bed next to him, she came and sat beside him. Her hands were clasped in her lap, her back rigid, like a schoolgirl awaiting a test score.

Redbird looked out at the river and the golden temple beyond. Gongs announced the appearance of a line of saffron-robed monks. "I did it because of you." He could not bear to look at her while he spoke of such intimate things. "Because a girl like you—no, that's not right—because *you* shouldn't have to bear the loss of your father, because he died alone and in darkness, because there was no justice in his death."

"He crossed the wrong people." Her voice was much softer than it had been in the bathroom, carrying with it the whisper of silk against skin. "My father was not a bad man, but nor was he a good one."

"He needed money for you and your brothers. As you say, he got caught up with the wrong people."

"He was foolish." There was no anger in her voice, only regret.

"And why should you have to pay for his foolishness?" Redbird looked at her now, because it had become impossible for him not to. "This man did not get the money your father owed him, so he took his pound of flesh. But do you imagine he would have stopped there? He wanted your father's death *and* his money. If we hadn't stopped him, he would have come after your brothers and then you."

"And you could not allow that to happen."

"No."

"And again I ask, why?"

"The brown loafers."

Dandy went and fetched them, along with a shoehorn carved from a water buffalo horn.

Redbird slipped the shoes on. They felt good, like being reacquainted with an old friend. There was nothing left to do. He set the shoehorn aside, took a deep breath, and let it slowly out.

He stood, looking down at Dandy. Then he held out his hand. As she slipped hers into it, he said, "I can't tell you what you already know."

[Engage Electronic Encryption Protocol OA-71937]

CONFIDENTIAL MEMO - TOP SECRET - EYES ONLY

FROM: G. ROBERT KROFFT, DIRECTOR, CIA

TO: WILLIAM ROGERS, NATIONAL SECURITY ADVISOR
    KINKAID MARSHALL, DIRECTOR, DCS
    TIMOTHY MALONE, DIRECTOR, FBI
    HENRY DICKINSON, ACTING DIRECTOR, DEPT.
       HOMELAND SECURITY

CC: ARLEN CRAWFORD, PRESIDENT OF THE UNITED STATES
    GEN. LUCIUS FORD BRANDT, DEPT. OF DEFENSE

SUBJECT: OPERATION ATLAS UPDATE

Gentlemen,

Please be advised, in response to the security breach surrounding the murder of Dennis Paull, the following changes in our ongoing preparations for Operation Atlas have been instituted, effective immediately:

1. New encryption algorithms have been substituted for communications with all Atlas personnel on foreign soil.

2. Encryption protocols are changed on a daily, rather than a weekly, basis.

3. Agents-in-place are directed to procure and secure new safe houses in their respective areas.

4. Six new Arab and Iranian handlers have been dispatched to confirm the loyalty and security of all of Atlas's agents-in-place.

5. J. J. Midwood, Chairman of Arclight, the black-ops security arm of the CIA, is given carte blanche access to assess every aspect of Atlas's infrastructure and personnel.

Sincerely,

G. Robert Krofft

[End Electronic Encryption Protocol OA-71937]

"What the hell do you think you're doing?" Henry Dickinson said.

"Think?" Krofft said. "I *know* what I'm doing, Dicky. I'm trying to clean up the mess you made. What are *you* doing? Where's Jack McClure? Do you have him? Do you even know whether he's in the country?"

Krofft had been on his way out of the office. Coat in hand, he had just stepped across the threshold when he'd been accosted by a raging Dickinson.

"You tried to hijack my crime scene and now you're hijacking Atlas." Dickinson stood spread-legged squarely in front of Krofft, blocking his escape.

"Let's go into my office and discuss this rationally."

Dickinson shook off the offer. "I'm not going anywhere until I get an explanation."

Krofft glanced down the hallway, which was, mercifully,

deserted. "First of all, the crime scene is being run by the FBI, which is as it should be. Frankly, Hank, homeland security's forte does not lie in crime scene investigation. Why do I have to tell you that? Oh, yeah, you're the *acting* director. Second of all, Atlas no longer belongs to DHS; it belongs to all of us. I'm just doing my job, which is more than I can say for you." His face darkened as he swept Dickinson out of his way. "What the fuck are you doing here when you should be tracking McClure down?"

High over the Himalayas, Jack sat back and tried to relax. Easier said than done. He had lost his best friend and mentor, he was accused of killing him, and he was now an international fugitive without a home or visible means of support, and, frankly, very little chance of vindicating himself.

He had considered calling Nona Heroe with the satellite phone he had picked up. She was his one slim lifeline, but there was only so much she could do for him without endangering herself. He was now so toxic that any known contact with him was perilous and so he decided against it. The only bright spot was that Alli was on assignment and, consequently, wouldn't have heard of his predicament. The last thing he needed was for her to come riding to his rescue, only to be targeted by the same person or group that had framed him for Dennis's murder.

Thoughts of his forced isolation inevitably led him to Annika. The last time he had seen her was in the Syrian's villa outside Rome a year ago. At that time, she had had a chance to escape with him. Inexplicably, she had refused, choosing to stay with the Syrian—a man Jack had been tracking, a man, as it turned out, with whom Dyadya Gourdjiev had been in business. What kind of business could Gourdjiev have had with a known terrorist? The kind of business that could have had him killed? Could Jack have misjudged Annika's grandfather so completely? Did that mean he had misjudged Annika to the same extent? It was true that she was an inveterate liar when it served her purpose, but could any female, even

Annika, train her body to respond to his the way hers did?

There was no doubt that she had the ability to break his heart. The question was, how many times? Endlessly? That he loved her was beyond question; but given all that had happened, how many times she had lied to him, he couldn't understand why.

Then there was Annika's half-brother, Radomil, who last year had helped him escape the Syrian's villa. Since that night, Jack had had no contact with Annika or Radomil, though he'd tried several different ways to track their whereabouts. And then Jack's busy life had overtaken him, and he had tried to put Annika out of his mind.

The truth was he could not bear to think of his link with her being broken. No matter what she had said, no matter what she had done, he simply could not let her go.

"*This woman,*" Paull had said, "*is perhaps the most dangerous female on the planet. This is the woman you love.*"

"*Loved,*" Jack had said. "*Past tense.*"

"*You can turn it on and off at will.*" Dennis's tone had made his skepticism clear. "*You'd tell me if it were otherwise, wouldn't you, Jack?*"

"*I would,*" Jack had lied.

Dennis had been right to distrust Jack's motivation when it came to Annika. He knew it, too, when he had said, "*If push comes to shove, Jack, would you be able to kill her, or would she kill you?*"

Jack, staring down at the ice and snow-encrusted top of the world, wished he knew the answer.

EIGHT

"None of us on your memo distribution list ever heard of Arclight," William Rogers said.

Krofft smiled. "You mean *you* never heard of Arclight."

The two men, hands in the pockets of their raincoats, strolled along the length of the Reflecting Pool. It was a visible measure of the importance Krofft gave to fishing the rotten apple out of their collective barrel that he insisted these meetings take place in public places, rather than in anyone's offices. A spotty drizzle was falling, and they hunched their shoulders against it.

"I'm all for stronger security," Rogers said. "I just don't like being blindsided."

"Couldn't be helped, Bill. Time was of the essence."

Rogers looked away, toward the National World War II Memorial. He was unclear whether he believed Krofft's explanation. "Tell me a bit more about J. J. Midwood," he said, after a time.

Krofft waited until a mother and her daughter passed by. A red-white-and-blue-striped balloon danced above the child's head, tied by a string to her wrist. Three young boys on skateboards, whooping it up, went whizzing by.

"Jonatha is an exceptional agent," Krofft said. "I recruited her; I trained her."

"So, in effect, she *is* you."

Krofft's eyes glittered behind his lenses. "My eyes and ears, anyway. If there is a rotten apple, she'll find him."

"How do you figure?"

"She has a nose for stink, no matter how slight," Krofft said. "That's how I figure." His flat tone made it clear that he was irritated with the national security advisor.

"But she's a *female*, G.R. I don't understand—"

"You don't have to understand."

Rogers blew air out of his mouth. "What I was going to say, is that I don't understand what makes her so special."

Krofft shot Rogers a withering look. "I just told you."

"Pretend I'm thick. Tell me again."

"She has an uncanny intuition."

"What, like a human lie detector?"

"If you like."

Rogers stopped and turned to Krofft. "What the hell is going on? Are you sleeping with her? And don't give me that 'I don't shit where I eat' crap. I know you better than that, even if your wife doesn't."

"You may be right about me," Krofft said, "but you're dead wrong about Jonatha."

"You tried, or she looks like a Mack truck, which is it?"

"You think you have all the answers? She's not the type to make a move on."

"So you did try." Rogers appeared genuinely taken aback.

"To be truthful, it never crossed my mind."

"Why?'

Krofft smiled. "I'll set up a meeting. You'll find out for yourself."

———

Chaat Pradchaphet's restaurant was named Blue Lagoon, but the regulars invariably referred to it as Chati's. It occupied a space more or less midway down a block in posh Soi Pichai Ronnarong, where, the later it got, the more packed the street was with young, wealthy Thais, Singaporeans, Russians, and Japanese.

The red and black lacquered interior was carved up into three spaces, sectioned off by bamboo and translucent glass-block dividers: the bar, the main dining room, and the exclusive club section in the rear, presided over by Chati himself. Sometimes, a guest or two would be invited to sit with him, at other times, a dark-haired bombshell drank and fondled him under the table. But, mostly, he sat by himself, smoking reeking cigarettes and poring over spreadsheets, like an accountant or a bookie.

Redbird was happy to let Dandy lead the way from the moment they stepped into the restaurant. She chatted a few minutes with the manager, blew the bartender a kiss, smiled at the waiters as they passed. Best of all, she was well known to the muscle Chati employed to keep the rowdies out, also to protect him from anyone who might seek to do him harm. She had even been known to stop on their way to buy a complicated-looking Transformers toy for one of the bodyguard's sons, who was ill.

They were allowed access to the club after hugs and cheek kisses. One of the bodyguards must have alerted Chati via a wireless network, because he raised his head to look directly at them. The moment he recognized Dandy a smile broke out across his broad face. He dismissed the bombshell sitting next to him with a curt gesture, and she slid out, rose, and made her way across the polished rosewood floor, her buttocks rolling like the ball bearings of a well-oiled machine.

Chati was a big man, tall for a Thai, and by Redbird's expert estimation, weighing somewhere between three hundred and four hundred pounds. He had small black eyes, like raisins sunk in a vat of suet. His lips were small, thick, bowed, and possibly rouged, like a girl's. Dandy introduced Redbird as Ken Douglas, an agreed-upon legend, and the two men shook hands. Chati invited them to sit. As they did so, a waiter appeared as if out of thin air and took their drink orders.

The big man and Dandy made small talk for several minutes. Redbird listened with one ear while he checked out the patrons. He neither saw nor felt anything out of the ordinary.

"Dhandyamongko tells me you're looking for a man by the name of—" He snapped his fingers.

"Pyotr Legere," Redbird said. "He's a bookstore owner and art dealer from Moscow."

"He's a long way from home," Chati said. "Plus, the art here is the shits."

"He didn't come for the art," Redbird said. "He was meeting someone."

"Does this someone have a name?"

"Leroy Connaston."

Chati cocked his head. "Shot-to-death-twelve-days-ago Connaston?"

Redbird's interest quickened. "Do the cops have a suspect?"

Chati laughed. "Fuck, no. This is Bangkok, man! The only time the cops can follow a lead is if they're paid to do it."

The drinks came, along with several plates of bite-sized snacks.

Redbird concentrated on the big man rather than the food. "Do you have any ideas?"

"You want to know who killed Connaston?"

"I might be interested," Redbird acknowledged, "but it's Legere I'm after."

Chati grunted. "What's it worth to you?"

"Plenty." Redbird was playing with Dickinson's money. Experience had taught him that the people Dickinson worked for had very deep pockets.

"You got a figure in mind?"

Redbird threw out a sum that left him plenty of room to maneuver.

"Huh," Chati said dismissively, "you must not want to find him that much."

Redbird was unfazed. "I need to know whether you can help me."

Chati plucked up a crisp morsel, popped it between his lips. "You still sitting here is proof of that."

Redbird wasn't budging. "So you say."

Chati swallowed, all the while eying Redbird calculatingly. "Because you're a friend of Dandy's I've decided not to take offense." Without taking his gaze from Redbird, he popped another morsel into his mouth. "I'm not going to eat all this food by myself."

Redbird ate slowly and deliberately.

"Good?" Chati asked.

Redbird nodded. "Very."

Chati wiped his grease-smeared lips with an oversize linen napkin. "I gotta guy who will tell you what you want to know."

"He in Bangkok?"

Chati's face was perfectly immobile. Then, like a detonation, he threw his head back and laughed. "Maybe I know why you like this one, Dandy." His hand waved back and forth. "Okay, Mr.—what is it? Douglas?" He laughed again. "Very good. Let's consummate our deal. I have a very sexy lady waiting for me."

Jack plunged into the teeming currents of Bangkok. With Tweet and Hitch at his side, he'd had no trouble passing through immigration, the harried officials on the freight side of International Suvarnabhumi Airport giving him scarce notice.

After purchasing a sat phone in an ultramodern mall on the outskirts of the city, he proceeded to an Internet café, paid an hour's fee, and settled himself at a free terminal. Typing in the Internet address of the *Bangkok Post*, he scrolled back in time to the date Leroy Connaston was shot to death at WTF.

The resulting story was sparse, providing nothing in the way of the victim's background, other than he was a British national, but it included a photo of Connaston: a middle-aged man with thin hair, a receding hairline and chin. He carried a shabby air with him like an umbrella, as if he were a solicitor down at the heels.

Jack made a copy of the photo, using the café's public printer, and stowed it away. He checked all the Thai papers, but there was barely a mention, and no other photos. Before he left the terminal, he accessed the Options menu on the browser and deleted both the history and the cache, erasing any vestige of his searches.

Outside the mall, he grabbed a taxi. On the interminable crawl into the city, he used his sat phone to call Nona and was relieved when she answered her mobile.

"It's me," he said tersely.

"Hold on."

He could hear noise—people talking, mostly—fading out of the background and knew she was moving to isolate herself from whomever she was with, in order to talk securely with him. "Are you okay?"

He heard the anxiety in her voice. "Unharmed. I'm down." Meaning on the ground.

"That's a relief."

"How are things there?"

"Worse. The manhunt has intensified tenfold."

Jack tried to block the rapidly deteriorating situation out of his mind. "I need some help."

"Tell me."

"See if you can find information on a man named Leroy Connaston."

There was a small silence, during which he could hear someone speaking softly, but urgently to her.

A moment later, she came back on. "What can you tell me about him?"

"He was a British national, shot to death in a Bangkok nightspot called WTF eight days ago."

Another small silence. "That's it?"

"I'm afraid so." He took a breath. "Listen, Nona, it's okay if you can't—"

"Stop right there," she said. "I'll get right on it."

Relief flooded through him. "I call back in an hour."

"You're giving me that much time?" she said archly. "Really?"

He laughed grimly. "Thanks, Nona."

"Thank me when I get you something you can use."

Forty minutes later, he had the taxi drop him off on Phaholyothin Road, in Soi Aree. There, he found the area jammed with an insane number of people, jostling and laughing, hurrying, hanging out and smoking. He joined the flow, finding it impossible to go at his own pace. Within a four-block radius, he spotted six massage parlors, any one of which could have been visited by Leroy Connaston, Pyotr Legere's murdered contact, before their fateful rendezvous. He didn't want to go poking inside them until he had as much intel on Connaston as he could get.

Dusk had laid its velvet hand across the city, the neon lights brightening the streets in a rainbow of flashing colors. He chose a small restaurant because it was playing American rock music through its tinny speakers, went in, and sat down. He decided that he might as well take advantage of the wait to fill his stomach, which had started growling the moment he had successfully passed ghost-like through the airport.

A stick-thin waitress, who might have been twelve or eighteen, dropped a laminated menu onto the table. He ordered a beer. A cursory glance at the offerings was all he needed, and when she returned to set the bottle in front of him, he pointed to the dishes he wanted. She swept the menu up and took it away.

Opening the photo of Connaston, he stared at it again. It was far from ideal, a smudgy copy of the already blurred newspaper picture, but for the moment it was all he had and it would have to do.

He was still staring at Connaston's face when Otis Redding began to sing "I've Been Loving You Too Long (To Stop Now)." It had been one of Emma's favorite songs. He remembered listening to it on her iPod for months after she had died. Like a film he couldn't stop playing in slow motion, he saw the car she had been driving smashed into a huge tree off the side of the road. He had arrived just after the paramedics had used the jaws of life to pry her out of the wreck. It didn't matter; his daughter was gone the moment her car struck the tree. Staring down at her bloody face, fending off the paramedics, all he could think of was her voice on the phone, just—what?—forty-five minutes before, asking for his help. But he had been up to his eyeballs coordinating an ATF raid and had not concentrated on what she was telling him. How many times since then had he played that scene over and over, hoping this time he would listen, that he would save her.

"I love you, I love you in so many different ways . . ." Otis sang, and Jack wept bitter tears for all he had lost.

"Leaving us so soon?" Police Commissioner Lincoln Dye said with one eyebrow lifted.

Nona Heroe, at the head of the alley in NW Washington, turned back. "I won't be long." She glanced at the three bodies in the midst of the crime scene she had been studying for the last fifteen minutes. A triple homicide involving Senator Herren's aide; no wonder Dye had made an appearance. "I've got as much as I'm going to get until the autopsies come back." She glanced over her shoulder at the gathering news media. "Anyway, it's your press conference, not mine."

Dye shook his head. "Uh-uh. I want you by my side when I step up to the podium."

He was a solid-looking individual, whose face the camera loved. Being telegenic was part of his job description, but Nona, checking up on him, had been impressed with his CV, which included stints at a prestigious law firm and with IA. It was a cliché that everyone hated internal affairs, but the truth was the dirty cops hated them the most. Dye seemed cut from a different bolt of cloth, at least so far as she could observe.

"The department needs a united front," Dye continued. "That was part of the problem with my predecessor, he had no idea how to get all the gears to mesh." He checked his watch. "We're on in ten minutes. That's all I can give you."

Nona ducked under the yellow tape, went past the uniforms guarding the crime scene, into the maelstrom of reporters demanding exclusives and face time, trying to attach themselves to her like remoras to a passing shark. She wished she had a shark's powerful tail to flick them away.

Finally making it into her car, she pulled the door shut, locked the doors, and powered up her new iPad, another of Dye's innovations. He wanted all his chiefs to be networked, able to talk strategy at a moment's notice.

But this allowed Nona to have her own network up and running. Tapping an icon, she established a network connection to Deckard. It was of his own design, meaning that not only was it encrypted, but both their IP addresses were shielded from prying software.

A moment later, his face swam up out of the gloom of his laboratory, his halo of golden hair standing up as if he'd just received an electric shock.

"Hey, how's it going?" Deckard was not his real name, but the moniker he used, one he'd chosen from *Blade Runner*, his favorite film.

"I need intel."

"Of course you do." Deckard's fingers were poised over one of the multiple keyboards that surrounded his workstation. He had touch screens as well, but they were mainly for aggregating and manipulating JPEG and video files. "Shoot."

Nona related the sparse details on Leroy Connaston that Jack had given her.

"What do I concentrate on?" Fingers already dancing over the keys, his heavily freckled face looked spectral in the LED light from his computers.

"Anything and everything."

"And you need it three minutes ago, yes?"

Nona laughed. "Yes." She was keeping one eye on the time, another on Deckard's expression, with occasional glances at the head of the alley, where the scrum of press had ratcheted up a couple of notches, as the victims, invisible inside body bags, were taken out to waiting meat wagons to be transported to the ME's cold room, to be picked apart, discussed, and argued over.

"Hey," Deckard said, "I can do that."

"That's because you're a replicant."

"Damnit, Nora," he said good-naturedly, "I told you Deckard isn't a replicant!"

"You should've called yourself Roy Batty."

"The head Nexus-6. Ha ha! Maybe you're right, but it's too late now." Deckard's head nodded like a bobble toy in the back of a car. "Okay, I've wormed my way into the Bangkok police files."

"And?"

"Well, it's notable for what's *not* in there."

"Meaning?"

"The investigation into Connaston's murder was slow in starting and then abruptly cut short."

"Cut short? By whom?"

"Someone high up in the Thai Royal Police."

"The Central Investigation Bureau?"

"Well, you would think so," Deckard said. "But no. It was the head of Naresuan Two-sixty-one."

"I beg your pardon?"

"Naresuan Two-sixty-one is a special operations unit of Special Branch, in charge of counterterrorism."

"Jesus."

"Right response," Deckard said. "Was Connaston a terrorist—or a spook?"

"I'm hoping you're going to tell me," Nona said.

"Yeah, well, if there was a Special Branch file on him or his murder, it no longer exists."

"Great," Nona sighed. "I'm chasing a ghost."

Deckard switched to another screen. "Not quite. Okay, here we go. Connaston, Leroy. Age, forty-six at time of death. Body repatriated to Yorkshire, England, requested by his younger sister, Penelope Barrowwood, but everyone seems to call her Penny." He gave Nona a date two days ago. "Married to Duff Barrowwood—do you believe these Brit names? Anyway, Sir Duff is a solicitor of some repute in Yorkshire. No other family, it seems."

"What did Connaston do for a living?" Nona asked.

"Good question. Whatever it was, it earned him a boatload of money. The guy had a townhouse in Belgravia—veddy posh, don't you know," he said, at the end slipping into a deliberately over-the-top upper-class English accent. "But that's not all. He also owned a house in Tuscany and—get this!—a fucking castle in the south of Spain."

Nona frowned. Her time was getting short. "Are you telling me he had no visible means of support?"

"Not immediately visible, anyway."

"Maybe he inherited."

"His father was a Yorkshire coal miner, died of the black lung, and the mother came from farming stock, so cross that notion out."

The crowd had thickened around the neck of the alleyway. The uniforms were standing at attention, at any moment Commissioner Dye would appear, and her time alone with Deckard would be at an end.

"Come on. There must be—"

"Of course there is," Deckard said. "But considering the tangled web the intervention of Naresuan Two-sixty-one has made, it's going to take a bit of specialized digging."

"Deck—"

"I know, I know, time is of the essence."

"If you've got a clear photo of Connaston—"

Deckard made a show of striking a key. "Done. You'll have it inside thirty seconds."

"Now—"

He sighed theatrically. "Nona, because I love you like no other,

I'm going to link up with Ripley." Another geek of his caliber who lived in London. She'd named herself after the lead character in the *Alien* trilogy. "Even though she's a royal pain in the ass."

"You're the best, Deck."

"You got that right!"

"I gotta break off now. Shoot me the intel as soon as—"

"Gotcha," Deckard said, breaking the connection.

Nona waited until the photo and what intel Deckard had on Connaston arrived in her electronic mailbox, then immediately forwarded it to Jack. Then she slid her iPad under the driver's seat, got out, and picked her way through the heaving throng to where Commissioner Dye stood, waiting implacably for her.

Armed with the photo Nona had sent to his Samsung, Jack visited the six massage parlors. It took him an hour to discover that no one would admit to knowing, or even having seen, Connaston. He didn't necessarily believe them, but there was little he could do, beyond the offer of American dollars, to get them to change their minds.

He was half a block away from the sixth establishment, the Unlimited Happy Spa, a two-floor business like all the rest, where legitimate massages were performed on street level, while upstairs entirely different services were performed in cramped, airless cubicles, stinking of sweat and bleach, when he heard his name being called.

Pausing, he turned to see one of the younger girls, not more than a wisp, insinuating herself through the throng of pedestrians, sausage grillers, juice vendors, and fresh fruit sellers. Her eyes were big, her expression anxious as she made her way toward him.

"Yes?" Jack said.

A motorcycle taxi, going the wrong way, almost ran her down from behind, but she sidestepped it without a second thought.

"Let's go inside," she said, in her high, piping voice. "Please."

She led him into a music shop, festooned with shiny CD covers and bootleg DVDs of current American films, juddering with terrible

Thai techno music.

Under cover of looking through bins of vintage and new vinyl albums, she said, "I am in desperate need of money."

She was one of the legion of workers who had shaken their head when he had presented Connaston's photo. Her name was Dao.

"If you help me," Jack said, "I'll help you."

She nodded but said nothing. Her eyes darted about the shop while she worried her lower lip with tiny white teeth. Jack also checked their surroundings, especially the people who had come in after them, but he did not recognize anyone from the massage parlors.

Growing concerned about her obvious skittishness, Jack said, "You know this man Leroy Connaston?"

"No, but I know someone who does." Her fingers trembled atop the cardboard LP covers as she shuffled them back and forth. "She was on duty the night that man was in. He asks for her especially."

"So he comes in often?"

"In spurts." She shrugged. "I don't think he lives here. There are long months when he isn't seen. Then Jaidee is very sad, because the English *farang* pays her above the requested rate, and she can put rice on the table every night for her whole family."

"Did I see Jaidee when I was at Unlimited Happy Spa?"

Dao shook her head. "This is her night off. But I have called her. She has agreed to see you."

Jack's pulse quickened. "When?"

"In three hours." Noting Jack's expression, Dao added, "She's got to take her daughter to her mother's on the other side of the city."

Jack nodded. She paused long enough for him to understand her underlying motivation. Drawing out some American dollars, he gave her two twenties and a ten. The blood drained from her face so quickly, he thought she was going to pass out, and he grasped her elbow as she staggered against the plywood bins.

"This is so much!"

"It's all right, Dao," he said gently. "Tell me now where to meet Jaidee."

The rider came toward them out of the gloaming, his horse high-stepping through the coarse, unmowed grass. Behind him, the last of the cattle was being herded in from the far grazing fields.

Redbird, comfortable in his Western saddle, said to Dandy, "What is it with Thais and cowboys?"

Dandy, beside him on her black mare, laughed. "Did you ever see *Tears of the Black Tiger*?"

Redbird remembered it: a crazy spaghetti western that had achieved the highest cult status in Thailand.

"Before *Tears*," Dandy went on, "we had no idea what an American cowboy was. Now we can't get enough of the experience."

They were at Shinawatra, a working cattle ranch less than a hundred miles outside Bangkok. This was where Chati had sent them. According to him, one of the ranch hands had information regarding Pyotr Legere and Leroy Connaston.

Rangsan Wattanapanit came up to them. He was tall and thin, his skin very dark. He was dressed in boots, jeans, a red-checked Western shirt with arrow slash pockets, and a Stetson hat. A calico neckerchief was tied at his throat. He watched them, his crossed wrists placed atop the pommel of his saddle.

"Chati sent us," Dandy said, after the moment of mutual sizing up had taken place.

"He called," Wattanapanit said in a laconic drawl, as if he'd seen too many Gary Cooper movies. "You want to know about the *farang* who was shot to death."

"Possibly. I'm more interested in the man he was meeting."

"Why?"

"Forget why," Redbird said.

"I don't forget anything." Wattanapanit turned his head and spat onto the ground. "Least of all why one *farang* is looking for another *farang*."

Redbird felt the adrenaline surge through him, fueling the muscles of his arms and legs. Then he felt Dandy's long, slim hand slide over the back of his right hand, and he smiled. He could take this arrogant Thai cowboy out within three seconds, but Dandy's hand signal was right on the money: What would be the point? Besides, while in Bangkok it was best to be guided by her unerring instincts.

"So." Wattanapanit's horse snorted, pawing the ground as if it was impatient to be off. He patted its neck affectionately. "I would think, *farang*, that you would be more interested in Connaston than Legere."

Redbird's eyes narrowed, studying the cowboy hard, to make certain he wasn't being made the butt of some obscure Thai joke. "And why would that be?"

Wattanapanit looked smug. "I have heard—and very lately—that another *farang* is asking questions about Connaston."

"Another foreigner?" Redbird was nonplused. "Do you have a name?"

The cowboy shifted in his saddle. "He goes by the name of Edward Griffiths—at least that's what he told the staff at Unlimited Happy Spa."

"Let me get this straight," Redbird said. "Griffiths was asking about Connaston at a massage parlor?"

"He seemed already to know that the *farang* Connaston frequented one of the parlors off Phaholyothin Road."

Redbird wondered not only who Edward Griffiths was but why he was interested in Connaston and whether his interest had anything to do with Pyotr Legere. The connection seemed a foregone conclusion. He wondered if Edward Griffiths might in fact be Jack McClure.

"Okay, but Chati said you had information about Legere. Is that true?"

"Oh, yes." Wattanapanit nodded. "Legere is a terrorist."

Redbird steadied his horse beneath him. "And you know this how?"

The cowboy raised a forefinger. "Now, now, what good would I be if I divulged my sources? No one would ever trust me again."

Redbird saw Dandy shake her head minutely. She knew him

much too well. Briefly, he wondered whether there would come a time when that intimate knowledge would become a liability he could no longer afford.

They were alone in the fields. It was almost dark now. In the distance, bonfires were being lit, but all the guests had gone in to change for dinner.

"Then what can you tell me?" Redbird said at last, carefully keeping the exasperation out of his voice.

"Legere's legitimate business is a front," the cowboy said, "but it's useful inasmuch as it allows him to transship whatever he's selling inside his books."

Redbird gave a skeptical snort. "What the hell could he be selling that could fit inside a book?"

"Microchips."

Wattanapanit seemed so self-satisfied that Redbird dug his heels into his horse's flanks, simultaneously moving himself away from Dandy and toward the cowboy. When he was abreast of Wattanapanit, he reined in. They were so close their knees pressed together.

Redbird leaned over, his face close to the cowboy's, and said softly, "Listen, you little shit, if you continue to fuck around with me, I'll make sure your asshole swallows your head whole."

Wattanapanit reared back slightly. "I'm telling you the truth. Legere is a middleman. These microchips are controllers, for the most part, of advanced weapons systems."

"Whose systems?"

"American, I'm told."

"Legere is a terrorist, you said."

"A cyberterrorist," the cowboy said. All smugness had vanished from both his face and his manner. It was clear that he was taking Redbird's threat seriously.

"Who is Legere selling these stolen microchips to?"

"The highest bidder, but his favored client—the one he goes to first—is a man known as the Syrian. Have you heard of him?"

Redbird hadn't, but he wasn't about to admit his ignorance to the

Thai, whose voice box he still felt like crushing between his thumb and fingers. "Legere and the Syrian have a special relationship?"

"That's right," the cowboy nodded. "They have for some time."

"Do you know where Legere is now?"

"He must still be here in Bangkok. If he'd tried to leave I'd know."

"Are the feds after him?"

"The what?"

"The state police."

"Special Branch," Dandy said, urging her mare nearer to the two men.

"For some reason, Special Branch seem particularly interested."

Redbird grunted in acknowledgment. "So Legere's gone to ground. Still, someone must know where he is."

"Well, there might be someone," Wattanapanit said. "A girl from the Unlimited Happy Spa named Jaidee. She used to service the *farang* Connaston."

"Do you know where can I find this Jaidee?"

"I always know where to find her," the cowboy said, pulling out his mobile. "Jaidee's my sister."

By the time Annika returned to the waiting car, she was sure that the Syrian hadn't stayed put. For one thing, there was the same blue-gray gravel dust on his boots that were on hers. For another, she had received a text from Dr. Karalian asking her if she knew someone named Mr. Cardozian, who had just visited him, claiming to be her friend.

She smiled at the Syrian as she ducked into the backseat, leaning over to kiss him.

"Miss me?" she whispered.

"Always."

Then he leaned forward slightly, breaking the closeness between them. "Take us home," he ordered Fareed, who doubled as his bodyguard and driver.

She closed her eyes against the abyss of the present, a black pit she had been trying to fill ever since her father had ripped her from her mother's arms, ever since her mother had died, alone, of a broken heart. She realized with an internal lurch that this was precisely how she imagined she would die: alone, of a broken heart. More often now she seemed to experience the world through a sheet of glass—seeing but not feeling. An iceberg encased her heart. And when she and Iraj made love, she found herself far away, on a bleak shore, walking into mist that blotted out all sensation as well as all memory.

The Syrian sat back, stared out the window as they left the Altindere valley. "How did Dr. Karalian take the news of your grandfather's death?"

"Not well." Annika cut a glance in his direction.

"Curious that I never heard of Karalian," Iraj Namazi said in an offhanded tone.

Annika tensed, knowing his question was anything but offhanded. "My grandfather had many friends—people in his life you never heard of."

"Apparently so." Namazi shrugged. "It's just that this place—" he gestured vaguely at the Assumption of Mary Clinic, fast disappearing behind them "—is so out of the way." He paused, as if considering his next words. "It seems odd."

"What does?"

Namazi turned his head, his eyes fixed on hers. "Tell me, how did your grandfather meet Dr. Karalian?"

"I have no idea," Annika said, not missing a beat. "But I imagine it was through their mutual love of chess."

He nodded absently. "It's time we got back to business."

"My grandfather's business, you mean."

He stared at her, his eyes like glowing coals. "One of these days," he said, "you must explain to me what you mean."

"I can explain it right now." Having regained control of the conversation, Annika settled herself more comfortably beside him. "My grandfather parceled out information in discrete bits. No one person ever got more than a single piece of the puzzle."

"The puzzle."

"His legacy, Iraj. That would lead to the endgame."

"I know a piece of it," he said.

"And so do I." Annika monitored his face, ready to analyze the minutest change. "But between us, we only have one half of the design."

"Half should be enough—"

"But it isn't, Iraj. Do you know where he hid the legacy?" She lit a cigarette with a small gold lighter. On the exhale, she said, "I don't."

The Syrian pursed his lips. "He told you what his legacy was?"

"Again?"

"Again."

She closed her eyes for a moment. It was like dealing with a child who, night after night, refused to go to sleep without hearing his favorite story. "Money. I imagine quite a lot of it," she said after taking time to calm herself.

"But that's not all," Iraj said. "Not the best of it." His greedy eyes were alight.

"The best of it," she said, "are dossiers on various sins and misdeeds of the top people in business, finance, military, and government across the globe."

"Influence," Iraj said, getting as worked up as if she had set her mouth on him. "An endless supply of influence, to get us what we want."

"My grandfather's legacy. Hidden somewhere."

"Do you know the names of the other two people, *chérie*?" When he smiled, his teeth looked like the blades of a guillotine. "Because if you don't, you're of little use to me."

"Iraj, what is accomplished when you speak to me like that?" She studied his face. "Do you expect to intimidate me? Really? After all this time?" She placed her hand on his thigh. "And what would be the point, when you need my cooperation."

He looked down at her hand, then away, but she could feel his muscles tense and relax against her palm and fingers.

"Iraj," she said now, "we've always had a—how shall I put it?—a conflicted relationship, full of discord, love, and hate. The truth is we frighten each other—don't bother to deny it. And, anyway, what's the harm in telling the truth? It can only bring us closer together. That *is* what you want, isn't it?"

"What I want . . ." He looked straight ahead, and then, presumably because he felt that wouldn't work, he turned his gaze back to her. "Your grandfather and I embarked on a partnership two decades ago. I have waited, I have been patient. Now I want the fruits of my hard labor. I want to know these twenty years of patience were worthwhile. I want his legacy."

"And what about us?"

He grunted. "There will be no *us* as long as McClure is alive." A terrible smile flashed across his face and was as quickly gone. "I know that stony expression all too well. You have no answer for that." He shrugged. "But, then, how could you?" He moistened his lips, took her cigarette, sucked smoke deep into his lungs, letting it drift slowly out through his nostrils. "So you see we are at an impasse."

"Not really." She took the cigarette back, finishing it. "To answer your question, I do know the names of the other two people."

"And?"

"I know it's not in your nature, Iraj, but ask me nicely." She stroked his thigh. "That's the only way out of our impasse."

"There are other ways," he muttered.

She lifted her hand. "All right then."

"No, no, *chérie*." He took her hand and gently drew it back to him. "Bringing the other two people to us will benefit you as well as me. After all, you're as anxious for it as I am."

Knowing this was all the concession she would get out of him, she said, "Legere has the third piece."

"I hate that fucker. He's as duplicitous as he is malicious, just like his father." Iraj's expression was expectant. "And the fourth, the one who is in possession of the final piece of information that will lead us to Dyadya Gourdjiev's legacy?"

"Jack McClure."

"What?" The word fairly exploded from deep inside him. "I don't believe you!"

She shrugged, her eyes never leaving his, never blinking.

"How could he entrust anything to the American agent?"

"He liked Jack," Annika said neutrally, carefully. "He trusted him."

"More than you or me?" Namazi gave a harsh laugh. "I don't think so."

"So. Solve the mystery yourself. Tell me where my grandfather stashed the money and the files."

With a disgusted hissing sound, the Syrian turned away from her, to again stare out the window.

"If I see McClure again," he said softly, "I will kill him."

"That's your jealousy talking, Iraj." Annika put a hand on his forearm. "Don't be like that."

There was silence, then, just the soft hum of the car's oversized engine, the gentle soughing of the wind against the bodywork.

After a long time, he said, "If McClure has a usefulness, so much the better. But once he tells us—"

"He can't. Jack doesn't know he knows. His part of my grandfather's legacy is locked away inside his brain."

"When did Dyadya Gourdjiev tell him?"

"He must have told him when he was in the hospital in Moscow."

"Hmm." He turned back to her again. "But yet, there will come a time when you will extract the information from him. Then his usefulness will be at an end."

"You won't kill him, Iraj."

"No?" He nodded. "All right, then. You'll do it, *chérie*. You'll kill Jack McClure."

NINE

Kampaengphet Road was lit up like a souk. By the time Jack arrived on a motorcycle taxi, the nighttime antique furniture market was in full swing. Bare bulbs were strung up in shallow arcs above the jumble of stalls lining either side of the road. Gaily striped awnings were stretched out over offered goods, sporting tiny twinkling colored lights on their undersides, the better to entice shoppers to take a second look.

As Jack picked his way through the deluge of shoppers, gawkers, and hustlers, he kept a sharp eye out for Jaidee. Dao had described her to him: a tall, slim girl with a doll-like face and shining black hair down to the small of her back. She had a beauty mark at the left corner of her mouth and the tattoo of a dragonfly on the side of her neck.

He passed many shops selling furniture, new, old, and purported antique, but also vendors of masks, lurid costume jewelry, blank CDs, rope sandals, cheap-looking electronics, and, of course, food. Food was everywhere, from barbeques, where people stood and ate as the juices dripped down their chins, to restaurants with plastic tables and chairs, packed with diners scarfing down seafood and blazing hot noodle dishes.

Jack spotted Jaidee at almost the same moment she saw him. Their gazes locked, keeping track of each other even when shoppers hurrying to and fro interfered with their lines of sight. He hurried across the road to where she stood, at the edge of a rug stall, out of the strongest eddies of people and taxis.

He was almost to her when he spotted the motorcycle taxi weaving down the road. He noted it, but not with any degree of alarm. After all, only hours before it looked as if a taxi was going to run Dao down, until she stepped smartly out of the way.

This one wasn't anywhere as near to Jaidee. Not, at least, until it swerved at the last moment. The helmeted driver's right arm shot out and grabbed her. Swinging her up onto the motorcycle behind him, he took off.

Jack sprang after them, moving along the snaking path the motorcycle clove through the crowd. For the length of the night market, there was nowhere to go except along the road, the shops and stalls smashed in together cheek by jowl.

At lightning speed, Jack's brain had automatically mapped the scene in front of him in three dimensions, so that when a grocer pushed a wooden cart in his path as he crossed the street, Jack leaped atop it then vaulted across to the other side without missing a step.

The cyclist was hampered by Jaidee's constant squirming, forcing him to keep one hand off the handlebars in an attempt to keep her under control. This distraction, combined with the people slow to get out of the driver's way, allowed Jack to make a certain amount of headway.

But they were already nearing the far end of the market, where the cyclist could veer off in one of multiple directions and put on enough speed to leave Jack behind. Jack knew if he was going to get Jaidee back, he would have to do it within the next minute or two.

The crowd was even denser here, and dashing along the road had turned from difficult to virtually impossible. Veering to the right, Jack climbed onto the front edge of a stall, upending half the display of masks. The owner shouted, raising his fist as he came after him, but Jack had already jumped up onto the wire holding the series of lights that lit up this side of the street.

Pulling himself hand over hand, Jack used his lower body as a pendulum, building up enough momentum to launch himself forward. He flew through the air, over the heads of the shoppers and strollers. Grabbing a handful of a cotton awning, he ripped it off as he landed on the rear end of the motorcycle taxi.

He swung his arm in a twisting motion, like a toreador with his cape, and the section of cloth fluttered down over the front of the motorcycle. The cyclist had to let go of Jaidee in order to maintain control of his vehicle. The moment he did so, Jack wrapped one arm around Jaidee's waist and snatched her off the cycle.

They fell, scattering screaming pedestrians in every direction. Jack wrapped her in his arms, protecting her as their momentum propelled them along the street and into the front of a stall selling carpets.

With carpets rolling everywhere, Jack picked his head up, brushed aside a couple of piles of wool, and saw that the cyclist had managed to free himself from the twisted piece of awning. Jack pulled Jaidee to her feet, but before he had a chance to move her to a place of safety, the owner of the carpet stall grabbed hold of her, shouting into his face.

The cyclist had turned his vehicle around and was heading at full speed toward Jack, Jaidee, and the vendor. Jack waited, judging distances and vectors as the motorcycle hurtled toward him through a field now clear of people who had already scrambled away.

The cyclist loomed larger and larger as he charged on. At the last instant, Jack took up a tightly rolled carpet and, bending his upper torso back as counterbalance, swung the heavy mass in a blurred arc. It struck the cyclist on his shoulder, knocking him sideways off the vehicle, which spun on, riderless, into two stalls across the road.

The cyclist skidded on his side, struck a shopper, and his helmet popped off. Now Jack saw that the cyclist was a young woman. She saw Jack staring at her, scrambled up, and ran, weaving through the crowd whose collective curiosity had brought it back, lapping at the empty circle in the road beside the carpet shop.

Jack took advantage of the rising chaos to shove the shop owner away from Jaidee. Taking her hand, he headed into the heart of the throng, where people were packed most closely, eeling their way through, even though the occasional hand clutched at them and, here and there, a voice was raised. But those querulous few were soon drowned out by the congestive roar of those many at the back, clamoring for a view of the incident, about which they knew nothing.

At the far end of the market, Jack turned left, heading down a narrow lane fronted by dilapidated buildings, filled to overflowing with multiple families, festooned with washing on grimy lines.

"Are you all right?" Jack asked as they sped down the alley.

Jaidee nodded.

"Did you see the cyclist's face? Did you recognize her?"

"I saw her," Jaidee said in the high, piping voice of a songbird. "I don't know her name, but I've seen her. She hangs out at a club called WTF."

"The one at Thonglor Soi 10?"

"That's the one." She glanced at him briefly. "Do you know it?"

Leroy Connaston had been shot to death at WTF. Now the same girl who hung out there had tried to abduct Jaidee before she had a chance to talk to Jack. Dennis was right: there was a local leak here in Bangkok.

He would need to think about the connections, but first he had to get them to a safe spot, where he could question Jaidee without fear of interruption.

He turned to her. "Do you know a place—?"

She nodded. "Follow me."

"Thank you," Jaidee said.

"You never would have been in this position if it weren't for me," Jack told her.

"I don't know. Ever since Leroy was killed I've felt eyes on me."

She had taken him to a small café perhaps a half-mile from the night market. No street in Bangkok was quiet, but this one came as close as was possible. They settled onto rattan chairs on opposite sides of a small bamboo table.

"Have you actually seen someone following you?"

"No," Jaidee said. "It's just a feeling I can't shake."

She ordered them Thai iced coffees, a plate of dragon fruit, and *Khao Niaow Ma Muang*, sweet mango sticky rice. The coffees arrived almost immediately. Jack dumped in two packets of sugar, slowly stirred the liquid with a long spoon, and took a sip. He had directed them to a table in the rear, having first located a rear exit to the café. He had no desire to be trapped in this small space in case the cyclist had somehow managed to follow them.

"But who would want to follow you?" Jack said, thinking of Naresuan 261's interest in Connaston.

Jaidee shrugged in the peculiarly Thai manner. "This is Bangkok. Everyone is followed at some time or other, whether the surveillance is official, semi-official, or the object of a bribe. There are too many people in Bangkok with secrets. In fact, people come here to bury their secrets."

"Do you have secrets, Jaidee?"

She laughed softly. "What I do is secret. As far as the authorities are concerned, I am a masseuse, but that isn't where I make a living."

"But no other secrets."

She looked at him with an odd expression. "Not like Leroy. He was a basket of secrets."

"Really? What sort?"

"Do you think he'd tell me?"

"I believe in pillow talk, Jaidee. Many a secret has been lost in the aftermath of sex."

It seemed to Jack that she was looking at him in an entirely new light. "In my line of work, the time after sex is used to dress and leave the spa. No one lingers."

"Not even Leroy Connaston? Dao tells me he was one of your best clients."

"Clients." Jaidee shrugged again. "You could call them that, I suppose. I wouldn't." She shook her head as the desserts were set before them. "The people who come to the spa are lowlifes. There is an entire group that wants only virgins. There's a doctor we take the youngest girls to, over and over. Eternal moons, we call them." Her mouth twisted in distaste. "Dao and I came to the spa when we were older, so we never had to go through that phase of the moon.

"But you're right." Taking a spoon, she scooped up a bite of the sticky rice. "Leroy was different. He was a gentleman. He wanted to stay afterward, always. He liked to lie with me, to hold me." She sighed wistfully. "I liked it, too."

"And what did he tell you during those times? I'm betting he didn't fall asleep."

A slow smile of remembrance curled her full lips. "No, he didn't fall asleep. He claimed he never slept. Maybe that was an exaggeration, I wouldn't know. But with me he never closed his eyes, not for a moment."

"What did he whisper in your ear?"

"He poured out his anxieties. Maybe because he liked me, or, more likely, because he thought me ignorant, that I wouldn't understand most of what he told me. But I did. I understood it all." She showed him a shy smile. "I educated myself."

"And yet you're—"

"I *chose* my profession. I'm the sole support for my family. I have a small child and no husband. It's a matter of money, you see. I make more in a week than I could make in three months doing something else."

Jack, as impressed with her as he was, led her back to Connaston.

"He was worried."

"Yes, always."

"About what?" Jack asked.

"For one thing, about this man Legere. Leroy was tied to Legere, but he never explained how."

"And you never asked?"

"He would have become wary, then, you see. No, I said nothing."

This girl was clever as well as smart, Jack thought. "Go on."

"He told me Legere was dangerous—very dangerous."

"In what way?"

"He had contacts in high places, powerful men who would move heaven and earth to protect him, even though Leroy said that Legere was involved in some very dicey business."

"Dicey?"

"That was his word. I don't know it, exactly, but—"

"It's slang," Jack said. "Connaston was saying that Legere was involved in something that was both dangerous and illegal. Did he say what it was?"

"No. Only that Legere had involved him."

"Was Connaston anxious about anything else?"

"He was afraid he was being followed, at least that last day— the day he was murdered."

"Did he say by whom?"

She shook her head. "It's so sad."

Jack knew she was speaking of Connaston's death. Could he have been shot by one of Legere's enemies? But then why kill Connaston and not Legere? Besides, Jaidee had told him that Legere was protected in high places. He shook his head; he was no closer to finding Pyotr Legere.

"Jaidee, I need to find Legere," he said. "Do you have any idea where he might be?"

She thought for a moment. "I don't. Unless . . ."

Jack's head came up. "Unless what?"

"Leroy had a flat here. Even though he was in Bangkok for only short periods of time, he came here often enough to want a place of his own. He used to tell me that his life was made up of one anonymous hotel room after another." She shook her head. "Anyway, it's possible Legere is hiding there."

"Do you know the address?"

Jaidee gave it to him. She balanced her spoon on the pad of her thumb. "Leroy was so sweet," she said in her little girl voice, "always buying me presents from all over." Her fingers went to a locket on a thin gold chain around her neck. "He gave me this the last time I saw him." She held up the locket on its chain, a gold heart.

"What did he put inside?"

She frowned. "What?"

Jack pointed. "There's a hinge on one side of the heart."

"I . . . I don't know." Jaidee tried to look at it, but couldn't find an angle. "I never noticed."

"Why don't we have a look?"

She hesitated for a moment, then, nodding, opened the clasp at the nape of her neck, set the heart on its chain on the table between them. But her hands withdrew, her fingers interlocked, the knuckles growing white.

"Don't you want to look?" Jack asked softly.

"I don't . . ." Her soft brown eyes lifted to his. "I don't know whether I want to."

"Do you mind if I look?"

Again, she hesitated before nodding. Her tiny white teeth gnawed at her lower lip.

She watched, her eyes staring as Jack took the heart between his fingertips. His nail found the tiny indentation along the seam of the two halves, pried them apart.

He laid the open heart down on the table.

"What's that?" Jaidee said. "What's in there?"

It was a tiny paper, rolled up very tightly. Jack used the tine of his fork to lift it out, then he carefully unrolled it. The paper was very thin.

"There's writing on it," Jaidee said, craning her neck. "Can you read it?"

"It's an address."

"Here in Bangkok?"

"No," Jack said, as he struggled to get his mind to read the single line of tiny letters and numbers. "It's thousands of miles from here." He looked up at her. "Zurich, Switzerland."

Jonatha Midwood, surrounded by tourists taking pictures, shrieking school groups, and wide-eyed families with toddlers, stood on the sidewalk of Constitution Avenue, a stone's throw from the Lincoln Memorial, waiting. She had heard plenty about William Rogers, the national security advisor. She'd seen his face on TV and in the press countless times, but she'd never actually met him. She'd had no reason to. She was wholly Krofft's creature, and Krofft, recognizing and nurturing her particular talents, had kept her hidden behind so many layers that most of the Langley CIA contingent had no idea she even existed.

Jonatha's path to the CIA was a circuitous one. She had graduated Yale with a double master's in political science and fine arts. She began working at Christie's auction house in New York, where she familiarized herself with the works of contemporary artists and then forged friendships with the artists themselves. With her brains, personality, and exceptionally fine good looks, this was, for her, an easy and enjoyable task, but it caused no end of jealousy in those above her, so she left.

The *New York Times* employed her as its art critic, but the first time she went on assignment to Washington, she became enamored of life there. She changed horses again, hired away by one Beltway lobbyist after another, but never for long, growing ever more restless the faster she mastered the methods of each firm. She could have had her pick of posts, then, but chose to go another route, entering a PhD program at Georgetown in computer science. She was so skilled that she was allowed to build her own curriculum in a form of electronic statistical analysis that she invented. One of her professors was good friends with Krofft, who had longtime contacts among key academicians throughout the country. Over the years, this elite coterie had been his best recruiters, able to evaluate candidates on psychological as well as academic merit. At the professor's urging, Krofft was present when she defended her thesis and was so impressed that he offered her a position in the CIA on the spot.

He was in for a long, convoluted negotiation. He scarcely minded; he enjoyed observing Jonatha's meticulous nature, as well as her wealth of knowledge on subjects that surprised even him. He had never been party to a contract such as she insisted on, and he believed he never would again. There was no one like her. Her professor was correct: she was a polymath, and an exceptional one at that.

Now she was head of Arclight, a construct wholly of her own design. Krofft had only to tell Jonatha what he needed and she, like a sorcerer, would create the method seemingly out of thin air. She never failed any assignment, so she was the logical choice for Arclight, perhaps the only choice to run it.

Now, waiting for the appointment Krofft had set up for her, she wondered what form of grilling she was going to get from the national security advisor. She had achieved a status in a world where such levels were normally closed to women. A world where women toiled in the trenches below their male counterparts. To their male bosses, women were basically family-oriented nesters, not hunter-gatherers, like men. One moment women were working at their job, the next they were home breast-feeding their baby. But Jonatha had discovered another, deeper level of distrust. The men were frightened of women. Women possessed something between their legs men desired. Women could lead them off course. Women could make them feel emotion. What more potent threat to a man could there be?

Jonatha knew all this when she came to Washington, but what she was quick to learn was just how insecure politicians were. And, much to her astonishment, the same held true for those set in high places inside Washington's shadowy, sprawling clandestine community. For the first time, her instincts about men had been challenged. Logically, spies and their handlers should be the most self-assured people on the face of the earth—how else could they do their dangerous work? But the opposite held true. These outsiders had cut themselves off from family, home, and their own personal history. In becoming ciphers, they were unmoored, adrift in a sea of eternal darkness, without a sense of self to anchor them.

All of this ran through her mind like a bright ribbon as she saw the national security advisor striding toward her. William Rogers held himself erect in the manner of an ex-military officer. Hands plunged deep in his unbuttoned overcoat, hatless, his thinning hair plucked by gusts of wind, he looked like an accountant or a salesman, which, she supposed, in a way, he was.

He had not yet seen her, but before she could enjoy sizing him up, a gleaming black Ford SUV pulled in to the curb directly where she was standing. Before the vehicle could come to a complete stop, the front curbside door was flung open, and a suit with a cordless earpiece and a sidearm at his hip stepped out, opened the rear door, took her elbow, and said, in a low but commanding tone, "This way, Ms. Midwood."

She turned, startled rather than alarmed. "Who are you?"

"This way, please."

His grip was firm, his expression insistent.

Still, she resisted. "I have an appointment."

"Ms. Midwood, it's a matter of national security. Your presence is required now."

She took one last look at Rogers, then sighed, and, ducking her head, slid into the rear seat. Immediately, the door slammed shut, dimming the interior further. The suit climbed into the front seat, closed his door. The SUV sat there, idling.

"Good afternoon, Ms. Midwood," said the man sitting beside her. "My name is Henry Dickinson, director—"

"I know who you are," Jonatha said curtly. "You've got a helluva nerve. I was on my way to meet the national security advisor."

Dickinson nodded. "Having spotted Bill Rogers, I surmised as much. You have my most sincere apologies, but—"

"Bullshit," Jonatha said. "This—what shall I call it? Intervention?—was planned."

"Even if it was," Dickinson said evenly, "my apologies *are* sincere."

She turned part way toward him. "Listen, Dicky—that's what my boss calls you, isn't it? Dicky." A smiled curled her lips. "Now I can see why." Even in the dimness of the vehicle's interior she could see the color rushing to his cheeks. "So listen to me, Dicky. My time is exceedingly valuable. Say what you have to say and then I'll be on my way—hopefully before Rogers takes me for a flake who hasn't the sense to show up on time."

"Tell me about Airgas."

"I beg your pardon?"

"Sorry, I meant Arclight." He projected a predatory smile onto his face. "It's your program, right? I want to hear about it."

"Talk to my boss, Dicky."

"I chose to talk to you. Was that a mistake?"

"Yes. I don't know anything."

"What you mean is you won't tell me what you know."

"If you had come to me and asked—"

"Please."

Jonatha considered a moment, trying to put aside her personal animosity toward this man. He had frightened her, if only momentarily. The innate female instinct to be cowed by a male of the species astonished her. It was fueled by the fear of being aggressive, which would inevitably label her as a bitch.

She wanted out of this situation, and she saw the quickest path was to give him what he thought he desired. "Director Krofft came to me three days ago," she began. "He was concerned about a leak—maybe inside homeland security—"

Dickinson's features grew dark, his brows knitted together. "He should have come to me."

"It was Atlas that was on his mind, and Atlas, as I understand it, is an umbrella operation."

"We both know that's not why Krofft took the lead on this."

Jonatha took a breath. "In any event, he gave me the guidelines and left the rest to me. I've worked up a schedule of interviews, psychological and polygraph tests."

Dickinson seemed taken aback. "We have already ID'd our bad apple—Jack McClure."

"We need to be absolutely certain there isn't another," she said.

"But this method—it's so old hat."

" 'Those oldies but goodies remind me of you,' " she sang lightly. "Little Caesar and the Romans. Nineteen-sixty-one." She slid away from him. "There's a reason the protocol is still around. It works." She reached for the door handle. "That's it, there's nothing more."

"What kind of psych tests?"

"You can't expect me to divulge details. Everyone in the Atlas program is suspect."

"Even Krofft?"

She smiled as she opened the door and stepped out.

Leroy Connaston's apartment was in a run-down neighborhood of Bangkok, where cars cruised alongside pedicabs and ancient motorcycles, whose two-stroke engines spewed blinding exhaust into the already hazy atmosphere.

Jack stood on the corner opposite, watching not only the entrance to the building but also the motor and foot traffic, looking for anomalies. The building looked like a drunken prizefighter that had spent too long in the ring, shoulders hunched and heavily sagging against its neighbor. In fact, it might have fallen down had it not been for the spiderweb of bamboo scaffolding around the facade.

Within a few minutes, Jack gave the surveillance up. The truth was, any number of people could be staked out here and he wouldn't necessarily know it. All he could say for certain was that no one seemed suspicious, and the female cyclist was nowhere in the vicinity.

Still, he waited. He was unhappy that Jaidee had insisted on accompanying him, ignoring his warnings of the danger.

"Leroy wasn't just another client, as you say," she told him. "I cared about him. If there is some clue as to who killed him in his apartment, I want to find it."

"You still don't see anyone suspicious?" Jack said to her now.

"I don't."

He nodded, having decided to trust her. This was her city, after all. For the moment, at least, he was in her hands. Together, they crossed the teeming street, heading into Connaston's building. It smelled of *mee krob* and overboiled rice.

According to Jaidee, Connaston's apartment was on the top floor. As they ascended the cramped, almost vertical staircase, they heard voices raised in argument, a baby crying, hip-hop music, and then, as they neared the top floor, silence.

They passed a small window on their right, covered in grime and soot, before they reached the landing. Jack could just make out a narrow alley, strung with so many electric and telephone lines the pavement below was encased in eternal night.

Four doors marked apartment entrances. Connaston's was the last apartment to their right. They went silently down the dreary twilit hallway. Jack put his ear to the door, listening for any sounds from inside. He heard nothing.

The lock was one of those so easy to pick it took him less than fifteen seconds. When he heard the tumblers turn over, he grasped the knob and, with a quick toss of his head at Jaidee to move her back, he opened the door no more than a sliver. He heard nothing, no movement inside the apartment. The air was stale, smelling of abandonment.

Standing to one side, he pushed the door, letting it swing wide until the doorway gaped at them. He went in then, still cautious, feeling Jaidee close behind him. He had expected the apartment to have been gone over by a police forensic team, but the place had clearly been tossed. Sofas and chairs were upended, their cushions punctured, the stuffing pulled out in handfuls, pictures hanging every which way, their backs slit open. In the bedroom, the wallpaper had been forcibly stripped back and now hung down like fillets of flesh. Drawers had been pulled out, their contents strewn across the floor. Connaston's bed had been overturned, the mattress completely in ribbons. Nona's information had been correct—the police investigation had been short-circuited so that Naresuan 261 could implement their own.

"Who did this?" Jaidee said, her voice sounding very small.

"Special Branch, I think." Jack, standing in the middle of the chaos, could find no sign of sheets or pillows. Had the officers of Naresuan 261 taken them away, perhaps for DNA analysis? "What could they have been looking for?"

Jaidee shook her head, but Jack wondered whether he already had the answer in the slip of paper that Connaston had secreted inside the gold heart he had given Jaidee just before he went to his fateful rendezvous. Did Connaston suspect he was going to die that day? He must have had an inkling, to take the precaution he did. But for what purpose? For whose benefit? Did Connaston plan for someone to meet with Jaidee to get it in the event of his death?

Jack had come to Bangkok searching for Legere, but now found himself in the midst of a larger puzzle. Connaston had told Jaidee that he was bound to Pyotr Legere. Legere was doing more than running a bookshop out of Moscow. Connaston had been the key that opened the door to Legere's business. If that were so, Jack's next stop needed to be Zurich, but not until he discovered whether Legere was still in Bangkok.

"If Legere was in this apartment," he said, "he certainly isn't now." And Nona's mysterious contact surely would know if Legere had been picked up by Naresuan 261, so either he was still in the city or he had somehow slipped through the antiterrorist cordon and flown the coop. Coming here was a dead end.

At that moment, he heard the buzzing of a fly, and turned. Jaidee, on her haunches, was poring over what was left of the contents of the wardrobe, picking through slashed clothes as if she wanted to take them home with her.

The fly should have been batting itself against the windowpane, but it wasn't, and now Jack heard a more consistent sound, as other flies made their presence known. He saw them then, a small black cluster, whirling like a miniature galaxy. One of them peeled off, vanishing into the bathroom. Others followed.

Picking his way through the debris, Jack stepped into the bathroom, which was far less of a mess than any other room in the apartment. At first, he assumed it was because there were fewer things here to pull to the floor. But then he saw where the sheets and pillowcases had gone—they were in the bathtub, set up like a bed.

He called Jaidee's name, and she appeared almost at once. When she looked at him, he pointed to the makeshift bed. The flies were settling onto the pillows, ingesting the minuscule bits of hair and skin shed by the occupant while he slept.

"Someone was here after Special Branch left."

"Pyotr Legere?"

Jack nodded as he went over to the small window, which looked out on the same alley as the window in the stairwell. The glass was cleaner here, giving him a better view of this small section of the city, forgotten and forlorn.

Turning away from the window, he approached the tub. "Once the police had left, they'd be unlikely to return. This was perhaps the safest place in Bangkok for Legere. Your hunch was a good one."

Brushing the flies away, he bent over and sniffed at the pillow. The scent of a masculine body was still fresh. He turned, then, saw the toothbrush and half-empty tube of paste on the rim of the sink. Also, a bar of soap that was not new.

"He's still here," Jaidee breathed, "isn't he?"

Jack shrugged. "Impossible to say."

"What do we do now?"

"Either he comes back tonight or he's already out of the country. So we wait." Jack turned to her. "At least, I do." He smiled. "There's really no point in your staying any longer."

"There's no point in my leaving, either."

"You're losing money every hour you stay away from the spa," he said only half-seriously.

Her reply, however, was without any irony. "This is not my night to work, otherwise I couldn't have met you." The smile she returned was melancholy. "Besides, just now I have no heart for the spa."

He nodded. "All right, then." He glanced at his watch. "It's after midnight. Legere will be coming back here soon, if he comes back at all."

They returned to the living room, and while she tidied up the snowfall of newspapers, magazines, and broken pottery that littered the floor, he righted the chairs and returned as much of their stuffing as he could. Then they sat down facing each other, occluded by the gloom of the apartment, which was part real and part psychic.

When Jaidee shivered a little, Jack said softly, "You can go any time, if you wish."

She stared at him, stone-faced.

After a lengthy silence, he said, "I don't understand why you don't leave."

Jaidee's eyes were half-closed, but she fingered the gold heart around her neck. "Leroy trusted me. Should I abandon him now because he's dead?" Her eyes opened and she looked at Jack. "You haven't and you never even met him. How can I do less?"

Her eyes closed and, after a time, her breathing slowed and became regular. Jack rose and made sure the front door was locked. When Legere came back he didn't want to give away their presence.

He returned to the chair. A glance at his watch told him that it was close to one a.m. He rested his head against the chair back. As was usual in the small hours of the night, he was flooded with memories of Emma, the life he lived too fast, blind to what was going on around him, what he was missing, until it was too late.

Her death had done something irrevocable to him, diminished him in a way he had yet to understand fully. No parent was ever prepared to bury their child; it was a horror incomprehensible until it had been visited on you. At the moment of her death, something was torn out of him, a phantom limb, a certain destiny, a future into which she would have grown, while he watched, becoming, if not contented, then surely a better person.

Destiny had other plans for them both.

There were times, after her death, when Emma had come to him, either as a vision or a disembodied voice. At the beginning, he was certain he was losing his mind, but that was a function of his deep and abiding grief. Talking with her, knowing that she didn't blame him, assuaged his grief, which, he realized, was underlaid with a terrible guilt.

But she had been silent for a while and he wondered whether he had imagined it all or whether, having fulfilled the task she had assigned herself—to help dispel his guilt—she was now truly gone. What was enduring—what was eternal—was his abiding love for her.

Listening to the shouts and traffic noises from outside, the more muted sounds rising up the stairwell from the apartments below, he wished she would come back to him, even just one last time. It was selfish of him, he knew. He had to let her go, to wherever she was now meant to be. But still, he couldn't help hoping . . .

His twilight world must have plunged him into sleep, because the next thing he knew he was started awake by a sound inside the apartment. He sat up straight, instantly alert. When he tapped Jaidee's knee, her eyes snapped open.

Jack was signaling toward the door when a tinkling crash in the bathroom brought them to their feet. Pushing Jaidee aside, Jack stepped into the bathroom and was immediately struck on the side of the face. Staggering back, he saw the petite figure and cat-like face of the cyclist. She was crouched on the tile floor, amid a welter of glittering shards of glass from the window she had smashed through.

The cyclist made a feint with her left hand, and Jack saw the glimmer of a knife blade. Her right hand, balled in a fist, caught him on the side of his neck, jolting him. Then she came closer with the knife, its point tipped upward.

Retreating, Jack grabbed a pillow from the tub, swung it directly into the path of the knife. The blade ripped open the pillow, embedding itself in the feathers. At once, Jack let the pillow go, and as the cyclist was working the blade out, he slammed the heel of his hand into her nose. She flew back against the wall, trailed by a fountain of blood. He was on her in an instant, jamming his forearm into her throat, pinning her against the wall, as he scrabbled to contain the knife, which she had managed to extricate from the feathers.

He missed, and the blade swept through layers of clothing, drawing blood from his chest. He slammed her, hard. The back of her head bounced off the wall, her eyes momentarily glazed over, and he wrenched the knife from her grip, slamming the hilt against the side of her face. She fell backward into the tub. Her insensate body dislodged something that had been hidden in the bedclothes.

Jack snatched it up and was pocketing it when he heard Jaidee's shout. Without another thought, he turned and sprinted out of the bathroom, through the living room in time to see Jaidee gripped by an unfamiliar man. Behind them, the front door sagged open, its top hinge busted off its spindly pin.

Jack led with the cyclist's knife, but the man swung Jaidee around, slamming her against the right side of his body, which he presented to Jack. Jack could already see him preparing to deflect the blade he expected to come from his left side, could see how the man would spin, disarming Jack in the same motion.

Sometimes the best offense was extreme offense. Jack feinted to his right, appearing as if he was, indeed, coming at the intruder from the man's left. Jack saw him shift his weight for his spin, and, at the last moment, Jack transferred the knife to his left hand, lunging in toward Jaidee and her captor.

She screamed, which was all the better for Jack. It distracted the intruder, freezing him while Jack pushed the knife blade in under Jaidee's armpit, through to the intruder's side. He got his arm inside, but Jack twisted the blade, deepening the wound.

Jack peeled Jaidee away from the intruder.

"Watch—!"

The cyclist crashed into him, climbing onto his back. He swung himself around, but she clung to him tenaciously. Her fingernails were clawing at his eyes. For an instant, he saw the wounded man trying to find the grip of a gun holstered in his left armpit. The gun was slicked with his own blood, but it would be only a matter of seconds until he drew it out.

Jack raised his arms, slammed the palms of his hands against the cyclist's ears. She screamed in pain, lost her grip long enough for Jack to grasp one of her wrists and sling her off him and into the wounded man.

As they crashed against the wall, he grabbed Jaidee and ran out of the apartment, down the hall, and into the stairwell. He could hear the sharp echoes of footsteps behind them and knew, while they might outrun the cyclist and her partner, they would never outrun his handgun.

They were trapped, finished.

TEN

"One down," Jonatha said into her mobile as she walked toward the waiting national security advisor.

"Rogers?" Krofft said in her ear.

She laughed. "That meeting's about to happen. No, Dicky shanghaied me in the middle of Constitution Avenue, if you can believe it."

"That man really is a dick." But Krofft was laughing, also. "Nothing would make me happier if you discovered he was rotten, along with McClure."

"Don't influence me, Robby. You know better."

"I'm encouraged you're taking your assignment so seriously."

"How else should I take it?" Seeing Rogers looking in her direction, she raised an arm, signaling him. He nodded in return.

"Arclight is the most public assignment I've ever entrusted to you," Krofft said.

"When have I ever let you down?"

"That's one of the reasons I chose you."

"That and my unique resource."

"Ah, yes, Ripley—your mysterious hacker contact," Krofft said. "Has she finished devising the psych tests?"

"The psych tests are my dominion, Robby. Ripley is ferreting out any anomalies in our suspects' financials."

"But we have our own people—"

"They can't dig the way Ripley can," Jonatha said. "Trust me when I tell you that Ripley can massage out any money trail, no matter how well hidden." She was only steps away from the national security advisor. "I have to go. Rogers is waiting."

"Keep me up-to-date on what Ripley finds."

"Always."

Jack saw the window to their left. If the cyclist could do it, why couldn't they?

"Jump!' he shouted to Jaidee.

"What?"

"Cross your arms over your face!" Taking hold of her hips, he hurled her through the glass, then, amid a blizzard of glass shards, followed her.

As he had seen, the narrow alley was thick with cables and wires, strung from wooden poles anchored in the ground. Jaidee had both arms around a cluster of these, and Jack followed her lead.

They were four stories above the ground, but all they needed to do was get to the pole just ahead of them and they could shimmy down. The problem was Jaidee was paralyzed with terror.

"Move!" Jack said from right behind her.

"I can't! I hate heights!"

"Jaidee—"

"No! If I move I'm going to fall, I know it!"

"That's what your brain is telling you, but it's a lie."

"Please don't ask me—"

Hearing a sound behind them, Jack risked a look over his shoulder and saw the intruder at the blasted-out window. He held a

Glock 9mm in his left hand. Jack had wounded his right arm, and from the awkward grip, Jack could tell he was right-handed.

The man braced himself against the side of the window sash and, aiming, squeezed off a shot. He missed, but Jack couldn't count on them being that lucky next time. Leaning forward, he wound one arm around Jaidee's waist.

"Let go," he whispered in her ear.

"Let go? Are you crazy?"

"Trust me."

"I don't—"

"If you don't let go now," Jack said, "we'll both be shot to death, just like Leroy."

The moment she let go, Jack swung them back and forth, gathering momentum with each pass. Then he too let go and they flew through the air. Jaidee bit her tongue to stifle her scream. They slammed into the pole, and Jack using his knees as well as his free hand to grip the rough wood, scooted them around so the pole was between them and the man at the window.

Jack could feel her trembling against him. "Down we go now," he whispered.

When they were almost on the ground, he glanced up to the shattered window. Only blackness greeted him; the man was gone.

William Rogers was the polar opposite of Henry Dickinson, Jonatha thought, as they ambled through the strip of trees guarding the Reflecting Pool from the constant traffic on Constitution. He was calm rather than jittery, his voice soft and as well-modulated as a TV announcer; his watery blue eyes held her gaze seemingly without guile, as opposed to sliding away to the left. He was not a big man, nevertheless he cut an imposing figure. He possessed an outsized personality. That he kept it in check so effortlessly impressed her further.

None of these observations made him any less of a suspect. On the contrary, a man like Rogers, so in control of both his thoughts and his emotions, clearly relaxed around strangers, might have been a heartbeat away from becoming her prime suspect if she were disposed to prejudge her subjects. She'd never make such a rookie mistake. When embarking on this kind of probe it was imperative that she remain impartial.

"So," Rogers was saying, "I hear excellent things about you from Director Krofft. He doesn't give compliments easily."

"He's been very good to me," Jonatha said neutrally.

"What I can't fathom is how successfully he's kept you under wraps. If you're half as good as he says you are, I'd think your name would have entered the lexicon of us mandarins before now."

Jonatha gave him a sideways glance. "I don't know whether you're praising my boss's skill at hiding me or doubting my abilities."

"To be honest, it might be a bit of both."

"I appreciate your candor, though I doubt Director Krofft would feel the same way."

Rogers chuckled. "I'm certain he wouldn't." He cleared his throat. "Still . . ."

"Is this about my position inside the Company or my being a woman?"

"To be honest, I've never known Krofft to rely on a female agent."

Jonatha made a mental note of his repetition. In her experience, people who repeated a phrase often meant the opposite. The jury was still out on Rogers; she'd have to keep an eye on where the rest of this interview went.

"I don't believe the director thinks of me as a female agent."

Rogers raised one of his eyebrows. "Oh? And why is that?"

"I've proved myself under fire. That's the director's benchmark for whom to put his faith in."

"Explain please."

They walked on. Jonatha could see, in the periphery of her vision, certain suits whose lips moved every so often as they communicated with each other wirelessly. They moved at the same pace as the national security advisor.

"When I was teenager," she said at last, "I never lacked for suitors."

"I can understand that," Rogers said, seemingly ignoring her odd, anachronistic language. "With your flaming copper hair and green eyes, I'd imagine all the boys would have been buzzing around you." He raked her with his gaze. "Even if you didn't have those long, shapely legs back then."

Jonatha released a small smile, like an aura, into the air around her. "Well, they never got anywhere."

"Never?"

Jonatha felt the need to gauge his coming reaction. "There was someone outside of high school, someone who interested me. She was an auto mechanic, loved to restore vintage wrecks to gleaming works of pure genius."

Rogers nodded, never missing a beat. "Later on, when you became a woman, didn't you worry about your—choice?"

"First, it wasn't a choice. Second, if I worried about everything, I'd never leave my house."

He laughed. "True enough." Then his face clouded over. "But, still, especially in politics—"

"I'm not in politics," she said. "I'm in the business of secrets." She tilted her head. "You see the irony."

"Indeed I do." Rogers considered a moment. "So Krofft doesn't mind."

"I think the director is amused. He enjoys watching the guys try to hit on me."

"Why?"

"He says it gives him an inner sense of satisfaction."

"That they can't have what he can't have."

Now she laughed. "I like you, sir. I like the way your mind works."

"Come on," Jack urged. "We have to get out of here before—"

"I don't know whether I can."

They moved through the patchy shadows cast by the jungle of

draped lines over their heads. Jaidee was still shivering uncontrolla-bly, and he threw an arm across her shoulders in an effort to calm her.

"Jaidee," he whispered, "you have to shake off your fear. You're on the ground now, but if we don't get out of this alley right now—"

It was too late. The gunman, blood dripping from inside his jacket, appeared at the end of the alley. As he began stalking toward them, Jack retreated, pulling Jaidee with him.

"What are we going to do?" she said.

Looking up behind them, Jack saw how the cyclist had reached Connaston's bathroom window. There was an iron ladder that led up along the side of the building all the way to the roof.

"Quick!" he whispered. "This way!"

Taking her hand he pulled her to the ladder, then, hands at her waist, lifted her up. To her credit, she didn't cower, but, understand-ing their dire predicament, began to climb. Jack waited for the gun-man to come in range, then overturned a galvanized metal trash can and, kicking it hard, sent it rumbling toward him.

Then he turned and leaped up the ladder after Jaidee. The first shot dislodged a chunk of wall to their left when they were halfway up. Moments later, a second shot pinged off a rung of the metal lad-der. But by then, Jaidee had launched herself over the low parapet, onto the roof. A third bullet took a chunk of cement off the top of the parapet just as Jack went over.

For a moment, he lay beside Jaidee, breathing heavily, then they began to get up. Jack was on his hands and knees when something crashed into him, driving him backward against the parapet. His head slammed against the cement. For an instant he blacked out, then he recognized the face of the cyclist. Her lips were drawn back in a rictus of rage. She had her hands around Jaidee's neck, squeezing so tightly the girl couldn't draw breath. She bore down on Jaidee with such savageness he thought, *an instant more and she'll kill Jaidee.*

Black lights flashed behind his eyes and he could feel his veins pulsing, see their branching, on and on, reaching from his eyes to his brain.

Then, he had his arms wrapped around the cyclist's waist. He heard a scream, not of pain so much as frustration. With a surge of fury, he ripped the cyclist away. The cyclist, squirming, almost jabbed Jaidee's eyes out, but at the last instant, Jack hurled her sideways, away from them both.

The cyclist stumbled hard against the parapet. Jaidee, scrambling up, kicked her in the chest. The cyclist screamed again, her clawlike hands shot out, grabbing Jaidee in a desperate attempt to regain her balance.

Jack struck her so hard on the nose her hands flew to her face, and over the parapet she went, tumbling head over heels through the air, plummeting down, crashing into the electrical lines, which acted like a webbing to cradle her fall. But then one of the lines broke, the live ends sparking and fizzing. Somehow the cyclist had the presence of mind to scramble away, but as if it were alive, the fizzing ends pursued her, arcing through the air, then dropping onto her back.

The electricity shot through her, and she arched, spasming, her eyes popping in their sockets, her feet drumming uselessly. Then she fell through the rent in the wires, crashing headfirst into the pavement of the alley.

Jack heard the gunman's curses rising up the side of the building from below and turned away.

"Are you all right?" he said to Jaidee. "Can you walk?"

"I . . . I think so." Her voice was no more than a hoarse croak.

"Then come on." He supported her as she rocked back and forth. "We need to go."

It was then he heard the high-low wail of a police siren approaching the building with alarming rapidity.

Ripley was hip-deep in Leroy Connaston's life, pieced together from various clandestine sources she had hacked online, when she came across something that gave her such pause that she immediately began to back out of every site. As she worked to leave no electronic fingerprints, she prayed that this wasn't the time she finally made a mistake. She desperately wanted to remain unseen.

When she was done, Ripley sat back in her task chair, staring at the blank screen. Then, on an impulse that was as paranoid as it was irresistible, she shut down her computer, unplugged it, and closed her eyes for a moment. Her hands were in her lap, and when she became aware of how violently they were shaking, she stood up, crossed the room where she lived and worked, ran the hot water in the kitchen sink, and put them under the cascade. As the warmth penetrated her chilled flesh, the quaking subsided, along with the accelerated beating of her heart.

She stood, bent over, elbows on the sink, staring out at the Place des Vosges. The sight never failed to calm her. It was the oldest planned place in Paris, and, to her mind, at least, the most beautiful, with its symmetrical lines of trees, like sentries standing guard over the four fountains at its corners, bubbling like flutes of champagne. Part of its exquisite charm was that it was surrounded by royal house fronts of red brick, stone quoins, and elegantly vaulted arcades, which now housed restaurants and cutting-edge art galleries, as well as, on the weekends, itinerant musicians and singers, unfailingly of exceptional quality.

Ripley's large, lofty apartment was ensconced in one of these buildings. Though her various employers believed her to be living in London, Gibraltar, or Geneva, these were fictions she had created to keep her whereabouts secret after she decamped from Washington, D.C., a year ago.

Ripley was her hacker's moniker, the name by which all her clients knew her. Her real name was Caroline Carson. She had been a computer hacker all of her adult life. Nothing else interested her as much as delving into other people's secrets. She had worked her cybermagic for a number of people, the last of whom was the Syrian. She had left him, abruptly and without warning, when Jack McClure was closing in on him. No one knew more about the Syrian's business than Caro. In D.C., just before she left, she had helped Jack find the Syrian. That he had been unsuccessful in killing the master terrorist had sent Caro to Paris and into complete anonymity. She had no idea how seriously the Syrian was hunting for her, but with his obsessive, narcissistic nature, she had no trouble imagining the worst. No one could protect her, no one could save her. In her mind, it was just a matter of time before the Syrian, or, more likely, one of his professional assassins, found her and put an end to her life. She had considered staying on the run, but she'd be damned if she was going to spend whatever time was still allotted to her fleeing from country to country. She had made a life for herself in Paris's Marais; she loved it here, so here she would stay until the end.

Shaking off these morbid thoughts, she turned off the water, dried her hands on a dish towel, and went back to her computer, plugged it in, fired it up, and got back to work. She regretted taking the Connaston commission now that she knew he had been involved up to his neck with the Syrian. She never would have agreed to it if her connection with Deckard hadn't been so tight. She had met him five years ago at DEFCON, the hacker's convention. Later, they had met once more at the Hacker's Secret Ball, a yearly event, a movable feast, whose location was so closely guarded it was only revealed twenty-four hours in advance. It was up to its invitees to find their way to it. Not very many received invites. Only the top-tier hackers, the crème de la crème from DEFCON even knew it existed. That year, it had been held in Abu Dhabi, a place she hoped never to re-turn to. There were almost fifty attendees that year—a high-water mark that had yet to be equaled. Deckard was a dead-eyed man with the skin of a lizard, but he had a mind that dazzled Caro. No one used their real names, no one was allowed to ask personal questions. The ball was to have fun, trade secrets, and, best of all, learn new ways into increasingly unhackable software. Deckard was in charge of a demonstration that year, and his was the one Caro found most fascinating. They had been cyberfriends ever since.

Now, staring at a summary of the material she had purloined, she wondered why she hadn't heard of Leroy Nathaniel Connaston before. It was he who had created the proprietary software she had used when she was working for the Syrian. She vividly recalled asking Iraj who had built the program, but he had never answered. Once, she had picked a fight with him over the dead air of his deliberate silence. The argument had ended abruptly and stingingly when the Syrian slapped her so hard she lost her balance. He had stared down at her where she fell on the Isfahan carpet, as if she were a soiled rag someone had forgotten to throw away. She never forgot that look, which was almost worse than the blow, and that was the moment she had decided to jump ship. She waited for the right moment, when he would be sufficiently distracted to allow her to escape. She would be eternally indebted to Jack McClure for providing that distraction, though she had never admitted it to him and never would.

Now, as she prepared the document on Connaston for Deckard, she scoured her system for any signs that she had been caught out while hacking into a server that belonged jointly to Connaston and the Syrian. To her relief, she found nothing, but as she was e-mailing the file, she heard the telltale *ding* of her alarm.

Someone was trying to gain entrance to her encrypted network.

Jack's head was clearing faster now. "Make for the front of the building," he said.

"Of course," Jaidee cried. "The bamboo scaffolding!"

They hurried across the roof, over the parapet, and onto the scaffolding just as a police vehicle pulled up below, disgorging a pair of uniformed men. But as they were heading for the front door, another car—this one unmarked—arrived from the opposite direction. Four suits got out, one of whom went up to the uniforms and showed them his ID. A short discourse from him sent them back to their cruiser, which backed up to a cross street and vanished.

"Special Branch?" Jaidee whispered in Jack's ear.

He nodded. They had remained motionless, hanging high above the street, their presence hidden by the webwork of bamboo poles.

The moment the suits went into the building, Jack and Jaidee descended to one of several platforms. Though narrow, it was long enough to accommodate half a dozen workers. At one end, Jack saw, neatly folded and stacked, a pile of canvas jumpsuits the workers had left overnight.

Moments later, he and Jaidee had climbed into a pair of them. Hers was comically overlarge for her petite frame until she turned up the cuffs on legs and sleeves, and, in the end, the two of them could pass a cursory inspection as maintenance workers.

Invisible beneath their camouflage, they made their way down to the street as quickly as was practical.

"No sign of the gunman," Jack said after a quick but thorough scan. "He must have fled the moment he heard the sirens."

"They're coming!" Jaidee said, listening at the front door.

She and Jack strolled across the street, joining the crowd that was shouldering one another to check out the unusual activity. At Jack's urging, Jaidee asked several bystanders what was going on. Drug bust, prostitution ring, terrorist hideout were some of the guesses. No one, however, was in a position to know the facts.

Taking her hand, he wormed them back toward the fringes of the crowd, and by the time the officers of Special Branch's Naresuan 261 had emerged from the building at a run, sprinting into the alley where the cyclist had landed, Jack and Jaidee had melted away into the greater chaos of the city.

Dr. Karalian stayed late at the Assumption of Mary Clinic, as he often did, to play a game of chess against himself. Over the years, he had discovered that he needed several hours to decompress from his long, psychically stressful day, before he ventured home to deal with his ongoing family issues. Nothing relaxed him the way chess did. He became instantly absorbed in the board warfare, in the complex strategy that would lead to victory or the death of your king. This was one of the reasons he treasured his friendship with Dyadya

Gourdjiev. Karalian was a chess master. In fact, such was his skill that he might have become a grand master, had he not chosen to pursue medicine. In all his playing time, he had not encountered anyone who could match his skill at long-range strategy, save for Gourdjiev.

Even as he worked on strategy, Karalian mourned the passing of his friend. He was thinking of the envelope Gourdjiev had left with him, which had "To Be Opened in the Event of My Death" scrawled across it in Gourdjiev's cramped hand. Inside were just a few lines, along with another, smaller envelope sealed with a blob of red wax. He had memorized the lines before burning the letter, as Gourdjiev had instructed him. The ritual, though brief, had only exacerbated his sorrow. Hearing his friend's voice again, from beyond the grave, had reminded him with great poignancy of how much they had meant to each other. His sadness was mitigated somewhat by the knowledge of how completely the old man trusted him. The moment he had read the letter, he was determined to justify Gourdjiev's faith in him.

He was mulling these thoughts as he took one of black's bishops with his white knight, an unorthodox move whose virtue and influence he and Gourdjiev had spent hours debating. He smiled to himself, the echoes of their friendly arguments resounding in his ears. Their last titanic struggle would forever remain an unfinished match.

It was at just this moment that a shadow fell across the lamp-illuminated chessboard. He looked up to see a familiar figure standing over him.

"How on earth did you get in here, Mr. Cardozian?"

The Syrian smiled, not unkindly. "There are ways into every place, even fortresses," he said. "And this is hardly a fortress."

Karalian sat back and sighed. Then he gestured to the chair opposite him, where Dyadya Gourdjiev used to sit during their matches. "Now that you're here, what can I do for you?"

The Syrian pointedly remained standing. "I came for the truth, Dr. Karalian."

Karalian's brows knitted together. "The truth about what?"

"About why Annika was really here."

"You told me that you were her protector."

"Among other things."

"It's been my impression that Ms. Dementieva is someone least likely to need a protector."

"You're wrong in your assessment."

"I am not," Dr. Karalian said. "I know her better than you think." He rose now, standing face to face with his visitor. "And as for truth telling, I doubt very much your real name is Cardozian."

"My name is irrelevant," the Syrian said.

"I doubt Ms. Dementieva would think so." Karalian looked around. "Is she here?"

The Syrian's arm moved in a blurred arc, sweeping all the chess men onto the floor.

"That was rather childish," Karalian said, "don't you think?"

"How about this?" the Syrian said, drawing a 9mm Glock from its shoulder holster and aiming at Karalian. "Is this childish?"

Karalian's gaze held steady on his visitor. "According to whom? Freud says it certainly is."

"Freud is dead, doctor. And so will you be unless you answer my question."

For a long, drawn-out moment, Karalian was silent. Then he licked his lips and said, "I didn't lie. Ms. Dementieva came to tell me about her grandfather's death."

"But that's not all she came for, is it?"

Again the hesitation, shorter this time. "No," Karalian said. "It isn't."

"Enlighten me, then."

Karalian glanced away for a moment, then cleared his throat. "Ms. Dementieva came to see someone here."

"An inmate."

Dr. Karalian winced. "They are patients, Mr.—Whateveryour-nameis—they aren't inmates."

"Are they free to leave whenever they wish?"

"For the vast majority of our patients, a premature release would not be advisable."

"In other words, they are inmates." The Syrian sneered. "So who did Annika come to see?"

"Her husband, Rolan."

"You're lying." The Syrian took a threatening step toward Karalian; nevertheless, all the color had drained from his face. "Rolan is dead."

"Well, it's true that he was on the point of death when he was brought here," Karalian said. "But he survived his terrible ordeal." His bright eyes surveyed the Syrian's face. "I was never told precisely what happened to him, but I'm willing to bet you know."

The Syrian waved his Glock. "Take me to him."

Karalian appeared alarmed. "Now? I don't advise it."

"I don't give a shit. I want to look him in the face."

Karalian acquiesced. "Very well."

Annika awoke in the Usta Park hotel suite she shared with Iraj Namazi to find him gone. She had jerked herself awake from a dream where she had been systematically slaughtering a lamb, whose bleats of terror and agony had followed her into her waking life.

The open door to the bathroom revealed only darkness. All at once, she was gripped by a sense of foreboding. Ripping aside the bedclothes, she dressed, then went down the silent, deserted hallway, stopping in front of the door to another room. She pounded on the door, called Fareed's name, but there was no answer. By this time, she didn't expect any.

Taking the elevator to the lobby, she inquired of the night clerk, who told her that both Iraj and Fareed had left the hotel over an hour ago. She cursed under her breath. She had a pretty good idea of where they had gone.

"I need a car," Annika said to the night clerk.

"I'm terribly sorry, madam, but—"

He stopped in his tracks as she put down three hundred-dollar bills. Instantly, they were swept off the countertop. In their place, the clerk plunked down a set of keys. "Dark-blue Fiat. Fourth car from the front in the employees' car park. It's my car so be careful—" But Annika was already past the sliding glass doors.

The hotel was twenty miles from Altindere National Park and the Assumption of Mary Clinic. For a terrorist, Iraj liked his creature comforts; not for him the fetid Damadola caves of Afghanistan. But then Iraj was nothing if not a knot of contradictions. It seemed to her that only her grandfather fully understood him.

The night wind brought with it the mineral smells of the Black Sea, as well as the ephemeral scents of areca palms and sand, which carpeted much of the red topsoil. The Fiat started up without difficulty. Grateful for the full tank of gas, she let out the clutch, geared up, and got herself out of the parking lot.

The moment she was outside the hotel grounds, she floored the accelerator, going flat-out down the two-lane highway toward the Altindere valley. A drive that would normally take forty minutes was accomplished in twenty-five.

She arrived at the clinic only to see Iraj emerging with another man. At first, she assumed it was Fareed, but then, as her headlights flooded them, she saw that the man with Iraj was Rolan, stumbling along beside him, blinking like an owl in sunlight. Behind them was Dr. Karalian, his head lowered in defeat.

Heart in her mouth, Annika stamped on the brake, threw the Fiat into neutral, and flung herself out of the car.

"Iraj, what do you think you're doing?" She rushed toward them. They looked like figures out of a nightmare, and she saw again her bloody hands wrist deep in the lamb's impossibly soft, bloody coat. She felt her world tilting away from her, sliding out of her control. "Iraj, are you insane?"

"On the contrary," the Syrian said, "I'm liberating an inmate who was being held against his will. Someone who is as sane as you or I."

"No, Iraj." Out of the corner of her eye, she saw Karalian trying to signal her, but her concentration was fixed on the Syrian. "You can't."

"But I have. It's done, Annika."

Tears stung her eyes. She could not imagine Rolan being able to control himself in the outside world. She had seen the havoc his rages had wreaked. There was no telling how he would react or interact with others once the knowledge of where he was began to seep in. Rolan was extremely dangerous, not only to others, but also to himself.

She recalled Dr. Karalian saying to her, *"Your husband's brain has been physically damaged. There is quite literally no available method to understand which path his mind might take."*

"What are you implying, doctor?" she had replied in dread. *"Is Rolan insane?"*

"Not yet," Dr. Karalian had said. *"And, one hopes, never. But I'm afraid one must be prepared for this eventuality, Ms. Dementieva. I understand your desire to bring him home, but in my opinion it would be a grave mistake. Rolan must stay here until we can assess the new pathways his mind is forging."*

Now Iraj had taken Rolan out, without any understanding of the implications or possible consequences. But her grandfather would have known, her grandfather would have known she could not sneak off here on her own without Iraj getting suspicious. Perhaps it would be Rolan who would kill Iraj; perhaps this was her grandfather's wish. Because she could not take over the Syrian's position if she herself killed him. His lieutenants would turn on her and kill her.

Was this the path to rid herself of Iraj and take over? If so, it was both ingenious and elegant.

All her life, she had been manipulated by men—for both good and evil. Not one of them had ever asked what it was she wanted, what it was that would make her happy. Consequently, she realized, she had never been happy—until she had met Jack McClure.

ELEVEN

The BTS Skytrain was hurtling past Benjasiri Park when Jack's mobile downloaded from Nona the packet on Leroy Connaston that Ripley had pieced together. Jack, and Jaidee as well, felt safer staying on the move. They had boarded the Sukhumvit Line at Thong Lor station and were now traveling east toward Siam station. It was just after 7:00 a.m., and already the Skytrain was jam-packed, taking commuters to work in the central districts. The sky was slate gray and formless. There was almost no wind.

Before he opened the packet, though, he took out the pad that had been secreted in the bedclothes Legere had been sleeping in at Connaston's apartment. It was a small oblong of thick cream-colored sheets backed by a slab of cardboard. Leafing through the sheets, he found them all blank, but when he ran his thumb over the top sheet he felt indentations. The paper was so thick Legere must have been pressing down hard to make such an imprint.

Reaching down, Jack swiped up a fingertip of soot from the floor and gently smeared it across the face of the top sheet. What appeared in reverse relief was a line of eight numbers: 24026188.

There were no spaces or any punctuation to give a clue as to what the number referred to.

"A bank account?" Jaidee said, peering around his shoulder.

"Possibly."

The BTS pulled into the Asoke station, surrounded by ultra-modern monolithic high-rises. Jack studied each person who entered. When the doors closed and the Skytrain sped on, he closed his eyes and said to Jaidee, "Read off the numbers to me."

She did as he asked without question.

"Again," Jack said.

"Twenty-four, zero—"

"Stop," Jack said. He opened his eyes and looked at her. "How do we know Legere meant twenty-four, zero, and not two-forty."

Jaidee shook her head. "We don't."

"Well," Jack said with a sly grin, "maybe we do." In his mind's eye, he saw the numbers in three dimensions. "Going forward gives us twenty-six, eighteen, eight."

"Or one eighty-eight," she pointed out.

"I don't think so." He had already parsed the puzzle. "Let's suppose this is a simple substitution code, numbers for letters. Twenty-six, eighteen, eight would give us what three letters?"

Jaidee counted on her fingers. "ZRH."

Jack's grin widened. "Do you know what those three letters stand for?"

When she shook her head, he said, "It's the airport code for Zurich."

She gasped. "The address on the slip of paper in my gold heart."

"Correct," Jack said. The train slowed, entering Nana station. "Now the first three numbers, two-forty, make sense."

"A time!"

He nodded. "A flight time boarding here in Bangkok, going to Zurich, Switzerland."

"But how can you be sure?"

He took out his mobile and brought up Orbitz. After a bit of hunting, he said, "There's an Air India flight that left Bangkok at two-forty this morning."

Jaidee's face fell. "While we were waiting for Legere to come back to Leroy's flat—"

"He was on his way to Zurich." Jack looked around. "How do I get to the airport from here?"

"We change at Phaya Thai for the Airport Rail Link."

He shook his head. "No, Jaidee. This is as far as you go."

Her eyes grew wide. "But I know I can help."

"You've already helped, more than you know." He took her small hands in his. "Jaidee, the best thing you can do for me now is to keep yourself safe. Is there somewhere you can go, where you will be absolutely out of harm's way? Your mother's house, maybe? That's where your child is."

"I don't want to be near her until I know everything's back to normal." She considered a moment. "I'll go to my brother. Rangsan is a cowboy. He works on a ranch." She ducked her head, as if abruptly ashamed to meet Jack's gaze. "He has many ties to powerful people in the underworld. He won't let anything happen to me. I'll be safe with him."

"All right then," Jack said. "It's settled." He watched her clutching the gold heart around her neck. "I'm sorry about Leroy."

"He was a good man." Her voice could scarcely be heard above the sounds of the BTS traveling along its tracks. "When he was away from Bangkok, maybe not. But when he was with me . . ."

Her voice trailed away. Jack understood. There was nothing more to say.

Ploenchit and Chit Lom came and went, and then the train slowed for the Siam stop.

"This is where I get off." Jaidee stood. "Phaya Thai is two stops farther on. You'll see signs in English for the connection."

He nodded. "Good-bye, Jaidee."

"Good luck," she said, before stepping off onto the platform, where she was swallowed up by the crowd even before the doors closed and the BTS continued on.

Jack took out his mobile and accessed the packet of information on Connaston. The swimming letters took some time to resolve into words, then phrases, and finally sentences.

It took him two minutes before he came across evidence of Connaston's involvement with the Syrian. At that moment, he knew everything had changed.

The moment she reached the street, Jaidee pulled out her mobile and punched a number on speed dial.

"Well?" the voice on the other end said.

"We were attacked." Jaidee was jammed in the ribs by an old woman with knife blade elbows. "Twice. You were right, Dandy was involved . . . yes, I said 'was.' She's dead. No, I didn't recognize the man with her." Jaidee went on to describe him in detail.

"I know him," the voice said with a grating of ice against ice. "Continue."

"Nevertheless, everything went as planned. Your man is very, very smart and very, very resourceful." Jaidee moved back into the doorway of a building, removing herself from the jostling throng filling the sidewalk to overflowing. "I fed him the story about Connaston and the gold locket, but it was difficult with him staring into my face. I couldn't risk him becoming suspicious." She kept her eyes moving this way and that along the street. She preferred to be a moving target; that had been another of the man's suggestions.

"Yes," she said in answer to a question, "he found the paper you wrote and folded up inside."

"Where is he now?"

"On his way to Zurich." Jaidee wet her lips. "But there's something else, something you didn't anticipate. Legere had scrawled something on a pad he had hidden. Even though the top sheet had been torn off, McClure was able to trace the imprint on the next sheet. Pyotr Legere somehow managed to slip through the cordon here. He left this morning at two-forty."

"Where is he headed?"

"Also Zurich."

A string of flavorsome Russian curses filled Jaidee's ear just before the connection was severed.

The instant Caro saw the red light flashing at the bottom right corner of her screen she knew everything had changed. For four hours, she had been laboring to run a trace on the program seeking to infiltrate her firewalls. And after all that time she and the intruder program were at a stalemate. Somehow her recent activity within Connaston's and the Syrian's servers had been flagged. Though it had not been traced back to her, neither could she find a way around the program to get to its source.

She stared at the computer screen like a general surveying a battlefield, searching for the path, no matter how circuitous, no matter the cost in lives, to victory. She made some hurried notes, then shut down her system completely, taking it off-line.

Stepping over to one of her tall windows, she glanced down at the Place des Vosges where laughing children played, lovers lounged on benches, members of a Japanese tour group in long white cotton gloves snapped photos incessantly, and grandpas and grandmas, cheeks flushed, turned their faces into the lowering sun. For several minutes, she watched a heavyset man in a ratty overcoat and scuffed boots without laces feeding pigeons bits of stale bread from a creased paper bag.

She turned away from the window, snatched up her coat, and went down to the square, mingling, matching her pace to the leisurely stroll of those around her. She circled one of the fountains in which a boy was sailing a tiny plastic pirate ship. Was that Johnny Depp at the helm?

Eventually, she sat down on the bench where the heavyset man was feeding the pigeons.

"Hello, Elady," she said in Russian.

"Please," Zukhov said with a wince. "My French is quite good enough." He threw out a couple of crumbs to the fat pigeons, who began their squabble all over again. "Look," he said, "just like politicians." He chuckled, his multiple chins wobbling. "And what have you done to your hair?"

"Dyed it black," Caro said, switching languages. "Don't you like it? It suits my mood." She had a beautiful Parisian accent, which was more than she could say for Zukhov, whose French, though fluent, marked him indelibly as a foreigner.

Zukhov leered at the fat-breasted pigeons. "Girl with your looks, the color of your hair doesn't mean squat."

"These pigeons look like they're about to explode from all the food you're feeding them."

"This is bread from Poilâne. Only the best."

Caro decided it was time to get down to business. "I need help."

"Did I teach you nothing?"

"You taught me everything. Almost."

"Almost," he repeated. "Like any master worth his copper."

"Nevertheless, now I'm at a loss."

"Sooner or later," Zukhov said, brushing crumbs off his stained pants, "it happens to even the best of us."

"To you?"

"Please," he said. "Not to me."

Caro watched the Japanese tourist group climbing like good soldiers into their hermetically sealed bus. "How often do you come here?"

"As often as I can," Zukhov said vaguely. "I am inspired by the magnificent symmetry. Also by that young countertenor who sings under the arches like an angel fallen to earth."

"You Russians," Caro said. "So poetic, so melancholy."

"We can't help it." Zukhov continued to dole out the stale bread for the pigeons' insatiable appetites. "It's in our blood."

"Along with cabbage and vodka."

Zukhov laughed shortly. "Do you want my help or not?"

He was the only person she had ever met who could scowl while laughing.

"I do."

"Speak, then."

A blue ball sprinkled with big white stars came merrily bouncing her way. She stopped it with her feet, bent, and threw it back to the little boy to whom it belonged.

"The Syrian is looking for me."

"This is news? He's been looking for you ever since you left him." Zukhov grunted. "Why d'you imagine I really come here so often?"

The watery light of afternoon had thickened, like flour and water, the slanting sunlight already tinged with evening lavender.

His admission left her momentarily at a loss for words. On her own since she was fourteen, she was decidedly deficient in accepting others' caring for her. She cleared her throat of confusing emotion. "I'm on a job, searching through the servers of a man named Leroy Connaston."

"For whom?"

"The important thing is one of those servers is jointly run by the Syrian."

"The Syrian, the gift that keeps on giving." Zukhov reached into the paper bag, which lay on his more than ample lap. "I'll bet a month's salary the moment you breached the firewall on the Syrian's server a nasty little netbot came looking for you."

Caro watched the young boy tossing the ball into the air. His thick hair was thrown back. The white stars kept spinning. "No bet."

"I'm sure not," Zukhov grunted again. "Did it find you, this little vermin?"

"Of course not. We're in a Mexican standoff."

Zukhov shot her a look. "A Mexican what?"

"Stalemate."

"Well, that won't sit well with him. He'll sent a second netbot, and then a third, and on and on, until one of them breaks through."

"We can't let that happen."

"Naturally. So you want something to eat the vermin."

"No," Caro said with some vehemence, "I want something to turn his netbots against him."

Now Zukhov's laugh was genuine. "Are you sure you're not Russian?"

"Fuck," Redbird said. "Fuck, fuck, fuck!"

"Hold still," Farmington said. "You'll rip the stitches and start bleeding all over again."

Redbird didn't care. Dandy was dead, and it was his fault. He dearly wanted to know who the fuck the man was with Jaidee, the cowboy's sister. And what were they doing in Connaston's apartment? It was true enough that Dandy had botched the snatch, which, considering Dandy's skill, should have been a snap. But that man had interfered. Now Dandy was dead, his upper right arm was dog meat, and he was no closer to finding Pyotr Legere.

He sat on Farmington's surgical table at Dickinson's Bangkok safe house. Farmington was Dickinson's agent-in-place. He was eyes and ears only, not a foot soldier. Though lacking a degree, he had a great deal of medical experience. Over the years, Dickinson's people had needed a great deal of patching up; the violence in and around the city was at an astonishingly high level.

Even when Dennis Paull was running homeland security, Redbird was Dickinson's man in the field. They were tied together by a particular strand of rope Redbird would prefer not to think about, though he was quite sure Paull knew nothing about his commissions. What he did for Dickinson was so far outside the bounds of legality, even by federal government standards, Paull would never have approved. Dickinson was corrupt in a way all of Redbird's clients were—with a sense of entitlement and a license to commit havoc.

A sudden searing pain in his right arm caused his muscles to involuntarily twitch.

"I told you to hold still," Farmington said, still working on the stitches. "Whoever delivered this knife wound knew what he was doing."

Redbird's ruminations were simply a way for him to stop thinking about Dandy. He had contacts in virtually every major city in the world, but she had been far more than a contact. He had crossed a line with her, had come to see her as a real person, rather than a thing to help get him from point A to point B. More fool him. He knew better than to involve himself in the lives of his contacts, who were, by definition, if not quite cannon fodder, then expendable. That included Dandy. He knew that, but he had refused to acknowledge it. Now he was paying the price. Her death weighed heavily on him, as did the thought of revenge on the man who had caused her demise.

"This commission is different," Dickinson had told him at the outset. *"You are to find one man, but as you'll see, the commission could turn out to be a complex one."*

He hadn't been exaggerating.

He winced again, said, "How much of the muscle is damaged?"

"The muscles in your arm are both dense and outsized," Farmington said, threading another stitch, further drawing the edges of the wound together. "Your muscles are what saved you from an open fracture, which would have put slivers of bone through your skin. That would have been beyond my skills."

"Fuck that," Redbird snapped. "How bad is it?"

"That depends," Farmington tied off the last stitch, "on how much pain you can tolerate."

Redbird shook free of him and, cocking his arm, punched a hole in the wall. "How's that?"

Farmington tried and failed to not look impressed. "Okay, given that demonstration, I'd say you can do whatever the hell you want. It'll hurt, and the longer you continue aggressive action, the worse the pain will get."

"Not relevant."

"But the bleeding will be. Here, take these." He handed Redbird two capsules, along with a glass of water.

"What's this?"

"Antibiotics." He placed a small vial on the table next to his patient. "Two a day. Ten days' worth. No alcohol. Clear?"

Redbird swallowed the capsules, put the vial away. "Bleeding, you said."

Farmington nodded. "And I damn well meant it. I told you whoever was working the knife knew what he was doing. The wound is deep. If you use the arm too much—particularly violently, as in a hand-to-hand combat, or putting your fist through a wall— the stitches may tear apart the edges of the wound. The resulting blood loss would be disastrous."

Ignoring the pain in his right arm, Redbird shrugged his shirt back on.

"I need you to focus," Farmington said. "Having a high threshold of pain is all well and good, but that isn't going to help you when blood loss or infection sap your strength."

"Okay, okay," Redbird said. "Message received."

His mobile sang out, and he looked up at Farmington, who shrugged and went into the next room, closing the door behind him.

"You missed your update," Dickinson said from the other end of the call. "Everything all right?"

"Fine," Redbird said. "But Legere remains elusive."

"That's because he's no longer in Bangkok." Dickinson's voice was as tart as a squirt of lemon juice. "And we just got a hit from the CCTV at Bangkok airport. McClure is on his way to Zurich, which means that's where Pyotr Legere went." His voice had turned dark and threatening. "How McClure discovered that and you didn't is anyone's guess."

So McClure was the man with the Thai girl, Redbird thought. "How McClure got out of D.C. scot-free is also anyone's guess."

"Just get the fuck over there yourself," Dickinson barked. "Your commission now includes two people: Legere and McClure, who, I have been informed by Bangkok immigration, is using the name Edward Griffiths. Obviously a legend. I want you to bring Legere *and* McClure back to D.C."

PART THREE

ENEMIES IN THE MIRROR ARE CLOSER THAN THEY APPEAR

TWELVE

"Why have you done this?" Annika cried. "Why have you taken him out of his sanctuary?"

Iraj Namazi eyed her calmly. He was holding Rolan by the hand, as if he were a bewildered child. "Why did you lie to me?"

"I never lied to you," she retorted.

"I thought Rolan was dead. That's what you and your grandfather led me to believe."

"Neither of us ever said—"

"Lies by omission," the Syrian said, "are lies nonetheless." His lips turned down in contempt. "And you grieving—"

"My grieving was—is—real. My husband was taken from me. By your raid, your men."

"And yet—" Namazi raised Rolan's arm, as if in victory "—here he is."

"Do you think he's the same as he was? Undamaged? My Rolan?"

The night wind, blowing in off the Black Sea, rustled the date and areca palms. To their right rose the immense bulk of the mountain, the fiery eyes of Sümela Monastery three-quarters of the way up. Above them all, the goddess face of the moon was wreathed in scarves of cloud.

Namazi lowered his arm with Rolan's. "He was caught in the gears."

"Collateral damage, yes." She stood before him, legs at hip width, knees slightly bent. She could see him assessing her battle stance, wondering if she would move against him or if her posture was just an act. "Happens all the time in war, is that what you'll tell me next?"

"It's the truth," the Syrian said, unblinking.

Annika bit back the invective that filled her throat and almost made her gag. "Iraj, let Dr. Karalian take Rolan back inside." She despised the pleading tone her voice had taken on. "He needs—"

"I know what he needs, better than you," Namazi said firmly. "He needs a purpose—we all do—otherwise life is meaningless. And, believe me, *chérie*, Rolan's life was meaningless chained to his chair."

Annika felt each word as if they were stones hurled at her. "This can't be guilt talking. You don't feel remorse."

Namazi smiled. "No, *chérie*. I have liberated your beloved husband for one reason: to control you." He took a step forward. "You see, as long as your grandfather was alive, he kept you on a tight leash. Now that he's gone—" Iraj shrugged "—another means had to be found to leash you." Stepping back, he clapped Rolan on the back. "It wasn't easy to find a suitable one, believe me. But it was you who led me to him, *chérie*, so it's you I must thank—"

"Fool! You don't know what you're doing."

"On the contrary."

"You don't get it, Iraj," she persisted. "In his current state, Rolan is dangerous."

The Syrian laughed. "Really, *chérie*, this is beneath you. Surely you can do better than spout dire warnings." He turned. "Look at him! Rolan is as docile as a lamb."

"You're judging him by his exterior, Iraj. You—"

"This is how you speak of your husband?" The flat of his hand swept through the air like a scythe. "Not one more word from you, understand?"

Annika understood, and so, it appeared from the expression on his moon-kissed face, did Dr. Karalian.

"I trust this interview won't take long." Tim Malone sat down across a narrow table from Jonatha Midwood. "My duties as the director of the FBI leave me little time for frivolities."

"Is that what you think this is?" Jonatha said. "A frivolity?"

"If what you're asking is whether this mole hunt is useful, then the answer is no."

Jonatha smiled like a sphinx. "You would say that if you were the mole."

"I'm not Jack McClure."

There didn't seem to be an iota of humor to Malone. She made a note; lack of humor was often an indicator of certain other traits useful in building a profile. Now, looking down, at the hard copy of the psych test she had prepared, she pretended to read, waiting.

After a time, Malone shifted from one buttock to the other. His hands were clasped before him on the tabletop. They were in a room within CIA headquarters that Jonatha had designed, overseeing every detail of its construction. It was painted a dull battleship gray, and was absolutely neutral—no windows, pictures, or wall hangings of any kind to distract the subject from her questions. The overhead fluorescent lights had a deliberate liminal flicker, a tape loop of barely audible whispers and footfalls emerged from speakers hidden in the floor. A scent of hot metal and electronics, manufactured to Jonatha's specifications, was pumped in through a vent to give the impression of a vast amount of machinery at work hidden behind the walls.

At last, Jonatha lifted her head, smiled at Malone, and said, "Tell me, Tim—do you mind if I call you Tim?"

"In fact, I do."

"Resisting will only make the process difficult."

"What process?"

"All right, Tim, let's begin."

It was always a good idea to ignore the subject's questions. A specific hierarchical order existed in this room. It was her dominion, and the sooner the subject understood this the better.

"I told you—"

"When did you join the Federal Bureau of Investigation?"

"Surely you know the answer already."

She stared at him, silent, unmoving.

He shrugged. "Three years ago this March."

"And where were you before that?"

He started at a whisper snaking through the room like smoke.

"Don't you people insulate your offices?"

"Budget cuts," Jonatha said.

Malone grunted and could not mask a smirk. "I came from the DoD," he said.

"You had military training."

"I was a captain in the Navy, yes."

"And then?"

"I was asked to join the DoD as part of their antiterrorist task force."

"Why did your wife leave you?"

"What?" Malone was clearly taken aback. "I've been happily married for seven years."

Jonatha studied his face. "Your first wife didn't leave you?"

Malone's brows knit together. "That was a long time ago."

"Why did she leave you, Tim?"

"I wish you wouldn't do that."

"Ask that question or call you Tim?"

He stared at her for a moment, his lips pursed.

"Please answer," Jonatha prodded.

"I . . ." Malone coughed into his fist. "At the time, I had a mistress."

"Stella Rodnina."

Malone's cheeks colored. "Are you objecting to her being of Russian extraction?"

Silence.

"Her grandparents were White Russians. They—"

"Since, according to you, you're 'happily married,'" Jonatha broke in, "I'm questioning why you still see her."

"We're friends."

"Friends who from time to time share a room at the Colonial Inn, on, let's see, New Hampshire Avenue, in Takoma Park, Maryland."

Malone glanced to his left for a moment, a sure sign he was about to lie. "It's nothing."

"Well, you see, Tim, that's where we differ. I believe it *is* something." She turned a page of dense typescript, scanning the next. "I'll tell you why. You've kept on with the affair, even after you remarried. You've kept that a secret, Tim. That's not good. But I'll tell you what's worse. You met while you were both in the Navy. She was a lieutenant, and not just any lieutenant, Tim, an officer in Navy Intelligence."

"What of it?"

"If I have to tell you, Tim, you're in the deep end."

Malone bristled visibly. "Stella was fully vetted by the Navy. D'you think intelligence would have—"

"You tell me. You know Ms. Rodnina more intimately than anyone."

"This intrusion is outrageous."

"This evaluation has Atlas priority."

"Fuck that shit; this is Krofft flexing his muscles. I'm going to have him reprimanded and you fired."

"This isn't school, Tim." Jonatha continued to scribble notes in the margins of the test sheet, even while she kept a sharp watch on Malone, who was trying to see what she was writing. "Do what you feel you must."

"You can be sure. As soon as I return to my office."

She gave him a perfectly neutral smile in return.

"We're done here." He rose, crossed the room to the door.

"Tim, we're not."

He ignored her, pulled open the door, and vanished down the hallway.

Humming Dylan's "All Along the Watchtower," Jonatha made some more notes in Malone's file, closed it, took it off the low stack, and set it aside.

"Next victim," she said into her mobile.

"No," Fareed said curtly, "you cannot see him."

"He's my husband," Annika said. "Iraj cannot keep Rolan from me."

"I have orders." Fareed crossed his arms over his burly chest. "Your husband is under Namazi's protection."

They were in the salon of their hotel suite. Beyond Fareed's broad back was the locked door to the bedroom in which Namazi had locked Rolan while he was out on business. Normally, Annika would have gone with him, but now matters between them were anything but normal.

"Protection from me? His wife?"

"He is asleep," Fareed said. "Namazi has seen to it."

"Namazi the god."

Fareed regarded her with dumb curiosity, as if she had spoken in a language he could not understand.

Annika turned, went across the thick carpet, and sat down on a chair facing Fareed. She had changed into a short sheath skirt of champagne-colored shantung silk that hugged her hips and butt and a black low-cut knit pullover.

"Fareed, you must get bored."

"I do not." He had the deep-throated growl of a wolf.

"But Iraj works you eighteen hours a day."

"I'm used to it."

"I'd never get used to it," she said. "So much time, so little to do."

"There's always something for me to do. Often, many things."

"Yes. Driving." Her full lips curved in the arc of a smile. "And watching."

"I watch all the time."

"Really. Like this?"

When she crossed her legs, the skirt rode up farther, revealing the taut, shimmering flesh of her thighs. Fareed contrived not to look, but she saw that he could not help giving her a furtive glance, so she bent over to remove her high-heel shoes, exposing the perfectly tanned tops of her breasts. She was not wearing a bra, and despite his best efforts Fareed's increasingly heated gaze was caught by the slow revealing of her lush body.

"And this?"

She raised one leg to massage her foot, her thighs opening just enough for him to see that she wore no underpants, either. She heard the tiny catch of his breath. His black eyes seemed to burn like coals beneath the ridge of his formidable brow.

"You like to watch, don't you, Fareed?" She rose and, on bare feet, picked her way across the carpet to where he stood, a stolid sentinel keeping her from Rolan.

He stared over her head. "I do what Namazi orders me to do."

"But you *do* like to watch. I see it. I *feel* it."

"Feel what?"

"Your eyes on me like hands." Her lips curved again. "You have large hands."

She moved close enough for him to inhale her scent. "What else about you is oversized, Fareed?"

His nostrils flared as he breathed her in, then his gaze dropped to her glistening lips. She turned her back to him.

"This sweater is irritating me, Fareed. I need to take it off." She raised her arms over her head, her voice rising to that of a little girl. "Will you help me? Please?"

When he made no move to put his hands at her waist, she spun back and said, "Come on, Fareed. We both have needs."

Unable to engage his eyes, she held out her hand. "Let me have your knife, Fareed. I know you always carry it, I've seen it often enough."

His gaze came down to her level. "I'm not going to give you my knife."

"Fair enough," she nodded. "Just take it out then."

He did as she asked, even though she could see he was dubious. Curiosity had got the better of him. Curiosity along with the sight and smell of her.

"Now open it."

When he did, she slowly wrapped her fingers around his wrist, drawing his fist and, with it, the tip of the naked blade, toward her. She could feel him resisting, but now she had locked up his gaze. He could not look away. Beautiful, she thought, relaxing fully.

She guided the tip to the center of her neckline, then increased the pressure. She heard the fabric separate, felt the bite of the steel edge, like the nip of an insect bite, at her skin, the warmth, the coppery odor of her own blood. She guided his fist and the blade downward in a straight line until her pullover was bisected, the two sections falling away to either side, revealing her heavy breasts and the light line of blood along her breastbone. A tiny drop, like a liquid ruby, wandered down her abdomen to pool in her navel.

Fareed, mesmerized, followed its path with his eyes. His thick lips were parted, and she could hear the soft animal pant of his breath. His fingers opened, the knife fell to the floor, the edge of its blade covered in a ribbon of her blood.

"Fareed," she breathed.

As if obeying a silent order, he knelt before her. His hand cupped her breast. His lips opened, his tongue traveling down the superficial wound she had granted him. He licked the drop of blood from her navel.

Reaching down, Annika slowly raised the hem of her skirt, revealing just the point of the vee between her thighs. Fareed sighed as he burrowed his tongue into her. Annika's head went back, her neck arched, the tendons rising against her tender skin as her hips rocked back and forth. She took his hands, sliding them around her hips until they grabbed her buttocks, and she gasped, bending over him as she came.

Then she reached behind her, unzipped her skirt. He shivered at the sound of metal against metal. The skirt writhed down her thighs as she slowly rolled her hips, pooling at her slender ankles. She lowered herself, kneeling, as she undressed him.

When he entered her, she was already elsewhere. Her body reacted on its own while her mind moved over what she wanted, what she needed, and how to get it. Her thoughts inevitably strayed to her grandfather, to his overarching plan, which, like the chess master he had been, spanned not years, but decades. There were times that she had doubts, when she had been downright skeptical, especially when she had discovered that she did not know every aspect of his dream, but her profound devotion to him kept her to the path he had laid out. When, precisely, had she intuited the key role Jack would play? She did not know, or maybe did not want to know.

Above her, Fareed groaned deeply, bucking his hips into her like a bull. He rolled off her, taking some of her sweat with him.

"Fareed," she whispered, "I want to see my husband."

Fareed stared up at the ceiling, then his head turned toward her and he stared into her eyes. "Is there anything you won't do for him?" he asked.

Though she was startled by the insight of his question she did not show it. Instead, she smiled. "I love him, Fareed."

He stared at her a moment longer. Then he rose to his knees, rummaging in his trouser pocket. He handed her the key.

"Be quick," he said. "Namazi will be back shortly."

Nodding, she stood and stepped past him, the chimera guarding the gate, to the door, inserting the key. She stepped across the threshold, closed the door at her back.

Contrary to what Fareed had told her, Rolan was standing by the window, looking out. He did not turn when he heard her softly call his name. He did not move at all. She thought about what he had been in the summertime of their love, what had happened to him during the Syrian's terrorist raid, and not for the first time thought it would have been better if he had been killed there in the street with the others, covered with shattered glass and the ball bearings used in the vest bombs. Not better for her grandfather, but better for her, and surely better for Rolan.

Now she went to Rolan, naked, coated with another man's sweat, and placed the bloody knife in his hand. "It's time," she said.

Rolan did not look down as his fingers grasped the hilt, but he turned and looked at her, through her, past her, and Annika's heart contracted once again, though she had promised herself it would never happen again. She had to remember that the Rolan she knew, who had laughed and held her, slept peacefully beside her and made love to her, was dead, destroyed by the ball bearing that had struck his head, the shrapnel that had pierced his body. He had died, and when he had returned to life it was as a different person. A miracle of medicine or an abomination? Rolan might never have existed. He was now something . . . other.

It was her grandfather who had recognized this first, even before Dr. Karalian, and had devised a use for what Rolan had become. At first, she had been filled with rage—rage that Rolan had left her prematurely, though being in the wrong place at the wrong time was not his fault. Gradually, the new reality sank in, but her irrational rage at Rolan for being in the wrong place at the wrong time consumed her. For three months she had not seen or spoken to him. And her grandfather had wisely stayed away, letting her passions cool.

Annika turned now, watching Rolan cross the bedroom, swing open the door, and step out into the salon. She could see Fareed, already dressed, sitting on the chair she had used, bending over to tie his shoelaces.

His head came up when he sensed someone approaching. His eyes grew wide, surprised that it was Rolan, not her standing in front of him. She saw Rolan's arm swing out in a shallow arc, perfectly calibrated and incredibly fast. Fareed had just enough time to register alarm, but not enough to rear back, before the knife blade slid across the width of his throat, left to right, so deeply that, in a geyser of blood, his cervical vertebrae were severed, his entire head dangling at an impossible angle.

THIRTEEN

Dr. Benjamin M. Scheiwold, the discreet brass plaque by the right side of the door said. The brass was so highly polished Jack could see his face in it. He didn't particularly like what he saw. He looked haggard, dark rings bruised the flesh beneath his eyes, as if he had been in a fight, which he was, a fight for his life. But his skin looked bleached and his hair was disheveled from his adventures in Bangkok and the long flight to Zurich, during which he had read in detail Nona's material on Leroy Connaston. He looked like a hunted man, though he knew that he must present himself to the world as perfectly normal.

A doctor, Jack thought now as he drew away from his reflection. He took out the slip of paper Connaston had secreted in the gold heart he had given Jaidee, checked the address again. Jack had expected it to lead him to one of the great Swiss banks. Why was Scheiwold so important to Connaston he felt the need to leave his address in Jaidee's safekeeping before what he must have suspected might be his last rendezvous?

Jack rang the bell next to the brass plaque, but there was no immediate answer. He turned, staring out at the busy street and the city.

Zurich, hunkered like a neoclassical *burger* at the northwestern tip of a cerulean blue Alpine lake, was founded by the Romans more than seven thousand years ago. Millennia later, in 1519, to be exact, it had given painful birth to the Protestant Reformation. At the moment Jack had stepped out of the Kloten Airport into a brisk, dry wind and a clear, high sky, Zurich was still one of the major financial centers of the world, which was very possibly why he had chased Pyotr Legere here.

With its plethora of high-steepled churches and steep-roofed houses, Zurich studiously maintained a certain Middle Ages charm. Across the placid surface of Lake Zurich could be seen boatyards and, farther inland, settlements that might still belong to German barons with storied, long-tail histories. Beyond, the vista widened out onto azure mountains towered over by the razorblade shoulders of snow-capped Alps.

Turning back, he rang the bell again, and this time received an answering buzz. He pushed the heavy wrought-iron and glass door inward, and stepped into a circular marble foyer, on the far side of which was a wide staircase with a polished brass banister. Above his head hung an ormolu chandelier, like a multifingered stalactite. On a small antique marquetry console to the left of the door to the doctor's suite stood a fluted crystal vase out of which exploded like fireworks two dozen white calla lilies, exuding the unmistakable scent of money.

Jack crossed the small space, opened the wide door, and stepped into Dr. Scheiwold's office. The moment he saw the frame with a digital display of women before and after facial surgery displayed on a glass coffee table in front of a plush semicircular sofa, he heard Legere's voice, an echo from the tape Paull had played for him:

"... he swung the M82A3 Special Application scoped rifle right into my face. I'll need plastic surgery. I can't go back into the field with this on my face. How would I ever melt into a crowd? It's like a neon sign."

It was clear now. Legere had been desperate to escape Bangkok and the attention of Naresuan 261 as quickly as possible so he could get his damaged face repaired.

"May I help you, sir?" A blond, blue-eyed woman in her early thirties who could have been a model, and no doubt was a living advertisement for Dr. Scheiwold, glanced up from whatever she had been doing. Her exquisite face was reminiscent of an alabaster statue, the features so perfect they were blinding.

"I'd like to see Dr. Scheiwold," Jack said, stepping up to the marble counter behind which she resided, and which reflected the expectant expression on her face.

"May I have your name, sir?"

"Edward Griffiths."

The receptionist glanced down at her tablet, then back up at him. "I'm sorry, sir. I don't see your name in Dr. Scheiwold's appointment book."

"Pity," Jack said. "In any event, I need to see him now."

"I'm afraid that's impossible, sir. The doctor is in with—"

"Tell him it's about Pyotr Legere."

The most extraordinary thing happened to the receptionist's face. An instantaneous flicker, like the briefest of power drains to a computer screen, passed across her eyelids. Otherwise, she remained motionless until her head moved from side to side.

"I'm sorry, Mr. Griffiths, but I don't recognize that name."

Jack glanced at the door to the offices, saw that it could only be opened by the receptionist buzzing him in as she had done with the door to the street.

"Dr. Scheiwold will," Jack said, "I assure you."

"I'm sorry." Her expression indicated that she wasn't in the least sorry.

At that moment, the door to Scheiwold's inner sanctum swung open and a fragile-looking woman, so thin she looked like a whippet, came through and began to engage the receptionist regarding payment and booking her next visit. Her face was a blotchy red, still swollen from the doctor's procedure. Like the receptionist, she looked far too young for plastic surgery.

Jack took the opportunity to grab the door before it closed, and step inside.

"Sir," the receptionist called after him. "Sir, you can't go in there."

She rounded the corner, but Jack was already at the doctor's consultation room and had stepped inside before she darkened the doorway with her perfect body.

"Yes?" Dr. Scheiwold looked up, peering at them both through wire-rimmed glasses with round frames.

"My apologies, doctor," the receptionist said, "but this man just barged in and—"

"I'm here," Jack intervened, "about Pyotr Legere."

"Doctor, I told him I had no idea who—"

"That's all right, Greta." Scheiwold raised a pink, manicured hand in which he held a slim gold fountain pen. "I'll take care of this." And when she hesitated, hanging indecisively in the doorway, he flicked his fingers at her. "I believe Fraulein Kirsch wants to come in next week."

"Very well, doctor." The scowl on Greta's face did not do her any favors.

When the two men were alone, Scheiwold put down his pen and tented his fingers. "Now who the hell are you?" he said in a tone reinforced with steel.

"My name is Edward Griffiths."

Scheiwold shrugged. "Means nothing to me."

"It doesn't mean anything to anyone," Jack said.

"Ah, you're one of those." Scheiwold nodded. "The moment you mentioned Legere's name I should have known." He extended one hand. "Well, then. You might as well make yourself comfortable, but please close the door first, if you don't mind."

Preferring a private interview, Jack closed the door, then came and sat down on an upholstered armchair facing the ornate polished walnut desk. For a moment, he studied Scheiwold. The doctor's real age could be anywhere from mid-forties to mid-sixties. He had the opulently polished look of all the marble and wood he had selected for his office, as if each morning he was massaged, barbered, bathed, and clothed by professionals. He wore an immaculate three-piece suit obviously made for him, beneath which Jack observed little fat. He had the aquiline nose of a Roman, the eyes of a hawk, and a loose-lipped rather feminine mouth.

"Now tell me, Herr Griffiths, what is your business with Pyotr Legere?"

"He's a patient of yours," Jack said, ignoring the other's question.

Scheiwold winced. "Please. Client."

"You worked on him, very recently."

Scheiwold shrugged again. "Why would I?"

Jack leaned forward. "Because last week in Bangkok Legere was struck on the cheek with the butt end of an M82A3 Special Application scoped rifle. Do you know what that is, doctor?"

Scheiwold picked up a lighter, flicked it open. "Do you mind if I smoke?"

"Shouldn't you know better?"

The plastic surgeon gave a snort as he opened a desk drawer. Jack was out of his chair in an instant. Reaching over, he clamped his hand around Scheiwold's wrist just as the doctor had taken hold of a wicked-looking gravity knife.

"You're not going to smoke that, Herr Doktor," Jack said, pocketing the knife. "And from now on, keep your hands on your desktop where I can see them." When Scheiwold had complied, Jack continued. "The rifle, Herr Doktor. Are you familiar with it?"

Scheiwold looked disgusted. "I go hunting up in the mountains. I have several sporting rifles. I don't know this one."

"It's a United States marine assault rifle. Pyotr Legere, your *client*, is in some very deep *Scheiße*. He's a wanted man. More specifically, he's wanted by me."

Scheiwold spread his hands. "I don't see how I can help you."

In one motion, Jack grabbed the doctor's wrists, pinning them to the desktop.

"Listen to me, Herr Doktor." He pierced Scheiwold with his gaze. "I know what you do and I know who you do it for. I'm not interested in your client list; I'm only interested in finding Pyotr Legere. I know you worked on him, possibly this morning. It would have been a rush job, we both know that."

"Legere . . . Legere . . ." Scheiwold said, as if trying to place the name.

Jack looked around the room. "This office must have cost a small fortune. How much do you take in a year?" Scheiwold made no move to answer, but then Jack hadn't expected him to. "No matter. It must be quite a bundle, what with your legit and not-so-legit *clients*."

He turned Scheiwold's hands so they were faceup on the desk. "You have long, slender fingers, the better to manipulate your instruments." He nodded. "I'm wondering how you'd make a living if you didn't have use of those talented fingers."

Scheiwold made a bleating sound in the back of his throat. He struggled to free his hands, but Jack pressed down even harder.

"What would a plastic surgeon with no fingers do with himself?" Jack stared into Scheiwold's face, which was now sheened with sweat. "Not a pretty future, is it, Herr Doktor?" He nodded. "So, your call: what's it going to be?"

When Annika stepped into the suite's salon, Rolan whirled around so fast, droplets of blood whirled outward in a series of concentric arcs, spattering the walls and a print of ancient Trabzon. Two people who had been husband and wife, who had once loved each other; but that was a long time ago, in a lifetime that seemed, at this moment, to be very far away.

"Rolan," Annika said, her voice pitched deliberately low.

He stalked toward her, shoulders hunched, staring at her from under his lowered brow. "You see how it is. Life has no meaning."

"Rolan, stand down."

"One act is as senseless as the next. I kill that man, I walk toward you, one act follows the other, there is no difference between the two."

She could smell him, his rich animal musk rising above the sickly sweet odor of Fareed's blood. He smelled like nothing she had ever encountered before, and for an instant fear rippled through her because she knew he was capable of anything

"I'm damned if I do, Annika, and damned if I don't. Where is the difference? Except I can't . . . not . . . do . . . it."

"Rolan." She held out an open hand, as if it were a peace offering. "Give me the knife."

He glanced down at it for a moment. "I want to keep it."

She could understand the request; she could accept it. She nodded. "Clean it before you put it away."

He went past her, into the bedroom, crossing to the bathroom. She heard the water running, then the shower. Good. He needed to scrub himself clean of Fareed's blood. Fareed. She looked at what was left of Iraj's trusted driver. Maybe not so trustworthy now. Fareed was grotesque, he no longer looked human, which, she supposed, was the point. At least, that was what Dr. Karalian had told her.

"If Rolan kills," he had told her one baking hot afternoon in the valley, *"he will make certain his victim is no longer human."*

Annika was shocked despite herself. *"How can you know that?"*

"Your husband no longer considers himself human."

Now she was even more shocked. *"But that can't be!"*

"He told me so himself, Ms. Dementieva. Those were his own words." Karalian's face softened with compassion. *"You see, his essential dilemma is that he knows what's happened to him, he's aware of how* changed *he is. That's the true horror of his life now, because he cannot help himself."*

"So he'll kill and keep on killing?"

"I don't know that, though it seems clear that your grandfather does. How he knows this is entirely beyond my ken, but my history with him makes it impossible to gainsay him. When my wife was

pregnant with our first child, he called me to congratulate me on the birth of my son. Not ten minutes after I hung up, my wife went into labor and five hours later gave birth to our son, Nator. Two years later, Illyusha called again, warning me not to get my wife pregnant again. Fool that I was, I didn't listen. Our daughter, Lila, was born with Alexander disease, a neurodegenerative condition that's fatal."

"I'm so sorry."

Karalian had given her a wan smile. *"Thank you, but feeling sorry is the one unalterable condition of my life. That's the main reason Illyusha brought Rolan here to me. He knew I would give him the best care. Also, that I wouldn't condemn him out of hand."*

"He means to use Rolan."

Dr. Karalian had nodded. *"This is my surmise, though he has not confided in me."*

Dyadya Gourdjiev had not confided in her, either. But, looking at what Rolan had done with such ease, she understood that her grandfather meant Rolan to be the hammer of God, the instrument of his revenge. And now that the monster had been unleashed, she was to be his guardian.

"You wanted to see me, sir?" Nona said, sticking her head in the doorway.

"Nona," Commissioner Dye said, "come on in."

When Nona was seated across from him, he said, "How's the Herren case coming? The senator is understandably anxious for a quick resolution."

"Understood," Nona said, "but I've been in the department for more than a decade and I've yet to encounter a triple homicide that leads to a quick resolution."

Dye nodded. "Senator Herren wields a lot of weight in this town of heavyweights."

"Let him solve the murder, then," Nona said dryly.

A twitch at the corner of the commissioner's mouth was all she received in return. "You know, my job is more political than procedural."

"That's why you get the big chair, sir."

Dye grunted. "Herren's put my nuts in a vise. Don't make me regret promoting you."

"Is that a threat?"

Dye leaned forward. "Nona, do you *want* my nuts in a vise?"

She rose. "A quick resolution. Got it, sir."

Just before she reached the door, Dye said, "Nona, I understand you've been nosing around the Paull murder."

She stopped in her tracks, took a breath while she thought, *What the fuck?* then faced him without expression. "I beg your pardon?"

"Don't pull that shit with me."

"Okay, what d'you want?"

"I want to know what you think you're doing?"

"McClure's a friend of mine."

"A fact that will get you in trouble." Dye stood up. "I don't want you in trouble, Nona."

"Am I? In trouble, I mean."

The commissioner came around from behind his desk. "You've got a high-profile triple murder to solve. That's more than enough on your plate."

"My own time, sir."

"Even worse." As he lowered his voice the tone became more intense, every word hammering home. "The tension in this town is palpable. I've received some calls from people I'd rather not hear from, especially when they're voicing complaints."

"This sounds like some terrible cliché."

"This town is one immense cliché, Nona. There is an immutable hierarchy, rules that are set in stone, one of which is Metro doesn't stick its snout in the feds' business. I shouldn't have to remind you of any of this."

"Jack helped me out when no one else would. I owe him."

"Dear God, Nona, I don't doubt your good intentions. But the fact is we're both new to our jobs. The last thing either of us needs is for homeland security and the Company to bust our humps."

"I understand, but—"

"I went out on a limb naming you chief of detectives," Dye pressed on, overriding her. "There were doubts, some objections. People are waiting to use the least excuse to wag their fingers in my face and say, 'I told you so. Fire the bitch.' Whatever you're doing that relates to Paull and McClure, stop, now. Am I making myself clear?"

"Like crystal."

Dye's face darkened. "I don't care for your tone," he said.

"Neither do I." Nona stepped out into the deserted corridor.

Zurich's Old Town, where Jack was headed, straddled the Limmat river, important in the south valleys, where in convenient stages it fell off, for hydroelectric power. Jack was taking no chances on Scheiwold calling Legere after he had left the doctor's office. To that end, he had pulled out the telephone cord and had taken the battery out of his and Greta's mobile phones, after tying them both up.

The taxi crossed over the Schanzengraben canal, which bordered the Old Town and which had been dredged to aid construction of one of the city's three great fortress walls between the seventeenth and eighteenth centuries.

Scheiwold's receptionist had booked Pyotr Legere into the Schloss Schnee. The hotel, used by the surgeon for his patients' post-surgery recovery, was more restful, not to mention discreet, than a hospital. It stood a block from the lake, the glittering opera house, and Bahnhofstrasse, Old Town's main thoroughfare, with its bustling shoppers, old-world trams running on a spiderweb of overhead lines, and, at night, lights twinkling like a constellation of stars.

Schloss Schnee was a modern building sheathed in glass and steel, an all-suite hotel, stocked with every imaginable luxury. Dr. Scheiwold had called the concierge before Jack had left his office, and the dapper young man had anticipated Jack's arrival with a cup of freshly made hot chocolate, topped with whipped cream.

"Herr Legere is in the spa," the concierge said as Jack sipped the rich, dark liquid chocolate. The concierge gestured as a lithe blonde, who might have been Greta's younger sister, appeared. She wore a sea-green sheath dress that hugged the outline of her well-toned body. "Hanna will guide you to the spa." He smiled, gave a little bow, and, Jack could swear, almost clicked his heels. "I wish you success in all your endeavors, Herr Griffiths."

Setting his cup onto the top of the concierge's counter, Jack followed the *Schöne* Hanna to the elevator bank, where they descended two levels, then down softly lit corridors. The odor of rose essential oil could not quite hide the chlorine smell.

They entered the spa through a wide rosewood door. Jack was surprised to find it deserted. When he remarked on the fact, Hanna told him that when Dr. Scheiwold's clients requested spa time, the area became theirs exclusively, in order to maintain their anonymity.

"Most of them choose to come here because they don't want to be seen until the bruising is gone and their cheeks and brows are sheened to perfection," she concluded.

"Is that what happened to you?" Jack asked.

Her laugh was like the tinkling of bells. "My genes are better than that." Her smile was as warm as buttered toast. "You should see my mother."

She led him past a fully equipped gym, beyond which was a steam room, sauna, a rubdown room that smelled powerfully of wintergreen liniment, and a small but cozy lounge, equipped with a half-fridge, healthful snacks, tall glasses, and two plastic pitchers, one filled with ice water, the other with iced tea. Several paces on, he could hear the velvety echo of water lapping against tiles.

"Three pools," Hanna said, "one cold, one warm, one hot."

"Where is Legere?"

"Right in here." She gestured. "Our tanning salon."

Jack almost tripped at the threshold, the toe of his shoe stubbing against the marble sill, his balance tipping so precipitously he surely would have fallen had not Hanna caught him. He was aware of her strength as he righted herself.

She peered at him, frowning. "Are you all right, Herr Griffiths?"

"Perfectly." But when he nodded, the vertigo overcame him again and he was obliged to grab hold of her to keep his balance.

"Herr Griffiths, you look unwell." Hanna led him over to one of the tanning beds. "Why don't you sit down?"

"Legere. Where is he?" Jack was dimly aware that he was slurring his words.

"Right over there, in the tanning bed across from us."

Jack turned his head, or at least tried to. Dimly aware that his body was acting as sluggishly as his mind, he said, "Maybe I should sit down."

"Considering your condition, I have a better idea." Hanna smiled her buttered toast smile as she lifted the lid of the coffin-like tanning bed. "Here we go," she said as she gave Jack's shoulder a push.

It wasn't much of a push, but to him it felt as if an avalanche had landed on him. His body canted over. He tried to right himself on his own, then, as he was going over, reached out for Hanna, but she had moved away and all he grasped was dead air.

He fell into the tanning bed at an angle, and Hanna, lifting his legs by the ankles, put him completely to bed. He stared up at her impossibly beautiful face. He willed himself to get up, but the flat of her hand on his chest settled him in place.

"I wish you success in all your endeavors, Herr Griffiths," she said, echoing the concierge, as she lowered the lid and snapped it into place.

A moment later, humming like a swarm of wasps, the UV lamps came on.

FOURTEEN

"WHAT PRECISELY is going on?" Iraj Namazi said into his sat phone. "Why aren't they convinced McClure is the mole?"

While he listened to the voice on the other end he watched three Egyptian kites wheeling high in the sky. He thought they must have spotted a dead animal—that's what they liked best, dead meat. Just like us humans, he thought.

"Who is this Jonatha Midwood?" he asked, hearing her name for the first time. "We don't want her mucking around in our business."

The kites were lowering, like storm clouds about to release their rain. He sat in his car, fifteen miles from the hotel, ten miles from nowhere. He didn't like Trabzon, a mixture of the touristic and the postmodern ugly. It bore no resemblance to Trebizond, the capital of the ancient Greek Byzantine Empire and, in its day, the most important trading hub linking the Eastern and Western worlds. How the mighty had fallen, he thought, as he watched the kites land and begin to feed on whatever poor animal was lying on the side of the road. Trampled by history, he thought sourly. A state into which he fervently prayed to Allah he would never fall. He longed to return to Fez, which he had made his home for the past year.

"In what ways is she vulnerable?"

"If we attack her," the voice in his ear said, "we'll only attract more unwanted attention. My position isn't under scrutiny—yet. I don't want to do anything to change that."

"Disruption is our business," the Syrian said. "I trained you well. Figure something out. Act in a way that will throw suspicion on one of your colleagues. The more confused these Americans are, the better for us."

"I'll do my best."

"I know you will."

Namazi put the car in gear, drove to where the kites were feeding. Their keen eyes had spotted a polecat that must have been hit by a speeding vehicle. He watched them, greedy birds, feasting on the beast's flesh. Death came to everything, he thought, and everyone.

"About Atlas," he said.

"These things take time."

"Even for you?"

Laughter rang in his ear. "You've been away from the States too long. You've forgotten how paranoid we Americans are."

"This is why I rely on you," Namazi said. "Don't make me use what I have on you."

There was a short silence, during which Namazi, like a preening carnivore, basked in his supremacy.

"The first operational phase of Atlas is about to be deployed," the voice said.

"I need the names of its operatives," Namazi said. "The people who hired me need to disrupt them, feed them disinformation, then pick them off, one by one."

"Disinformation works both sides of the street."

The kites' sharp beaks were bloody, strung with bits of flesh and organs. This was life at its most elemental. There was no hate in the kites' hearts, no envy, no bitterness for injustices done them or their kin. They were driven simply by the need to eat, to live.

"Meaning?"

"I have heard the whisper of a rumor that someone—CIA, DCS, I don't know—is sending out disinformation regarding Atlas."

"An attempt to smoke you out."

"Yes."

Namazi's laugh was as harsh as a jackal's. "What a joke these people are!"

"And yet it would be a mistake to underestimate them. Dennis Paull was definitely onto something, after all."

"And now Dennis Paull is dead," the Syrian snapped. "Leaks are only dangerous until they're stopped up." He made an animal noise in the back of his throat. "Go on then. Get on with it."

Elady Zukhov, standing in the deep mansard shadows thrown by the Paris roofs in twilight, had never married. He had no children of his own. His protégés were his children; he could love them no less than if they were blood of his blood. In his lifetime, he had trained three; Caro was the last and the best.

Zukhov took Caro's concerns very seriously. It was inconceivable that he would stand by while something untoward happened to her. Like a wolf—his hacker handle—he would rip the throat of anyone who threatened her.

There were many ways to trap a stalker, but none more effective than putting yourself between him and his intended victim. This path was not without danger, but Zukhov had been raised on a steady diet of danger from the time he was eleven years old, when he lived in the great shaggy cemetery-city in Prague, where the ghosts of murdered Jews built their golems in the hours between midnight and dawn.

These were the stories the night watchman used to tell him, trying to scare Zukhov away from witnessing the unholy business from which the watchman made his living—grave robbing and drug dealing.

Far from being frightened, Zukhov, an enterprising orphan whose parents and siblings had been killed shortly after arriving from the Russian heartland, wanted to believe in avenging ghosts and their undead instruments of revenge. But since he never encountered avenging spirits—never even caught a glimpse of them—he decided to become one.

Someone needed to protect the dead, so it might as well be him. He figured there must have been a reason that he was left washed up in that cemetery. That was the closest Zukhov ever came to believing in a divine power, and at last, some weeks later, he took up a rusty, dirt-clotted shovel and stove in the side of the night watchman's head. What else but the divine spirit could have lent such power to a child's hand?

Now, watching the night steal over the jewel-like square far below, he recalled those ancient days in Prague with the painful fondness one feels for a lost love.

His head turned. With the darkness came movement, just a blur at the edge of his field of vision, but it was enough. Zukhov had had enough experience with the Syrian to know what—if not who—was coming for Caro. Over the years, as his weight ballooned, he had taught himself to compensate. He moved like a sumo wrestler, like a dancer, his weight centered in his lower belly. Despite his size, he was as deceptively quick as he was agile. When he wished it, his weight seemed to melt away.

This time, however, as he stood on the rooftop of Caro's building, he had no need to move. Raising his right arm, he fired a bolt from a mini-crossbow he had manufactured himself. The release made virtually no noise. The bolt, traveling almost as fast as a small-caliber bullet, buried itself just below the stalker's sternum, thrusting him backward, so that he staggered.

Zukhov, springing forward across the canted tiles, caught him before he could pinwheel over the parapet. For a moment, their eyes were at equal level, before Zukhov dropped him to the rooftop. He slid down a little, curled around Zukhov's feet like a stricken cat.

Lowering himself to his hams, Zukhov slapped the man's cheek, causing his eyes to flutter open. His face revealed his Middle Eastern origins to Zukhov, who could see that he had recently shaved off his beard, no doubt before he had entered France. His expression, though stoic, could not completely hide the terrible pain he was in.

"You had no chance to get to her," Zukhov said softly, as a night bird sang on a nearby chimney pot. "No one the Syrian sends to kill her will."

"He didn't send me to kill her, or even to hurt her," the man said slowly and haltingly. "He wants her to come back."

Zukhov grasped the fletched end of the bolt. "I don't believe you."

The man licked his parched lips. "He needs her; no one else can fathom the algorithm protocols she created and set in place. Without her, his financial empire is in shambles. Soon, if he cannot access his money, he will be in real jeopardy."

"All the more reason for Caroline to stay away."

"He believes she will return. The financial rewards are substantial."

"I can only imagine," Zukhov said dryly. "And if she were to refuse? Then what?"

The man closed his eyes. His blue lips were trembling. "I don't know."

Zukhov moved the bolt as if stirring a pot of stew. "Of course you know."

The man groaned. He seemed to be bleeding from his eyes.

Zukhov searched him for the weapon the Syrian had given him to use on Caro should she refuse his offer. What he found chilled him to the bone: it was a lead vial.

"What is in this?" Zukhov said, though, being Russian, he suspected he already knew.

The assassin shuddered as his breath sawed in and out of him. "I had orders to poison her," he said, "with plutonium."

What would it be like to be broiled alive? Jack, sweltering in the heat emitted by the powerful UV, awoke to the groggy feeling of being a lobster in a pot with its claws bound with stout rubber bands. The difference was, he'd probably go blind before he was fully cooked.

Keeping his eyes squeezed shut, he reached up, fumbled behind his head. Every tanning bed had a kill switch embedded in the lid. He found it, after a short search, but when he depressed the button nothing happened. The lamps were still burning brightly. The kill switch on this bed had been deactivated.

Now he pushed with both palms against the lid, but it was firmly shut. He could not budge it. The adrenaline pumping through his system was working overtime at dissipating the drug he had ingested with the hot chocolate. As a result, it was running its course prematurely. He could feel an unmistakable lethargy beneath his frenzy, and this, more than anything, terrified him. When his overtaxed system stopped producing adrenaline, he was finished.

He tried to move faster, but that only resulted in him becoming even more aware of how debilitated he was. Between the drug, the UV lamps blasting him, and the confined quarters, he felt himself drifting away on a tide of resignation and, worse, surrender. He recalled reading accounts of people on the verge of freezing to death feeling exactly this way just before they were saved. But there was no one to save him here. The invidious hotel staff was arrayed against him.

He felt his lips peeling, then splitting painfully. His ears and forehead were blistering, and he was having trouble breathing. He forced himself to concentrate, but the drug was still working its way through his system and he kept having three- and four-second blackouts, after which he had to spend precious moments gathering thoughts that had exploded away from him, toward the dark margins of his consciousness.

He managed to raise one hand over his head. Turning his head to one side, he curled his fingers into a fist, smashed it into one of the UV tubes. It didn't shatter, as he had expected. He tried again and again, but the glass was thick, coated with a special material that spread the UV rays evenly over the length of the lamp, and on his back he lacked both the leverage and the space to bring all his strength to bear.

Tears of frustration creeping out from between his squeezed-shut lids seemed to sizzle on his cheeks, evaporating almost instantly. The vault of artificial suns continued to beat down on him, determined to be his sole companions into death.

"Is that all?" Dickinson said. "Is that all there is to it?"

"That's all," Jonatha said, as she collated papers on her side of the table at which Henry Dickinson had been sitting, answering her questions for the past twelve minutes. She regarded him from beneath long lashes. "You seem disappointed."

He laughed. "Relieved. Bemused, maybe. But not disappointed."

"Tell me." Jonatha laced her fingers together. "What were you anticipating?"

"I don't know. Something more along the lines of an interrogation. Especially after . . ."

Jonatha's eyes sparkled in the overhead lights, which she had softened to a rosy glow before Dickinson had stepped into the room. The whispered voices coming from the hidden speakers in the floor were all female, like the cooing of doves. "Imagine interrogating the acting director of homeland security!"

He laughed again, this time with a measure of uncertainty. "It's in the realm of possibility. After all, Dennis Paull was killed on my watch and, of course, we're talking about Atlas."

"Yes, Atlas." Jonatha tapped the butt end of her pen against her papers. "Tell me about Atlas."

Dickinson shook his head. "Atlas is strictly need to know."

"Do you think Director Krofft would have assigned me to head up Arclight without briefing me on Atlas?"

"I have no idea," Dickinson said. "But if that's so, then you have no need to ask me about it."

Jonatha smiled, as if to herself. "You're free to leave, Director."

He stood up. "Did I pass?"

She stared up at him impassively.

"Of course." He nodded and turned to go.

"Henry . . ."

He turned back, his hands gripping the back of the chair on which he had been sitting. "Yes?"

"What is it you wish to ask me?"

"What are you, some kind of . . . ?" He waved away his words as if paddling upstream. "I did want to ask you something."

She tilted her head his way, the subtlest of gestures. "Please."

"We got off to a rocky start. My bad. Maybe there's some way . . . I was wondering if you'd have a drink with me sometime."

"How about tonight?"

Dickinson stared at her, his mouth partly open. "I didn't—"

"Well, what would life be without surprises?" She stood. "Shall we say eight, at the St. Giles's Club?"

"I'm not a member," Dickinson said.

"No worries," Jonatha said with a farewell smile. "I am."

Jack woke, passed out, only to rise again into his living nightmare. His situation was now desperate and he concentrated all his energy into a single point, like a dark blade, in an attempt to push the drug through his system, metabolize it faster and faster. This was easier said than done. Certain endorphins, which caused the metabolism to speed up or slow down, had to be activated, either through pain or fooling the autonomous nervous system into believing it was in imminent danger of dying. And yet, Jack possessed the ability to accomplish this difficult task.

Was it his imagination or was his mind clearing? Marshaling his thoughts, he put them into action. The cramped space made maneuvering his arms terribly awkward, but after several false starts, he managed to get one hand back down by his side. Jamming the hand into his pocket, he drew out Scheiwold's gravity knife. Securing it between his teeth, he manipulated one hand to open the blade, which was beautiful, blinding in the UV light, and narrow, which suited his purpose.

Using the same hand, he took the knife out of his mouth and applied the tip of the blade to the locking mechanism, working the tip back and forth, praying that the force required wouldn't snap it off.

Behind his tightly closed lids, brights spots were blooming, blinding flowers, spreading their petals, proliferating at an alarming pace as the UV rays penetrated the thin skin and started to effect his eyes. If he didn't get out of here soon, he'd be permanently blind.

Sweat rolled down the sides of his face from both the heat and the intense concentration required to get the knife tip through the lock. Once or twice, he was sure the tip was going to snap, and even though it cost him in fear, he eased off, allowing the steel to come back to true. Then he began all over again, listening to his heartbeat, the blood rushing in his temples, his shallow breathing, and, beyond all of that, the tiny telltale sounds of metal against metal that told him his progress was slow but steady.

He needed for it not to be slow, he needed to find a way to speed up without endangering the blade. Turning his body just a fraction allowed his other hand to assist, and now with both hands guiding the blade, he felt the lock give, then give again.

A moment later, he pushed the lid up, and still with his eyes squeezed shut, climbed out of his would-be coffin.

When Iraj Namazi returned to the hotel suite, Annika was sprawled on the sofa, smoking a cigarette. She wore a sleeveless top and a lightweight pleated skirt. On the other side of the salon, Fareed sat in a chair, surrounded by a pool of his own blood.

"What the fuck?"

"We should leave, Iraj. Now." Annika let out a stream of smoke. "And you'll have to grease a few palms before we do."

After giving his dead driver a cursory examination, he strode over to her. His face was dark, filled with blood and rage. "What the fuck happened here?"

"I warned you about releasing Rolan, didn't I?"

"Your husband did that?"

"He's very good at killing, Iraj. An expert." She gestured with her cigarette. "As you see."

"And where is he now?"

"Gone. Do you think I was going to question him, the state he was in?"

He slapped the cigarette out of her hand. It rolled, burning, across the marble floor until it came to rest at the pool of blood, where the glowing end died, hissing like a cornered animal.

"Get up! Are the bags packed?"

"I wasn't idle while you were gone." She rose off the sofa. "Where did you go, by the way?"

He went into the bedroom, careful to sidestep the bloody wreck of Fareed. In a moment, he reappeared with their suitcases, handed over hers.

"Don't glare at me like that," Annika said, following him out of the suite. "You only have yourself to blame for Fareed's death. Besides," she added, "Rolan was just protecting me."

The Syrian stopped in his tracks, then turned to face her. "What did you say?"

Annika, who had deliberately waited until the last minute to drop her bomb, said, "You heard me. Fareed had me pinned against the wall to the bedroom you had him lock Rolan into. Rolan heard my voice and he—"

"The door lock wasn't broken, Annika. Someone unlocked it from the salon side. I know it wasn't Fareed. He had strict instructions—"

"Did you give him instructions to molest me?" She put a lot of venom into her voice.

"Don't be absurd."

"Why else would he assault me?" Annika had calculated this counterattack while smoking her cigarette, waiting for Iraj to return. "I got the key off him while he was fumbling under my clothes. I pushed him away and unlocked the door. Rolan was already on the other side. He rushed out and, well, you saw for yourself what happened."

"All I see is a dead man, Annika. The rest is coming out of your mouth, and as I know better than most, you're an accomplished liar."

"What can you do, Iraj? We both like lying better than telling the truth. We do what we do until a situation like this comes along and then we're suddenly in no-man's-land."

He appeared to hesitate. "I don't know what to believe, but now's not the time to sort it out. One thing you are right about: we need to get out of here."

They stepped into the elevator together. While she pressed the button for the lobby level, Namazi dug in his pocket. "Luckily, I have more than enough money to cover the baksheesh. Death happens here all the time. Given the right payouts, another one will mean nothing."

Annika stepped past him and pressed the emergency stop button.

"What are you doing?" Namazi said as the elevator lurched to a halt.

He watched as Annika knelt beside her suitcase, snapped open the metal tabs. Inside, on top of her other clothes, was the skirt she had been wearing earlier, wrapped in a clear plastic dry cleaning bag. She took it out and, standing up, turned the skirt inside out. The silk lining contained a large, thick stain.

"Here," she said, holding it out to him, "smell it."

"The fuck?" Namazi took an involuntary step back.

"You know what this is, Iraj. It's Fareed's—"

"Shut up," he said.

"Look at it, Iraj. *Look*." She waved the skirt like a matador waves his cape in the *corrida*. "This is Fareed's semen, so you know what he did to me, so you know what he did to me was real."

Namazi turned his head. "Put that away."

She did, snapping the suitcase shut.

His head swung back now that the offending garment was out of sight. "Burn it when we get home."

As she leaned past him to set the elevator in motion again, she was acutely aware that he was looking at her in an entirely different light.

When Redbird was a young boy, long before he had taken on his code name, he had had a younger sister, Angel. As he traveled from Bangkok to Zurich, he entered a part of reality he refused to acknowledge in his waking life. He dreamed of his brief time with Angel, when he'd made her laugh by pushing her high in the swing in their backyard, how he'd make her shriek by pulling grotesque faces on her, how he fed her when his parents were out, put her to bed, read her the stories she liked best, and when those stories were at an end fabricate more stories with her favorite characters. She liked best tales of little girls who found their way into the land of the fairies and had adventures there. She was still too young to understand, but like Redbird she yearned to be far away from her own home, which was sad and desolate even when their parents were present. Some people should never have children. Their parents were such people.

When she was a little older and could read her children's books on her own, Redbird began to read to her from his favorite book, *Kitāb alf laylah wa-laylah, One Thousand and One Nights*. He was already fascinated by Arabia, and, much to his delight, Angel was, too, from the moment he began to read her the first exotic tale.

Redbird woke once to use the toilet. The terrible thing had not yet happened; returning to his seat, he closed his eyes, praying that it would not happen. But, of course, it did, as it always did when he dreamed of Angel.

He saw her on that late summer day, the lawn sprinklers spraying rainbows and kids on tricycles clattering along the baking sidewalk. She wore a red dress with ruffles here and there like undersea coral, but her face was white even in the speckled sunlight beneath the elms. Red and white, blood and bone, like a frame from a film he was watching in the safety of a dark air-conditioned theater, smelling of popcorn, the concrete floor sticky with spilled Coke.

But this was no film, there was no safety here. There was a peculiar odor about her, like an aura. Years later, the same odor came to him again at his job, and he knew it for the smell of death.

He was in her hospital room, looking down at her, holding her pale hand. She was white as the ghosts in *Kitāb alf laylah wa-laylah*, but far more frightening. The leukemia wasting her body had seemingly drained her of blood. He had asked the doctors and nurses, anyone who would listen to him, whether he could give her his blood. They all shook their heads, looked at him with a pity that further enraged him. He wished he could transform her into an Arabian wraith, put her into a brass lamp, to keep her safe. But all he could do was hold her hand and watch her slowly fade away. When death finally took her from him he had already retreated behind a rock-hard wall that, years later, served as midwife to the birth of Redbird.

He awoke just as the plane landed in Zurich. Looking out at the quintessentially Western buildings he felt, as ever, like an outsider, a nomad who belonged in the desert, a brass lamp hooked to his belt, waiting for a return that would never come.

Somewhere, deep inside him, on the other side of the stone wall inside his mind, he was aware that he had not been able to curtail his attachment to Dandy, that when he looked at her, when he spoke with her, he was with Angel. With Dandy's death, his sister died a second time. This was something he could not tolerate.

On the way into the city, which was as alien, as malignant to him as a planet without atmosphere, his rage reached fever pitch, boiling like a storm-driven sea against a rocky shore. All thought of money, of loyalty to Dickinson, of following orders, of having a job to do vanished in that dangerous tide.

For the first time since she had died, he wanted to remember Angel, he wanted to remember how helpless he was to save her, he wanted to remember the outrage he had felt at everyone and everything in the world for taking her from him. These memories and the emotions behind them at last burst through the stone wall, obliterating it. They became fuel for the assassin that entered the heart of Zurich, who now had a single focus for the decades-long outrage filling the imaginary brass lamp clipped to his belt like a holstered gun.

"I'm sorry to say I won't be participating in this charade," William Rogers said.

Jonatha stared at the national security advisor from across the table in her specially prepared room. He seemed different to her, sterner, more businesslike, though the difference was not readily apparent. The lights in the room were a subtle blue, the scent like that of burning paper. The sounds of faraway traffic, of, now and again, sirens drifted out of the hidden speakers.

"Why do you consider this interview a charade?"

"Call it whatever you like," Rogers said. "I won't be a part of it."

"I don't believe that's possible, Bill. You already are a part of it."

"Only my friends call me Bill, Ms. Midwood."

"As you wish."

He slid a burnished calfskin briefcase onto the table and pulled out a slender folio, opened it up in front of him. "Your lover's name is Lale, isn't that right?"

Jonatha turned gimlet-eyed. "My partner."

Rogers appeared to ignore her. "Lale Serezo."

"We're not actually going down that road, are we, Bill?"

"A Moroccan Jew, isn't she?"

"An even worse path."

He looked up sharply. "I told you—"

"I don't give a fuck what you told me," she said softly, pronouncing each word precisely and violently.

Rogers nodded. "Now that the gloves have come off, I have no qualms about showing you this." He spun the top sheet from the folio over to her.

Jonatha's gaze dropped to the police report.

"We're going to go down a path not quite of your imagining." Leaning over the table, he tapped the sheet. "Did you know about this?"

Jonatha said nothing; she had no intention of admitting to Rogers that Lale had never told her that she had committed grand larceny—that she had stolen a car, taking it on a three-state joyride before abandoning it in western Pennsylvania.

"She stated she went to see Frank Lloyd Wright's Fallingwater," Jonatha read from the arrest report. "She was sixteen."

"Under the legal age to drive without an adult, besides all the other offenses she committed."

"She was a minor."

"And now a convicted felon," Rogers said. He took back possession of the police report. "How do you think this would play with Director Krofft?"

Jonatha stared at him, saying nothing.

Rogers smirked. "So let's stop playing games, *Jonatha*. This isn't about your sexual orientation, it isn't about your lover being a Jew, it's about you cohabiting with a criminal."

Jonatha spent the next small silence setting aside the fact that Rogers had sandbagged her, instead calming herself and, like a professional pool player, calculating the array of bank shots open to her.

"So we have reached the end of this particular path, a short though painful one." Rogers placed his hands atop the folio. "You write up your report on me as if I took all your psych evals, and I bury this police report so deep no one will ever find it." His pearly teeth appeared between his pulled back lips. "Does this agreement meet with your approval?"

Half-numb, she nodded.

"Excellent." Rogers checked his watch, stowed the folio in his briefcase, and stood up. "It's almost time for my four o'clock." He gave her an ironic mock-bow. "So I bid you adieu."

At the door, he turned back. "Oh, and Midwood, don't fucking contact me again."

Deep underground, Jack stumbled to the doorway of the tanning salon, holding on to the frame, his head hanging down, chin against his chest. When he cracked open his swollen lids, everything looked hazed, and for a moment he panicked that the UV lamps had done him some permanent damage. Then he realized his slitted eyes were overflowing with tears.

He started to blink rapidly, wanting to clear his vision, then realized the longer he kept his eyes bathed in tears, the more quickly he'd be able to shake off the effects of the UV lamps. He didn't know who he wanted to find first, Legere or Hanna. Remembering that Hanna had said Legere was in the tanning bed opposite him, he went back into the salon and lifted the bed's lid. Not surprisingly, it was empty, as was every other one in the salon. For a moment, he had to hang on to the lid as a powerful wave of vertigo swept through him. Taking deep breaths, he began to stalk forward again, slowly at first.

Out in the corridor and moving like a man half blind, using one outstretched hand on the wall to guide him, he found the lounge he had passed coming in, drank deeply from the pitcher of ice water, then dumped the remaining contents over himself. Kneeling, he gathered two handfuls of ice cubes off the floor and lowered his face into them.

He sat for another moment, his back against the mini-fridge, gratefully feeling the coldness stealing through his clothes and into his flesh. Then he rose and, checking to make sure the spa corridor was still clear, began to make his way back to the elevator bank. His senses were on high alert—surely someone, the concierge or Hanna—would be returning shortly to check on him. He needed to be out of the hotel before then. With the hotel now a red zone, he was ill-equipped to locate Legere. His best course was to withdraw to a safe place where he could keep the hotel under surveillance in hopes of catching up to Legere as he exited.

The elevator was in sight when the vertigo hit him again. His legs gave way and he half fell, sliding down the wall in a heap. He sat like that for a time, his head lolling, consciousness spinning.

At some point he became aware of someone bending over him. He smelled perfume, a female presence. Instinctively, he flicked open the gravity knife, sure it was Hanna, but when he opened his eyes he saw it was Dr. Scheiwold's patient, Fraulein Kirsch, her whippet's body curved as a comma. She reached for him and he flinched away.

"Don't," he heard her say. "It's all right."

Nothing was all right, he thought, as he felt her hands under his arms. He was certain she couldn't pull him to his feet without his own help, but she was far stronger than he had imagined.

He leaned against the wall, breathing hard. He felt as if a pair of fire-breathing dragons had taken up residence in his lungs. Her outlines moved in and out of focus. Even squinting, he couldn't be sure, but she seemed to be beckoning to him. He watched her with suspicion, but this only seemed to make her impatient.

"Hurry!" she said in a low, urgent voice. "This way, Herr Mc-Clure."

FIFTEEN

The St. Giles's Club occupied a stupendous limestone structure of palatial cake-box beaux arts style on the posh northern curve of Dupont Circle. It was originally the home of Stanley James Fortune, a tycoon in the truest sense of the word, who began in railroads, then segued into minerals, most notably diamond mines in the Belgian Congo. Fortune died prematurely of dementia praecox, after which his home was handed down to his son. Subsequently, his great-grandsons commenced a thirty-year war with one another, which led to the building being sold to the St. Giles's Club of Kensington, London. Its directors had been looking for a suitable venue for their foray into the colonies, as they only half-jokingly referred to America. The price had been high, but the directors had made up their minds, and for them money was no object. The deal was quickly consummated, after which they began a tedious three years of renovations, following which they deemed their colonies' outpost ready to open its doors.

Of course it was expensive to be a member, but in accordance with their credo, the directors' eighteenth-century criteria had more to do with your station in life than how much money you were worth. As an adjunct, it was also whom you knew, for you had to be nominated in order to be considered for membership.

For Jonatha, whose net worth would impress no one, membership in St. Giles's was nevertheless a snap. She knew Sir Edward Enfield-Somerset, a London director, who had been anointed director of the St. Giles's Club in the States. Sir Edward was a big bear of a man, six-foot-six, with the rough, reddened skin of the inveterate outdoorsman and drinker of fine single malts and other powerful spirits.

Jonatha had met him through a mutual friend. To say that Sir Edward was taken with her would be to do his emotions a grave disservice. He was bedazzled by her—not only by her physical appearance but by her intellect, which he took advantage of every chance he got. In return, he named her a member of the St. Giles's Club in perpetuity. In short, she had the run of the place. The one time she had paid for dinner, he had been so upset she never did it again, though having someone else pay her freight was against her principles.

"You're the daughter I never had," he had told her. *"You must consider St. Giles's your home."*

She appeared at the club precisely at eight and found Henry Dickinson waiting for her in the marble, gilt, and crystal entryway. Dickinson had obviously gone home and changed his clothes. He wore a dark suit, rather than the bland gray one from earlier in the day. This one fit him better, and his shirt and tie were first-rate and freshly pressed.

His face split in a wide smile as the doorman ushered her inside. The evening had brought a slight mist, and her hair seemed to be sheathed in tiny diamonds glittering in the light splashing down from the immense Victorian chandelier Sir Edward had imported from a London antiques dealer.

After the manager greeted Jonatha by name, he escorted her and her guest to a private nook of the library, where a liveried waiter, as ancient as the chandelier, took their drinks order while leaving them with a pair of oversized menus, hand-written in flowing purple script.

"We order here while enjoying our drinks," Jonatha explained. "Philippe, our waiter, will come for us when our first course is ready in the dining room."

"Thank you for inviting me here," Dickinson said, craning his neck.

Like all the club's spaces, the octagonal library was a dazzler. The walnut panels were over a hundred years old, as were many of the first-edition books that lined the floor-to-ceiling shelves. Every major philosopher and scientist and a majority of the minor ones were represented. Several antique library ladders that could be rolled on brass rails were in evidence beyond the groupings of high-backed wing chairs, standing lamps, and small round tables.

Jonatha clandestinely studied Dickinson as he sipped his bourbon while perusing the menu.

Philippe appeared—slender, elegant, a gorgeous Burmese man in his late twenties, with long, agile fingers, perfect skin, and dusky, heavy-lidded eyes. Dickinson looked up and ordered the Caesar and a club steak. Jonatha chose fois gras and the bone-in rib eye with bone marrow.

"Very good," Philippe said, gathered their menus, and departed.

"You must know," Dickinson said, after a time seeming to listen to the muted buzz of conversations around them, "Dennis Paull's death wasn't due to negligence."

Jonatha, instantly interested, said, "I don't remember anyone saying it was."

"Kinkaid Marshall said as much," Dickinson acknowledged, "in our first briefing."

"Marshall's the head of DCS," Jonatha said. "He's like a Marine DI." She scanned the room, as she always did periodically. "According to him, everything is negligence."

Dickinson grunted. "I'm under no illusions. Your boss agrees with him."

Jonatha looked up. "And what's your opinion?"

"Mine?"

"Yours is as valid as anyone else's—probably more. You knew Director Paull and Jack McClure better than any of us."

"Dennis was a friend."

"And McClure?"

"I don't know." He sipped his drink, then shook his head. "A closed book, maybe. I'm not sure even Dennis knew him well enough."

"Then why did he trust him?" Jonatha said.

"The billion-dollar question," Dickinson admitted. "But to answer your question, I followed protocol all the way down the line. Paull had our two best men protecting him that night. The meeting with McClure was completely unscheduled—it wasn't on any time sheet."

"Someone wanted it that way. Paull or McClure?"

"Only McClure had enough juice with Dennis to request an off-sheet meeting."

"Everything was meticulously planned."

"That's McClure to a T."

"Do you know where McClure is hiding out?"

"He was seen passing through immigration in Bangkok on his way to Zurich." Dickinson allowed a small smile to curl his lips. "I've got my best field operative on his tail. He'll soon run him to ground. Bringing McClure back here for interrogation will vindicate me, even with Marshall and Krofft."

At that point, Philippe reappeared at Jonatha's elbow, bent down, and whispered in her ear. Her eyes opened wide, then she nodded, "We're ready anytime."

"What is it?" Dickinson said when Philippe had departed the library.

Jonatha drained her glass. "It seems the POTUS is dining here tonight. Philippe will show us in to dinner as soon as the Secret Service finishes its usual security protocol."

"More power flexing." Dickinson leaned forward, elbows on knees. "Can I tell you a secret?"

Jonatha laughed softly. "My life is constructed of secrets, what's one more?"

"I don't much like power flexing."

"Neither do I."

For a long moment, Jonatha looked at him, wondering what they were really talking about.

"How do you know my name, Fraulein Kirsch?"

"Kirsch," the whippet-woman said. "I despise that name. Don't you despise that name?"

"Fraulein Cherry."

"You can imagine the jokes at my expense." Her lips twitched in an ironic smile. "Call me Romy. Please."

"All right. How do you know my name, Romy?"

They were in her suite at the hotel, which, she had told him as she had taken him upstairs via the service elevator, was the safest place for him.

"The moment Hanna discovers you're gone, they'll be looking for you all over Zurich."

"Okay, let's start with who 'they' are," Jack said.

He sat on a chair in the kitchenette while Romy mixed up a poultice of baking soda, water, and one of the wound-healing creams Dr. Scheiwold had prescribed for her after-surgery regimen. She had made him take off his shirt, and now she bustled around him applying the cooling poultice on his face, ears, neck and hands.

"They," she said, as she worked, "are Legere's people. Zurich, along with Paris, is Legere's home territory."

"I thought he was based in Moscow."

"Oh, you mean Pyotr," she said. "I was speaking of his father, Giles Legere."

"Wait a minute," Jack said, turning to get a good look at her expression. "I thought Pyotr's father was dead."

"So do a lot of other people." Romy continued slathering on the paste. "That's the way the Legeres—*Vater und Sohn*—want it. Giles has moved into the background, but Pyotr does what the old man tells him to do." She went to the refrigerator, poured a tall glass of water. "Not that the son likes that arrangement. There's a certain strain between them that we have been working to increase."

"We?"

"Yes." She smiled at him as she handed him the water. "We who work for Dyadya Gourdjiev."

"Gourdjiev is dead."

"Regrettably. But everything that surrounded him, everything he built is still very much alive."

Though in his heart he knew the answer, Jack couldn't help asking the question: "Who is running the show now? Who is Gourdjiev's designated successor?"

"I think you know, Herr McClure," Romy said. "His granddaughter, Annika Dementieva."

"Look who's at the POTUS's table," Dickinson said as Philippe escorted them into the dining room. The president's Secret Service contingent was deployed at strategic points around the glittering room, and all the surrounding tables had been cordoned off, isolating the president's party, which included Senator Herren, Director Krofft, and Alix Ross, the president's press secretary.

"I have no doubt Herren and Krofft are pitching a way to spin the triple murder away from the senator and his dead aide," Jonatha said as they sat down at a table set with sparkling crystal, silver service atop snow-white linen.

Dickinson shook his head. "Your boss has a way of insinuating himself into every nook and cranny."

Jonatha laughed softly. "He was born for his position; it's all he knows."

"That sounds sad."

"Yes," Jonatha said, as Philippe set their first course in front of them, "doesn't it?"

"But then the world we live in is sad."

"Is it?"

"How could it not be, surrounded as we are by suspicion, betrayal, and death?"

Jonatha forked a cube of fois gras into her mouth. She thought of Lale's past. Her eliding over it was a betrayal, a secret she had kept hidden. A dark, angry part of her didn't want to see Lale now, let alone confront her.

"I can hear you thinking," Dickinson said.

"I was wondering whether you're right, whether we need to be suspicious of even the people closest to us."

"It's been my experience that we do."

She did not need to be clairvoyant to pick up on the rueful tone of his voice. "What happened to you, Henry?"

He gave her a lopsided smile. "So we're done with 'Dicky'?"

"I'll leave that to Krofft and Marshall." She bit into his fois gras with her even white teeth. "As for myself, I never much cared for it."

Something seemed to clear across his face. "My wife left me three years ago."

"I'm aware of that."

"It was with my best friend."

"And now you don't trust anyone."

"I can't afford to."

She nodded. At that moment, she saw Alix Ross leave the president's table. She found her eyes following Alix all the way into the corridor that led to the toilets. Without allowing herself another thought, she excused herself.

As she passed the president's table, she saw Krofft and Senator Herren pleading their case. The president looked tired, like a fox who'd been harried all day by a pack of hounds. In the corridor, she pushed open the door to the women's toilet. She was as familiar with this room as she was with every other in the building. There was a line of three stalls to the left, to the right, two sinks over which hung a long mirror with the superior lighting women required to reapply their makeup.

She stood by one sink, alternately staring at herself and the single closed stall. She was reapplying her lipstick when the toilet flushed and Alix emerged. She was wearing a plum-and-cream striped dress. She was tall and athletically slender. Jonatha knew she jogged four times a week in Rock Creek Park before she arrived at the West Wing; she had passed her several times on the same winding path during her own runs. Jonatha had long admired her square shoulders and long neck. In the artificial light, her hazel eyes looked more tan than green.

"Hey," Alix said. She wore her thick, dark hair at shoulder length in a sexy retro-sixties style.

"Looks like Herren has roped in my boss to hammer at you and the POTUS."

"Hammer and tongs," Alix said as she stepped up to the sink next to Jonatha and began to wash her hands. "Why on earth do you work for the man? He's relentless."

Jonatha smiled at Alix in the mirror. "That's precisely why I work for him."

Alix shook her head. "I don't get it."

"There are very few men in this town who really understand me. Robby is one of them."

"Oh, Robby, is it?" Alix said with a mock-smirk.

"Not what you think."

"No? Your Robby has a certain behind-closed-doors rep with the women." Alix's gaze moved up and down Jonatha's body. "I seriously doubt he could resist you."

"I have no trouble resisting him."

Leaning over the sink, Jonatha deposited an open-mouthed kiss on the mirror. When she moved away, the imprint remained, an erotic emblem branding the glass. Alix looked from the lipstick to

Jonatha's face. Her lips were wet, slightly parted. Her eyes seemed to burn into Jonatha's flesh.

Reaching out, Jonatha took her by the hand and led her into one of the stalls, shutting and locking the door behind them.

"Really?" Alix said. "We're going to do this? Here? Now?"

"Men always wonder," Jonatha said, "what we do in the bathroom that takes us so long."

Feeling the blood rising up into her face, she pressed her lips against Alix's, felt her lips soften, then open. When their tongues met, it was like an electric shock passed between them. Jonatha felt Alix's hips lurch toward her. Her hands came up, cupping Alix's small, hard breasts, and she could feel her nipples rising to meet them. A small moan escaped Alix's throat, passing into Jonatha's mouth as a vibration.

One of Jonatha's hands stroked downward, lifting the hem of Alix's dress, searching out what was underneath. Alix's hips bucked again, pressing the hot core of herself into Jonatha's palm. Jonatha's middle finger curled in. Alix was already wet with desire.

Jonatha's heart beat fast as she slipped to her knees, burying her face in Alix's surprisingly chaste underpants. The Catholic schoolgirl undergarment only inflamed her further, and she hooked her fingers over the waistband, feeling Alix's soft flesh give. But before she could push them down, she heard Alix sigh, "No, leave them on. I want to feel your tongue through the cotton."

Jonatha thought she would lose her mind. Alix's scent made her dizzy. Alix was leaning back against the wall, her legs spread on either side of the toilet. They were both breathing hard. Jonatha reached up and grabbed one breast, rolling the erect nipple back and forth with her palm. Alix let out a little squeal.

They both heard the *clip-clop* of high heels on the tiles and they froze. Both had been too lost in their sex haze to hear the door open. The water ran briefly on the other side of the room, but no one stepped into the stalls on either side of them.

Jonatha started her tongue moving again.

"No," Alix whispered. "Wait."

Jonatha kept at it, and Alix threw her head back, closed her eyes. Her fingers twined in Jonatha's hair, pulling her head hard against her groin. Jonatha was dimly aware of the door sighing closed.

Then Alix cried out, a sound cut off by her hand in her mouth. She lost control of her hips and her thighs began to shake as she slid down until Jonatha caught her. Her forehead pressed against Jonatha's hard, flat belly as she gasped in breaths, shuddering still.

Jonatha held her, gently, tenderly, but when Alix's fingers began to seek her out, she put a hand over hers, caught it, held it still.

"No," she said quietly. "No."

Alix looked up at her. "But I want to."

Jonatha took Alix's head in her hands. "And I want you to."

Alix stared into her eyes. "You have someone at home."

Jonatha's mouth twitched, her heart lurched painfully.

"And I can't tempt you the way you tempted me?"

Leaning forward, Jonatha kissed her on the forehead, but it was a chaste kiss.

"We're all tempted by something, Jonatha." Alix reached up, traced a sinuous path down Jonatha's neck with the pad of her forefinger. "I know what you did to me was real, I know you felt something, you can't lie about that."

"I never said—"

"Then let me," Alix put a hand on Jonatha's lower belly, slowly moving it in an ever-widening circle. "Why should I have all the fun?"

Jonatha felt a return of the furnace between her legs. "We all lie about something."

"We have to." Alix continued her caress with admirable concentration. "We're dirty creatures, at heart. We all have things to hide, things we're afraid to show to anyone else. Lies protect us; they're necessary."

A muscle in Jonatha's inner thigh began to jump and flex, and

Alix ran her fingertips over it. "Oh, I know that response," she whispered. "I know it well." Her fingertips continued their journey. She gave a tiny squeal. "You're wearing a thong. To work. I love that."

Her fingertips were making circles again, small this time, and light as a breath of air. Then she rose, extended one leg, inserting the long powerful muscle of her thigh between Jonatha's. Pressing in, she started a slow rocking motion, applying pressure to Jonatha's mound.

Jonatha emitted a little gasp, and her arms flew around Alix, the nails clawing at her back.

"Lies," Jonatha breathed into Alix's ear. "We'll have to lie about this."

"We lie for a living, we lie about everything, even our identities," Alix said. "What's one more lie to blur the lines between true and false?"

Jonatha, panting like an engine, rested her head on Alix's shoulder. "We live in a world where all the lines are blurred."

Alix, intoxicated by Jonatha's intimate scent, rubbed her sex against Jonatha's hip bone. "But what happens when the lines disappear?"

"How did you know I'd be here at the hotel?" Jack asked.

"Why don't you lie back and rest?" Romy gave him a concerned look.

"I need to find Pyotr Legere. Do you know where he is?"

"Right here two floors down." Romy put her hand against his chest as he began to rise. "Not now. You don't have the strength yet, and he's not going anywhere."

"How can you be sure?"

Romy's lips twitched in the semblance of a smile. "He won't leave without me."

Jack stared up at her. "And why would that be?"

She shrugged. "He sees something in me other people don't." Then she burst into laughter. "Or maybe he likes what I do to him in bed, or the shower or the living room floor or the park or—"

"I get the picture," Jack said.

"Not really, you don't." Romy put her hands in her lap. "But that's as it should be."

"You're just doing your job, is that it?"

She watched, possibly to see if he was serious.

"I don't judge anyone," he said, "not in this line of work, anyway. You didn't answer my question."

"My dear Herr McClure, your whereabouts have been monitored from the moment you called Ben King."

"Dennis's pilot."

She nodded.

"You've been monitoring me?"

"Just since you arrived here in Zurich."

"And before that?"

Romy turned away and was pouring him another glass of water when he took hold of her wrist, turning her back to him.

"What are you keeping from me?"

She put the water down, sat on a chair across from him, her back curved, elbows on her knees. "Is this necessary? Isn't it enough—?"

"No," Jack said, "it isn't." His eyes searched her face. "If you were me wouldn't you want to know?"

"Please let me go," she said softly, but she would not meet his eye.

"Why don't you want me to know who's been tracking me?"

Her hands were busy doing nothing. "Did you mean what you said before, about not judging anyone in this line of work?"

"I did."

She took a deep breath, let it out slowly. "Annika has been monitoring you."

Jack felt as if an icy sword had passed through him, and his mind leaped ahead. "Did she have Dennis killed?"

"No," Romy said. "God, no."

"Then who did?" He gripped her harder, making her shudder. "Do you know? Does Annika?"

"I don't. And as for Annika, if she did know, the murderer would be dead by now."

Back to square one, Jack thought. But then again maybe not. The whole picture was starting to form in his mind, and at the center of it, like a spider in its web, the identity of Paull's killer becoming ever clearer.

"Tell me about Pyotr Legere."

Romy glanced down at where his fingers encircled her slender wrist. At once, he let her go, feeling ashamed when he saw how her skin had been marked.

"I'm not that sort of man."

Romy's smile was as pale as her skin. "But Pyotr is. I'm not too much of a lady to call him a sick fuck." Her eyes slid away again. "The things I do for Dyadya."

"Dyadya is dead," Jack reminded her again.

She shook her head. "He lives on in Annika."

"Still," he said, "nothing is stopping you from walking away, starting your life over."

She sat back now, seemingly more comfortable with him. "I could say, 'and do what; this is all I know,' and that would be correct, but it wouldn't be entirely correct. I owe my life to Dyadya. There is nothing I wouldn't do for him, even after he's gone—especially now."

Jack sat up, the initial dizziness vanishing quickly now. "What d'you mean?"

Romy frowned. "Are you Annika's friend or enemy?"

Jack thought for a moment, wondering what to say. "I'm both," he said truthfully. "I suppose she'd say the same."

"That's not possible."

"You would think it's not possible," he said. "My experience with her and with Dyadya says otherwise."

"He loved you like a son." She smiled sadly. "I see how shocked you are that I would know such a thing."

"I'm more shocked that he genuinely felt that way."

Her smile broadened. "Yes, for some people it was impossible to believe that Dyadya was genuine about anything. For others, just the opposite. This was the kind of man he was—one of the astonishing consequences of knowing him. He was a chameleon—it was his nature. But you have to know that he gave himself to very few people—he trusted even fewer. You were one of the ones that had both from him."

"Why?" Jack said. "Why should he trust me?"

"Dyadya was a shrewd judge of character. I believe he understood you better than you understand yourself; he certainly did me."

"He misjudged his granddaughter's feelings about me."

She cocked her head. "How can you be sure?"

"How often can you be betrayed by one person?"

"By someone you love."

Jack said nothing. Slipping off the chair, he padded into the small kitchen, found bread, cheese, and fruit in the half-fridge, and began to eat standing up.

"You can't walk away from this," Romy said. "From her."

"I have."

"There's no point in fooling yourself." She rose, came up beside him, but seemed indifferent to the food. "I'm proof of that."

"Everyone's different," Jack said around a bite of cheese.

"And yet we're all human." Romy took up a paring knife and cut an apple into segments for him. "We're all subject to the same laws of desire and destiny."

"You really believe that?"

She rinsed the knife blade, wiped it, and set it aside. "You would do well to believe it."

"And what are your feelings toward Pyotr Legere?"

Romy laughed. "Other than disgust, I have none."

"You let him handle you."

"My mind is far away, in a place he can never reach."

"And your body?"

"My body recovers, as from a strenuous workout." She raised one leg and kept on raising it until her ankle rested on his shoulder. "It's flexible that way."

Jack swung her leg, the odd, unspoken invitation, away from him. Finished with the bread and cheese, he packed them away. He took up a slice of apple, crunching into it. "About Pyotr," he said. "I'll need an edge when I confront him."

"There are three things you need to know about him," Romy said. "First, he's exceedingly clever. Second, he's exceedingly cruel. His cruelty has trapped him, as it always will. Evil is inherently stupid, Herr McClure. Its refusal to change is part of its nature."

"And the third thing?"

"Ah, well, the most important of the three. He's quintessentially Russian, despite his family name."

"Meaning?"

She turned to him. "He's not afraid to die."

SIXTEEN

When Jonatha passed through the pair of Secret Service suits and strode over to the car idling in Dennis Paull's driveway, the blacked-out rear window slid down and she saw DCS Director Kinkaid Marshall's lined, sour face.

"Have you been waiting long?" she said.

"Too long," Marshall barked.

"I'm terribly sorry, but dinner went on and on." She stepped back as the door opened and Marshall got out.

"I can't fathom why you wanted to meet here, of all places," he rumbled. "And at this hour."

Jonatha went by him, picking her way across the gravel to the front door. Krofft had given her the key. Now she turned it in the lock and they both went inside. She led him through, turning on lights as she went. The place smelled of books and hunched men in overcoats, the agents who had been pouring through the house like locusts.

In the study, she threw open several windows, letting the night in.

"Paull was shot to death near this time," Marshall said, glancing around with obvious distaste. He was the kind of military man who looked uncomfortable out of uniform, the kind of military man who wore his career on his sleeve, who knew his best days were behind him, that no matter how high he had risen, his current position was the penultimate step to being let out to pasture, like an old stud who could no longer fulfill his duty.

"To answer your question," Jonatha said, settling herself in Paull's chair behind his desk, "I thought, since this interview is largely window dressing, it would be more comfortable for both of us outside the office." She gestured for him to sit.

"What shall we talk about?" Marshall said, glancing at his watch. He remained standing.

"What would you like to talk about?"

He gave her a sharp look. "Frankly, I'd like to get home."

"Why?" she inquired.

"Sleep."

"I heard you don't sleep."

"Would you care to come home with me and find out?"

"How would your wife feel about that?"

He opened his mouth to answer, then closed it, his lips almost disappearing as he pressed them together.

She stood up. "Maybe I *will* come home with you."

Marshall's eyes slid away from her. "I wasn't serious."

"I am." She came around from behind Paull's desk. "Shall we go?"

He stood stock-still. "Is there something you're trying to prove? Some female thing?"

"That's the typical male response, isn't it, to try and defuse difficult questions by framing them in terms of gender."

"What do you want me to say?"

"How long have you and your wife been sleeping in separate bedrooms?"

"None of your business."

"That's not entirely true."

He pulled a face. "I snore."

"Mmmm."

"If you're on a fishing expedition, Midwood, you're bound to be disappointed."

"I'm not looking for mistresses in your closet."

"Then what are you looking for?"

Turning, she opened a file, slipped out a sheet of paper, part of the intel Ripley had sent her, and handed it over.

"What the hell's this?" he said, glancing down.

"You tell me."

"How did you even find this account? I made sure it was a double-blind." When she made no reply, he said, slowly and grudgingly, "I didn't make these withdrawals."

"I know you didn't," Jonatha said, taking back the sheet and returning to the chair behind Paull's desk. "Your wife did."

"She's a profligate woman," Marshall said stiffly.

"In fact, she's quite frugal." Jonatha put the sheet away. "But your son-in-law is another matter entirely." She studied the director's face. "He's an inveterate gambler."

Something crumbled behind Marshall's stony facade. He suddenly looked ten years older. "My daughter's family wouldn't get by without our help. That's what the account was for."

"Your son-in-law wouldn't be able to continue gambling without your help, either."

Marshall turned, stepped to the window closest to him. "He got in over his head. He was desperate—and unbelievably foolish."

"He borrowed from the wrong people. It's such a cliché, but people still do it. That's why those people still exist."

"Not those particular people," Marshall said with some vehemence. "I wiped them off the face of the earth."

"That must've made you feel good."

"What if it did?"

"Did it stop your son-in-law from gambling?"

"I should've locked him up years ago." Marshall stared blindly into the darkness. "I was going to, but my wife—she said it would break my daughter's heart. . . . How she could love that dead-beat . . ." He shook his head.

"It would've broken your wife's heart, too."

"There was a time," Marshall said, as if to himself, "when that would've stopped me."

"But not now."

"Things have changed." He shook his head slowly. "My son-in-law wouldn't stop, so I had to do it for him. The night I had him put away my wife moved into the guest bedroom, but the fact is she's never there. These days she prefers to stay with our daughter and grandkids."

"All part of a soldier's lot in life."

Marshall squinted at her. "Are you mocking me?"

"Your current situation is too sad to mock."

Marshall studied her for some time. "You're a strange creature."

"I'll take that as a compliment."

"Take it any way you want," he said.

It was clear to her the wound she had explored was still open. She sat with her elbows on the desktop, her hands clasped in front of her. She looked at him, wondering whether she could afford to empathize with him. She knew that whatever happened next would tell her which way to proceed.

"It occurs to me that Paull sat just that way when he was at this desk," Marshall said in a softened tone.

"Really? Tell me about him."

Marshall spread his hands. "What could I tell you that you don't already know?"

"I never met him," Jonatha said.

Marshall nodded. "He was a good man. Smart, insightful, a good administrator."

Jonatha picked up on his hesitation at once. "But?"

Marshall sighed. "He liked to get out into the field, but he was too old for that. And he had his blind spots, I think Jack McClure was one of them."

"Is that what you think—or believe?"

Marshall raised his eyebrows. "What? Is there a question?"

"There's always a question," Jonatha said, "when you don't find the killer standing over his victim with a smoking gun or a bloody knife in his hand."

Marshall laughed. "If we went by that criterion no one would be prosecuted."

"Not without a proper investigation, anyway."

"Meaning?"

"I'm positing the question: What if Jack McClure didn't kill his boss?"

Marshall looked at her for a long, silent moment. "Funny, I've had the same thought."

"Really."

Marshall nodded. "Odd, isn't it, since we've all been given the same facts."

"Which means," she said, "we're missing something."

Fez was a city of red walls and closed doors. Waves of war immigrants from Tunisia and Córdoba, in the south of Spain, had for centuries leant the city a distinctly Arabic aspect. Nowadays, it clung to its historical character far better than Morocco's other imperial cities, Marrakech, Rabat, and Meknes.

When Annika and Namazi arrived in Fez, they went straight to his house, a large, rambling structure with a fountain-cooled courtyard. During the Ottoman Empire it had been a prison. Even now, there were corners dark as night, even when sunlight flooded the rooms, where layers of blood had built up like plaster, impossible to scrape off. The history of Fez resided in every room, like a guest who never leaves, recounting silent stories of the past at all hours of the day and night.

Namazi had said not a word throughout their journey. Annika

could feel the electric current coming off him, like a storm of tiny needles pricking her flesh. Several times, she had tried to engage him, without success. She had seen him like this only once before, in the smoking aftermath of the disastrous terrorist raid in Aleppo, and she did not like the implications.

The house smelled musty, though his men had been living in it during their absence. Though it was raining, he called for the windows to be thrown wide open. The floors and shutters, even some furniture, were soon soaked, but he did not appear to notice.

Instead, he strode through the house, shouting orders that to Annika seemed petty and, at times, contradictory. When they weren't carried out immediately and to the letter, mayhem ensued—shrieks, curses, and, once, Namazi's fist connecting with a confused man's jaw.

However, nothing that came before prepared her for what ensued when he reached the small room, crammed with computers and other electronic equipment. It stank of hot metal, silicon components, and male sweat. Two heavily bearded men sat hunched over their workstations, toiling away, trying to break Caro's labyrinthine algorithm. Heavy metal shutters closed off the windows; the room was illuminated only by LED task lamps, blue-white spots penetrating the gloom like bullet holes.

"What progress have you made?" Namazi demanded of his operators.

At first they were silent, and Annika could feel the tension pressing inward like a constrictor coiled about its prey. When, at length, they admitted that they had made little or no progress, Namazi grabbed one, lifted him bodily out of his seat, and slammed him against the wall. Then he began the real beat down. Annika waited until he had buried half a dozen punches and the blood began to flow before hauling him off the half-unconscious man.

As the victim slid down the wall, Annika said to the other cryptographer, "Now you see what will happen to you if you fail to solve that algorithm."

Namazi shook free of her and was about to turn on the second cryptographer when one of his armed men entered the room and handed him a note. Peering over his shoulder, Annika read: "Isaam dead. Caroline no longer in Paris."

"Iraj—" she began, but he shot her such a fierce look that she bit her lip in order to keep her own counsel.

Namazi turned to the armed man. "You may go."

"Yes, *sidi*," the man said in a low voice.

When he was halfway to the door, Namazi called out, "Your sidearm. Is it clean?"

The armed man turned. "It is, *sidi*. I clean it every morning."

Namazi snapped his fingers. "Let me see."

The man retraced his steps, then pulled the handgun from its polished holster and handed it butt first to Namazi.

"Is it loaded?" the Syrian said.

"It is, *sidi*."

Namazi thumbed off the safety, aimed the weapon at the man's chest, and pulled the trigger. The resulting report was deafening. Shot at close range, the man was catapulted across the room before he slammed into a wall of electronic equipment. The Syrian walked over to him and shot him three more times.

Dropping the gun, he strode out of the room, shouting for someone to clean up the mess.

For a long moment, Annika stared at the two men—one dead, the other badly beaten. Then she, too, left the room. She could not bear to remain in the house a moment longer, so she left the Syrian to the remainder of his rageful frustration and went out into the delicious chaos of the medina, where she was sure to clear her head.

It was times like these when she hated her grandfather more than she could ever imagine hating a human being. She was trapped in his vast, decades-long plot, his queen's gambit, as he liked to call it.

Colors, sounds, and the scents of exotic spices and oils slowly dissipated her black thoughts. The rainstorm had passed, lamps had been lit, their flames casting dancing shadows between the milling shoppers in every direction. She passed myriad stalls selling every-thing and anything the heart desired. From one, she bought a pat-terned silk scarf, which she tied around her head. From another, she bought six blood oranges. She stopped to look at several gold neck-laces. The many gold shops were modern-day reminders that Fez had once been the northern terminus of the ancient gold route that began in Timbuktu.

At the far edge of the medina, she caught a taxi, which took her out of the old walled city to Fez Jdid, home to the *mellah*, the old Jewish ghetto. The Jewish population in Morocco had steadily dwin-dled following the establishment of Israel and, in the last two de-cades, the growing animosity of Moroccan Muslims against their Jewish brethren. While she stared out at the passing city, she peeled a blood orange, used her nails to separate the sections, then popped them into her mouth, one by one. She savored the bittersweet taste, which brought to mind memories of sun-soaked Mediterranean coasts and verdigris-green Venetian canals.

At the iron gates to the Cementiri Jueu, Annika had the taxi stop. She handed the driver enough money to ensure he would wait for her. Stepping out of the cab into the starlit golden evening, she felt a furtive breeze stir against her bare calves. She had had enough experience entering the cemetery at night that the lock provided no problem.

Soon enough, she was surrounded by a surf of low, white mark-ers, as ugly as they were efficient. They stretched away from her in ordered ranks, like waves rolling onto a flat sandy beach. Apart from the names engraved on them, they all appeared identical, sadly anonymous, almost an afterthought of lives lived in Fez's ghetto and the deaths that had overtaken them.

To any outsider or even casual visitor, finding your way would seem impossible, but Annika was an old hand here. She knew pre-cisely where she was going. She stopped in front of Rolan's father's marker. Kneeling down, she placed four of the blood oranges in a square, then topped it with the fifth one. When she whispered parts of the Kaddish, the Hebrew prayer for the dead, her lips barely moved. The wind took the words away from life into death, where the old man dwelled with his God. Annika was not a believer in any organized religion, and neither was Rolan. But his father had been devout, and Rolan had been a bitter disappointment to him. Rolan had never visited his father's grave, but Annika did every year, more often since Namazi had made Fez his new headquarters.

The old man had died before she had met Rolan; nevertheless he loomed large in her life. Whether Rolan liked it or not, parts of the old man remained inside him, had changed him, for better or for worse. His father had been a scholar. Annika had realized that the more quickly she familiarized herself with the old man's letters and papers, the better equipped she'd be to deal with Rolan. Soon after they had married, she had realized that Rolan was like two people in one, and his father's rejection of him had sundered those two parts of him irrevocably. Her solution was to try and placate the ghost of his father. Of course, Jews didn't believe in ghosts, but they believed in golems—in the undead—which was what both she and Rolan imagined his psychically powerful father to be.

She stared down at the blood oranges, arranged in a three-dimensional quincunx, an ancient design thought to have magically curative powers. *"Oseh Shalom—rest in peace,"* she whispered, in conclusion, only dimly aware that it was an order, not a request.

Something flew by her ear, a beetle or a moth, and she batted at it. A hand slammed down on her shoulder, pinning her in place as an arm wrapped around her neck and throat, cutting off her breathing.

"Why me?" Marshall said.

Jonatha shrugged. "It no longer matters."

"I think I deserve to know."

"Ideology, sex masquerading as love, money—these are the reasons people betray their country. I ruled out the first two fairly quickly; you're not that kind of man."

"I'm not the kind of man to betray my country, period."

"But the third—well, the withdrawals, the trouble your son-in-law was in, these were markers—red flags, if you like."

"Must we return to this?" Marshall growled.

"I'm simply doing my job," Jonatha said. "Just following orders."

He smiled grimly. "I understand. I do."

"Then help me," Jonatha said.

"What?"

"That was what Dennis Paull must have said to Jack McClure, at, yes, just about this time of the night."

Marshall's eyes opened wide, as if at that very moment he realized why she had chosen this place, this time for their interview.

"Why do you need my help?" he said. "Hasn't Krofft given you all the tools you need?"

"Krofft believes absolutely in McClure's guilt."

"Why don't you?"

"I'm naturally suspicious of airtight cases. Life is a messy affair, I've found. A veritable shit-box."

"Too true." It seemed clear Marshall was thinking of his own personal situation. "What are you proposing?"

"An alliance of sorts."

He looked at her askance. "Krofft will surely see that as a betrayal."

"That's why we won't tell him."

"I have to say, Midwood, betrayal is behavior unbecoming."

She leaned forward. "Listen to me, Director. We have entered the labyrinth; without me, you'll never get out."

Marshall shook his head. "You're awfully sure of yourself."

"To be honest, life has never allowed me a choice."

Marshall considered her for some moments. "Continue," he said at length.

Jonatha nodded. "I've been thinking that Paull's murder might be an attempt to stop Atlas's deployment." She stared out the window for a long moment. "If that is, in fact, the case, then the Syrian knows less about Atlas than he needs to."

"Yes," Marshall said thoughtfully. "On the other hand, the threat still exists, and with time passing and Atlas continuing its rollout, the Syrian is likely to become desperate."

Jonatha turned back to him. "Maybe that will lead to a mistake."

With arms like iron bands, the faceless male continued to solidify his grip on Annika's neck by increasing the torque. At that point, she realized he was about to break her neck. She knew the technique—it had been taught to her by an Israeli spymaster years ago. She also knew that if he managed to lock the grip in place, she would never get out of it. She arched her back, but he pulled her off her feet. She used her elbows, the heels of her feet, knowing she was expending her last reserves of energy. But even as her elbow struck her assailant she knew it was useless; his side was as hard as corrugated steel.

The smell of his wintergreen breath wafted over her as he laughed softly, strangely, deep in the back of his throat.

"You're done, darlin'," he said in the slurry accent of the American South. "Dead'n'buried."

Annika's vision grew spotty, her lungs were desperate for oxygen, and a terrible weakness invaded her extremities, negating any counteraction. The trouble was she wasn't thinking clearly. Her thoughts had been muffled in the past, in the ritual of placating the Jewish undead. She had allowed the present to slip away, her usual vigilance subsumed by a superstition she only half believed.

She was fast losing consciousness. Her fingers felt cold and unresponsive. A sharp pain gathering in her neck pointed to her life being over within seconds.

And then she heard something—a sound only a golem could make—inhuman, undead. A gout of hot blood drenched her right shoulder and cheek, stuck in her hair like sleet. An evil, retching sound invaded her right ear, then was just as quickly ripped away. Bones cracked from behind her. More blood fountained, and then the terrible weight of her assailant fell away, as if he had been a cardboard cutout set aflame. She turned, despite the sea of pain in her chest and neck, and saw the face of her savior—her golem, risen from the dead.

It was Rolan.

All along, Nona had her suspicions about who had committed the triple murder that included Senator Herren's aide. When the autopsies came back, she was certain. By the pattern of the mutilations, which happened postmortem, Nona had her perp. He hadn't been after Herren's aide—the aide had been collateral damage. The murders weren't political in nature, as everyone including Dye suspected and feared, but they were just as inflammatory. The perp, a neo-Nazi who went by the street name Hella Goode, had been after the two men with Herren's aide. They were gay; Hella Goode had a history of involvement in hate crimes, though no one had been able to pin anything on him, save being drunk and disorderly or pissing on the front door of a police precinct.

Now, however, Nona had Goode. A partial fingerprint had been recovered from the eyelid of one of the men. It was a match with Goode's. Nona, knowing Goode better than she would have liked, took with her a squad from Tactical, fully armed and armored. These precautions were critical; Goode did not go easily or well. Half-a-dozen of his men were either killed or severely wounded before Nona, with a pair of Tactical, dragged Goode bodily from his headquarters along a burned-out street in the dangerous southeastern quarter of D.C.

Downtown, as she was processing Goode and what was left of his gang, Dye appeared, trailed by a larger than usual posse. She noticed newspeople from all the local media trailing after him.

"Good work, Chief." He pumped her hand, his telegenic smile broadcast throughout the ground floor. "Go get yourself cleaned up and then join me back here for a press conference."

Nona spent no more than ten minutes in the restroom. She

looked in the mirror and congratulated herself on a job well done. She wondered if she would get a commendation for keeping Dye's nuts out of the fire lit by Senator Herren.

Returning to the headquarters rotunda, she found the press conference already under way. Dye was in the eye of the media storm. She was further stunned to see Senator Herren standing by his side. She heard Senator Herren's sanctimonious eulogy to an aide he scarcely knew or cared about. She heard Dye in full political smear mode talk about the successful wrap of the case. He made no mention of the two gay men with the aide or that the murders were hate crimes. Instead, without stating it outright, he implied that the murders were politically motivated, that the perpetrator was in custody, and that justice would be performed to the full extent of the law.

"This is the heart and soul of the democratic process," he wound up his web of omissions, misleading statements, and outright lies. "We cannot, we *will* not allow those who seek to attack our great system of government to go undiscovered or unpunished. Write that in large type. That is the unyielding backbone of my administration."

Nona turned around, pushing through the throng, making her way back to the restroom, where she made it into one of the stalls just in time before she vomited.

How do you look for a needle in a haystack? This is what Redbird sometimes did. While it was true that the bulk of his assignments were what he called "straight shots," where Dickinson sent him the identity, location, and movements of his target, there were times, as now, when it was up to him to find the target and liquidate him.

So how do you look for a needle in a haystack? Redbird chose to magnetize the haystack, so that the needle he was searching for would be drawn north. This was an inexact analogy, to say the least, nevertheless it best described Redbird's methodology.

Having arrived in Zurich, his first stop was his armorer, a man named Heinrich. Redbird didn't know his surname, and didn't care to. Heinrich was a technician at an upscale watchmaker on Bahnhofstrasse. Redbird had become aware of him in the usual manner of his kind—through a personal recommendation, in this case, a very dangerous Welshman of Redbird's acquaintance. Over the years, Heinrich had proved absolutely reliable.

He was a rotund, affable German-Swiss with ruddy cheeks, huge blue eyes, and ginger side whiskers that made him look like he'd stepped out of a previous century. He was always pleased to see Redbird because, as he once put it, "you arrive with the most unusual requests."

"And what is it this time, my friend?" Heinrich said, when he had led Redbird into his cramped workshop in the rear of the store. "How can I help?"

Redbird set out a thick wad of Swiss francs.

"Must be something special." Heinrich eyed the pile, but did not touch it. To do so would violate propriety and his image as a gentleman of the old school.

"I want to be police," Redbird said. "Someone high up—an inspector, perhaps."

"But not from around here."

"Indeed not."

Heinrich nodded. "Geneva, then. The other side of the country."

"How soon?"

Heinrich eyed the thick wad of francs. "Three hours."

"Fine. I need to be armed."

"You will be," Heinrich said.

"Also, I need the name of the dirtiest detective in the city."

Heinrich laughed. "This is Switzerland—we have no dirty police." He gestured with his head. "Now go get cleaned up or have something to eat or pray—whatever it is you people do in the silences between acts of violence."

Redbird grinned and strode out of the shop.

Bahnhofstrasse was a whirl of regimented energy. There was something about the Swiss that rubbed Redbird the wrong way. They were such hypocrites—wallowing in their reputation as upright law-abiding citizens, detached from the petty rivalries, conflicts, and antagonisms infecting the rest of the world. But underneath that facade, they could be as devious, underhanded, and treacherous as anyone else he could think of, possibly more so.

Checking his mobile, he found a nearby branch of the bank he used. He was running low on cash—he had mostly euros, anyway. While he was on an assignment he used local currency to pay for everything. Cash was impossible to trace, unless it was counterfeit. Accessing the account Dickinson had set up for him, he withdrew approximately a third more than he thought he'd need. Early in his career, he had been caught short, and he'd vowed it would never happen again.

Outside, he watched the trams wheeling by like stately nineteenth-century women in their extravagant bustle dresses. He strolled down the wide boulevard until he came to the large corner building whose second-floor iron balcony was festooned with pink flowers. Its large street-level plate-glass windows were filled with chocolates of every variety. He turned into Sprüngli, Zurich's most famous chocolatier, bought himself far too much, and began eating even before he had left the shop.

Down at the lake, he watched a young Italian woman laughing as her lover fed her ice cream. He instantly thought of how deeply Dandy had loved ice cream, and this reminded him of how everything had gone to shit in Bangkok. Abruptly sickened, he threw the remaining chocolate in a trash bin and walked away.

Three hours, to the second, after he had left the watchmaker's establishment, he returned. Heinrich was waiting for him.

"Everything in order?"

Heinrich, beaming, set before him the complicated ID.

"Florian Birchler," Redbird said as he picked it up. "Inspector,

Federal Criminal Police, Einsatzgruppe TIGRIS." He looked up at Heinrich. "Nice touch. You've outdone yourself."

"And as a member of the special operations unit, you're required to carry a sidearm." Heinrich slid a 9mm Glock in its sleek black leather holster over to Redbird, along with a Ka-Bar Marine knife. "Just in case," he added.

Redbird nodded. "And the last?"

Heinrich smiled thinly. "That would be Detective Quentin Gensler." He showed Redbird a xeroxed photo of a man who looked like a baked potato. "Quite a character is Herr Gensler. Runs an illicit gambling and prostitution ring on the side, maybe drugs, too, I'm not sure about that." He spun across a sheet. "Here're some interesting facts about him." Heinrich shrugged. "As you can see, he's as dirty as they come."

"You've earned your pay, Heinrich," Redbird said, gathering what he had come for. "Be seeing you."

Pyotr Legere, staring at his face in the hotel room mirror, saw someone he did not recognize. He had peeled off the bandages, despite Dr. Scheiwold's express orders to keep it undisturbed for at least three days. He was confronted by the thoroughly unpleasant sight of his swollen cheek, black and blue, the black stitches like railroad tracks keeping his flesh from bursting through the inflamed skin.

How was he ever going to recover from this? How could he ever look at himself in the mirror again? He'd have to live the rest of his life like a vampire, all mirrors banished from his residences, both temporary and permanent.

Then he began to laugh, not only at his situation but at himself. Over the years, Legere had discovered laughing at himself was often the best medicine. In the darkest hours it put his mind in a place of calm that allowed him to think his way back into the light.

And this was a very dark hour, indeed. He had warned his father not to involve himself with the Syrian, but the elder Legere had been dazzled by the promises of riches the Syrian had dangled. Not that the Syrian had lied. In the five years of their business marriage, riches had, indeed, come the Legeres' way—more even than the Syrian had promised. But at what cost?

Swollen with money and power, his father pushed him down even further, keeping secret key elements of the partnership that, try as he might, Pyotr could not ferret out. This humiliation was what he saw when he stared into the mirror. His wound was the cost writ large and right across his face. No matter how skilled Dr. Scheiwold was, Pyotr would know what was there, as if each separate affront, each abasement was written there under his skin, like the multiplied arms of an unwanted tattoo.

He had borne the humiliations while the money was rolling in, but starting eight months ago, the gravy train had jumped the tracks. He had contacted the Syrian numerous times since then but had gotten only nonanswers in reply. They all amounted to one thing: have patience.

It was about six weeks ago when Pyotr's father had called.

"We have a problem with our major supplier." He meant the Syrian.

"How serious?"

"I think he's running out of money."

"How is that possible?" Pyotr had asked. *"He's richer than we are."*

"Two possibilities," his father had replied. *"Either he's not as rich as we believed—which I doubt, considering the vastness of his organization—or he's run into a problem accessing his cash hoard."*

"What about continuing cash flow from his businesses?"

"That's sufficient to fund his organization, his purchases of guns and war materiel, and the baksheesh involved in the intricate planning of his terrorist raids."

"Meaning he's got nothing to spare for us."

"That's right," his father had said. *"And something must be done about it. I have no intention of embroiling us in whatever difficulties he is experiencing."*

Pyotr had bitten back the "I told you so" he so dearly wanted to utter. Gloating would get him only a moment's satisfaction, especially when weighed against his father's wrath. But his father would not always be the head of the company. *My time will come*, Pyotr thought, anxious to push the old man from his lofty perch.

He was replacing the bandage when he heard the particular knock on his door announcing Romy. Immediately his mood shifted. She was just the ticket. He could take his frustration out on every part of her. Choking her while he came was one of his favorite pleasures. Maybe, he thought, as he crossed to the door, he'd start choking her right away this time.

Jack shoved him back as soon as he flung open the door. Romy shut the door behind them.

"Who the hell—?"

"Jack McClure, Herr Legere." Jack had him firmly by the front of his shirt. "Surely you know who I am."

"Should I?"

"Your people tried to kill me in the spa an hour ago."

Legere shook his head. "You're mistaken. I have no knowledge—"

The sentence ended in a sharp squeak as Jack slammed the back of his head against the wall.

Legere's eyes went briefly out of focus, then, clearing, his gaze shot past Jack to Romy.

"How could you? Jesus, who the hell are you?"

"Someone you'll never know," Romy said.

Legere's gaze switched back to Jack. "What lies has the bitch been telling you?"

Jack slapped him hard across the face, and Legere howled as blood bloomed between his stitches. "Let's cut the crap, Legere. I've been following your trail all the way from Bangkok."

"Now I know you have the wrong person," Legere said. "I've never been in Bangkok in my life."

Jack grabbed his jaw. "Dr. Scheiwold does good work." He

caught Legere's eye. "You were injured in Bangkok, where you met with Leroy Connaston. That's why you came here."

"I didn't—"

"In a nightclub called WTF at Thonglor Soi 10."

"You're insane."

"Shall I play you the tape of your debriefing with Dennis Paull?"

Legere's hands were behind him, and Jack felt his intent just before he produced the Luger. Knocking it aside, Jack slammed the edge of his hand down on Legere's wrist. He wrested the Luger away from him, checked that it was loaded, then jammed it into the waistband at the small of his back.

"Dennis Paull is dead," Jack continued. "He was my boss and my friend. Now everyone believes I shot him."

"How does it feel to be a fugitive, McClure? Not good, I imagine."

Jack shrugged. "It doesn't matter now. You're coming with me, back to Washington."

"With my men all around you, I'm not going anywhere with you." Legere's face broke out into a sly grin. "You're a dead man, McClure, but your death will have more meaning—a terrible meaning—when I tell you that you were set up from the very beginning."

Legere's eyes were alight with a kind of glee. "I didn't work for your boss, Paull. Well, I did, but only as a double for the Syrian."

Jack felt his stomach clench. "Was there ever really a mole?"

"Oh, yes, but now everyone is convinced it's you."

Jack hit him. Blood spattered from Legere's split lip.

"Having fun yet?" Legere said, as he spat out more blood. "Just wait until my men catch up with you."

"I'm going to make sure they don't."

"Actually," Legere said, "it won't matter."

"He's right," Romy said to Jack. "It will be your word against his. Taking him back without tangible proof of your innocence will only entangle you further."

Jack felt the web of lies around him drawing in, leaving him no room to escape. He dearly wanted to get on a plane now and haul Legere home, but Romy was right. That wasn't going to solve his problem. If anything, it might make his situation worse.

"What d'you suggest?" he said to her.

"That's right," Legere said, "ask the conniving bitch for advice."

Romy stepped up to him, placed her hand against his cheek. "Poor, poor Pyotr." Then she grasped his neck so hard he began to retch. "But surely this can't be the first time you were lied to."

He spat into her face. For a moment, something dark and convoluted squirmed behind Romy's eyes, then she smiled wickedly. Taking a handful of his hair, she drew his head back, wiped his bloody spittle off her cheek.

"You're such a little boy, Pyotr. You're riding high as long as everything goes your way. But when you encounter even the smallest pothole you go to pieces. What kind of a porcelain doll did your mother raise?"

"Don't you say a word about my mother!"

"Not a man, surely." Her voice was mocking, steely, cruel. "She fucked up, Pyotr. What did she do to you? Keep you at her breast too long? You liked her breast, didn't you?"

Legere, growling, lunged at her, but Jack had a firm hold on him, restraining him from reaching Romy, though she remained near him, undeterred and unafraid.

"Now we come to the nub of things, Pyotr," she continued. Her eyes were blazing, her expression triumphant. Some long-held emotion had been unleashed by his gesture of utter contempt. "You and your mother were closer than—what?" She snapped her fingers repeatedly. "I need a word to describe—"

"SHUT UP!" Pyotr screamed, struggling against Jack's restraining arms.

"You have no idea how disgusting it was to feel you on top of me," Romy said. "To feel you penetrate me made me gag."

"That's enough, Romy," Jack said. "We need a next step."

Romy was breathing as hard as Legere was. She stared at Legere like a gorgon. "The chimera is powerless without his body."

Jack understood. "So we need to get Legere out of here."

Romy nodded without taking her eyes off Legere. "They all work for him here—that is to say, they work for his father." Her lips screwed up. "No one actually works for you, do they, Pyotr? No one respects a porcelain doll."

"Let's get him out of the building," Jack said. "Fetch me a washcloth and surgical tape." When she hesitated, he added, "Romy, now!"

Breaking her poisonous visual contact with Legere, she crossed to the bathroom, returning a moment later with the required items. Jack wadded up the washcloth and jammed it into Legere's mouth, sealing it with a length of the surgical tape.

"Okay," he said as he pushed his prisoner toward the door. "Ready."

Caro was scanning for the intel that Jonatha had requested when her mobile buzzed. She picked it up and was about to answer when she got a hit.

"Gotcha!" she said, capturing the carrier e-mail on which the intel was piggybacking. She flashed off the raw data to Jonatha, along with a hastily typed note, while simultaneously answering the call.

It was Zukhov.

"I'll buzz you in," she said.

"Not necessary."

"Wait, what?"

Hearing his sharp knock, she crossed the room, and threw open the apartment door.

"How did you—?"

Zukhov pointed up above their heads as he closed and locked

the door behind him. "The Syrian knows where you are. He sent someone."

"Is that blood on your coat?" She reached out for him, took his hands, which were also bloody. "My God, are you hurt?"

"Not my blood." He smiled like a shark. "I'd better wash up."

She followed him across the living room, stood in the doorway to the bathroom, watching him run the water in the sink.

"What the hell happened?"

"The less you know about it the better." Zukhov scrubbed the splashes of blood off his jacket and hands.

"Looking at that blood I know all I need to know," Caro said uneasily. "I promised myself I wasn't going to move from here, but I guess I have no choice."

"Oh, yes, you're going to move." Zukhov dried his hands. "Come on, we'll do it together."

Caro stepped back so he could exit the bathroom. She followed him to her laptop, put her hands on his meaty shoulders as he sat down, his fingers dancing over the keyboard.

"Physically, you're staying right here," Zukhov said, "but as far as the Syrian is concerned—"

Caro leaned over him. "You're rerouting my IP address."

"Indeed. You've just decamped to—hmm, where shall we put you?"

"Singapore," Caro said.

Zukhov's fingers were a blur as he worked. "Good one."

"And then Beijing."

He nodded, laughing. "Even better. That will keep his people running in circles."

Romy stuck her head into the corridor first. After looking both ways, she gestured to Jack, who pushed Legere out the door. They encountered no one on their short walk to the service elevator at the back end of the corridor. Jack listened for the sounds of conversation or footfalls.

When the elevator door opened, Legere tried to lurch away, but Jack spun him around, slammed the side of his head into the edge of the door frame. Inside the elevator, Romy leaned forward, pressed the button for the basement.

"There's a car park under the building," she explained. "We can use my Audi."

Legere struggled against his gag.

"Look at him. He's nothing more than a thug." Romy put her hands on her slim hips. "A thug with bad hygiene."

Legere glared at her.

Romy leaned against the padded wall. "Herr McClure, do you know anything about Pyotr's mother?"

Legere made desperate grunts.

Romy paid him no mind, which infuriated him all the more. "Galina Yemchevya, chief translator at the Kremlin, a position she enjoyed from the time she was nineteen years old. Any idea why she was elevated to this lofty post at such a tender age?"

She stared at him without pity. "She was a prodigy. She had a brilliant talent."

Romy's smile was cruel. "Oh, she was talented, all right," Romy said, "with her mouth, her hands, and her vagina. The men she pleased. The powerful and the wealthy knelt before her, argued over her, fought over her, purge after purge." She ran her tongue over her lips. "Galina Yemchevya, chief translator at the Kremlin, the most notorious courtesan of her time."

She turned to Jack. "You see the truth of it, Herr McClure. Poor Pyotr has no evidence to prove he's Giles Legere's son. There are so many possibilities, so many famous and infamous men who could be his father. I very much doubt if even Galina Yemchevya knows."

At that moment, the elevator lurched to a stop. It hung, a sealed cage, shuddering on its cables.

Then the lights went out.

SEVENTEEN

Needless to say, Detective Gensler was not happy to see Inspector Florian Birchler, Federal Criminal Police, Einsatzgruppe TIGRIS step into his office. He hid his anxiety well, Redbird thought, give him that. In person, he looked even more like a potato—ovoid, leathery, and green-eyed.

Mustering a smile, even after Redbird had produced his credentials, Gensler gestured to an uncomfortable-looking chair. Redbird pointedly ignored him.

"What can the Zurich police do for you, Inspector?" he said, massaging the backs of his hands, which were raw and red with a nasty case of eczema.

"Not the police, Detective," Redbird said with icy venom. "You."

Gensler sat down as if Redbird had pushed him. "I . . . I don't understand, Inspector."

"No, I don't suppose you do."

Redbird stepped to the desk, picked up a glass paperweight, put it down in a different spot, then did the same with a brass-and-leather letter opener, and every other item on the desk. Gensler eyed him with what looked like mounting alarm.

"Gensler," he said at last, "you have a thoroughly undistinguished record." Redbird looked up sharply to see the potato holding its breath. He almost laughed. "On the other hand, your extracurricular activities show initiative."

"I beg your pardon?"

Gensler's face had turned the color of ash. Redbird wondered whether he was going to lose his lunch.

Looming suddenly forward, Redbird jammed his knuckled fists onto the desktop. "Don't fuck with me, Gensler. I can take you into custody this minute if I choose to. Do we understand each other?"

Gensler swallowed convulsively.

"Answer me, damnit!"

"Yes, sir."

"Good." Redbird stood up straight. "I've come to Zurich to find two people." He held out his mobile screen-first, so the detective could get a good look at Jack McClure and Pyotr Legere. "Either of these men look familiar?"

"Actually, I know that one." Gensler pointed to Legere.

Redbird frowned. "How's that?"

Gensler wiped sweat off his broad brow. "I mean I don't *actually* know him. I know *of* him."

Redbird's brows knit further together. "That's not the same, Gensler. You're not helping me." Intruding on the following silence, he said, "Tell me, how much do you treasure that summer chalet of yours on the lake?"

Gensler made a stricken animal noise in the back of his throat.

"Or the Mercedes convertible you keep hidden up there?"

"All right, all right," Gensler blurted out. "I know where this man—Pyotr Legere—is staying."

"What are you not telling me?"

Gensler blew air out of his pursed lips. "He's a big spender—a payday whale, as it's known in my world. He comes to Zurich three or four times a year. When he does, he avails himself of my services—gambling and the girls. He's pretty tough on the girls, but he leaves them big enough tips that they don't complain."

"Listen, Gensler," Redbird said, "if you withhold anything from me, I'll shut you down and put you away so fast your wife will have a stroke. I'll strip her of everything—the chalet, the Mercedes, the lifestyle she's become used to. If you don't cooperate fully, you're looking at your own personal Armageddon."

Gensler nodded. "When Legere got into town, he had a wound on his cheek. It was bad enough for him to seek out a skin job doctor. Following the procedure, the doctor stashed him at a hotel by the lake set up for his patients. So far as I know, that's where he is now."

"And you know this how?"

Gensler, apparently feeling himself at last on firm ground, grinned. "Legere's got a favorite girl. He called for her while he was in the hotel. She went to see him there."

"Address," Redbird said, holding out his hand while Gensler frantically scribbled on a notepad.

"How did it go?" Krofft said when Jonatha checked in by phone.

"Perfectly. Marshall and I have an alliance."

Krofft shook his head. "You could recruit a nun to kill her mother."

Jonatha laughed. "You know me, I'd give it the old college try."

Krofft laughed with her. "Over the next week, I'll be feeding you intel you'll pass on to Marshall. At some point, knowing him as I do, he'll go to the president with it. When I prove the intel's disinformation, he'll have made such a fool of himself with the president, the POTUS will have to act. I'll finally get Marshall off my back. Ever since DCS was initiated, he's made it his mission to meddle in Company affairs. He thinks DCS is a reaction to my failures." Krofft made a sound akin to a cat purring. "The sooner I'm rid of him, the better."

Annika took Rolan to the taxi and got them out of the ghetto as quickly as traffic would allow. At the edge of the medina, she paid the driver, then led Rolan into the labyrinth, until they became lost in the cacophonous ebb and flow of the immense market, a city within the city.

They walked, seemingly aimlessly, long enough for Annika to make certain they weren't being followed. Rolan's body was close beside her. At times, in the dense crowds, they touched, even, once, pressed together, but she felt nothing. It was as if the man she had known, the man she had once loved, had died in the bomb blast. The creature who had been released from Dr. Karalian's care was as hollow and dead as a golem, a thing created from clay in the shape of a man.

At a tiny café she knew, she ordered sweet mint tea and a plateful of small pastries. Rolan sat next to her, staring out at the endless parade of people moving to the beat of drums, the bark of hawked wares.

When the tea had been poured from a copper pot with a spout as long and graceful as a swan's neck, she pushed the plate of sweets toward him. He said nothing and did not look her way.

After a time, she said his name just loud enough to be heard over the incessant clamor. His head swung toward her. His eyes were empty of love, of empathy, of any recognizable human emotion. He was a walking time bomb, another of her grandfather's chess pieces.

"I recognized the man who attacked me in the cemetery. He's CIA."

"Why is the CIA after you?"

"Rolan." She forced herself to extend her arm, take his hand in hers. It felt hard as marble and twice as cold. "Rolan, you shouldn't be here."

He stared at her for a long time. Annika had difficulty meeting his eyes.

"Where should I be, then?"

His voice was like nails over sandpaper, making her wince inside.

"I see you have no answer for me," he went on, "but you must. I have no answers for myself."

"Rolan, forgive me." She put her head down. "I didn't know you were so unhappy at Dr. Karalian's clinic."

"I was neither unhappy nor happy," he said in a curiously mechanical voice.

It seemed as if his thoughts were already elsewhere. "It's as if . . ."

His eyes slid away from her, much to her relief.

"I'm in a cage," he said slowly and carefully, "a glass cage. I can see out; I remember what the world looked like once upon a time, but now I can no longer make sense of it."

This confession only exacerbated her guilt.

"Everything is distorted," he continued, apparently oblivious to her pain. "I see people, but they mean nothing to me. I can't taste food, smell smells, feel pleasure—all that is gone."

"Rolan, what can I do to help you?"

"There's nothing anyone can do. I'm beyond Karalian's help, or even yours." His face seemed chiseled out of stone. He sighed. "At least I was able to save you."

When his eyes swung back to her they were dark and haunted. "I remember who you are, Annika. I remember a time when . . . but then the memory eludes me, slips through my fingers even while I try to hold on to it. I loved you once, I know that. I loved so many things. But now—now that seems alien to me, like someone else's dream. I want to go back."

"Rolan, you need to stay here with me. That's what Dyadya wanted."

"You said 'wanted.' Is he dead?" Rolan's eyes narrowed. "Is Gourdjiev dead?"

When Annika nodded, he said, "Better late than never."

She was taken aback. "What are you talking about? My grandfather loved you."

"He loved himself," Rolan said bitterly. "Possibly you, too, though he wasn't above using you." He paused to search deep within Annika's eyes. "Don't you get it? To him, people were chess pieces, and you can't have an attachment to pieces you put in jeopardy. On the next move or the one after you may have to sacrifice them in order to win the match."

"You must stop talking like this, Rolan. Dyadya didn't sacrifice anyone."

"He sacrificed me." Rolan's face grew dark. "Didn't you know? Your Dyadya wanted the Aleppo attack to happen."

"Impossible. Why would he provoke a terrorist attack?"

"It was a trap. He wanted to teach the Syrian a lesson. Think about it. How many of the Syrian's people returned from that raid?"

Annika felt as if she had lost the ability to breathe. "Not one." Her voice barely rose above a whisper.

Rolan nodded. "Those men weren't suicide bombers; the Syrian is not a religious fanatic—his motivations are purely venal. No, the men who were caught in your grandfather's trap were the elite of the Syrian's soldiers—and none of them survived."

Annika felt as if her head were about to explode. "But you were in Aleppo by accident. It was a coincidence that—"

"Annika, think back. What was I involved in then?"

"I . . . I don't remember." Her heart was hammering painfully in her chest. The past and present, colliding, rushed at her at light speed. "I . . . you were in Aleppo for a Mid-East economic summit."

"Yes and no. You recall that I was employed by the Saudi Royal Bank. But at the same time I was secretly working for the opposition to Syrian President Assad's regime."

"Why didn't you tell me?"

"How could I? But Gourdjiev somehow found out. He used me as bait to draw out Namazi. At that time, Namazi needed to infiltrate the Syrian opposition."

"I don't understand. Why would he—?"

"Assad had hired him to root out the opposition leaders," Rolan said, "for an obscene amount of money."

Annika bit her lip to keep herself from screaming. "How could I have known nothing about this? Dyadya—"

"Imagine what would have happened, Annika, if you had found

out. Your grandfather kept you out of it. You were completely in the dark, as was I, until I discovered afterward what he had done."

"This can't be," Annika said. "I refuse to believe it."

"You're far too smart not to believe the truth when you hear it." In his eerily detached way, Rolan watched the pain work itself across her face. "That's the way it went."

"You're telling me that Dyadya destroyed your life—*our* life together."

"Chess pieces, Annika. Sacrifices in the service of checkmate."

Annika looked away, no longer able to bear the thought of him knowing how her grandfather thought and acted.

Rolan bit mechanically into a small cake, chewed as if it were made of cardboard. "Annika," he said after a time, "you must know by now that we aren't alive unless someone loves us."

"Rolan, I love you."

"You once did, that's true enough. But you don't anymore. I see it in your eyes, in the way you can never quite look at me."

Annika shook her head, but she found herself thinking of Jack. "That's your injured brain talking."

He shook his head, his expression without a scintilla of sorrow or remorse. "It doesn't matter. I can't feel anything anyway." He pushed the plate of barely eaten sweets away. "Though I'm not quite dead, I'm beyond life now. I inhabit a place of darkness, a place where emotions don't exist, and never did."

In the darkness, Jack's keen hearing identified the harsh scrape of metal against metal. Reaching out to the seam between the doors, he felt the sharp edge of a crowbar. Romy brushed by him, pressed her ear to the door well away from the intrusion of the crowbar.

Another rustle and Jack felt her lips against his ear. "Pyotr's people are on the other side," she whispered. "They're saying they have us trapped."

Legere was panting. Jack could smell his sweat.

"He's claustrophobic," Romy said.

Jack nodded. "Get down on your hands and knees," he said, pushing Legere down. When Legere tried to resist, he added, "You want to get out of here, don't you?" He sensed, rather than saw Legere nod. "Then do as I say."

Standing precariously on Legere's narrow back, he stretched up until his searching hands found the emergency door in the roof. The squeal of the crowbar trying to pry apart the doors was unnaturally loud in the confined space. Jack didn't know how much time they had. He focused on the roof escape, turning the lever, unlocking the hatch and pushing it upward.

He hauled himself up through the square opening, onto the top of the elevator. In the dim light of the shaft he could see the cables. Beyond was the reinforced concrete wall of the shaft, into which horizontal steel bars had been set as rungs for maintenance workers and firemen to climb up and down.

In a whisper, he instructed Romy to get Legere to his feet.

"Raise your arms," he said to Legere, then pulled him up to the roof of the car.

Legere was ashen-faced, shaking, mumbling into his gag, crumpled into a useless pile. Just as well, Jack thought. In this state, he'd offer no further resistance. Reaching down a second time, he grabbed hold of Romy's outstretched hand and helped her through the opening.

"Now," he said, "all we have to do is get to those rungs, climb up to the next floor and use the emergency button in the shaft to open the doors."

"Are you kidding?" Romy said. "There must be a three foot jump from here to the wall."

"It's more like four," Jack said. "But we have no choice."

"I can't make it," she said.

"Sure you can." Jack lifted her to her feet and walked her to the edge of the elevator.

He could feel the tremors up and down her body. "Don't worry," he said. "I have you." With his hands on her waist, he heaved her across the divide.

She bit back a scream as her hands instinctively reached out, her fingers wrapping around the rungs. She lost one shoe, then shook off the other as her feet scrabbled for purchase on the rungs lower down.

"You bastard!" she cried.

"Climb up, Romy," he said. "Legere's people have pried the elevator door almost open."

Seeing her do as he ordered, he grabbed Legere. He seemed as light as if he were made of balsa wood.

Legere tried to shout a protest around his gag. Jack ignored him. With his arm around the other man, Jack leapt off the edge of the elevator. As he grabbed hold of the rungs, Legere almost slipped out of his grip.

"Grab on, man!" he shouted. "Grab it! Yeah, that's right."

The three of them began to climb. Romy, reaching the floor above first, slammed her palm against the emergency open button on the left side of the doors, and climbed back onto safe ground. Jack and Legere soon followed.

In the third-floor corridor, they raced to the fire stairs. As Jack threw the door open, he could hear a clutch of voices.

"They don't know where we are," he said. "Come on."

He drew Legere's Luger as he herded them down the stairs. They were approaching the second floor, when the hairs at the nape of Jack's neck stirred. With a gesture, he halted them. He put a forefinger across his lips. He took a step downward, then another. The flicker of a shadow came from below, just past the landing, where the staircase doubled back on itself.

A moment later, he saw Hanna ascending barefoot in order to keep her approach silent. Jack took another step down in order to block her view of Romy and Legere. Her long neck twisted as she stared up at him.

"Herr McClure," she said calmly, "you don't seem to appreciate our spa."

"I was disappointed, Hanna. Your treatment was somewhat overcooked."

Her wide lips twisted into the semblance of a wry smile. "But you left prematurely, Herr McClure. You didn't give us a fair chance."

"It doesn't seem as if a fair chance is on your hotel's menu of amenities."

It was then she produced a Beretta from behind her back, aimed at him. "Get down here, Herr McClure." The veneer of banter had disappeared, replaced by the steely resolve he had observed in her earlier. "Get down here now."

"As you wish," Jack said, and shot her through the heart.

Hanna, eyes open wide in astonishment and shock, pitched back down the stairwell, her body rolling over and over as her head struck the edge of each successive step.

"*Sheisse!*" he heard Romy exclaim from just behind him. "Is she dead?"

As Legere turned tail, Jack leapt back up the stairs, pulling him down with such force the other man tripped, his knees buckling. Jack dragged Legere behind him as the three of them continued down the stairs. When they came across Hanna's body, Romy bent down and retrieved her Beretta.

As they stepped over Hanna's broken body, they heard the frantic drumbeat of shoes against the concrete stairs.

"Get behind me," Jack said. "Here they come."

The moment she saw Jonatha jog out of Rock Creek Park, Alix Ross, behind the wheel of her black Chrysler convertible, leaned over and opened the passenger's side door. The early morning light was pink, glowing like mother-of-pearl. Stratus clouds, high up and far away, reflected the sun that had not yet risen above the horizon.

Jonatha saw the car with its open door first, Alix second. With her sport towel around her neck, she jogged easily over. Her hair was pulled back off her wide forehead, a plain rubber band binding it into a ponytail. Alix's eyes ate up every inch of Jonatha in her Spandex running shorts and sleeveless top.

Jonatha cocked her head. "I didn't see you on the trail. Did you finish your run already?"

"I passed on the exercise this morning." Alix gestured with her head. "Get in."

"Uh-uh. I've got to shower, change, and get to work."

"You can shower at my place." Alix fired the ignition. "I'll soap you down."

"I don't think that's a good idea."

"Why not?" Alix reached out, stroked Jonatha's flat belly. "You know you want to."

Jonatha stepped back, and Alix gave her a quizzical look.

"What is it? What's the matter?"

Jonatha shook her head.

Alix's mouth turned down. "Damnit, Jonatha, are you telling me I was wrong about what happened at the St. Giles's Club? *You* seduced *me*."

"At first," Jonatha said.

"What, now this is my fault?" Alix switched off the ignition, got out of the car. "I know what I felt, Jonatha. More important, I know what *you* felt." Her voice was by turns forceful and pleading. She took a step toward Jonatha, ringed her with her arms. "The body doesn't lie."

As her pelvis began to grind against Jonatha's, Jonatha unwound her arms and again stepped back.

"You're not the same woman I made love to," Alix said with a hint of confusion in her voice. "What's happened to you?"

"What happened at St. Giles's was a mistake."

"How can you say that?"

When Jonatha made no reply, Alix said softly, almost desperately, "How can you treat me this way?"

"Listen to me, Alix, whatever you thought happened, whatever's in your head, doesn't exist."

"So what happened, then? Was it a dream?"

"Two bodies meeting, that's all."

"That's *not* all," Alix wailed. "It *wasn't* a dream. Jonatha, please." And then, in a different voice altogether. "You're so cold."

"Alix, I meant you no harm, but I'm late. I have to get going."

"Wait!" The note of desperation in Alix's voice had broadened, deepened, until that was all that was left. "I can help you."

"What?"

"I know what you're working on. The POTUS has been briefed and so have I. There's information that could be of use to you. I can provide it."

"You have nothing of use to me."

"Then I'll get it. I'll do whatever you want."

"Alix, don't demean yourself." Jonatha shook her head. "I know what you want, and I can't give it to you. I love someone else."

"You loved me," Alix said, "if only for that moment."

But there was no one to hear her; Jonatha had already vanished down the twisty path.

Romy squeezed off three shots, wounding one man, forcing three others to retreat. The wounded man returned fire, and Jack put a bullet in his chest.

He held tight to Legere and, with Romy following closely, kept up his descent. They could not afford to give ground. They had to reach the underground garage in order to escape what had turned into a death trap.

They were on the second floor—two levels to go, but three armed men stood in their way. Jack knew he needed to change the odds.

"Romy," he whispered, "keep a hold on Legere and whatever happens don't let him go."

"What are you going to do?"

Without another word, Jack turned and vaulted over the railing. The instant he saw Legere's men, he opened fire. He had a quick flash of one man spinning backward, blood spurting, before he landed, knees flexed to absorb the bulk of the impact, on the floor at the bottom of the stairwell. He was on the basement level; the two gunmen still functioning were now above him.

One of them appeared and squeezed off several shots that, though missing him, sent chips of plaster at him, then ricocheted off the steel beams beneath. Crouched down, Jack got off a shot, the gunman ducking away. He was wondering why they did not continue to fire when he heard gunshots coming from the second floor, and he thought, *Romy! Goddamn her!*

Racing up toward the ground floor, he saw the gunmen with their backs to him, firing up the stairwell. Setting himself, he squeezed off a shot, catching one of the gunmen in the back. His arms flew up and he staggered back, off the tread, plummeting down, directly at Jack.

Jack tried to sidestep the hurtling body, was only partially successful, and threw up his free arm to protect his face. The gunman struck him shoulder-first, slamming him into the stairwell wall. He bounced off and, hearing more shots fired, shoved the body off him just in time to see the remaining gunman racing up the stairs toward Pyotr Legere. Where was Romy? Mounting the stairs three at a time, his angle of view changed, and he saw her sprawled facedown across two steps.

His next shot caught the remaining gunman in the shoulder just as he reached Legere. Ignoring the wound, the gunman took hold of his boss and, spinning around, fired off two shots at Jack. Jack ducked down as the metal railings sparked around him.

Then he saw Romy moving. He shouted for her to lie still but either she didn't hear him or she didn't care. She lifted her gun hand, squeezed off a shot that struck the gunman in the stomach. He went down onto his knees, forcing Legere down with him. Jack aimed and fired, but he was out of ammo. The gunman leaned to one side, panting, trying to stem the gush of blood even as he brought his weapon to bear and pumped three bullets into Romy.

She was still spasming when Jack, running full tilt, vaulted over her and kicked the man in the head. His torso arched back, his head struck the edge of the tread two steps above him, staving in his skull.

Legere took advantage of the chaos to scramble upward, but Jack lunged out, caught him from behind, and hauled him back down the stairs. He glanced sadly at Romy. There was no point in checking; she was clearly dead.

Stooping, he closed her eyes, then rooted in her handbag for the keys to her car. He snatched up one of the gunmen's Glocks, then, as quickly as he could, he dragged Legere back down to the basement, entering the underground garage with a great deal of caution.

No one was about.

Pressing the unlock button on Romy's remote caused headlights to flash on a dove-gray Audi sedan eight ranks away. They crossed the concrete floor, Jack sometimes having to half carry the recalcitrant Legere.

They reached the car without incident. Jack hauled open the driver's side door, shoved Legere across the center console into the passenger's seat, then got in himself, slammed the door shut. The Audi's powerful engine sprang to life immediately, and Jack backed out of the parking spot, following the signs for the exit.

The car gained speed as he drove up the ramp, past the manned toll booth, and roared toward rain-gray daylight. He was halfway out onto the street when men on both sides of the door opened fire with SIG-Sauers affixed with noise suppressors; Switzerland was not a place to be firing off guns in public.

Jack stepped down hard on the accelerator. The bullets slammed into both sides of the Audi. Safety glass spiderwebbed, then cracked through. Jack, the car's tires squealing in protest, made a hard right onto the street, accelerating so fast he went through a light beginning to turn red.

Rain pummeled the windshield, streamed in through the shattered windows. Jack made an immediate left, hurtled down two blocks, then pulled a hard right. Glancing up to see if more of Legere's men had mounted a pursuit, he noticed droplets of blood spattered over the right side of the rearview mirror.

"Legere," he said, reaching out to his passenger. "Legere!"

But there was no hope of Pyotr Legere mumbling through his gag. A bullethole in the side of his head assured that he wouldn't be answering anyone's questions. Jack's one hope of exoneration had just gone up in a puff of smoke.

PART FOUR

BLOWBACK

EIGHTEEN

"Just before dawn is the best time." Annika stood beside a stall selling antique lamps, along with knockoffs for the tourists that looked like the classic illustrations of Aladdin's lamp. "Iraj barely sleeps, and never before four."

"What keeps him occupied?" Rolan asked.

"A restless mind."

"Someone once said that those who can't sleep walk on the bones of their victims."

"In Iraj's case that very well might be true," Annika said. "He'd enjoy walking on the bones of those he's slaughtered."

"In that case," Rolan said in his curious inflectionless voice, "I'll bring him something to enjoy."

Annika left him standing there, staring past the copper and brass pots, past the colorful awnings, the bearded men, the covered women, looking at something invisible, possibly even to himself.

She made her way back to the Syrian's house. Well-guarded, as fortified as a castle keep, the home was nevertheless vulnerable to someone like her, who had sniffed out every nook and cranny, for all castles could be breached by knowledgeable people given proper tools.

But when she arrived it was to a whirlwind of preparation.

"Where have you been?" Iraj said. "Never mind, pack your things."

"What, why?"

"I've arranged a midnight flight to Zurich."

"Zurich?" Annika's heart beat a little faster. Romy had texted her that Jack was in Zurich. "What for?"

The Syrian looked up at her, his eyes alight with fury. "Pyotr Legere is dead."

Fuck me, she thought.

"And once we get to Zurich?" she said. "What then?"

"I discovered a certain art gallery in Zurich had become the middleman in our highly lucrative business of trading secrets hidden in Pyotr's book shipments," Iraj said, "as his father had done using the paintings he sold. I tried to find out more about this gallery, but your grandfather stopped me."

Iraj watched her carefully, his paranoia clearly spread across his face. "You did not know this?"

"No."

"Your grandfather didn't tell you?"

Annika tossed her head. "What did I just say?"

He held out one hand, palm up. "There are things you say." Then held out the other hand, making a scale, weighing the meaning of his words. "And things you mean."

"Who are you, all of a sudden? The Dalai Lama?"

Iraj gave a barking laugh, much like a deranged seal, then shrugged. "Why did Dyadya insert the gallery into the pipeline? I think I know."

She looked at him with a fair amount of curiosity.

"The gallery," Iraj said, "is where I think Legere stashed the key to Gourdjiev's legacy."

———

Jack ditched the Audi—and its dead passenger—as soon as he was far enough away from ground zero. The moment he had run the red light, he had put the car on the police CCTV. The Swiss police were überstrict as well as übereffcient, and the last thing he needed was to come to their attention.

He had no blood on him, which was a blessing of sorts, but the filthy weather made roaming the streets a difficult and thoroughly unpleasant proposition. Ducking under the awning of a shoe store, he drew out the Samsung Nona had given him and went through the short list of numbers of people who would help him that she had programmed in. Not surprisingly, there was no one anywhere near Zurich, so he punched in her speed dial number. She didn't answer. Instead, he got her voice mail, but he was reluctant to leave a message.

He thought a moment while the rain came down and people hurried by, hunchbacked as beetles, beneath a bobbing sea of black umbrellas. At last, he made up his mind and, punching in a number from memory, waited while the line connected.

"Who the hell is this?" the voice said after the fourth ring.

"Caro," he said softly, "it's Jack."

"Jesus, Jack!" There was an audible inhalation of breath. "Where the hell are you?"

"I need your help."

"You're damn right you do. You're in the center of a cluster-fuck of monumental proportions, man." Then she laughed, not unkindly. "Whatever you need, okay?"

"Thanks, Caro." The relief he felt carried over to his voice. "I'm in Zurich."

"And up to your ass in alligators, I'm guessing."

"That's about the size of it."

"Okay, sit tight. I'll be back in two or three."

"Caro—"

But she had already disconnected. Jack shook his head, but at the same time he smiled to himself. After what they had been through, he trusted Caro with his life. Good thing, because his life was exactly what she had in her hands now.

An approaching police siren caused him to turn his back to the street. Ostensibly checking out the footware on display, he watched the reflection of the police car zoom by, blue lights flashing. Without realizing it, he had been holding his breath; he let it out now in a deep sigh. He had to be extra careful now. Everywhere he went the local authorities were after him; the situation was only going to get worse now that Pyotr Legere was dead.

His mobile buzzed and he answered it immediately.

"Got someone," Caro said. She gave him a name and an address that, as he could tell from his mental picture of the city, was only a few blocks away.

"Thanks, Caro. I owe you."

"Don't be an idiot, and, listen, call if you need anything else. I'm more than happy to help. I mean it."

"I know you do."

He shivered a little, wet despite the awning. Pocketing his mobile, he moved off at a brisk pace, matching his stride to the people around him. Once, he passed a cop. The cop was talking to a man whose face Jack couldn't see. Jack sensed something false about their stances, the very brief snatch of conversation he overheard, but who could really tell? He hurried on, eager to get space between him and the two men.

The address Caro had given him was an art gallery. Shaking the rain droplets out of his hair, he entered the space, which was bright, neat, and coolly ultramodern, with spotlit artwork on the whitewashed walls: paintings of colored splatters, attenuated figures with grotesque faces, and an incredibly large canvas by Kehinde Wiley of a woman luxuriating in a bed of flowers that curled around her like a family of Arabian serpents. An elegant matchstick-thin woman and her elegant gray-haired escort were moving somnolently from painting to painting, occasionally whispering to each other.

A beautiful raven-haired young woman in a short, skintight black dress that showed off the tops of her breasts and her long, powerful legs appeared from the back of the gallery, smiling warmly at him.

"I'm Noemie," she said. "May I help you?"

"Just looking around," Jack said.

Noemie nodded. "Take your time, but if there's an artist you're particularly looking for, ask. Not everything is on display."

Jack thanked her, watched her walk away before he turned to the pieces, moving slowly, his eyes on the paint splashes, but his mind far away. It seemed to him that from the moment Dennis Paull had summoned him to his house in the middle of the night he had been falling down a well of unknown depth. The farther he fell, the darker his surroundings became. Mysteries multiplied like images in opposing mirrors, and he felt no closer to solving any of them.

And yet, he had been given clues: Leroy Connaston's involvement with the Syrian, Pyotr Legere's odd parentage. Romy's perplexing revelation that Annika had been monitoring his progress ever since he fled Washington. How had she done it? How could she have known where he was going?

Unless . . .

Jack put his head in his hands. Unless she was behind everything. Annika had aligned herself with the Syrian, as, apparently, had her grandfather. Jack thought back to his time with Dyadya Gourdjiev, but nothing came to mind that might make sense of that partnership. In fact, just the opposite. It seemed inconceivable to him that either of them would have anything to do with the terrorist.

If he was right, then something else was in play, something he had not yet seen. All at once, he recalled the conversation he'd had with Gourdjiev in the Moscow hospital where the old man had been taken following his heart attack.

"*Jack, do you trust me?*"

"*I think the question is, Do you trust me?*"

Dyadya Gourdjiev had smiled. "*You wouldn't be here now if I didn't. Now, come, answer me.*"

"*Trust. That depends on what you mean,*" Jack had said truthfully. "*You've lied to me in the past.*"

"*Did things turn out badly?*"

"*No.*"

"*And it's always turned out for the best, no?*"

"*That doesn't stop me from feeling used.*"

The old man had taken a moment to digest this. "*Do you trust me to do no harm?*"

"*It depends on your point of view. I'm never certain whose side you're on.*"

"*Do you trust me to protect Annika, whatever the cost?*"

Jack's alarm had escalated exponentially. "*Protect her from whom?*"

He had never gotten an answer, but what if Gourdjiev meant the Syrian?

"*You love my granddaughter, yes?*" the old man had asked, almost plaintively.

Jack had never heard him sound like that, vulnerable.

"*Yes,*" he had said.

"*Because she loves you. This is my beacon in the dark, the only thing I pay attention to now. This is the depth of my trust in you, Jack. Words—words mean nothing, an actor's lines. I want you to remember that. No matter what may occur, you must remember that you love each other, that that love will never change, that it is your true strength, your only salvation.*"

Gourdjiev had looked deep into Jack's eyes. "*You don't understand this now, but I have faith that one day you will.*"

Now, standing in the Zurich art gallery, Jack wondered if that day had come. "*I can't go with you, Jack,*" Annika had said, before leaving him. *Words mean nothing, an actor's lines.* Had Annika been acting, had her words meant nothing? Did she, indeed, still love him? But how could she, betraying him time and time again.

This is what Annika did to him: his feelings for her muddied the waters, making his usually agile mind lose its way. In this sense, she was like a poison he had ingested and couldn't get out of his system. It kept recirculating in his brain, blurring the edges of right and wrong, good and evil, the means and the end.

He turned away from the headache-inducing artwork and made his way to the rear of the gallery, where Noemie sat behind a sleek black marble desk, listening to someone on her mobile phone. Her head rose at his approach. She said something indistinguishable into the mobile and cut the connection.

"Have you found something?"

"I have," Jack said. "I'm looking for you."

Alix was in her office just after 9:30, late for her, but the POTUS hadn't asked for her, thank God. There were six calls she had to return, but when, forty minutes later, she had put those to bed, she was, for the moment, at least, free.

Jonatha had been on her mind ever since Jonatha had parted from her in Rock Creek Park. Alix's cheeks were still burning with the humiliation of that shocking encounter. The fact that she had been willing to prostitute herself, to trade intel she clearly did not have for a return of Jonatha's affection was almost too pathetic to bear.

Without another thought, she put her head down on her desk and wept hot, bitter tears. Her phone rang; she ignored it. Finally, it stopped ringing and, a moment later, when she picked her head up, she saw her voicemail light was blinking. She snatched up the phone, dialed in, hoping against hope that it was Jonatha who had left the message. It wasn't. She put down the phone, no longer interested in who had called or what they wanted from her.

Everyone wanted something from her; everyone except Jonatha.

As she dried her eyes an idea came to her. She knew it was a terrible thing to do, but wasn't what Jonatha had done to her terrible? An eye for an eye. That was all that was left her.

For the next three hours, she worked diligently without so much as a coffee break, and when she was done, she printed out her findings, stuffed them in her briefcase, grabbed her coat, and left the office, on her way to Langley.

"How do you know Ripley?" Noemie asked.

Jack shook his head. "Who?"

Noemie looked alarmed. She had taken him into the back room, a large open space with monstrous wooden racks between which the artwork was stored. In the rear were massive doors. Now Jack understood how the Kehinde Wiley had entered the gallery. Noemie, who had been standing beside one of these racks, slipped a slim hand into a niche. When she withdrew it, she aimed a small, silver-plated .25 caliber pistol at his head.

"You don't know Ripley. Who the hell are you?"

The moment Jack McClure walked past him on Heinrichstrasse, Redbird turned away from the cop Gensler had given him. Their desultory conversation had rapidly become intolerable. With the cop at his heels Redbird followed McClure, careful to keep at least four or five pedestrians between them. With the kind of irony that only happened in his line of field work, McClure's interference had proved the death of Pyotr Legere, leaving Redbird a clear field to concentrate on McClure. It seemed curious to him that death followed in McClure's wake just as it did his own.

It occurred to Redbird that when he killed McClure it might be like killing himself, a notion not unknown to him. It was like living in a hall of mirrors, where reflections took on the solidity and power of their real-life counterparts.

Several blocks later, he watched McClure enter an art gallery. Moving a little to change his angle only brought slight streaks across the large plate-glass window to the right of the door. In any event, he could see nothing beyond the large canvas that dominated the window. Redbird couldn't decide whether the painting was offensive or incomprehensible, two mutually exclusive descriptions that existed only in the world of contemporary art. *Give me Caravaggio's* The Entombment of Christ *over this slop,* he thought.

He waited for McClure to come out. After ten minutes, his senses began to tingle. At once, he turned to his cop. "Go get your vehicle," he said.

"Listen to me, Noemie, Caro gave me your name and address," Jack said as calmly as he was able. "Caroline Simpson." He used the surname of Helene Simpson, the alias Caro had been using last year, knowing she wouldn't be using Carson, her real family name.

The concern leached off Noemie's face, leaving it clear again. "Her hacker moniker is Ripley." She put the pistol away. "You didn't know?"

"She never told me. When we were together I knew her only as Caro."

Noemie's eyes narrowed. "You mean you've actually *met* Ripley?"

Jack nodded. "I helped her out of some trouble."

Noemie's eyes narrowed further and she took a step toward Jack. "When was this?"

"About a year ago. We were in Washington, D.C."

"Well, she isn't there now."

"No? Where did she go?"

Noemie shrugged. "I don't know and I don't want to know. It's too dangerous."

So Caro was still under threat from the Syrian. That she hadn't mentioned it when they spoke was typical of her, Jack thought. She kept everything inside, especially her fears. Her terror at appearing vulnerable was always palpable.

"The reason I'm here," he said now, "is there's been an incident nearby, and I need a way to get out of Zurich as quickly and invisibly as possible."

"Where will you be going?"

"I don't know," Jack said. "I haven't had time to consider a destination. Somewhere, anywhere. What's easiest for you to effect?"

"It's not a question of what's easiest." In her skyscraper-heeled Christian Louboutin pumps, Noemie crossed to a long, thick wooden framing table, on one end of which was a tray with three bottles of liquor, a frosted ice bucket, and several fresh lemons, along with a paring knife, and a selection of cut-crystal bar glasses. "We have vodka, scotch, and tequila. What can I get you?"

"Nothing, thanks."

She turned, putting her back against the table. "I see you *are* in a hurry." She nodded decisively. "All right, then."

Picking up an iPad, she brought up a map of Switzerland on Google Earth while he came over to stand beside her.

"Here's where we are." She pointed to Zürich. "And, here—" her fingertips moved the map east, moving ever closer to the Alps that lay to the west of Geneva "—here is Méribel, a rich man's hideaway, filled with luxe ski chalets."

Thinking he had caught her drift, Jack said, "You have clients who spend winters there."

"I do," Noemie said, "and as I think you have guessed I have access to a number of chalets that are used infrequently, if at all. But that's not the only reason you're going there."

Jack regarded her inquisitively.

"Méribel is where my most special client now lives full time."

"You're sending me to his chalet."

"Ah, if only it were that simple." An enigmatic smile wreathed Noemi's face. "No, you'll be using the chalet of a couple who are in Ibiza at the moment. But you *will* be within walking distance of Giles Legere's home."

NINETEEN

Alix Ross sat in her car, stewing in her own whirl of thoughts. If only, she thought, the world was black and white, if only it wasn't filled with shadows all too eager to lead you down the wrong path. But the world she chose to live in was all shadows, some deeper and darker, some mysterious and toxic. The trick was figuring out which ones could help you and which ones would signal your demise.

She turned off the ignition and sat staring out the windshield at the opaque blandness of CIA headquarters. Nothing in its skin would ever lead you to believe what went on inside, which was precisely the point. A house built on lies was never what it seemed; on the other hand, it could appear to be all things to all people.

Gathering her courage, she stepped out, went into the echoing lobby, with its immense CIA emblem embedded in the center of the floor.

"Alix Ross to see Director Krofft," she announced.

The receptionist dialed an extension, spoke softly into the microphone of her headset. Then she looked at Alix. "The director is in a meeting. Is he expecting you?"

"Just tell him the POTUS's press secretary has something for him."

The receptionist whispered through the headset again. "Please have a seat, Ms. Ross. The director will be with you shortly."

"Shortly" turned out to be an hour, by which point, Alix supposed, Krofft had ground his superior position into her face. Yes, she was little people. Let's get on with it.

She stood before a computer camera to have her photo taken, then was issued a laminated plastic badge, which she held up for the various security guards stationed at each stage of her ascent to the director's office. She was placed in an outer office for another fifteen minutes. *Like seeing my doctor*, she thought wryly. But Jonatha had already humiliated her beyond her limit. There wasn't anything this man could do to her to make her feel worse about herself than she already did.

But when she was ushered into his office, Krofft rose from behind his desk and, smiling broadly, strode across the carpet, hand outstretched.

"Ms. Ross—"

"Alix. Please."

"All right. Alix, it's a pleasure to see you. To what do I owe this visit?"

"Atlas," she said.

Krofft's smile faded and his eyes grew hooded. "Shall we make ourselves comfortable?"

He directed her to a sofa on which they both sat.

"Now," he said. "What is this about Atlas?"

Alix, her briefcase on her thighs, dug out the papers she had prepared. Without a word, she handed them over.

Krofft looked hard at her before glancing down at the top sheet. Then, more and more engrossed, he read the material through to the end.

Finally, he looked up at her. "Where did you get this?"

Her smile was both thin and sly. "The POTUS has any number

of files he never bothers to look at. They're updated all the time, but—" she shrugged "—he's an extraordinarily busy man." Her smile broadened. "You know how that is, Director."

Krofft returned her smile. It was warm and inviting. He tapped the document. "You've done your country a great service, Alix."

"Thank you, sir."

"Robby. Please."

A laugh bubbled up from her throat, and all the humiliation she had endured today circled the drain and vanished. She nodded, her cheeks reddening.

He cocked his head, clearly considering a decision. "You seem to have a natural nose for ferreting out secrets. Tell me, are you happy in your job?"

"Of course, sir."

"Robby."

"Of course, Robby, but—"

"But what?" he pressed.

Her sly smile was back. "Opportunities are where you find them, don't you agree?"

"I most certainly do." He checked his watch. "I'm late for a meeting and, to tell you the truth, I'm up to my ass in meetings today."

She laughed again, and he looked pleased.

"But I have a proposition to make you. Would dinner tonight suit you?"

"Tonight? I don't know what to say."

"Of course you do." Krofft rose, and she with him. The interview was almost over. "My car will pick you up at eight." He held out a hand and she took it. "In the meantime—" he rattled the papers "—this is just between us, yes?"

"Absolutely."

When she had left, Krofft rose, recrossed the room, and, with a grim face, fed the document into a shredder.

"Giles Legere," Jack said. "You expect me to believe Giles Legere is your client."

Noemie shrugged. "Why not?"

"Let me count the ways." Jack ticked them off on his fingers. "The world believes Giles Legere is dead. I have been following his son, Pyotr, from Bangkok to here in Zurich. Pyotr's people almost killed me not an hour ago. They killed a woman named Romy Kirsch. I tried to escape with Pyotr, but he was shot to death, presumably by his own men. I call my friend Caro and she sends me to perhaps the only person in the entire city who knows Giles Legere is alive." He shook his head. "These are coincidences that defy logic."

"Annika said you'd say that," a male voice replied. "She must know you as well as you know yourself."

Jack turned and immediately recognized the tall slim man.

"Radomil," he said.

The last time Jack had seen Radomil Batchuk, Annika's half-brother, he had mysteriously helped Jack escape from the Syrian's villa, just outside Rome. That was a year ago. A lot had changed since then; but then again, Jack realized, some things would never change.

Noemie was smiling. "Now do you see it?"

"The circle," Jack said.

She nodded. "Yes."

He looked from her to Radomil. "You all belong to Gourdjiev."

"To Annika now," Radomil said.

"But Annika is in league with the Syrian."

"Because Dyadya was." Noemie was watching him with undisguised curiosity, as if he were a new species whose responses to stimuli were unpredictable.

This was the question Jack had been asking himself—one without a suitable answer. "All of you," he said now. "Even Ripley."

"Even Ripley," Noemie nodded again.

"Then how—?"

"A means to an end."

Jack took a deep breath. "And if the means and the end are the same?"

"Then," Radomil said, "we're all damned."

Jack turned to him. "That night at the Syrian's villa in Rome, when I ran into you outside—you were prepared to keep the dogs at bay, you knew the way out. Why did you save me?"

Radomil jammed his hands into the pockets of his trousers. "I was ordered to save you."

"By whom?"

The smile had never left Noemie's face, as if this new species in front of her was an endless source of surprise and delight. "By this time," she said, "you shouldn't have to ask."

Krofft was behind her desk when Jonatha returned to her office. He was stretched out with his feet up on her desktop. When she stepped in, he glanced up from a sheet of paper he had been scrutinizing.

"Don't be shy. Come on in." His voice was uncharacteristically gentle.

Following a small hesitation, Jonatha dragged a chair over to the space in front of her desk and sat down.

He spun the sheet across the table to her.

Jonatha picked it up. It was Lale's arrest sheet with which Rogers had threatened her. Her heart seeming to beat in her throat, Jonatha looked up at him. Curiously, he was smiling.

"Calm down," he said. "It's a fake."

"What?" She looked from him to the arrest report, back to him.

"D'you really think my people would've missed something like this?"

Jonatha swallowed. Relief and anger vied for the upper hand. "I wasn't thinking."

"Of course you weren't. You love Lale; your only thought was to protect her. Which is what Rogers was counting on. Emotions cloud judgement, Jonatha, you know that as well as I do."

"Damnit," she said bitterly, "emotion often is what I myself use against suspects."

"We all have a blind spot. Even you."

"Rogers—"

"I know you're going to want to take care of him yourself," Krofft said. "But trust me on this. I know how to deal with the fucker."

Caro, riding the Métro's 2 line, thought about Dyadya Gourdjiev. She had met him in Paris, where all runaway girls go when their bitter hearts are filled with fury. She had fled her life in D.C., fled her mother, a woman who had once been her father's mistress, who had never treated her like a daughter. Never held her, comforted her, provided solace in any form. *Would it have killed her,* Caro had often thought, *to have shown me a modicum of affection?* Caro's assumption was that she had never wanted to give birth, never wanted to be burdened with a child. But Henry Holt Carson, with his outsized ego, hadn't allowed her to abort her fetus, and with money and, perhaps now and again, his cock, had kept her in close orbit until his tastes led him elsewhere.

What kind of life would she have led were it not for Gourdjiev's intervention? She had run into Elady Zukhov in one of those louche Left Bank cafés that in those days was filled with smoke, laughter, and fuzzy beards and talk of anarchy that amounted to nothing but navel-gazing. Although, in hindsight, it was clear that Zukhov had run into her. The meeting had not been coincidental.

When Zukhov had sat down at her table, Caro had almost gotten up and walked away. Even in those days he was none too appealing to look at, but when he began to speak something changed. He offered her not only an income but a way of life that appealed to both her talents and her mind-set. It was only much later that she learned she had been working for Gourdjiev all along.

Caro got off the Métro at the Père Lachaise cemetery stop. Crossing the street, she entered the cemetery, known affectionately to Parisians as *la cité des morts*. Within its beautiful precincts, among serenely winding paths and thick, clattering foliage, lay the remains of so many of history's famous, from Chopin to Edith Piaf, Oscar Wilde to Seurat, Molière to Jim Morrison.

Here in the city of the dead Caro felt more alive than she did out on Paris's wide streets and leafy boulevards. She felt a kinship with the dead, and in Père Lachaise she could listen as they spoke to one another, their quavering voices lifting and falling on the breeze.

She sat on a bench across from an old pergola that was in the process of being rebuilt. Raw boards lay across sawhorses, temporary posts held up part of the roof, which would otherwise have collapsed. At one time, birds had nested under the eaves, but their eggs had hatched, the fledglings fed by their doting parents until the time came for them to take wing and fly away.

The sight of that nest, once filled with activity, now abandoned, caused tears to sting Caro's eyes. She'd had neither a mother nor a father; she had fled the nest before either of her parents had had a chance to eat her alive.

This last attempt on her life seemed to have acted as a final straw, pushing her into darkness. In this unfamiliar state, she saw her life reflected back at her, and didn't like what she saw. Who was she, always running, looking over her shoulder for knife-edged shadows bent on her destruction. Zukhov was as close as she would ever come to a father figure, but he was getting old; how much longer could she count on him?

She heard the flutter of wings and lifted her head, looking around for the bird. She saw it then, a male cardinal, bright body, inquisitive face, hiding in the shiny dark-green foliage of a boxwood. It seemed to be watching her. She stared at its obsidian eye, polished as a bead.

The cardinal seemed to want to communicate with her, or perhaps it already had. Because she was wrong; there was someone else who had treated her with respect and genuine affection. Jack.

Hauling out her mobile, she punched in the number nine. The speed dial did the rest, connecting via an eleven-digit number. The line rang for such a long time Caro was on the point of hanging up instead of leaving a message she knew would not be returned.

Then she heard the voice, familiar even though she hadn't heard it in some time.

"Yes?"

Caro felt a flutter in the back of her throat, her voice quavered like those of the dead who continued to converse all around her. "Can you talk?"

"Not really."

"Then I'll do the talking."

"As you wish, but there's not much time."

"I don't understand," she said.

"Speak."

"Annika," she said, "you have to stop these mind games with Jack. They're evil and they're dangerous. One day you'll go too far and it will mean the death of you."

Silence.

"Are you still there?"

"Barely," Annika said in her ear.

Her voice was sharp, metallic. Caro knew Annika must be annoyed at this breach of protocol. She didn't care.

"Unlike me, you have a chance for happiness," Caro said, her voice growing desperate because she wanted—needed—Jack to be safe. He never would be if he and Annika were at odds. "It's so rare—so rare. You have to take it."

"It's too late."

"Why do you say that? You know it's not true."

"You have no conception of evil."

Caro ignored her. "No matter the cost, Annika. Do you hear me?"

"You're shouting."

Caro rose off the bench. She could no longer see the birds' nest. "I need you to understand me clearly. If you destroy what you've built, you'll never forgive—"

She stopped abruptly, sensing a subtle change on the line. "Annika? Annika!"

The air around her was more alive than the connection. The call was lost, the link severed from the other end. Reluctantly, she put her mobile away. *Would nothing in the world work out?* she wondered. She broke down, then, weeping in earnest, while the dead, oblivious, continued to chatter away about nothing and everything.

When Annika saw Rolan step out into the crowded Fez street in front of their car, she heard Iraj curse as he slammed on the brakes.

"He murders one of my men and now he comes back?" Namazi said. "He must really be insane." He threw the car into neutral and began to open his door. "I'll fucking kill him."

Annika put a hand on his arm. "How many times do I have to tell you that he was defending me?"

"I have only your word for—"

"If my word isn't enough for you," Annika said with steely conviction, "then we're done, right here, right now." When he continued to glare at her, she added, "You decide, Iraj, once and for all. I am fucking exhausted by your suspicions, your innuendos. I have more discipline, more backbone, than three-quarters of your men. But now you force me to ask myself what I'm doing here with you."

"Doing your duty. Following your grandfather's wishes."

"My grandfather is dead. Every day that goes by he's more dead. Do you understand what I mean, Iraj? I'm not a disillusioned Islamic youth. I'm not blindly following orders—either yours or his. Either you trust me or you don't. This is my line in the sand."

Iraj turned, staring through the windshield.

"We may need Rolan," she said.

"Really? What for?"

Annika looked into Iraj's eyes. "He's a killing machine. We're going to Zurich to kill, let's not pretend otherwise."

"He's unpredictable."

"Not with me."

"I don't like this."

"You don't have to like it, you just have to accept it." She smiled coolly. "Let me handle him."

She was out of the car before the Syrian had a chance to continue the argument.

"What are you doing?" she said as she approached Rolan.

"I'd ask you the same question. I was supposed to . . ." He put a hand to his temple, rubbing the skin so hard it turned red.

"What is it?" Annika said. "What's the matter?"

"Hurts," Rolan said. "I've been having bouts of . . . pain . . . ever since your shitbag lover pulled me out of the clinic."

"Iraj isn't my lover."

"Please."

"He's my business partner."

"What the fuck kind of business are you in all of a sudden?" The patch on Rolan's right temple was beet red. His eyes were slitted with pain.

"It's not all of a sudden," she said. "And you're better off not knowing."

"I don't know about that." Rolan's eyes were slowly clearing. He seemed to be breathing better, as well. "But then these days I don't know about anything, do I? I've been in prison for seven years."

Annika stared mutely up into his face. There was no point in answering.

"I missed my chance to snuff him," Rolan said. "Where are you and the shitbag going?"

The cacophony of bleating horns, as the traffic backed up farther and farther, was on the verge of becoming overwhelming.

"Zurich."

"You're in such a rush it must be important," Rolan said. "I'm coming with you."

"He's peering over my shoulder," Namazi said.

Annika, sitting next to him on the plane, said, "He's two rows behind us and he's asleep."

The Syrian twisted in his seat, rising up over other people's heads so he could see Rolan. "Well, he looks asleep," he said.

"Trust me, he is."

He turned to her. "We'll be landing soon." He placed a hand on her thigh. "Let's take advantage and get ourselves into one of the restrooms."

She shook her head. "It's too dangerous. If Rolan wakes up while we're gone he'll come looking for us."

Namazi's hand moved upward. "Let him. He won't find us."

"Once he's gone up and down the aisle, he'll know where we are and what we're doing."

"So?"

"Iraj, he's my husband."

"He stopped being your husband seven years ago when your grandfather admitted him to the Assumption of Mary Clinic."

Annika stared at him. Her face was a perfect mask, revealing nothing of the emotions that battered her like a fierce storm. For the first time, she understood why Dyadya had insisted on keeping alive the lie that Rolan had died during the Syrian's raid. He was playing God, giving her a clear field to seduce first Namazi and then Jack. The trouble came when she discovered that she had fallen in love with Jack—a sad, doomed love between two people on opposite sides of history. Once he saw her align herself with the Syrian—a man he was pledged to destroy—there was no chance of reconciliation. They were enemies, now and forever—beloved enemies. She did love him deeply, with a passion she had never felt for anyone before, not even Rolan. What cruel fate had set them at odds with each other and kept them that way? There were times when she was desperate to find a way out, a way for them to be together, but there was none, no matter what Caro said. She knew it, but she couldn't accept it.

"Annika." Namazi's voice, though lower, had become urgent. "Annika, come on. While we have the chance. The more we fight the more I burn for you."

She rose from her seat and, feeling him trailing after her, went to the unoccupied lavatory.

Iraj closed and locked the door as soon as he had followed her in. He pulled her to him, his hips molding against hers. She could feel his heat and his size prodding her like a great mailed fist.

She reared back over the tiny oval sink and struck him across the face as hard as she could. After a moment's shocked paralysis, he locked his hand around her throat. He snarled at her, his lips drawn back from his teeth.

"That's right," she said as his other hand slithered inside her blouse, "take me right here, rape me. That will surely cement our partnership."

"I could," he said. "You know I could."

"Says every man to every woman down to the dawn of time." Her disdain for him was unmistakable. "You do what you have to do, Iraj, and I'll do the same."

There was a moment then when they were locked together, the gulf between them, having been revealed, of unutterable depth.

"I never should have . . ." Namazi began.

"Never should have what?"

He stared at her with blank eyes, his mind seeming far away. Then, with a feral grunt, he let her go, turned his back on her, unlocked the door, and stepped out.

Annika relocked the door, even though the plane was already in its final descent toward Zurich Airport. For long moments, she stood absolutely still, listening to her heartbeat, the breath soughing in and out of her lungs.

Had Iraj changed or just her perception of him? What did it matter? Iraj had become his own most adoring fan; with every day that went by now, he spent more time burnishing his own legend than seeing to business—a business that was shrinking because Caro had presciently locked him out of his own trove of funds. Having become larger than life, Iraj had turned inward, becoming, in the process, a hollowed-out straw man, no longer fit to rule his vast regime.

She stood inches away from the shining precipice of the future—a future without Iraj, a future with her at the helm of his regime, restructuring it, turning it to her grandfather's design. Or was it her own? She could no longer tell. She felt it now as one feels a sudden rush of blood to the head. She was dizzy with the revelation that there was no limit to which she would not go.

When she lifted her hand to smooth back her hair, she saw someone in the mirror she did not fully recognize and for some reason felt a terrible fear grip her.

Bending over, she vomited up everything that had been inside her.

"What does she want from me?" Jack said. "There are only so many times she can betray me."

"Annika wants what her grandfather wanted," Noemie said.

Jack looked at her. "And what is that?"

"We don't know," Radomil said.

"You don't know." Jack looked at both of them in turn. "You're spending your life taking orders from an old man and now from his granddaughter, and you don't know why." He shook his head. "I don't get it."

"But you do," Radomil said. "You knew Gourdjiev."

"I spent time with him," Jack said. "That's hardly the same thing."

"He trusted you, Jack," Noemie said.

Jack gave her a bitter smile. "I keep hearing that. The trouble is, I don't believe it."

"If he didn't trust you, he never would have allowed you to get near Annika." Radomil drummed his fingers against the art racks. "Listen to me, four years ago, when you were in Moscow with the president, he sent Annika to fetch you, to bring you to him."

"Through trickery and lies."

"Would you have come of your own free will?"

"I was with the president; I had a job to do. Gourdjiev didn't figure into it."

"Well, in fact he did," Radomil said. "It was through his indirect help that the president was able to sign the security treaty with Russia. True or false?"

"Okay, but that seemed to be a by-product of Gourdjiev getting what he wanted."

"Does that matter?" Radomil asked.

"We're back to means and ends," Jack said, "and being damned—all of us whom he's involved in his schemes."

"All this talk is meaningless," Noemie said.

"If you were in my position," Jack said, "you wouldn't think so."

Radomil cocked his head. "Annika tells me you have an uncanny ability to see patterns before anyone else."

It's hardly uncanny, Jack thought. "She isn't wrong," he said, "but this puzzle is impenetrable. I have no idea what Dyadya Gourdjiev's endgame might be."

"Then let's ask Giles Legere," Radomil said.

Jack shook his head. "I'm going after Legere alone."

"Radomil will drive you," Noemie said firmly. "He'll also protect you, should circumstances warrant it."

"I don't need a nanny—"

"We have our orders," she interrupted. "Besides, you're a wanted man."

Alix stepped into the back of the car Director Krofft had sent for her at precisely eight o'clock. The sky looked ghostly gray, stark against the apartment buildings. Not a breath of air was stirring.

Alix, in a sea-green tube skirt, white blouse, open at the throat, soft leather ankle boots, sat back against the plush seat. She was aware that she was dressed more like Jonatha, but thought, Fuck it, why not?

"Where are we going?" she said to the back of the bulky driver's head. "Are we picking up the Director at work?"

"He had a late meeting."

Alix chuckled, thinking of Krofft—Robby—saying "*I'm up to my ass in meetings.*"

"He'll meet you at the Inn at Little Washington."

Out in the country, Alix thought, *at one of the best restaurants in the D.C. area. Just the director of the CIA and me.* She stared out the window as they crossed the Potomac on Route 66. Up ahead, the lights of Virginia sparked and glistened. *And he's going to offer me a job. Oh my God, not to be constantly hounded by hordes of reporters, all wanting scoops. Not to be held hostage to the POTUS's idiot whims.* She was elated. It amazed her how unknowable life was. One minute she had been cast into a black pit, the next she was scaling new heights, lifted up by Robby's helping hand.

She saw the driver's eyes regarding her in the rearview mirror and she smiled, almost preening. *I am the honored guest*, she thought. *Consort to the director of the CIA, even if only for this one glorious night.*

Feeling an eerie sense of power flooding through her, she leaned forward. "Would you turn on the radio, please? I'd like some music."

"Sure thing, Ms. Ross."

A moment later, Dusty Springfield was singing "Twenty-Four Hours from Tulsa," a terribly sad, terribly exciting song that had always been one of her favorites. She was so happy she sang along for a few bars. "I hate to do this to you/But I found somebody new . . ."

She hummed along for the rest of the song.

They crossed over into Virginia and, soon enough, were in the countryside, on the last lap to the Inn at Little Washington and her starry, starry night.

"Ms. Ross," the driver said, "I wonder if you wouldn't mind." His eyes engaged hers again in the mirror. "I haven't been out from behind the wheel in hours."

"Sure," she said. "Of course."

"Hey, thanks." He smiled. "My bladder is bursting."

He slowed, pulled over to the verge of the road, and stopped. It was darker here the night more true to its foundations, starlit.

Star-crossed, she thought with a smile.

The driver turned. "Ms. Ross?"

"Yes."

She was staring right at him when he pointed the silenced pistol at her and shot her point-blank between the eyes.

"*Hold on, Alix.*"

Was that Jonatha's voice?

But it didn't matter now. Alix's irises rolled up into her head. There was no breath left inside her.

Lana Del Rey was singing, "Born to Die."

TWENTY

Galina Yemchevya, now in her late forties, had lost none of the singular glamour or heady sensuality that had made men weak-kneed around her for the past thirty years. Time had worked one of its inscrutable miracles, so that, if anything, she was now even more transfixing than she had been in her youth.

Emerald-eyed Galina, skiing down the vertiginous, serpentine black diamond course outside Méribel, was as fit as any twenty-year-old athlete. With the limbs of a swimmer, the face of a goddess, and the heart of a lion, she was a modern-day griffin. As Arthur Conan Doyle wrote about one of his most indelible characters, Galina possessed "the face of the most beautiful of women and the mind of the most resolute of men."

She had been skiing all morning, starting in the eerie oyster darkness just before dawn, carrying a torch, like the ancient Olympians, the flame guiding her through the crystalline wind and powdery snow. Galina, who looked Aryan rather than Russian, was, in fact, a great admirer of Leni Riefenstahl. Galina owned a 35mm copy of Riefenstahl's *The Blue Light* and her infamous Nazi propaganda film, *Triumph of the Will*, a chronicle of the Nuremberg Rally, as well as several of her lesser-known works, including an extremely rare twelve-minute reel of her interpretation of *Tiefland*, Adolf Hitler's favorite opera, a project the director never completed.

So far as Galina was concerned, nothing except a strenuous bout of sex beat a run down the snow-covered mountains of Méribel just as the sun was rising, flooding the slopes with bloody light. But by ten o'clock, she was ensconced in her massive chalet, enjoying a multicourse breakfast prepared by their private chef. By her left hand was, as always, a pack of cigarettes, a chunky, masculine lighter, and a thick cut-glass ashtray.

Her newspapers were spread out for her, each page ironed the way English butlers in the nineteenth century used to do so their masters' hands wouldn't be dirtied by the ink.

She was scanning the papers, in her opinion, the way news was meant to be disseminated, and was halfway through her leisurely breakfast when Giles Legere made his appearance. Unlike her, he was still in his purple silk jacquard dressing gown. His sandy-gray hair was tousled and there were still night creases on one cheek where his head had met the pillow.

"For God's sake," Galina said without looking up, "the least you could do is make yourself presentable for breakfast." She reached for a cigarette and, with a practiced motion, lit it.

Legere shot her a poisonous glare before seating himself. "Just coffee," he snapped at the maid, who had brought over a copper chafing dish of scrambled eggs and sausage. Shuddering as she let smoke drift from her nostrils, he said, "It's barbaric the way you smoke at this ungodly hour."

"It's going on eleven," Galina said. She was absorbed with the story of the massacre in the downtown Zurich hotel, for which the police claimed they had no leads. "God has been awake and active for ages."

All Legere could produce was a noncommittal grunt. He stirred his coffee absently, though he had leavened it with neither milk nor sugar. Guiding the spoon was simply a way to keep himself occupied while he tried to outshine Galina. He scarcely knew why he tried; he'd never been successful before, and now, of course, it was impossible.

"Pyotr's dead," he said, because he could think of nothing else to say.

"Clearly." Galina stubbed out her cigarette, looked up at last. "You seem to have taken it well."

"Not as well as you, I daresay."

"Stop trying to sound like David Niven," she snapped. "It ill becomes you."

"You have no idea what becomes me," he said dully.

She stared at him for a moment. "Perhaps you're right," she said, returning to the unhelpful and, in her opinion, poorly written news story and then muttering something.

"What was that?" he said.

Her emerald eyes rose above the top of the paper. "I was just musing on why you would build a vertical ski chalet."

"We live in a vertical world. Méribel is a vertical town, this mountain is vertical."

"Who cares? You could have just as easily cut across the mountain as others did."

"If the house makes you uncomfortable," he said slowly, "why don't you leave?"

Their eyes locked for a moment, then went their separate ways. As it always seemed, nowadays. Of course, she wouldn't leave, and Giles knew why. She was hanging on for a piece of Gourdjiev's legacy. He shouldn't, in all fairness, blame her, though he did, with a vengeance.

Legere drank some coffee. "Things are bound to change now," he said after a time. "In that, at least, Pyotr was useful."

Galina turned a well-ironed page. "Say this for him, your son made an adequate duck blind."

"If he *was* my son."

"Well," Galina said conversationally, "now you'll never know."

Legere took his cup in his two hands, tipped some more coffee into his mouth, and swallowed. It tasted like bile, but, then, these days most things did.

"Doubtless," Legere said, "the Syrian will be coming now."

"Who can blame him? But he and Annika Dementieva won't be the only ones coming."

Legere's brows knit together. "What do you mean?"

"There are more layers to this than you can imagine."

"Explain, please."

Galina directed a smile at her newspaper.

Legere put down the cup with a clatter.

"Careful," Galina warned.

"You seem inexplicably unconcerned."

"Unconcerned? Hardly." Having reached the end, Galina folded the paper in two and set it aside. "On the contrary, I've been planning assiduously for this day."

Legere blinked heavily, like an owl in sunlight. Legere looked nothing like Pyotr, which added to his angst. He was big, his face aggressively mobile with its long, patrician nose and close-set eyes. Once heavily muscled, he had now turned to fat, especially around his middle. His body was still powerful, though not as much as it had been in his prime. Unlike Galina, time had been unkind to him—exceptionally so, by his lights. His body wasn't the problem, though; his mind was. He was in the early but unmistakable stages of Alzheimer's.

Ever since he had been diagnosed, Galina's contempt for him knew no bounds, but, he thought ruefully, perhaps she had always felt this way about him. Then why, he wondered, did she keep coming back to him after all her fucking around in high places? It was a mystery to him, like the many things around him that had become opaque, unrecognizable.

"What about Annika?" he said, struggling to keep his thoughts from squirming away from him.

"What about her?"

Galina's eyes seemed like miniature suns, burning his face. He wanted to look away, but he couldn't.

"She's as dangerous as . . ." He groped for the name he knew so well.

"The Syrian." Galina's voice felt like acid thrown in his face. "She's far more dangerous, Giles. You once knew that."

He looked away, ashamed despite his resolution not to allow her that victory.

"When the time comes," Galina said more conversationally, "Annika Dementieva will be dealt with, as well."

He believed her. He had to believe her, she was all he had left to anchor him to the shifting ground that each moment threatened to swallow him whole. There would come a time, he knew, when he would ask himself the question, *Who am I?*, and not know the answer. That moment terrified him far more than death.

"I can feel them coming," Giles said, because since the onset of the Alzheimer's he thought he could feel the advent of future events—of death, really—the way others felt the first raindrops before a storm. The future plucked at him with a plangent tone, causing long-buried emotions to swirl into his consciousness, roiling it like heavy weather.

"How soon?" Galina said, because she had learned to take note of his presentiments, using them to her own advantage.

"Soon. Very soon," was all he could manage, before his head lowered, chin resting on the bow of his chest, as he fell away into a deep sleep.

Radomil drove a large, late-model Audi sedan the color of oxblood. Jack, sitting beside him as they left Zurich and the rich, reflective light of the lake behind them, was sunk deep in thought. Radomil drove very fast, but also as expertly as a professional.

"I must have some Italian blood in me," Radomil said, but having failed to garner a smile from Jack, he lapsed back into silence.

In this desultory way, the miles sped by. They stopped to refuel and to grab a bite to eat, then pressed on. Neither of them was in any mood to linger.

"When Annika ordered you to save me that night at the Syrian's villa," Jack said at last, "what did she have in mind for me?"

"How d'you know she had anything in mind?" Radomil said. "She loves you."

"If you continue to treat me like a lovesick suitor, you can pull over and let me out."

"What, here, in the middle of nowhere?"

"At least here I can see where I am," Jack said, "and where I have to get to."

Radomil grunted. "You know, the thing of it is, even though she's my half-sister, I'm not of Gourdjiev's blood. I'm only part of this because she needs me."

Jack turned to him, and when he spoke his voice was sharper than he had intended. "Needs you for what, exactly?"

Radomil's eyes flicked to the rearview mirror before returning to the road ahead. "Ah, well, I suppose you could say I run interference for her."

"In other words, you're the djinn who lights the way."

Radomil's black brows knit together. "I beg your pardon?"

"There's a legend concerning an Arabian prince. He was young, this prince, and his father had been murdered—poisoned, I believe, an excruciating death—by his trusted vizier, who, it turned out, was in the pay of the family's enemies.

"Given the circumstances, the prince wasn't inclined to name a new vizier from within his father's court. Instead, against his advisors' wishes, he went outside the walls of the palace, into the worst part of the city. Hiding out there for three weeks, he learned the meaning of poverty, thirst, hunger, pain, and humiliation, while witnessing all manner of violence and mayhem.

"At the end of this instructive period, he chose the most violent and unrestrained of the villains he had encountered. Bringing this man back to the palace, he offered him an end to his own poverty, thirst, hunger, pain, and humiliation if he followed the prince's orders.

"The villain said, 'What makes you think you can trust me?'

" 'I am going to ask you to do what you like best, in perfect safety. Furthermore, I will reward you for it.'

" 'And why,' the villain said, 'did you choose me?'

" 'You are not blood of my blood,' the prince replied. 'You know no one inside the palace walls. Therefore my will becomes your will, pure and unbiased. And when you are finished, you will teach me both to defend myself and to kill those who wish me harm. I would not have you do it all yourself.'

"This pleased the villain no end, and he readily agreed. Within twenty-four hours, every advisor, courtier, and nobleman hanger-on inside the palace walls lay dead. That night, for the first time since he had come to power, the prince slept deeply and dream-lessly, guarded by the djinn who lighted the way for what would be his long and fruitful reign."

Radomil, who appeared impressed by this tale, pursed his lips. "I think you give me too much credit."

Jack stared out the window. "Like the villain in the story, your entire purpose is to bring the hammer down on enemy after enemy, after they make the mistake of giving you no credit at all."

Radomil shook his head. "At last I know why she loves you."

"While it's true that on occasion Annika can give the impression of loving someone," Jack said, "I seriously doubt she's capable of actually loving anyone. In that, as in many other ways, she's just like her grandfather."

"I have to disagree." Radomil's gaze flicked again to the rear-view mirror. "There's a very good reason why she can only show you how she feels in tiny segments."

"What's that?"

"Her husband," Radomil said, slowing for a moment.

Jack felt as if he were in a plane that, wing over wing, was going down in flames. For a moment, he felt weightless, then gravity slammed into him with the force of a pile driver, setting up a fierce pounding in his head.

"Annika is married?" he said in a voice he didn't recognize.

Radomil nodded. "Her husband almost died in a terrorist attack some years ago. His brain was damaged. He's been in a psychiatric facility ever since."

"She never told me."

"His incarceration is a secret," Radomil said. "Gourdjiev wanted it that way. I suppose Annika does, too."

"You know."

"Only because she needed me to bring something to him when she couldn't get to the facility."

"She's married," Jack murmured again, scarcely believing it. "She's lied to me again."

"About Rolan, she and her grandfather lied to pretty much everyone." Radomil shifted uneasily in his seat. "But right now we have a more immediate issue. I wasn't sure before, there are so many of them on the road, but a moment ago I got a second look at the license tag. The same silver BMW has been following us from the time we left Zurich."

As the cop's BMW was fueled by gas, Redbird was fueled by rage. This was unfamiliar territory for him, a man who made his living detached from all human emotion save lust. But for him there was no going back. His desire to kill Jack McClure consumed him like fire.

He did not like having the Swiss cop with him, liked even less that he himself wasn't driving, but he had been trapped by his subterfuge. A first. He'd wanted the cop to drop him at an auto rental office, but there had been no time. McClure, accompanied by another man, had exited the gallery minutes after the cop had pulled up in his BMW. When they got into the Audi, Redbird knew he'd have no chance to ditch the cop without also losing McClure. This he could not tolerate even though he was aware of the heightened risk posed by his not being alone. These Swiss cops, he thought, run totally by the book. No deviation was possible. Redbird was not foolish enough to offer the cop a bribe—leaving a loose end on a commission was simply not in his vocabulary.

But, hours later, he saw his opportunity when the Audi pulled into a gas station. The cop pulled in as well, steering well clear of the Audi. Redbird directed him to a remote corner of the lay-by and, as the cop rolled the BMW to a stop, reached over and snapped his neck like a dry twig. The cop's body arched up, his limbs twitching for a moment.

Redbird got out of the car, stretched his cramped muscles, then went around the front of the BMW, opened the driver's side door, and hauled the cop out. He wound one arm around him, as if providing support for an ill companion.

At the rear of the lay-by were three huge Dumpsters, shielded from sight by two concrete buildings. Hoisting the corpse onto his shoulder, he threw him over the lip of the Dumpster farthest away from the buildings. He spent the next couple of minutes transferring armloads of trash from the adjacent Dumpster until the cop was covered completely.

Then he slid behind the wheel, backed up, and, engine thrumming, followed the Audi as it nosed out into the rocketing traffic. When he had slipped fully into the traffic he called Gensler on his mobile.

"There's one more thing I need from you," he said.

"There's no reason to hurt her," Annika said.

Iraj, who had hold of Noemie by her hair, said, "There's reason and there's need."

Annika looked at him askance. "Not everything has to be accomplished with brute force."

"Brute force works." He jerked Noemie's head back, exposing the vulnerable length of her throat. "Always."

Annika tried another tack. "It's messy, Iraj. We're in a high-end art gallery in Zurich—in *Switzerland*, for God's sake, not Waziristan. Mayhem will likely be more dangerous to us than it will be to her."

The Syrian appeared to consider this for a moment. "I have a better idea." He tossed his head in Rolan's direction. "I'll let the zombie off his leash. Let him do the damage, our hands will be clean."

"Don't be stupid," Annika said, successfully hiding both her alarm and her outrage.

Blood filled Iraj's face. "You talk to me like that again—"

"What?" she said. "What will you do?"

He spat on the floor between her feet.

God, I hate him, she thought.

"Let me have a crack at her," she said in her sweetest voice, seeking to calm the waters she had foolishly roiled. "If she knows what happened to Pyotr and where Galina is, I'll get it out of her without the mess."

She did not look directly at Noemie, nor had she since they had entered the gallery, locking the door behind them.

"All right," he said at last.

He shoved Noemie into Annika's arms, then grasped Annika's shoulder. It was like being snatched at by a reptile. Annika could barely hold down the vomit. Instead, she smiled winningly at him. "You won't be sorry."

"I know I won't," he said, every word a naked threat.

"They're going to Méribel," Annika said, ten minutes later.

"She's playing you." Iraj shook his head. "Why the hell would they be going there?"

Annika produced an ironic smile. "Giles Legere is still alive. That's where he's living."

The Syrian smashed his fist against a wall, making a good-sized crater between two paintings.

"Your grandfather knew all along, didn't he?"

"Possibly."

Iraj advanced on her. "Don't give me that. He probably arranged the whole thing."

"I wouldn't put it past him."

He glared at her. "But you didn't know."

"Will it matter what I say?"

"Answer me," he grated.

"I'm as surprised as you are."

Iraj turned away. Annika wished she knew what he was thinking.

"We'd better get going," he said, turning on her.

Here was the moment she had been waiting for. "Let me go on ahead."

Iraj laughed. "Why would I do that?"

"Because Jack is here. You need him and I know where he is."

"Another one of your secrets." He shook his head. "How am I ever to fully trust you?"

"All right," she said. "You tell me all your secrets and I'll tell you mine." She waited, but not for long. "No? I thought not."

"I don't want you out of my sight. I'll go with you."

"You won't, he's too smart, he'll suss out you're there," she said with a certainty that stopped him cold. "I can deliver him, Iraj. Only me. I know how he thinks."

He stared at her.

"Plus, he trusts me."

"After what you've—"

"He loves me, Iraj. That's all that matters."

The Syrian glanced over at Rolan, who was leaning against a wall, staring at the newly made crater as if it were a piece of art that consumed him. He seemed oblivious to them both.

Shaking his head, Iraj looked back to Annika. "Why would you do that, deliver him to me?"

Annika, prepared for this, said, "A year ago, at your villa outside Rome, I made a decision. You think it was a difficult one, but it wasn't. I was never going to go with Jack; my place is here with you. That was my commitment to my grandfather while he was alive and it's my commitment today."

"Not even love will sway you?"

"His love for me? No."

"I meant your love for him."

"I don't feel love, Iraj. You know that better than anyone."

Now was the moment of truth, she knew. Either he'd acquiesce or he'd break with her, something he could ill afford to do. This was her power over him, the skill Dyadya Gourdjiev had taught her.

Something dark and unknown shifted behind his eyes. "Go ahead then," he said. "Bring him to me."

"Do you know who's driving the BMW?" Radomil asked.

"Not for certain," Jack said. "But I have a good idea. He's been trying to kill me since I arrived in Bangkok."

"Who is he?"

"Before I kill him," Jack said, "I'm going to find out."

Radomil shot him a quick glance. "It's going to come to that?"

"The people who framed me for my friend's death will go to any lengths to ensure I'm not cleared."

"What's their endgame?"

"Not *theirs, his*. There's a mole in the upper echelons of the U.S. government. If I'm fingered as the mole, his real identity is safe-guarded."

Radomil was keeping one eye on the following BMW. "You know who's running the mole?"

"I've been told it's the Syrian," Jack said. "I have no reason to doubt the intel, plus, since then, I've sorted the data in my head. I've come to the same conclusion."

Radomil shook his head. "I had no idea."

"But Annika must; she's his partner."

"I'd know if she did, believe me." Radomil looked increasingly concerned. "This is very bad news. If Namazi is running something without her knowledge, then Annika's lost control of him. That's the last thing she wants or needs."

"It was a grave mistake to partner with him in the first place."

"She had no choice."

"Now you're making excuses for her."

"Hey," Radomil said, "no one knows better than I do what a prickly bitch she can be, but that's just a facet; it's not all of her, not by a long shot."

"You and Noemie have to trust her." Jack stared into the side mirror, where the silver BMW could be intermittently observed. "I'm not in that position."

"You are if you want my help," Radomil said. "I'm going to exit the A3. I'm not going to be able to lose this cocksucker while we're on this straight and narrow."

"Stay where you are." Jack had spent no little time checking out the countryside, which was hilly but unforested. "I need a large swath of thick trees."

Radomil nodded. "You see that spire there, across the river to the right? That's Wettingen Abbey. In a few minutes, we'll be passing through the northern end of Neuenhof. A couple of miles beyond is an enormous forested area."

"Roads running through it?"

"Only a few paved ones," Radomil said. "But this Audi can handle any of the earthen paths there."

"Perfect," Jack said. "Get us there as quickly as you can."

Jonatha was lying on her bed, thinking about Lale, working to all hours on the paintings at the Corcoran, when her mobile rang. It was Marshall.

"I just heard about Alix Ross," he said. "The POTUS just about shit a brick."

Jonatha sat bolt upright. "What about Alix?"

"She's dead. Found shot in a field in rural Virginia."

"What the hell was she doing in rural Virginia?"

"One shot between the eyes," Marshall said.

Holy Mother of God, Jonatha thought. "A professional hit? How is that possible?"

"These days I've discovered that anything's possible." He paused. "Jonatha, are you all right?"

"Fine, yes. I'm fine." But she wasn't fine, not by a long shot. Why would Alix be murdered, shot to death by a hit man? Unless . . . Jonatha's chest constricted. She felt as if she couldn't breathe. Her heart hammered in the back of her throat. She thought of the last time she had spoken to Alix, that dreadful morning in Rock Creek Park.

"*I can help you*," Alix had said at the last. "*I know what you're working on. The POTUS has been briefed and so have I. There's information that could be of use to you. I can provide it.*"

"*You have nothing of use to me*," Jonatha had replied. It had been a complete dismissal. At the time, all she could think of was extricating herself from a liaison she had had no business entering into in the first place.

She had scarcely heard Alix say, "*Then I'll get it.*"

But now those four words came back to her with the impact of a locomotive. What if Alix *had* found something? But she hadn't come to Jonatha with it. Who would she have gone to? Not the POTUS, that's for certain. Then who?

All at once, Jonatha knew, and she began to break out into a cold sweat.

Quickly, she ended the call, then lapsed into a deep, contemplative silence. She lay, arms folded across her breasts, like an Egyptian mummy. She stared up at the ceiling, as she had done in her childhood bedroom, turning cracks into rivers and their tributaries, tracing them to the sea, as if she were about to weigh anchor, embark on an epic journey through an unexplored continent. She imagined herself aboard the ship, a captain supervising the lading of provisions, watching the crew scuttling up and down the masts, hanging from the spars as they checked the rigging. She felt the wind in her hair, smelled the bracing tang of the open sea or the wide river.

This was a game she had made up when she was little, taking

her away from the fixtures of the everyday world she hated and feared. Over the years it had become her singular pleasure of solace. But this evening she was reminded of why she was embarking on this trip, why she so desperately needed to get away. It wasn't working. She could see Alix standing in front of her car, alone and forlorn, her teary eyes begging for the love Jonatha didn't feel.

She thought of Roy, the white-haired Replicant, sitting on the rooftop in the Los Angeles of *Blade Runner*: "*. . . those moments will be lost in time, like tears in the rain.*"

No! It didn't have to be like that.

She swung out of bed and, crossing to her closet, slammed all the clothes she thought she'd need into a weekend suitcase. "I've been a bad, bad girl. Please forgive me," she scribbled on a piece of paper, which she left propped up on Lale's pillow. Moments later, she was taking the elevator down to the lobby of her building.

She walked in a square pattern, two blocks on each side, standard procedure to see if she were being followed. When she was reasonably certain she was in the clear, she called for a taxi, stood in the deepest shadows of an art deco doorway that looked like the entrance to the Bat Cave. Six minutes later, when her taxi drew up, she stepped across the sidewalk, trying her best to keep out of the streetlights' glow. The moment she ducked inside, she told the cabbie to take her to the north side of Dupont Circle.

The hour was late, the streets dark and eerily deserted. The monuments' glow, as it often did, seemed to define the city of power.

In due course, she found herself outside the St. Giles's Club. She went up the marble steps, used her key to open the immense door, and, stepping quickly inside, shut it, and the ills of the city, behind her.

The chandelier over the vestibule was turned down to its dimmest level. By its illumination, the wood wainscoting, the intricate marble floor, the pair of Louis XVI marquetry side chairs, the giant spray of lavender and roses in the oversized crystal vase all took on a certain verdigrised sheen, so that they appeared to have been transported intact from the nineteenth century.

Not surprisingly, no one was about. Without members milling, power brokers' conversations, and the clinking of champagne flutes the house felt hollow, like an ancient tree before its fall. As she mounted the curving polished staircase, she heard the deep, barrel-chested British voice. "The city must have done you some hurt, for you to arrive so late in the evening on little cats' feet."

Only Sir Edward Enfield-Somerset would call midnight "evening." As she raised her gaze, she couldn't help but smile. He wore a purple smoking jacket, cashmere slippers with his family crest embroidered across the toe box, and, of course, in one hand he held a cut-crystal snifter of Napoleon brandy, his nightcap of choice.

"You looked peaked. Have you had supper? I'll have Emmeline heat up some—"

"I'm not hungry."

"You must be tired," he said, waving her up, "but taking a few minutes to talk couldn't hurt, eh?"

At the top of the stairs, she followed him into his private library, which existed en suite with his bedroom and enormous bath.

"Choose your poison," he said crossing to the bar.

"Not tonight, thank you." She almost sighed out loud as she collapsed into one of the huge upholstered wing-backed chairs.

Sir Edward shot her a jaundiced look. "No food, no drink. I don't like this."

"A woman I knew was shot to death."

"You mean Alix Ross? I just heard. How well did you know her?" He waved his free hand. "No, no, never mind. The point is, surely that sort of thing doesn't often happen, even in your line of work."

"It *never* happens," Jonatha said bleakly.

"Well, it's happened now." He padded across the priceless antique Isfahan and sat in the wing chair facing her. "No use crying over it." They were so close their knees were almost touching.

"I'm not crying!" she fairly yelled.

"On the other hand, there's no shame in having feelings. Rum business, all right." He spent another moment settling himself. "There's more than death to it, isn't there?"

Jonatha nodded miserably. "This woman and I had sex—she fucked me, I fucked her . . ."

Sir Edward arched an eyebrow. "Were you ordered to do this as a function of your job?"

"No. I indulged in a selfish moment. I fucked up. I lost my head. I enjoyed it."

Sir Edward shrugged. "All that proves is you're human."

Jonatha put her head in her hands. "I don't know if Lale will forgive me."

"Do you love Lale?"

"I do."

"Does she love you?"

Jonatha nodded.

"That's all that matters," said Sir Edward.

"But what if it isn't? What if she won't forgive me?"

"Are you speaking of Lale now, or of yourself?" He took her hands in his. "You know, you have to begin this process by forgiving yourself."

A long silence ensued, punctuated by Jonatha's small, stifled sobs.

"So," Sir Edward said at length, "have you come here tonight only seeking solace?"

Jonatha shook her head, looked up into his kindly eyes.

"I pushed Alix away and because of that she was killed."

Sir Edward made a noise. "That's a mighty harsh judgement. Are you certain of it?"

"I'm not certain of anything anymore." She shook her head. "But it seems to me . . ."

"You're in a serious line of work, Jonatha. Always a rough patch to get through."

Jonatha's eyes seemed to flare in the lamplight. "This is more than a rough patch," she said. "I might not get out of it alive."

Now real concern darkened Sir Edward's face. "Jonatha, what in the name of St. Augustine is really going on?"

Jonatha looked at him bleakly. "I think I know who had her shot."

Sir Edward reared back. "Someone you know?"

She nodded. "The man I work for."

"We need a destination," Jack said, as they neared the exit that would take them to the Oberforst, the forest preserve. "We need to make it seem like we're meeting someone here."

"I have just the place," Radomil said.

Behind them, they heard the oncoming high-low siren of an ambulance. Radomil glanced in the rearview mirror, then moved to the right to get out of the speeding vehicle's way. The exit came up and he took it. The ambulance, moving to its right, followed them down the ramp. Radomil was about to pull over to the curb, when the ambulance struck them from behind so powerfully that Radomil was catapulted through the windshield in a welter of safety-glass shards. Jack slammed out of the Audi and grabbed Radomil, whose face was scratched and bleeding.

Three men armed with Lugers poured out of the ambulance. Behind them, the BMW came rocketing down from the A3 and screeched to a stop. One of the armed men aimed at Jack as he was trying to steady a staggering Radomil. Jack shot him and he went down. The other two men took cover behind the ambulance's open rear door.

As they began to fire, Jack dragged Radomil into the trees.

"Go left," Radomil said, wiping his face on the sleeve of his jacket, smearing blood over his cheeks, nose, and mouth. "Left again, and in three hundred yards, go right."

Jack could hear the men slashing through the undergrowth in their frantic pursuit. Then a commanding voice lifted over the noise, ordering the men back to a spread perimeter. The assassin he had encountered in Bangkok was mounting the pursuit alone, his men guarding the exits to what he hoped would be the killing field.

Following Radomil's directions, Jack led them on a final turn to the right, heading ever deeper into the Oberforst. Looming pines crowded either side of the track, the tips of their graceful branches overhanging the path, occasionally brushing against their legs. Though the sky was still mostly clear, what little sunlight penetrated was tinged a poison green. Black shadows lay everywhere, like felled soldiers on a long-abandoned battlefield.

Several hundred yards further on, Radomil called a halt. "We're very near now," he said.

They continued down the increasingly narrow track. The air was clear and fresh, the pine straw beneath their feet providing fragrance as their shoe soles crushed the needles underfoot.

"You think he's tracking us," Radomil said.

"I'm staking my life on it," Jack replied.

As Radomil took them around a bend in the path, Jack said, "Quick, exchange coats with me."

He slid on Radomil's bloody dun-colored raincoat, while Radomil donned his dark-blue trench.

"You think this will fool him?"

"He's never going to get a good look at either of us until it's too late," Jack said. "But still . . ." Reaching out, he transferred some of Radomil's fresh blood onto his own face, smearing it like war paint.

"Collar up," he said, as he pulled his up around his ears.

They continued on until Jack saw the low concrete structure half-covered over in vines and foliage, its long side covered with graffiti.

"What the hell is that?"

"*Der Bunker auf dem Baregg*," Radomil said with a thin smile. "Named after the Baregg, that mountain you see in the distance. I have no idea what it was once used for, but to me it looks like a reminder of the war that never came to Switzerland."

"When we get beyond that stand of pines, you go on ahead."

"What will you be doing?" Radomil asked.

"Circling around behind our pursuer. In the meantime, try to match your gait to mine."

Radomil produced a vulpine smile. "I will present to him your perfect doppelgänger."

———

After Sir Edward had tucked her into the high wooden four-poster like a father with his beloved child, Jonatha fell fast asleep for an hour or so. Just after dawn, she rose from a dream that seemed disturbingly real. As she had done in her dream, she took up her mobile from the night table at her right elbow, made a couple of calls, then punched in a number on speed dial.

When Ripley answered, she said, "I need you."

"Anything," Ripley replied.

"The mole issue just got wet."

"Pity."

"You don't know the half of it," Jonatha said, briefing her on the little she knew of Alix Ross's murder.

"Okay, it was a professional hit," Ripley said. "What makes you think Krofft ordered it?"

"Two things. First, Alix was desperate to keep the infidelity going. She offered to get intel on Atlas for me. Second, if you were her who would you take the Atlas intel to?"

"You."

"She didn't. Instead, she showed up at CIA headquarters this afternoon. She told the receptionist she had something to show Krofft."

"Well, that's a smoking gun."

"I need you to dig deeper."

"No kidding."

"Also, I need local help."

"You *are* local, Jonatha."

"For obvious reasons, I can't use my normal sources."

"Got it. Not to worry," Ripley said. "As it happens, I have just the answer."

———

Once, Redbird had tracked a quarry through frigid Siberian waste-land; another time, through marshy equatorial jungle so overhung with thorny South American vines and deadly serpents masquerad-ing as vines that every step was an adventure. As such, the Swiss Oberforst proved minimally invasive to his task, a benign labyrinth within which he was certain to find his quarry. His conviction was absolute. He would find his way in and out, but Jack McClure would not leave the Oberforst alive.

He had seen McClure pull the driver through the smashed windshield. The driver was in a light-colored raincoat, smeared now with his own blood, the easier for Redbird to track him. Mc-Clure, in his dark-blue coat, would still be easy enough to spot among the forest's greens and browns.

However, such was not the case. It took him far longer than he had expected before he caught a flash of dark blue, moving from right to left. Cutting through on the diagonal, he was able to slowly collapse the space between them. Even so, the woods were so thick, he never got more than a partial glimpse of his quarry, apart from one or two flashes of what looked like blood. That was all he needed, however, to continue stalking his prey.

At length, he could see up ahead a whitish, brutalist structure covered in equal measure by foliage, vines, and graffiti. As he drew closer, the structure resolved itself into what looked like some kind of bunker, though what it was doing in the middle of the forest was anyone's guess. In any event, McClure was heading right for it, as if he was late for a rendezvous.

Redbird kept on, doggedly following McClure. And then, all at once, he spied the flash of McClure ducking and disappearing around the far side of the bunker. Not wanting to lose him, he pushed on through the underbrush, hurrying faster and faster, his urge for vengeance expanding inside him like a black sun, blotting out all other thought or emotion, even his well-honed sense of con-trol and command.

It was at that precise moment that he was struck from behind, an immense blow that took him off his feet, laid him low, pressing his face into the dense mat of pine straw.

Nona was on her way to work when she caught the call. She had never been to the St. Giles's Club, let alone been a member. In fact, barring a murder of one of its distinguished constituents, she had been quite certain she would never set foot inside the club. Now, out of the blue, Deckard called her, urging her to get over to St. Giles's ASAP. She was to be the guest of Jonatha Midwood. Nona had never heard of Jonatha Midwood, but her relationship with Deckard was such that she would not disregard a request from him.

Jonatha Midwood herself let Nona into the club's imposing vestibule. Looking around, Nona wondered whether the club had any black members. It sure didn't look like it to her. Still, she was ready with a smile as Midwood offered her hand. Nona took it, somewhat surprised at the offering as well as the woman's stunning beauty.

"Thank you so much for coming on such short notice," Midwood said in her creamy contralto. "I know this detour in your busy day must be as inconvenient as it is mysterious."

"Not at all," Nona said truthfully. She had no strong desire to return to the office or to see the boss whom she no longer respected. In fact, following his press conference, she had gone out of her way to avoid seeing or talking to him. "How can I help?"

"Why don't we talk over breakfast." Midwood led the way into what appeared to Nona to be a baronial hall that would not have been out of place in the seventeenth century. Since no one was in evidence, they had their choice of tables. Nevertheless, Midwood chose one on the far edge of the room.

The moment they sat down a waiter shaped like a question mark appeared out of nowhere to pour them coffee and fresh-squeezed orange juice. He set down a basket of warm rolls and pastries, then left them alone.

"I must say, you don't look like you'd need help," Nona said, dropping three cubes of sugar into her coffee and stirring slowly.

"I'll take that as a compliment," Midwood said. "Nevertheless, I do."

Nona sipped at a spoonful of coffee, found it more than agreeable, and said, "Maybe I'm not the right person to help you. I just got fucked over by my boss. Was I surprised? Hell, no. He's a politician, not police. Still, it hurt. He disappointed me."

"What happened?" Midwood asked, digging into the breadbasket.

Nona told her.

"You were the one who solved the triple murder?"

Nona nodded. "Me, myself, and I."

"Then I think you're definitely the right person to help me."

Redbird counted to ten, slowly, with the kind of deliberation colored by neither surprise nor fear. The attack from behind had, in fact, caught him by surprise, but it had served as a splash of icy water, bringing him back to himself.

The wounded driver was on top of him, he surmised. He was struck on the back of the head by a hard object, possibly the butt of a handgun. He groaned, not too theatrically, and, at the same time, drew the Ka-Bar knife from its sheath. He took three deep breaths, then jackknifed his body, torquing his torso as he did so. His left arm whipped around as he dislodged his attacker.

As he turned onto his back, he saw that his attacker wasn't the driver, after all, but Jack McClure. The two men had switched coats; he had been so intent on vengeance, he had missed the small, telltale signs that should have tipped him off.

Even as he fell backward, McClure was aiming a Luger at him. Without another thought, he flicked the Ka-Bar. McClure hurled himself to one side, but the edge of the knife struck his wrist, sending the Luger flying.

Jack saw the assassin coming at him. He raised his elbows in an attempt to protect himself. The assassin came on, and Jack feinted to the right, kicking out with his left leg. The man went down on one knee. At once, Jack was on him, but he misjudged the damage his kick had done. The assassin buried his fist in Jack's solar plexus and, when his guard came down reflexively, struck him on one cheek.

Jack's head snapped back as he crashed down onto the pine needles. As the assassin climbed onto him, he scrabbled beneath the needles with a hand, grasped a rough-edged stone, and swung it in a shallow arc. It connected with the assassin's forehead, gouging a horizontal slash from one side to the other. Blood sprayed in a crescent, splattering Jack's face and chest.

The assassin's muscle-knotted forearm slammed down onto Jack's neck. Jack drove the bloody stone along the assassin's arm, opening skin and muscle, causing blood to pour. He used the stone again, but the assassin's fist was coming straight at his face. He tried to turn away, but the forearm had his head pinioned, and when the knuckles slammed into him, he made his body go limp.

Redbird had just finished stringing McClure up by his tied wrists, using an old length of rope he'd found in a dank corner of the bunker, tossed over a concrete beam, when he heard a furtive sound from outside. Quickly donning the coat McClure had been wearing, he placed himself between the open, sunlit doorway and McClure, a mere shadow among others in the dim interior.

Radomil, pistol in hand, poked his head into the bunker. "Jack?"

"Right here," Redbird muttered.

Reassured, Radomil stepped inside, and Redbird slammed a board into his side. Radomil staggered back, Redbird came after him, but Radomil turned and ran in a strange, loping gait, vanishing between the trees.

TWENTY-ONE

As Nona came down the front steps of the St. Giles's Club her mobile phone buzzed. It was close to one o'clock. She had stayed a long time with Jonatha Midwood. Interesting, she thought, that a woman in the CIA needed her help.

"Hello?"

"Nona, it's Deckard."

"Hey."

"Are you with Jonatha?"

"Just left. Why?"

"I have something but I don't want to contact her directly."

"Too dangerous?"

"Right. A colleague I'm working with informed me . . ." There was a brief pause. "You okay to talk?"

Nona checked the immediate vicinity as she climbed into her car. "Hold on." She turned on her radio. "Secure."

"Okay. Jonatha asked my colleague to do some digging and, together, we found something. Leroy Connaston, who you asked me to get info on earlier, was involved with someone named Pyotr Legere.

Legere was with Connaston in Bangkok when Connaston was killed. And, Legere turns out to have been Dennis Paull's not-so-confidential informer. Seems he was working both sides of the street."

"Fuck. There's a breach a mile wide."

"It gets worse. Every piece of intel Connaston passed on to Paull, the Syrian knew first."

"So Jack—"

"McClure isn't the mole," Deckard said.

"That's the best bit of news I've heard all month."

"He was set up. It was the Syrian's plan, a misdirection."

"While the real mole—Krofft—could continue his work." Nona continued to use her side mirrors to monitor her environment. "But this is all pie in the sky. The man's the head of the CIA. What we need is proof—hard, irrefutable evidence that can be brought to the president."

"I've got something—maybe. I found a backdoor money trail from Connaston to someone in the D.C. area."

"Who?"

"Not who—what," Deckard said. "A company called Long-formz, Ltd."

"What does this company do?"

"No idea," Deckard said, "but I have an address."

Thirty-five minutes later, Nona drove up to the pale stone building on S. Wayne Street in the Penrose Park area of Virginia. It looked like nothing more than a private house in a residential area.

Nona got out of her car, crossed the sidewalk, and trotted up the steps. On the left side of the front door was an intercom with a single button. Beneath the button was a plastic strip that said: Longformz, Ltd. Beneath that was a yellow UPS notice. Peering at it, Nona discovered it was an announcement that a third delivery attempt had failed. The package had been returned to the sender.

Noting the invoice number, Nona called UPS on her mobile, read off the invoice number, was subsequently told the name of the sender: SouthEast Fashion. The address was somewhere in Bangkok.

Neither of these meant anything to Nona, but she quickly phoned Deckard and asked him to run them down.

Finally, she turned to the door, rang the intercom. She did not expect an answer, and she wasn't disappointed. She tried the door, but it was locked. Returning back down the stairs, she went around the block to the rear of the building. Trash cans littered the alley. There was a rear door but it was also locked. To the right was a window, the glass too filthy to see inside. The wooden sash was rotting, and it was of no moment for Nona to get through it, lift the window wide, and climb inside.

No lights were on. Neither did they work when she flipped the wall switches. The interior was so dim she brought out her flashlight with her pistol, following its focused beam down a hall, narrow, completely unadorned. The odors of neglect and mold caught in her throat, making her choke back a coughing fit.

The rooms on the ground floor were empty, completely bare. Cautiously, she went up the rickety staircase to the second floor, and immediately saw the body. It was lying facedown on the threadbare carpet of a room facing the staircase. She could see no stain of blood, but it might be contained beneath him. Only one way to tell.

The smell of rising damp was overwhelming as she proceeded into the room. She had crouched down beside the body, identifying it only as male, when she heard the click, as of an electronic device turning on.

A moment later, with a great whoosh that blasted up the staircase, a wall of flames came leaping up from the ground floor with so much force and heat she knew the fire must have been started with an accelerant.

No time to ID the body. As smoke was injected into the room, she leapt over the corpse and, without a second thought, she crossed her arms in front of her face and hurled herself through the window.

Glass shattered, following her down like a spray of hail. She was out in the fresh air, tumbling. She knew how to fall. Relaxing her shoulders, she rolled herself into a ball. Still, she struck the street with a force that knocked all the breath out of her.

For some minutes, she lay on her back, her vision shaky, her thoughts scattered. Slowly, she regained the use of her limbs. Then, above her, a gout of flame burst out of the window through which she had escaped, and she roused herself. Picking herself up, she ignored the pains throughout her body and limped to her car.

Before driving away, she called 911, reporting the fire. On the road back to D.C., she dialed Deckard. When he answered, she said, "Take special care. Someone's one step ahead of you."

Jack had feigned unconsciousness. When he opened his eyes, he looked for the assassin. Not finding him, he expanded his field of vision. He had heard Radomil's voice, but now there was no sign of him, either. He was, at least for the moment, alone in the bunker.

He saw the surrounding pine straw, the phalanx of tenacious weeds that had cracked open the concrete, infiltrating the bunker like a superior army host. Sunlight had pried open a thin rent in the ceiling. It seemed as if a bolt of lightning had frozen in the air and on the dirt floor, as if the interior of the bunker had slipped the bonds of time itself.

He smelled the remnants of fire, the dank, latrine odor, the scent of long dead animals, saw, here and there, the scattered bones of small mammals, the desiccated remnants of a lone bird, yellow-and-black beak and gray-and-brown feathers more prominent than its poor, hollow bones. One stained wall was tagged with the slogan "BEFRINAZIGULD," a Danish phrase meaning "Release Nazi gold," rendered in the splendid multi-scrolled artwork of a graffiti artist of the first rank. But there was no sign of the man who had attacked him.

He kicked out, starting a momentum that swung his body back and forth like the pendulum of a grandfather clock. He saw the vectors in three dimensions, calculated the angle at which he should jackknife his legs. Within seven swings he'd reached that point. Jack-knifing his legs over his head, he grasped the rope between his ankles, hauled himself up until he could take hold of the rope with his hands.

Resting his chin against the top of the beam to which the rope was attached, he relaxed, collapsed his shoulder muscles, drew his shoulder blades together. Doubling his legs up to his chest, he passed his hands beneath them. Now, with his hands in front of him, he was able to free his ankles, then his wrists. He slid down the rope to the concrete floor.

He heard the sounds of tramping boots; the assassin was returning. Jack quickly headed for the deepest shadows of the bunker, where he found a length of iron pipe. He worried that the assassin had gone in search of Radomil and prayed he hadn't found him.

The assassin entered the bunker. Jack used the instant of his shock at seeing the empty rope swaying gently from the rafter.

"Who are you working for?" Jack said, stepping out of the shadows.

Redbird whirled, gun in his hand. Jack slashed out with the iron pipe and the gun went flying.

Redbird, in a half-crouch, shook his head. "You caused the death of something precious to me. I was ordered to bring you back to Washington, but, fuck that, I promise I'm going to kill you."

Jack swung the pipe around and around. "You're in no position to promise anything."

Redbird licked his lips, looked from Jack to the gun lying on the ground not three feet from where he stood.

"Come on," Jack said. "Let's see if you can shoot me before I crack your skull in two."

A flicker of sunlight and shadow among the trees beyond the bunker appeared in Jack's peripheral vision. Someone was coming—Radomil? But, no, this was someone smaller, fast, and lithe.

And then Jack's nostrils dilated, and he knew.

Annika.

Redbird, noting the minute flicker in Jack's attention, leapt for the gun. His fingers had curled around the grips, his forefinger on the trigger, and he was bringing the gun to bear, when Jack let fly the pipe. Its side struck Redbird and he went down, but he did not lose his grip on the gun.

To Jack's left, Annika emerged from the trees. Redbird saw her and got off a shot toward her before Jack stove in his forehead with the pipe.

"Jesus, I didn't want to do that," he said as she came up to him, clearly unharmed. "Now I'll never know who sent him after me."

"Does it matter? He's dead."

"Of course it matters," Jack said. "Whoever he was working for will send someone else."

"Not if you disappear."

He eyed her warily. "You've been following my progress. Why?"

"I wanted to make sure you were safe." Her whisper was like the slither of desert sand lifting and falling.

"No, you were tracking me for the Syrian. Did he hire this man?" But before she could answer, he shook his head. "No, he's American—I know by his accent and his mannerisms. He belonged to someone in the American intelligence community." He stared down at the corpse.

"That kind of man would never have revealed an iota of information."

Jack felt anger climb in him, principally because he knew she was right. The only way to deal with people like this assassin was to kill them.

She looked at him with an expression of relief, but it held more than a grain of amusement as well. "We've come all this way to arrive at the place where we started."

"We started in Moscow, you and I." But he knew what she meant.

"You know I was watching you long before."

"You were my first and only stalker."

She laughed softly. When she touched the nape of his neck, he shivered.

"You see?" she whispered. "Nothing has changed."

"I can't just vanish," he said. "With Paull's death, I've become a liability to an elite group of people in my government. Most of them think I'm a murderer and traitor, and for at least one I know too much," he said. "Plus, my connection to you cannot make anyone in D.C. happy."

"Why? We're friends."

Jack laughed. "Is that what you think we are?"

She folded her arms beneath her breasts, levering them into even more prominence. "How do *you* see it?"

"We're enemies, Annika." He shifted uneasily. "You made that very clear when you chose to stay with the Syrian."

"I told you—"

"I don't care what you told me." He knelt down, started going through Redbird's pockets. "You lie more easily than you tell the truth."

"That night in Rome, I ordered Radomil to save you."

"So he said."

She watched him as he methodically searched the assassin. He came up with a bankroll of euros and a car key.

"How did you find me here in the middle of the forest?" he asked.

She smiled. "That phony ambulance was like a beacon on a moonless night. I followed my nose until I saw the armed men and slipped between them. It wasn't difficult."

"Not for you, I imagine." His fingertip found something hard, which he fished out of Redbird's pocket. A mobile phone. He pressed the on button and the phone's screen lit up. "Numbers," he said with an unmistakable note of triumph in his voice. There was only one in the phone book, the same number that was the last incoming call.

Jack pressed the redial button. After two rings, he heard the telltale hollowness on the line and knew the call was being rerouted to a secure government line.

A moment later, Henry Dickinson said, "Redbird, talk to me."

"Redbird is dead," Jack replied.

There was a sharp intake of breath, followed by, "Who is this?"

"I'm coming for you, Dickinson," Jack said. "You and all your kind."

"Who the fuck is this?!" Dickinson screamed.

"Precisely who the fuck you think it is."

Jack disconnected, then when the phone rang again, he dropped it to the ground and watched Redbird's blood flood greedily into the back, destroying the battery and the SIM card.

"Nicely done," Annika said.

"You," Jack said. "Shut up."

Jack squinted in the dappled sunlight. He breathed deeply of the piney, oxygen-rich air. "Radomil must be somewhere around here," Jack said. "Redbird hit him in the ribs."

"How badly was he hurt?" she said.

"I don't know. We need to find him."

She shook her head. "He's a master at hiding; we could search for a week and never find him."

"Still. You don't want to try."

"Iraj is waiting."

"Fuck Iraj. Today will be the end of him."

The trees were thick around them. The buzzing of flies rose and fell like the tide, as if they were approaching the ocean. Jack took several steps away from her as if to go on his own.

"Do you really hate me," she said, "or is this an act?"

He stopped, turned back to her. "You're married. Radomil told me. He told me the whole story."

"Ah." She came toward him, closing the distance.

"What the hell does that mean?" He turned his head to look at her, but they were too close. Her image blurred disconcertingly.

"It means nothing," she said. "And everything."

He felt her like a series of gentle electric shocks. He realized, to his shame, that if he acted on what his body was telling him, he'd take her this instant.

"There were so many times I wanted to tell you."

"Don't give me that."

She nodded sadly, stoically. "You're right. I never would have told you; I never wanted you to know."

"You're not divorced."

"No."

"Or separated."

"I was separated from Rolan less than a year after we were married. We haven't been together since."

"I want to meet him."

"No. You don't."

He thought about that for a moment. "You're right. I never want to see him."

They pressed on, through the thick stands of pines, whose tops bowed and spoke to the rushing wind. Here and there, high cumulus clouds could be seen through the gaps in the trees. Light fell like lances, striking the ground and seeming to sever it from itself.

Stopping them, she turned to him. She touched him in the intimate way only she could, and the core of him leapt like a flame ignited.

"Tell me you don't love me," she said. "Tell me you don't love me, and I'll believe it."

"I don't love you."

"I don't believe you." She leaned in and kissed him, her lips opening under his, in a way that made the two of them one. When she pulled away from him, she said, "I want to stop here."

"Here? Why?"

"I want you to make love to me. I've been dreaming about it for months."

"This place is full of death."

She nodded. "Yes. Now we change that forever."

He opened his mouth to say no, but, God help him, he couldn't. He didn't want to.

Radomil, palpating his side with extreme care, felt certain that a rib had been cracked, maybe two. He had run from the bunker in an asymmetric zigzag course no one would be able to follow.

He made his stealthy way out of the Oberforst. He did not look back over his shoulder, he did not think about the bunker. It was far too dangerous to go back there. Besides, his choice was now between Jack and his half-sister. He would press on to the chalet that had been Jack's objective. Now Namazi was his target. Killing the Syrian was the only chance he'd ever have now of saving Annika from a life that was eating her alive.

The icy tinkle of an Alpine spring lured him. He knelt beside it and, like a child, scooped the bracingly cold water in his cupped hands, splashing it again and again onto his face, until all the caked blood was sluiced away and his superficial lacerations were numbed.

Near the eastern edge of the forest, he spied one of the men the assassin had left to hem in his prey. Creeping up behind him, Radomil clipped him over the ear with the butt of his gun. The man bellowed as he went down. Radomil struck him again for good measure, harder this time, with a good deal of anger, then relieved him of his Luger before he dragged him roughly into the deep shadow within the trees.

He saw his crumpled Audi and the ambulance as soon as he hit the tree line. The moment he broke cover, a shot whined past his shoulder. He spun, shouted in pain as his cracked rib shifted, saw a second gunman advancing toward him and shot him with the Luger. The gunman, arms splayed, crashed backward and lay still.

Radomil, ignoring the pain in his side, sprinted over to the vehicles. His car was useless, but the ambulance's engine turned over just fine when he turned the ignition key the driver had left behind. Just as he was pulling out, the third gunman appeared. He aimed and fired. A bullet smashed through the windshield. Radomil ducked, trod hard on the accelerator. The ambulance leapt forward and struck the gunman full-on. Radomil felt the bump as the body was ploughed under first the front then the rear wheel.

Swinging around, he drove off, powerful engine thrumming, as he headed back onto the highway that would lead him to the posh ski resort of Méribel and Iraj Namazi.

The jagged shard of sunlight lanced through the trees.

Jack, whose heart had quickened even while his mind had slowed, was acutely aware of his body wresting control of his emotions, obliterating—or was it obscuring—past betrayals, desperately trying to fabricate a flimsy new present out of passion and what passed for love.

He watched her, drinking in her exquisite beauty—her large, wide-apart eyes that seemed to see him and only him, her half-parted lips, breath like honey and cloves, the press of her high breasts, her strong thighs, and the portal he knew so well between them. All these terrible, awesome, knee-weakening treasures he saw and smelled. He felt as if he and Annika were already both naked.

Two pairs of hands rose and fell, fingers working, and soon enough they were naked. He pushed her up against a tree as his lips closed over hers, as he felt her mouth open, felt her moan seep into him as her tongue wrapped his. Her nipples were hard even before he kissed them, but when he did, she threw her head back, and arched her neck. Her right leg rose, opening herself to him, and she guided him into her, cupping him tenderly as he thrust into her, as she gasped with the pleasure, holding him in her warm palm as he moved rhythmically, faster and faster, until he lost all control. When he shuddered, and she felt him high up inside her, she abandoned herself to her own pleasure, shuddering with him, her buttocks bucking back and forth against his warmth, against the cool concrete—hot and cold, hot and cold, the sensations setting her off over and over again, until she thought the ever higher waves of ecstasy would never stop, would engulf her completely, shatter her into a million pieces, and leave her for dead.

"Jack," she whispered, a long time later, "when I'm with you, I don't know who I am."

"You always know who you are, Annika. That's the problem." He shifted against her, not wanting to let go of the animal stickiness gluing them together. "You know, and I'm left in the dark, wondering. Always wondering."

She put a hand alongside his cheek, stroking it. "I don't want that. I swear I don't."

He shook his head. "I don't know what you want, Annika. I doubt you do, either. Your life has been twisted up with your grandfather's. He was everything to you—father, mother, mentor, confidant."

"But you—you're my friend, my lover."

"For other women that might be enough," he said. "But I wonder whether it is for you."

She smiled enigmatically. "You think I need more than other women?"

"I think you need everything."

"You judge me so harshly."

"How else should I judge you?"

"I was going to say . . . But no." She turned away and reached for her clothes, then abruptly changed her mind, coming back to him, her hands on his bare flesh. Her eyes were large and glittery, tears throbbing on her lower lids, as if revealing the anguished beat of her heart.

She kissed him, tenderly, but with passion, so that when she took his hand and grazed it against her mound he found it newly wet, and she pressed herself against him. He pushed her away, and now she wept openly, but she no longer protested when he stepped away.

"Don't go to Méribel," she whispered after him. "For the love of God, I'm afraid for you."

Jack could not think about that now. "Do you want me?"

"Yes." He could barely hear her.

"Then tell me."

"I want you."

He came back to her then, and she opened herself to him, and again there was no space between them. He was inside her, part of her, and she him. There was only the two of them, entwined on the precipice of an abyss so terrifying neither of them could look into its maw.

Much later, as they dressed, she said again, "You mustn't continue on."

"But I have no choice, Annika. The Legeres must know who murdered Dennis, who the mole really is. The son is dead; only the father can save me now."

"This is all conjecture on your part."

"No. I see the pattern, Annika. Your grandfather understood what I can do. Giles is the key to saving me."

"And if he can't—or won't?"

"I'll worry about that then. For now, I can only go forward."

"Iraj wants you dead."

"He's not the only one. But one way or another, we will be done with each other in Méribel."

She kissed him with half-open lips. "I'm not your enemy," she said. "I never was."

He touched her, staring into her eyes. "Tell me, how can I be sure?"

William Rogers, busier than ever, had quite consciously not looked at the clock on his desk, but then an image of Justin crossed his mind. He tried to wipe it away, couldn't, and saw that it was almost four o'clock. That, for him, was the witching hour. The time of day when his desire needed quenching and, no matter how much he fought against it, he knew he'd lose the battle. Already defeated, he rose and slipped on his overcoat.

No chauffeured car for him, no bodyguards, not even a taxi, blocks away from the office. Only public transportation would do, delivering him up onto M Street in Georgetown, where he walked, trembling hands in pockets, down to the canal. He turned right, went along the cobbled street until he came to a ramshackle brick building, next to a café touting Fair Trade coffee from Tanzania and Bali.

Rogers, who lived and breathed in a den of secrets and mysteries, was a mystery to himself. He had lived his adolescence and young adulthood in denial, the rest of his life in a dreadful duality that often struck him as being akin to Dr. Jekyll and Mr. Hyde. The one ignored the other, and vice versa. The strain this bifurcation put him under was immense. He had tried to abstain—repeatedly— without ever achieving an iota of success.

He paused on the building's crumbling stoop, feeling distinctly lightheaded. He looked left and right, but no one was paying him the slightest attention. He was about to ring the bell, when the door opened inward. Justin, half in shadow, barefoot and naked to the waist, beckoned him inside. Rogers was momentarily paralyzed. That is, until Justin pulled him inside, led him down a dingy, windowless corridor into the familiar small room.

There were the slightly grimy calico café curtains on the window, the brass bedstead, the homey quilt coverlet, and Justin's bluepoint Siamese, fastidiously licking his forepaws as if he had just eaten.

Justin's wide lips curved into a knowing smile. The bluepoint purred as Justin closed and locked the door, before returning to where Rogers stood in an agony of anticipation.

"I believe I know what Billy wants," Justin said, dropping to his knees.

Just over an hour later, Rogers was back in his office, running through electronic files, when the door opened and Krofft stepped in unannounced. He held a manila envelope under his arm. Rogers swung away from his computer terminal. "What are you doing here, Director?" Krofft laid the envelope on his desk.

"What is the meaning of this?" Rogers felt paralyzed again, but for an entirely different reason. A terrible premonition began to work its way through his mind, like beads of cold sweat running from his armpits.

"If you won't open it, Bill, I will." Krofft tipped out its contents. When Rogers saw the 8 x 10 photos of today's sexual encounter with Justin, he leapt up, his chair tumbling backward.

"How stupid of you to fuck with one of my people," Krofft said. "Copies of these have already gone out to the major political blogs. Next stop, the papers and the networks. Pack your bags—you're finished."

Rogers took one twisting, disoriented step, then another, before he fell to his knees and vomited all over himself.

TWENTY-TWO

"If you're determined to continue on to the chalet," Annika said, "then I have to go now."

Jack studied her. "Back to Namazi."

"I have no choice."

"There's always a choice."

"My grandfather—"

"Gourdjiev was a monster," Jack said.

Her eyes grew dark. "You're confused. My father was the monster."

"A different kind of monster—but still . . . Your Dyadya only thought of himself, of his plan, whatever the hell that was."

"He was a good man."

"He aligned himself with a terrorist—a gunrunner, a creator of cannon fodder, a man who helps manufacture wars, suffering, deformities, and death. My God," Jack said, "look at your husband—"

"Don't speak of Rolan. You know nothing—"

"Because you've kept his existence from me."

"You were better off. I was protecting you."

Jack's laugh was bitter. "From what? The truth."

She shook her head, as if shaking off his words. "I have to go."

"Now you've aligned yourself with him."

Her eyes sparked. "Iraj will be waiting. It will be difficult enough as it is to explain why I haven't brought you back with me."

"Tell him I threatened you." Jack put two stiffened fingers against her temple. "Tell him I was going to blow your brains out."

"He'd never believe—"

Jack struck her so hard on her jaw she staggered. Blood leaked from the corner of her mouth and her lips were already starting to swell.

"He'll believe you now," Jack said.

Annika took her sweet time leaving the forest, and drove slowly, in order to give Jack as much of a head start as she dared. She didn't wipe away the blood that still oozed from the corner of her mouth. She glanced at herself in the rearview mirror. The swelling continued, and the center of it was already discolored. So much the better. The worse she looked, the more difficulty Iraj would have disbelieving her. Her face hurt, but it was Jack who had hurt her, so the pain was only skin deep. He had done what she would never have asked him to do; he had done what needed to be done in order to protect her from Iraj.

She drove fast, with an expert's elegance, through the undulating countryside. Already, in the hazed distance, she could make out the jagged white shoulders of the Alps, among which Giles had made his exile's home. With the road unfurling like a black ribbon ahead of her, she thought about Jack—the fierceness of his outrage, the righteous fury he directed at her. And yet, they had made love, not once but twice, and in that cauldron of desire all other emotions were swept away. She had felt him melt—not only his body, but his heart, as well—until they merged, facing each other as their true selves, stripped of artifice, lies, the cloaks of deceit under which they both hid. He loved her—no matter what he said or how he acted, she *knew*—and this alone kept her going, not her grandfather or her vow to him or her sense of duty. But love.

Love.

She felt the place where Jack had struck her, felt the soreness, the heat as if it were a caress. The swelling was a secret badge of his love, his talisman hiding in plain sight.

Love, that strange and exciting beast, spread its wings, like a phoenix rising from the flames.

A text from Namazi pinged her cell. He was waiting for her at a small airfield close by, where a helicopter was ready to take them to Giles's chalet. He asked her whether she had Jack with her. She didn't bother to reply.

Soon thereafter, she spotted the helo, squatting like a vicious insect on the tarmac. Beside it stood Namazi, speaking on his mobile phone. The moment he heard her vehicle approaching, he ended the call and pocketed the mobile.

His expression was expectant, nothing more, when she pulled up and he saw that she was alone in the car.

"What happened?" he said as she climbed out from behind the wheel. "What the hell took you so long?"

She put her face—bloody and swollen—up for his inspection.

"He did this?"

She stared at him, not bothering to reply.

Sporting an unpleasant grin, he said, "Your vaunted charms are eroding, *chérie*. Must I also find a new lover?"

The threat made her sick to her stomach.

"And what of the information you claimed he had?"

"I have it."

"How did you get it out of him?"

"How do you think?"

"Even so." Iraj studied her critically. "I can't believe he would give it to you willingly."

"He had no idea what it was."

Namazi nodded in grudging assent, took her by the elbow, guided her into the helo.

Annika's flesh crawled at his touch. This turn of the wheel of her life, binding her to this man, was almost over. She and Jack had discussed the end before she had left. And if this wasn't to be the end? If something went wrong? she asked herself as she strapped herself in and the rotors began to turn, the violent engine revving up to a deafening pitch and a heavy vibration rattling her teeth. If her freedom failed to materialize? Then what? She turned to Rolan, who sat strapped into a rear seat. He stared vacantly at her, a vague smile on his face.

"Iraj, what is this?" she shouted. "What have you done to Rolan?"

Namazi bent over her, the better to be heard over the hellacious noise. "It seems your husband harbors a desire to kill me." He cocked his head. "That isn't what he confided in you, is it, *chérie*?"

Annika's heart skipped a beat. *Rolan,* she thought, *how could you be so stupid?* "What are you talking about?"

"While you were off having your tête-à-tête with Jack McClure, Rolan tried to knife me. I saw it coming; I sedated him. It took two injections; he has an exceptionally strong constitution, that one."

Iraj slipped into the copilot's seat and buckled up, leaving Annika in the rear, facing a man she once knew intimately, who was now as opaque to her as a block of clay.

The helo rose off the ground and, banking steeply, headed west, toward the Alps. What a great effort, Annika held back her tears.

TWENTY-THREE

Giles Legere rode the elevator from his basement wine cellar down to the subbasement. Halfway down, he forgot why he was making the trip. The blank space in his mind, like a flabby sheet of wet paper from which all the writing had been washed away, startled him, then terrified him so badly that he staggered, only the padded red velvet walls keeping himself from crumpling into a heap on the small square of inlaid marble floor. There were two elevators in the chalet. The large one he and Galina used to travel between the three floors and, on occasion, the wine cellar, when they did not feel like climbing the staircase, and this one, hidden away in a secret side shaft, which went down into the room carved out of the mountain's bedrock. This chalet that had once been the home of Giles's father now kept the secrets of both Giles and Dyadya Gourdjiev.

Giles knew why he was making this trip, and yet he didn't. Somewhere, in another part of his brain that was still functioning normally, was the answer. The trouble was, the harder he tried to get to it the less legible that sheet of wet paper became.

Secrets.

His lips curled into a sly fox's grin. The thought of keeping secrets from Galina gave him a warm feeling inside, as if he had taken a large swig of the slivovitz his father had kept in the highboy on the wall facing the head of the dining room table. Late at night, when he assumed everyone was asleep, the elder Legere would pour two fingers into a glass and down it in an instant.

Giles, crouched like a mouse on the stairs, had watched many times as his father drank and sang to himself in a language Giles did not know and had never heard since. Once, when he was nine, he had tried the slivovitz, pouring the clear liquid into the same glass his father drank from. The liquid fire had caused him to choke, gag, then vomit, making so much noise that he had roused his father, who had beaten him severely with the leather strap that hung on the back of his parents' bedroom door.

The elevator came to a stop, reminding him that he had a mission to accomplish. The doors opened, but he stood rooted to the spot, his mind as fog-bound as a seashore. As often happened nowadays, his mind, at an impasse, would dredge up another subject entirely. As he stepped out onto the polished stone floor, Pyotr popped into his mind. He had not shed a tear upon learning that Pyotr was dead—and why should he? Pyotr was not his flesh and blood, though Galina claimed that he was. In fact, by her very claim he suspected she was lying. Galina had brought the babe with her when she moved in with him. Giles had always suspected that Pyotr's father was some politburo big shot who wanted the child about as much as Giles did. A man who doubtless had a wife and children of his own. What need had he of a bastard?

Galina, he'd noted, had not shed a tear over Pyotr's death, either. But then she was a strange woman, deeply private, someone who excelled at keeping to herself. Not that Giles minded—he had more than enough secrets of his own, without peeking into her head. Anyway, he had a strong suspicion he wouldn't like what he found there.

Pyotr had been problematic from the time he could string together his first sentence, which, if Giles remembered correctly, was, "I want more."

Typical of the little bastard. No matter how much Giles gave him, he wanted more. There was no sense that he could ever be satisfied. And Galina was worse than useless. She was too busy spinning schemes to be bothered raising a child. Of all the women he had known, Galina Yemchevya was far and away the least suited for motherhood; her maternal instincts had so atrophied they might never have existed. On the other hand, she had refined her natural affinity for giving physical pleasure. But, as Giles well knew, her attributes could cause as much pain as pleasure.

Perhaps it was best that Pyotr was dead, Giles mused as he wandered the halls like a wayward mountain king. No more anguish, no more frustration. Only a peace, of sorts. Or then again a whole bunch of nothing. Who could know?

In the subbasement, closer to the glories and disappointments of his past, Giles grew calmer. He was better able to think, as if the ever-present fog inside his head had lifted enough for him to glimpse slivers of the person he had been, the person he had wished to be.

His father, a highly successful surgeon, had insisted that Giles follow in his footsteps. When Giles showed a distinct aptitude for downhill and slalom skiing, his father had said nothing, but the next time it came for Giles to be punished, his father broke his leg.

"Let's see you ski with a pin in your knee," he'd said.

After he had been expelled from medical college for incessant fornication, to spite his father he did nothing at all. Following the old man's death, he had made it his life's work to sell off his father's prized art collection, one piece at a time. In doing so he amassed a fortune, after which he moved to Moscow, at the behest of one of his best clients, cementing his reputation as one of the preeminent art dealers in the world. The smuggling of politburo secrets along with the artwork came later, at the behest of the same client—his idea all along, or so Giles had thought, until, following the first few successes, the client had introduced him to Dyadya Gourdjiev, an individual as shadowy as he was charismatic. Never before or since had Giles encountered someone so able to effortlessly command a room and so reluctant to do so. Giles was instantly attracted to the charisma, and unwittingly became the latest in a long line of Gourdjiev's human shields. Of course, it wasn't long before he cottoned on to his role; but it didn't matter a whit. He was making too much money, had been introduced into too many power circles—in business, the arts, and politics—for him to care. After all, he was using Gourdjiev as much as Gourdjiev was using him.

Or so he had thought.

The essential takeaway about Gourdjiev was that when you thought you had him figured out, you were dead wrong, and by the time you figured *that* out, he'd already gotten what he needed from you. It was a perverse form of inversion: you bought into being a part of the Gourdjiev money-making regime, gladly did what he asked, were well rewarded, only to discover that your jeopardy was far greater than he had led you to believe and that he had used you for a purpose you could not have conceived of.

Case in point: Pyotr was dead because of Giles's involvement with Gourdjiev, which went far beyond using his legitimate business to transport Gourdjiev's secrets to clients all over the world. It was only after Gourdjiev's death that Giles had discovered that this very house, which Gourdjiev had visited any number of times—had become the repository of the secrets he wished to pass on to his designated heirs.

Those secrets were, in fact, hidden in these bunker-like rooms deep inside the mountain. Which, now that Giles's impaired mind was rolling in that direction, was the very reason he had come down here.

Finally recalling his errand, Giles began to whistle an old folk song his grandmother used to sing to him many years ago. Recently, he had tried to tote the secrets up, but like counting sheep to fall asleep, his mind clouded over before he could finish.

He was about to enter the chamber with the Dufy painting of horses in the Bois de Boulogne when, even this far underground, he felt the heavy vibrations running through the structural girders of the chalet, and he thought: helicopter! At last! He's here!

With an eagerness he hadn't felt in years, he hurried back into the corridor and sent the small elevator up to the roof.

When Jack heard the *thwop-thwop-thwop* of the helo's rotors he was within hailing distance of Giles Legere's chalet. The helo was not yet visible, passing through ribbons of low cloud, but he pictured it in his mind's eye and knew it was close.

He had driven hard and fast up the narrow road that wound around the mountain on which the chalet was perched like a clawed raven. The chalet was an odd structure, more like a medieval Tibetan castle—three stories, built of black rock, shiny as obsidian. At its corners—the four cardinal directions—what appeared to be titanic talons curved out and down. Most oddly of all, the chalet had a flat roof, impractical in snowy climes like this one but essential for the placement of a helipad, which was where the helo must be headed. What other surprises were in store for him?

Not wanting to announce himself, he abandoned Redbird's car just shy of the last bend in the road that ended at the chalet and proceeded from there on foot. It wasn't long before he came upon the ambulance that had plowed into Radomil's Audi. After Annika had left, he had checked outside the bunker for any sign of her half-brother, but without success. He had, however, stumbled upon the bodies of the three gunmen. As Annika had predicted, Radomil was alive and well.

As Jack had driven up, he had been afforded an almost 360-degree view of the chateau. Each changing angle had been recorded in his mind, one overlapping the next, and now, as he made his final ascent, he had a clear three-dimensional picture of the structure with all its quirks—rooms and interior staircases, illuminated through windows, balconies, drainpipes, and curious dead spaces—and had already determined the best way to gain entrance without being noticed.

Even though he was certain the helo contained Iraj Namazi and Annika, he was now grateful for the distraction it afforded him. All eyes inside the chalet must be on the descending helo, giving him a brief window in which to get inside the chalet without being discovered.

Racing around to the west side of the chalet, he climbed a mature pine and, when he was high enough, edged out onto a branch he deemed thick enough to hold his weight. Even so, the soft pine wood began to bend the farther out he inched, and he was obliged to leap off the branch before he wanted to. His body struck the edge of a balcony, his fingers grasped the lowest of the wood railings, and for a moment he hung there, gasping, his breath coming in clouds, condensing in the chill air.

Slowly and surely, he raised himself up until he was able to swing one leg then the other over the railing top, slithering, at last, onto the balcony. The curtains were pulled across a large picture window, making it impossible to see either in or out. Crossing to the slider, he was unsurprised to find it locked. Inserting a pick between the insulation strip on the stationary window and the locking mechanism on the slider, he soon had the lock open.

Carefully opening the window just enough for him to drop into the room, he slowly pulled aside the heavy damask curtains, only to be confronted with a Smith & Wesson Centennial 442 Airweight aimed directly at his chest. Holding it was a strikingly beautiful woman.

TWENTY-FOUR

As Namazi's pilot maneuvered the helo for landing, it came under automatic weapons attack as four men in white parkas spewed out of the elevator and began firing. Sliding open the helo's door, Annika tossed out a flash grenade, then turned her head aside as it exploded.

Moments later, Namazi leapt from the helo and, half bent over, hurled himself at the most forward of the men. Ripping the FN SCAR-H / Mk .17 out of his hands, he smashed the butt into the man's face, then, using short bursts of gunfire, took down the remaining three. Two were dead by the time he got to them. The last was not. Namazi slammed his boot down on the man's neck, crushing it.

After throwing the guards' weapons over the chalet's side, he and Annika trotted across the rooftop, opened the door into the chalet, and stepped into the elevator.

"Welcome to the Legere chalet," Galina Yemchevya said, the ghost of a smile playing around the corners of her wide, sensual lips. She wore black raw-silk slacks, a wide patent-leather belt, and a low-cut oyster-gray blouse that showed off the snowy tops of her admirable breasts. On her feet were velvet slippers. "I've heard so much about you, Mr. McClure, I'm pleased to finally meet you in the flesh."

She shook her head. "My name is Galina. Galina Yemchevya." A small laugh burst from her like a helium-filled balloon. "Dyadya Gourdjiev must have mentioned me many times."

"I'm afraid he neglected to tell me about you," Jack said. He was leaning back against the window sash, his hands behind him. "Perhaps he had forgotten you."

Galina's eyes narrowed, then she laughed again, but this time it was with an unpleasant edge. "I doubt that highly. We used to fuck like bunnies."

"But the lifespan of rabbits is so short."

Galina, angry now, waved the barrel of the gun. "Whether you've heard of me or not is of no consequence. Let's get going. Now that the Syrian has arrived, the conclave in the subbasement Giles has been waiting so long for is sure to begin shortly. I assure you we don't want to miss it."

As he complied, stepping forward, Jack said, "You sound like you don't share Giles's enthusiasm for this conclave."

"Why should I?" Galina scarcely bothered to keep the bitterness out of her voice. "For more than twenty years, he's been held hostage to that devil Gourdjiev's promise that he'd be part of the old man's legacy." Her mouth twisted, as if she were about to spit. "All Gourdjiev brought us was an inescapable alliance with the Syrian. I argued against it, to no avail. I want no part of the devil's legacy."

"Gourdjiev stashed his legacy here?"

"In a vault he had specially made. There's no key to the vault. It's opened by inputting a series of numbers. Giles has a part of it, Annika another, and the Syrian another."

"He couldn't have trusted the three of them to wait until he died," Jack said.

"Of course not. But he trusted Annika. Besides, all three of them were loyal, bound to him irrevocably, by either blood or money, as long as he was alive." Galina grimaced, almost, it seemed, against her will. "He exerted a kind of mesmeric control over people. But now he's dead, thank Christ." She waggled the gun barrel again. "Let's go."

As Jack came abreast of her, he sensed her movement, the raising of the S&W over her head to strike the back of his head. Ducking away, he shoved her into the heavy drapes. She staggered, regained her footing, and aimed the Airweight at him. Jack struck her, and she whipped the S&W around, the side of the barrel impacting his cheek. He knocked the gun out of her hands, and she raised them, thumbs outstretched to dig into his eyes. He tried to deflect her, but she was an athlete, hard-muscled and determined. She slammed his head against the windowpane, then her thumbs were at his eyelids, pressing inward.

Light flashed behind Jack's eyes. His hands felt along the edge of the curtain, grabbed the cord, and wrapped it around her neck. He pulled tight. The instant Galina's hands came away from his eyes, he whirled her around so that he was behind her. She arched backward, her mouth open as she tried to scream, but only a tiny bleat emerged. She whipped her head back and forth more and more violently even as she reached back, tried to slash his face with her nails. He reared his head out of the way, tightened the cord more, cutting deeply into her throat.

Now her thrashing became desperate, her strength increasing with her body's will to survive. She slammed her body into his, pitching him painfully against the window. Again and again she tried to dislodge him.

He kept his grip, bringing her to her knees, and then, all at once, she toppled over, her heels spasming weakly, before she grew still. Jack scooped up her S&W, stashed it in his waistband.

The elevator descended through the three floors and the basement. When it reached the subbasement and the doors opened, the first thing Annika saw was Giles.

"Come out," he said in a conciliatory tone. "We know why we're all here."

"Is that why your men tried to kill us up on the roof?" Namazi said, stepping out, Annika just behind him.

"Galina hired those guards, not me. She doesn't take kindly to her house being invaded."

"And you can't control that bitch?" Namazi said.

"You know the answer to that. No one ever could—not even Gourdjiev."

Namazi shook his head. "You're a pathetic excuse of a man."

"You really could use an attitude adjustment."

The Syrian whirled on him, glaring. "I should kill you right here."

"But you can't," Giles said, nevertheless stepping cautiously back. "We all need one another. That's how Gourdjiev planned it."

"I curse that bastard's black, shriveled heart to the lowest circle of hell," Namazi said.

"You don't believe in hell," Giles pointed out.

"Neither did he," Annika said.

"We should at least call a truce," Giles said, addressing the Syrian. "Our enmity only makes matters worse."

"There can be no peace among us," Annika said. "Only a need—an imperative—that's greater than any one of us."

Namazi shouldered past Giles. "The four of us are what matter. Where the hell is McClure? We can't complete the vault sequence without him."

"Four? What are you talking about?" Giles said. "Three blocks will open the vault. We each possess one-third of the number sequence."

Namazi turned to Annika, his face livid. "You said your grandfather had given McClure one of the number blocks."

"I lied," Annika said.

Slowly but surely the drug Namazi had administered to Rolan had worn off. Now Rolan unbuckled himself and walked to the helo's door.

The pilot turned in his seat. "Where d'you think you're going?"

Rolan turned, stalked back to him, held out a hand. "Gun."

The pilot looked up at him. "Are you crazy?"

Rolan struck him so hard in the face the pilot's body rocketed back and forth. Bending over, Rolan took the Mauser from the dazed man. Then he went out the door, jumped down onto the chalet's roof.

Like Annika, Radomil had been to the chalet before. His mother had taken him and his twin brother when they were boys. The chalet had been under reconstruction then, so Radomil had been witness to the workmen putting in the central elevator shaft, as well as a far smaller shaft that ran just within the northern wall. At that time, he'd had no idea what that secondary shaft was for, but now, inside the chalet, avoiding the armed mercenaries Galina had obviously hired to keep her and Legere safe, he encountered it again and realized it housed a second, smaller, secret elevator.

He'd seen Namazi's helo landing on the roof and knew that's where he wanted to be. That's where Namazi would be making his escape.

He pressed the button to summon the small elevator. He watched as it rose from the lowest level, the subbasement, then opened the narrow door and stepped into what looked like a vertical coffin, lined with plush red velvet, a little circular light in the center of the ceiling. He pushed the button for the roof. Before stepping out, he sent it back down so his use of it would remain unnoticed.

As Jack stood up, letting go of the curtain cord, he heard sounds coming from just outside the door. Then there was a sharp knock and a voice raised in concern.

"Ms. Yemchevya! Are you in there? Are you all right?"

Stepping over the corpse, Jack flattened himself behind the door an instant before it swung open. A guard, holding a Glock 9mm at the ready, entered the room, saw Galina lying on the floor. As he swung around, Jack landed a blow with the butt of the Airweight to the base of his skull. The guard went down and stayed down.

Jack stepped over him, peered cautiously into the corridor. It was deserted, at least for the moment. He stood in the doorway, the window through which he had climbed at his back. Closing his eyes, he oriented himself, as if he were looking at the chalet from his vantage point outside. He had noticed the solid walls where, in other chalets, there would have been windows. That area was to his right.

Moving out into the hallway, he made his way toward the windowless area, but before he could get there, he was stopped by a blank wall that, unlike the sidewalls, was papered in a busy cabbage rose, trellis, and vine pattern. He had reached the end of the hallway, but from his recon he knew more of the chalet existed on the other side.

Pressing his ear to the wall, he rapped with his knuckles, but could discern no hollow sound. Returning to the room, he rummaged through Galina's pockets, found a pack of cigarettes and a lighter. He had smelled the smoke coming off her hair and clothes.

Returning to the end of the hallway, he lit a cigarette and took several puffs, letting the smoke out slowly. It drifted up to the ceiling. He stepped along the wall. Suddenly, the smoke he released swirled toward the wall instead of the ceiling.

By viewing that section of the wall from different angles, lit by the flame from the lighter, he could discern a seam, cleverly hidden along the line of a trellis. Using his fingernails, he traced the seam into which the smoke was vanishing. He moved closer, felt the draft of air being sucked into the space on the other side of the wall.

He pushed on areas around the seam until a section of the wall, wide as a door, swung open, and he stepped into the hidden area beyond.

"I should kill you." Namazi shot Annika a menacing look.

"What a disappointing response." She shrugged. "But it's only what I expected."

Giles stepped between them. "We need to keep our personal animosities on hold or we'll never get this done." He looked from one to the other.

"This way," he said, after a moment's silence.

He led them to the room with Jean Dufy's prancing horses amid the leafy greenery of the park. Giles unlocked the door and flipped a switch. A spotlight illuminated the Dufy. Stepping over to it, he swung it aside, revealing a formidable-looking wall safe.

Iraj stood very near her. "This isn't over," he said under his breath.

"You're terrifying me," Annika said. "Input your fucking numbers."

"If you recall," Giles interjected, clearly uneasy with their display of hostility, "we were informed there was a certain order. I was to go first, then Namazi, and Annika last."

"Do it then," Namazi said without taking his eyes off Annika.

Stepping up to the vault, Giles typed in a set of numbers, then moved back so Namazi could input his. After he was done, Annika typed in hers.

The click of the tumblers opening sounded as loud as a rifle shot.

Iraj's eyes glittered.

Giles licked his lips.

Annika turned the lever and opened the safe's door.

Leaning forward, they all peered inside. At nothing.

The vault was empty.

TWENTY-FIVE

"What the fuck?!" Iraj said.

Giles scrabbled in the depths of the safe, unable to believe the evidence of his eyes.

Annika began to laugh. She laughed so hard tears sprang into her eyes and she began to wheeze. When she had regained her breath, she said with a biting savagery, "You fools! You're both fools to take my grandfather at his word. He despised both of you."

"You bitch," Namazi said, baring his teeth. "Don't you understand, he's made a fool of you, as well."

"I don't care. I don't want any part of his legacy."

The Syrian frowned. "Another of your lies. You've been bent on doing what Gourdjiev told you just so you could come to this moment."

"That was then," Annika said with an equanimity that clearly disturbed him.

"God in heaven, Galina was right." Giles began to pull at his hair. "I allowed Gourdjiev to lead me around by the nose. I did his bidding without question, no matter how abhorrent his orders seemed—beginning with you, Namazi. I curse the day Gourdjiev introduced us."

The Syrian turned to him. "Shut up, Giles!"

Giles shook his head, lost in his own thoughts. "All these years, I chased after a phantom—a dream he created for me."

"I said shut the fuck up!" Namazi drew a gun from beneath his jacket.

"No!" Annika screamed.

But it was too late. The bullet plowed into Giles Legere's chest, slamming him against the wall, like a pitched ball. He gave out a little sound as he slid down the wall to sit, splay-legged like a child.

"It's beyond me why you'd want to save that sorry sack of shit." Namazi grabbed Annika's hand, dragged her out of the room and into the vertical coffin. They rose up toward the roof and their waiting helo.

Jack flicked the lighter and the flame rose up, sending his shadow streaming across the wall. The odors of must and decay, mold and an unending damp that even the freezing temperature couldn't allay burned his eyes and the inside of his nose.

A light switch brought several bare bulbs to life. Jack found himself in a warren of rooms—no more than cubicles. What windows had once been there had long ago been removed, the rectangles walled up and papered over.

Cobwebs and dust balls were the only furniture. That was not to say were empty. In one, he found a metal box filled with vintage diamond jewelry, in the second, another box, this one covered in velvet the color of oxblood. Inside were piled handfuls of gold fillings, some still embedded in human teeth.

Farther back, he approached an object covered in a canvas drop cloth. Peeling it away, he discovered a painting of heart-stopping beauty. His dyslexic mind sorted through images he had seen at lightning speed. He looked closer and then was certain. He was looking at the *Portrait of a Lady*, by Caravaggio, believed to have been destroyed in Berlin's Friedrichshain Flakturm, in 1945.

Continuing on, he found statuary by Donatello, a painting by Raphael, one of the Virgin by Giotto. All thought lost or destroyed, each one in a small, square, windowless room, as if on display in an eerie, forgotten museum.

He stood back, heart pounding. Giles Legere's chalet was a storehouse of treasure looted by the Nazis during the war.

Giles was colder than he had ever been in his life. But, somehow, he didn't mind. He thought he'd sit here a while and enjoy Dufy's prancing horses, so noble and proud. He imagined them in another season, pulling a sleigh of laughing, red-cheeked people, warmed by drafts of hot buttered rum and red-and-white-striped candies.

With perfect clarity, he recalled a day snuggled between Christmas and New Year's. The Swiss Alps wrapped their mighty arms around him. He was bundled beneath a quilted blanket, sitting between his parents in an old-fashioned, horse-pulled sleigh. His mother was a month away from death. He was eight years old.

"Sugar," his mother had said, *"are you happy?"*

He remembered the Alps, the snow, the red noses, the high curved back of the sleigh, the horses, snorting and prancing through the drifts.

"Yes, Mama, I'm happy."

It was the last time he had been happy.

Until this moment of utter peace, watching Jean Dufy's horses, the riders, the park, remembering the snow falling, his breath steaming, his mother close beside him, asking the crucial question amid the utter, silent grandeur of the Alps. His mind traveling back in time, that winter moment and this one, conflated forever in a perfect fusing of future, present, and past.

The chalet seemed eerily quiet. It was time. Jack needed to find a way to reach the roof. Soon enough, he found it. This secret section of the chalet had its own staircase—a narrow spiral with worn stone treads rising up through a cramped, conical space.

The window he had entered was on the second story, so he had only two flights to reach the roof. He launched himself up the stairs. It seemed criminal to leave the hoard behind—both historians and art critics should have access to it—but that was hardly his concern now. Annika and the Syrian were uppermost in his mind.

He passed a door to what must be the third floor and hurried on, mindful that the stone walls surrounding him were starting to converge. Some way up above his head, the space was reduced so drastically it appeared a preteen would be hard-pressed to squeeze through it. From the picture in his mind's eye, he guessed the top of the conical space turned into one of the chalet's great curving iron talons he'd observed from the road far below.

The spiral stairs gave out just below the severely narrowed space, though the central column continued to climb all the way to the top. Jack stopped, stymied. There was no egress to the roof from where he was perched. He could go back down to the third floor and, perhaps, find another way up. But he could just as well find himself trapped in this secret, windowless section of the chalet.

The only way was to continue up.

Grasping the metal pole, he wrapped his legs around it and began to shimmy his way upward. The conical space continued to press in around him, until he could feel the freezing stone against both shoulders. He drew them in, compressing the width of his body as escape artists do when wriggling out of a straitjacket.

He continued upward until the space was simply too narrow for him to continue. But now he felt gusts of icy air flow over him and, like the cigarette smoke that had led him here, he followed it until he saw light ahead of him and knew that he was crawling through one of the massive talons at the corners of the chalet.

The brightness of the sky crept toward him, then, all at once, he was at the outlet, emerging into dazzling light after his long dark climb, all of Switzerland's Alps, it seemed, ringing the clear, cerulean sky.

Radomil had been on the roof for some minutes, hiding behind one of the mounds of snow that had been shoveled off to the edges. He had seen the sprawled bodies of the guards. They were all unmoving, undoubtedly dead. It was curious, though, that there was no sign of weapons. He saw the helo, crouched and waiting, its rotors revolving, ready for liftoff at a moment's notice.

There was no sign, however, of either Namazi or Annika, which meant they were still in the chalet. Then he saw a door slam open and his half-sister being dragged by the Syrian across the roof toward the helo.

At that moment, another man—big, eyes wild and staring—appeared, taking aim at the running figures. Radomil launched himself at the big man, knocking him sideways as he squeezed off a shot. Namazi and Annika ducked but kept running, reaching the open door to the helo and climbing in. He heard Namazi shout an order and the rotors began to revolve more quickly. The helo was ramping up to lift off.

The big man struck Radomil on the jaw, and he saw stars. He rose, kicked Radomil in the ribs, then aimed at the helo. Rolling over, Radomil kicked the back of the big man's right leg. Again, the shot went wide.

Then the big man turned, aimed his handgun at Radomil and shot him between the eyes.

A split instant later, he himself was rocked back by a bullet that struck him in the chest. He whirled. Jack sped over the roof toward him. He raised his Mauser, but Jack fired again, and he was taken off his feet. Jack fired a third time, leapt over the body, and sprinted toward the helo, which was now rising off the rooftop.

For an instant, he doubted he was going to make it, but at the last moment he put on a burst of speed, then leapt, grabbing onto one of the landing runners just before the helo took to the air. Immediately, it began to bank to the right.

Jack scrambled up onto the strut. From there, he could lever himself into the interior of the aircraft. As he began this maneuver, Namazi stuck a gun out through the doorway and fired. Jack spun away beneath the fuselage just in time, but the Syrian extended himself to fire again.

"McClure!" he shouted over the helo's noise and the rushing of the wind. "You're well and truly fucked now. You poor bastard, you shot Rolan! You killed her husband!"

Jack worked his way around the strut, but at that moment the pilot banked and dipped the helo. Jack's foot slipped and he began to fall backward. Lunging out, he caught the door handle just as he lost his footing altogether.

For a long, heart-thumping moment, he swung in the air, then, as the helo shuddered upward, he used the momentum to swing himself around to the fuselage. He was just scrabbling for a handhold on the rim of the opening when the door began to slide shut.

The helo banked the other way, shuddering in the wind currents as the pilot continued to try to shake him loose, but this last maneuver worked in Jack's favor, as the door slid back open.

Seizing the opportunity, Jack swung his lower body up and into the interior of the helo. Namazi was still hanging on to the door, in a vain attempt to close it. Jack struck him on the point of the chin and he staggered backward, landing on his shoulder.

"Didn't I warn you to stay away, Jack?" Annika, weeping uncontrollably, held her Bersa aimed at his head. "Why didn't you listen to me?"

"I couldn't stay away." He took a step forward. "You knew that."

"Sadly, I did. And now both Rolan and Radomil are dead."

"Ah, the lovebirds," Namazi chuckled as he rose to his feet. "United, only to be forever torn apart."

"God, I hate you, Jack!" Annika waggled the Bersa. "Stay back."

"You'd better do as she says, McClure," Namazi said. "Or maybe it doesn't matter. She's going to put a hole through you no matter what."

Jack took another step toward Namazi. "You won't shoot me, Annika."

"Oh, but she will. Bank on it."

The helo skimmed over the tiled rooftops of other chalets.

Jack moved a step closer to both of them. Annika was staring fixedly at Jack, or maybe through him. Jack saw his opportunity, saw what he had to do in a lightning flash. He faked to the left and knocked the Bersa away from her.

"Annika, Annika, listen to me!"

But she was past listening to anything he had to say. Witnessing Rolan's death had clearly unhinged her. There was only one other choice. Fighting her every step of the way, ignoring the strikes of her fists and feet, elbows and knees, he doggedly hauled her over to the door. He kicked it open and, as the helo passed over the roof of another chalet, he moved to shove her out. As she was toppling out, she lunged back and snatched the Airweight from Jack's hand, and it went tumbling down. She fell only six or so feet before she hit the snow piled on the canted roof tiles. She slid a bit, then grabbed on, pulling herself horizontally to the roof's edge, where she lay, staring after the receding helo. Jack bit back every emotion that threatened to rise up and overwhelm him.

"Now it's just you and me, Namazi."

As he turned, Namazi fired at him. The bullet put a hole in the fuselage and, for an instant, the helo wavered. Jack sprang at him, slammed his fist into the side of Namazi's head. Namazi turned in his seat. A thick-bladed hunting knife came whistling down, slicing through Jack's coat and shirt, drawing a line of blood across his chest.

The Syrian tried to turn the strike into a thrust, but Jack smashed his right shoulder with such force, it dislocated. Namazi gasped but still managed to transfer the knife to his left hand. Jack grabbed it and repeatedly slammed it down onto the instrument panel.

The helo went immediately out of control, veering downward at a terrifyingly steep angle. It plowed into a deep snowdrift, slowing its momentum somewhat before striking the rocky ground beneath. The two men slammed into the helo's windshield.

Jack must have passed out. He blinked, his lungs working like bellows. He looked around the shattered interior, saw the pilot crushed in his seat. Then Namazi was coming at him, both hands extended. Jack, cocking his right leg, buried his foot into Namazi's sternum. He felt the percussion all the way to his coccyx.

The Syrian was thrust backward against the helo's shattered fuselage. He stared at Jack, his lips drawn back from his hungry teeth. He looked like he wanted to eat Jack alive. A moment later, blood gushed from his mouth. Jack saw that he was impaled on a length of twisted metal.

"Fuck you," Namazi said. "Fuck you."

Jack pulled himself to his feet, every muscle in his body screaming in pain, and picked his way to where the Syrian hung. He smiled as he saw the light fading from the Syrian's eyes. It was a terrible thing, perhaps, but he couldn't find it in himself to feel remorse.

Iraj Namazi, the Syrian, was dead. Into Jack's mind came something that Gourdjiev had said to him: "Words mean nothing, an actor's lines."

Turning away, Jack made his stumbling way out of the wreckage and into the late-day sunshine, where already a crowd had gathered. Sirens were wailing, and someone put their arm around him to keep him from falling.

When he found her, she was lying in the snow where she had fallen. At some point she had moved her arms and legs, making a snow angel.

Jack hunkered down next to her. "Aren't you cold?"

"Numbs the pain."

"Annika, I'm sorry."

"Is he dead?"

He knew she meant the Syrian. "I made sure of it."

"Thank Christ." She closed her eyes for a moment.

He waited for her to speak.

At length, she said, "I thought I could handle him. As it turned out, I couldn't."

"You know, your grandfather made me promise to look after you."

Her eyes grew big. "When?"

"In the hospital, before we left Moscow." His gaze seemed to penetrate through her. "He was dying, wasn't he?"

"Yes. He hadn't long to live."

"So he sacrificed himself."

"It was the endgame he always envisioned." A lone tear leaked out of the corner of her eye. "Only I wasn't strong enough."

"So he enlisted me."

"And yet—"

"You pushed me away," Jack said, "so violently I didn't know what to think, say, or do. It seemed you had become my enemy. You made it impossible to keep my promise."

"And yet you're here with me now."

"Yes."

"You never lost faith."

"I suppose that's true. Deep down."

When she made no comment, he said, "Don't you want to get up?"

"Not now," she said in a small voice. "Not yet."

Jack looked at the snow angel she had made. Perhaps, he thought, she was remembering the one good moment of her childhood.

After a time, he said, "I had to choose between your husband and your brother. He was about to shoot Radomil. I tried to save at least one of them, but I was a second too late."

"I know."

"Now they're both gone. Annika, I'm so sorry. "

"Don't be. Rolan's life ended when he was hurt. He emerged from that a changed man. Better he should have died in the explosion."

"You must have still felt something for him."

She smiled sadly. "We all harbor dreams. Some of them are impossible dreams. Why do you think that is?"

"It's one of the things that makes us human, isn't it?"

She nodded mutely.

"And Radomil."

"Yes, Radomil. I've tried to shed a tear for him, but I can't. Why is that, do you think?"

Jack said nothing, knowing it was a question she was asking herself.

"Maybe," she said, after a time, "the tissue binding us was too thin. Maybe it wasn't there at all."

She stared up at him for a moment. Then she held out her hand and he took it. Together, they regained their feet.

She placed a hand on his arm. "I feel as if I failed him."

"Your grandfather."

"Yes."

"I imagine he felt he failed you."

"I can't believe that."

"You don't want to," Jack said. "But the truth is he failed to protect you from your father. He never could forgive himself for that."

She smiled again, warmly this time. It was clear she had turned her mind away from Dyadya Gourdjiev and her life with him.

"I did okay in the plane, didn't I?"

"You did great," he said. "I was able to get you out of harm's way. That's all that mattered."

"No," she said. "Without you it wouldn't have mattered whether I lived or died." She leaned her head against the crook of his shoulder. "You see? My grandfather finally succeeded in protecting me."

He put his arms around her. A bout of dizziness threatened to overwhelm him, but this time it was purely emotional. He kissed her—on the forehead, both cheeks, and, finally, on the mouth. Her lips opened under his.

The electrifying, familiar taste of her melted everything inside him, a balm that banished his aches and pains, an affirmation that everything he had been through was worthwhile.

EPILOGUE
May 5

Paris, France / Washington, D.C. / Altindere, Turkey

Caro had once read a novel about a man who had been sent to jail because he had hit a girl who had darted out in front of his car. He'd had no chance to stop, and yet, as an object lesson, he had been convicted and incarcerated in a hard-time prison. During her time in Paris, on the run from Iraj Namazi and his people, Caro had read and reread the description of his life there, recognizing his feelings of fear and despair, reconfirming to herself that not all prisons had high walls, razor wire, and steel bars.

Now, as she sat on a bench in the Place des Vosges, near the beating heart of old Paris, she tilted her head up to the early afternoon sky, realizing that, from the time she had fled Namazi's compound until this moment, she hadn't truly felt pleasure from the sun on her face.

The wind brushed her lips, ruffled her hair, and she bit into a buttery *pain au chocolat* with all the joy of a child on Christmas morning.

Iraj Namazi, the Syrian, was dead, his entire network destabilized and rapidly unraveling, as his lieutenants fought each other like hyenas over a corpse.

She had been living under his curse for so long she knew it would take some time for her to fully comprehend the width and depth of her freedom. She could go anywhere, do anything she chose. Freedom was such a new concept for her, for the time being it took her breath away.

She finished her pastry and, brushing the crumbs and bits of chocolate off her lap, decided what she wanted now was a large steaming cup of café au lait.

Rising, she crossed the magnificent square, past the fountains, the children playing, watched over by knots of young mothers, gossiping with one another. There was a sudden burst of babies in Paris, as if life were returning to a field that had lain fallow for years, patiently waiting for this moment.

As Caro walked, she breathed in the scents of the city she had grown to love and knew that, at least for the foreseeable future, she would stay here. As she passed the last bench before the swinging iron gate leading out of the square, a young man glanced up, looked at her, and smiled. He had a handsome, open face, with wide-apart eyes that regarded her inquisitively.

He was finishing a *pain au chocolat* as well, and she paused, wondering whether he, too, wanted a café au lait.

Toward dawn, Jonatha, exhausted from staying up all night checking and rechecking her proprietary intelligence, fell into a shallow sleep, slumped over in a chair at her kitchen table. Slowly, her mind sank into a dream-reality in which she had never met and, therefore, never fallen in love with Lale. She stood by the edge of a lake. Somehow, in the manner of dream logic, she knew the lake was very deep. Far out, she saw a ripple, repeating.

In her hands was a fishing rod. She lifted her arm up and back, casting the line far out into that part of the lake where she had observed the ripple. For some time nothing happened. Then, she felt the tug on the line, and she lifted the rod. The tugging grew in intensity as the hook was taken, and she reeled in the line a little bit at a time.

But at some point, the resistance on the other end of the line began to alarm her, and she could no longer reel in the line. The rod was bent almost double. And, now, with a terrible strength, whatever creature was on the other end began to drag her into the lake.

The water rose above her ankles, then to her thighs. When it reached her waist, she began to panic. She tried to throw the rod away, to free herself, but somehow she was unable to let go, as if it were she who had been hooked.

She was into the lake to the level of her breasts when she grabbed the line and, drawing it to her, began to gnaw on it with her teeth. Every second brought another slip, as she was dragged farther and farther into the lake by the unknown creature, which now seemed monstrously huge to her.

A jerk, more powerful than the others, almost wrenched her off her feet, and she dug in her heels with a desperate strength she didn't know she had. Then she bit through the line and the rod snapped back to its normal shape. The line whipped away from her, vanishing beneath the surface. But now something dark and menacing seemed to coalesce in the deepest part of the lake, rising up, coming toward her . . .

And she woke with a gasp and a shout that brought Lale at a run. "What is it?" She stood naked, hands on hips, her dusky skin burnished in dawn's rosy light. "What happened?"

"I dreamed I never met you. I dreamed I never loved you." She turned. "Lale, there's so much I can't tell you."

"Your job, I know." Lale perched on the edge of a chair. "But I wonder what it's doing to you, what it's turning you into."

She held out her hand, aware that it was trembling slightly. "It's you I love, Lale. Only you."

Lale rose and began to walk away. Jonatha felt a terrible sadness grip her, and a terror of the dream lake whose inhabitant wanted to draw her into it, drowning her.

At the doorway to their bedroom, Lale turned, looked at Jonatha, and said, "I know."

Jonatha watched her disappear into the shadows of the bedroom, a tightness in her throat. But her anxiety was not simply for her relationship with Lale.

She punched in a number on her mobile and waited, a hole widening in the pit of her stomach, until her call was answered.

"Thank God you're okay."

On the other end, Nona laughed. "Of course I'm okay. All in a day's work."

"Almost being burned to a crisp is definitely not in a day's work. I owe you—big time."

"You don't owe me anything," Nona said. "I couldn't find out who was killed at the house, nor could I discover a thing about Longformz, Ltd."

"But you did scrape up something of note. My contacts tell me that SouthEast Fashion is a legit business in Bangkok that Leroy Connaston used as a drop. He must have sent that package to Longformz, perhaps on the day he died."

"But we don't know what was in the package or who was murdered at the Longformz address."

"Just a matter of time now," Jonatha said. "The fact of the fire means we're getting close."

"Speaking of that fire, I've been working with the local fire department. We've confirmed that the fire at Longformz was deliberately set. Traces of butane and bits of foam, which would spread the fire in a heartbeat, were found in the rubble. I'm following up with the arson squad."

"So you're still willing to help me?"

Nona laughed again and said in her best street accent, "Sistahs gotsta stick togethah."

"So you're Jack McClure."

Dr. Karalian studied Jack's face as if he were a student trying to work out the complex formula chalked onto a blackboard. Then he pushed back his chair and crossed to the window of his office, staring out at the steep cliffs of Melá mountain and the ancient ruins carved into them.

"Tell me, Mr. McClure, have you ever been to the Sümela Monastery?"

"This is my first visit to the national park," Jack said, "and I came directly here."

"Pity." Karalian stood with his hands behind his back. "It's a remarkable place, not only historically. It's a power spot. Do you believe there are places in the world that radiate great power?"

"I don't know," Jack said. "I've never encountered one."

"Then you must go up the mountainside and stand inside Sümela."

Jack said nothing, waiting.

"I've been here over thirty years," Karalian said. "Apart from the renewed influx of tourists and Greek Orthodox clergy, the place is much the same as I imagine it's always been.

"It was founded in 386 AD, but it wasn't until nearly a thousand years later that it gained its present size and shape. Since then, the monastery has been overrun many times; the last time was in 1916 by the Russian Empire. The monks of Sümela were entrusted with a sacred icon, which they buried for safekeeping under the vaults of St. Barbara Chapel. It was smuggled out in 1930 by an intrepid monk. I've never seen it, but I wish I had."

Karalian turned from his contemplation of the past. Jack, expecting to see his eyes glazed over with the memories, was startled to see the doctor's keen, piercing gaze leveled at him.

"How do I know you're Jack McClure? These days, anyone can claim virtually any identity."

"I could show you my passport."

"It could be forged, as can any other piece of ID you might have on your person."

Jack spread his hands helplessly. "I am who I say I am."

Karalian grunted. "Tell me, why did you come here?"

Jack inclined his head toward the chessboard. "You were Gourdjiev's playing opponent, as well as his friend."

"There weren't too many things he was passionate about."

"Chess was one of them."

Karalian continued to study Jack. "So you came on a hunch."

"My mind told me that you would be the one person Gourdjiev would trust, that this place would be the one he deemed safest."

"Illyusha." Karalian shook his head. "He said you'd come." The doctor walked over to his desk and sat down. "He left something for you." His eyes did not waver. "If you are Jack McClure."

"How shall I prove it? A DNA test?"

Karalian ignored him. "Give me the number."

"Come again?"

"There is a number—a code, I suppose Illyusha would call it— you must give me. Without it, I cannot hand over the envelope."

Jack had no idea what he was talking about. Gourdjiev—or Illyusha, as Karalian called him—had never given Jack a number. Jack was certain of this. Or was he? Unbidden, from the depths of his subconscious returned a portion of the last conversation he had had with Illyusha.

"This is the depth of my trust in you, Jack," Gourdjiev had confided. *"Words—words mean nothing, an actor's lines. I want you to remember that. No matter what may occur, you must remember that you love each other, that that love will never change, that it is your true strength, your only salvation.*

"You don't understand this now, but I have faith that one day you will."

Perhaps, Jack thought, this was the day.

Making a rapid calculation, he said, "Twelve, fifteen, twenty-two, five."

L-O-V-E.

Dr. Karalian's face broke out into a smile. From a locked drawer he drew out an envelope sealed with red wax, which he handed over.

"You must be a very special man, Mr. McClure."

Jack held the envelope in both hands, as if it weighed far more than it actually did. "Why do you say that?"

Karalian nodded toward the envelope. "Illyusha trusted you absolutely."

"I didn't believe him when he told me that."

"And yet"—Karalian spread his hands—"here is the proof."

" 'Words mean nothing—an actor's lines.' "

Karalian leaned forward. "I beg your pardon?"

Jack shook his head. "Nothing." He looked over at the chessboard. "May I?"

Karalian lifted an arm. "Be my guest."

As Jack stepped over to the chessboard, Karalian rose and followed him.

"Do you play chess, Mr. McClure?"

"Some. I've read the books of the grand masters."

Dr. Karalian produced an indulgent smile. "Not the same, I'm afraid."

"Whose turn is it?"

"I play against myself now. I like to imagine Illyusha to be the black, however."

Thirty seconds after surveying the board, Jack moved the black king's knight.

"Have you suckered me?" Karalian said as he moved his knight.

They played six more moves until Jack moved his queen.

"Checkmate," he said, and Karalian laughed like a delighted child.

Annika was waiting for him outside. She sat in the car's passenger seat, studiously ignoring the building where her husband had been incarcerated for so long, where he had died and been born again as someone both less and more than he had been, a terrifying being without a soul.

"Was it there?" she asked when Jack slid behind the wheel.

When he nodded, she said, "So it's real—it isn't a hoax. My God."

He put the car in gear and drove off.

Jack could smell the eons of history the moment he stepped into the Sümela Monastery, could see it, as well, briefly held in the bright flashes of sunlight that filtered in through the roofless outer chambers.

He and Annika ignored the troupes of tourists, their respective leaders holding up small flags as if they were the standard bearers of the various armies that had conquered Sümela, only to be themselves conquered. In the end, only Sümela survived, mostly intact and now in the process of being restored to its thirteenth-century glory.

Taking her by the hand, he threaded their way through the hordes. He did not stop until they were in the St. Barbara Chapel. Its hand-hewn stone walls were covered with religious paintings of saints, crosses, and God on high, clutching what appeared to be the tablets of the Ten Commandments.

The doorway down to the vault had nothing to commend it, being small, of plain wood, cracked in places. It was almost invisible, hidden in deep shadows, and, therefore, bypassed by the tour guides and ignored by singleton tourists. The moment they slipped through, he was greeted by a waft of frigid air, sharply redolent of minerals, stone that had never been warmed by the sun. He switched on the flashlight Karalian had given him. He had asked for it after reading the letter Illyusha Gourdjiev had left for him.

He was still somewhat stunned that the old boy had been so genuinely fond of him. Given Jack's history with him, that he had been genuine about anything except his love for Annika was, frankly, surprising. And that was another thing. He hadn't trusted his beloved granddaughter with his legacy. Why? Perhaps because he feared that in the end she wouldn't have the strength to stand up to the Syrian?

Shivering in the semidark, Jack turned the flashlight's beam to the craggy walls of the vault beneath the chapel. Unlike those of the chapel itself, the vault's walls were composed of separate rocks and, at some sections, ancient brick, mortared together. This led Jack to believe that the vault, as it appeared to him, was far smaller than the cavern out of which it had been hewn. The walls seemed to be weeping the tears of the Virgin, whose face adorned the central section of the wall opposite the one beneath which the monastery's icon had been hidden and retrieved.

Following the instructions in Gourdjiev's letter, he knelt down and, at the base of the wall, measured off the requisite distance from the corner. This brought him to a roughly square stone approximately the size of a large man's shoulders. He laid out the other implements Karalian had given him and began to etch away at the surrounding mortar. This proved easier than he had imagined. Beneath the layer of "aged" mortar was mostly air.

Sitting down to give himself the proper leverage, he pulled at the stone, which, again, was easier than he had imagined. When he shone the beam on the sides, he saw why. The stone had been set on smooth stainless-steel tracks, which did most of the work.

The stone set aside, he shone the beam into the cavity. He'd been right. Beyond the vault's wall was another space, vast, shadowed, beckoning. Without another thought, he crawled through, Annika just behind him.

Soon enough, they found themselves in the true vault. It looked like a cathedral, with its double line of carved stone pillars that held up nothing. They walked down the center aisle between the pillars. There were six pillars on each side. At the center point, he stopped and shone the beam at his feet onto a circle cut into the floor.

"What is it?" Annika whispered.

In the center of the circle was a stainless-steel ring. Reaching down, he pulled on the ring, and the circle came away.

Inside was the repository of Illyusha Gourdjiev's legacy, wrapped in waterproof cloth. Jack pulled it out and unwrapped it. There was a brass key with a number on it to a Swiss bank account, what appeared to be an ancient icon of the Virgin, and then there were the documents, hundreds of documents detailing the misdeeds of a bewildering array of business leaders, military contractors, government officials, federal officers—the beat went on across borders and continents. But one document grabbed Jack's immediate and undivided attention.

A dossier on G. Robert Krofft, director of the CIA, whose attachment to Gourdjiev was assured through Illyusha's intermediaries, Iraj Namazi and a person whose ghost Jack had been chasing over thousands of miles: Leroy Connaston.

"According to this file," he said to Annika, "Connaston had been a freelance mercenary Krofft had recruited for off-the-radar wet work. Six years ago, Connaston had expanded his work to freelance terrorism, funded by Krofft's sizable stash of black ops money." The irony was mind-bending. "Gourdjiev had Iraj contact Krofft with the evidence of what his pet dog was up to and, from that moment on, he had Krofft in his pocket."

Senses reeling, Jack took a moment to catch his breath. He made a mental note to get this file to Nona as soon as possible. It would both exonerate him and indict Krofft.

But, of course, that wasn't the end of it. This tale had a far darker end. Yes, Krofft was the mole, but he wasn't Iraj's mole, as Dennis Paull and Jack himself had figured. As usual, Illyusha had bought himself a world-class stalking horse. While everyone was running around trying to bring down the Syrian, it was Gourdjiev they all had had to worry about.

Now Jack was in the center of the entire web, one so immense his mind could scarcely encompass it. It seemed likely, then, that

Krofft had murdered Paull because he had compromised Connaston, which he could not tolerate.

Jack, surrounded by an Aladdin's cave of postmodern riches, sat back on his haunches. He pulled out Gourdjiev's letter and, in the light of what Gourdjiev had left him, reread the final paragraphs:

I couldn't trust her with this. Better she believed, as the others who have survived do, that my legacy is a hoax. I made a tactical error in tasking her to take over Iraj's regime. It's too late now to reverse myself—she's in too deep—even I couldn't pull her out. But I believe you can. Only you. I believe your love for each other is stronger than the Syrian's power and influence—stronger than anything else you may encounter. If I've learned nothing else in my life it's the power love possesses. It can bring down the most powerful man just as surely as it can be his salvation. Or, in this case, her salvation.

Annika has been severely scarred. You know this, of course, but what you may not know is how deep the scars run. The depravity of her father knew no bounds. A child, Jack! She was just a child! And the things he did to her—they're unspeakable.

Only love can save her, Jack. Your love.

She loves you. Because of that you can raise her out of the dark void of herself. I fear for her; I have always feared for her—feared that one day, despairing of her past, she would take her own life. Watch over her, Jack. Heal her. With love, it will be easy.

Together you will use the tools I have provided in my legacy. They're yours now, Jack—yours and hers, if you want—to do with as you wish. I have given you the chance to ascend the great Pyramid, to be more, to be Other.

I trust you to wield the power of these tools wisely. You, better than most, know the corruption that lurks within such enormous power. I trust you to resist it. I trust you to use my legacy to help create a better, brave new world.

ABOUT
JACK McCLURE

Jack McClure is a government agent who has lost everything but his job. His daughter was killed in a terrible accident and his marriage disintegrated shortly after. And even at work he is an anomaly: as a guy who grew up on the streets, he always has one foot on each side of the law. But he's also a very gifted agent, with analytical talents that are unsurpassed in the service.

To discover more – and some tempting special offers – why not visit our website: www.headofzeus.com

MEET THE AUTHOR

ERIC VAN LUSTBADER has published more than twenty-five bestselling novels, which have been translated into over twenty languages. In 2003, he was asked by the estate of the late Robert Ludlum to continue the series based on Jason Bourne. His first contribution to the series, *The Bourne Legacy*, was published in 2004. Lustbader has gone on to write eight more Jason Bourne novels.

Discover more at
www.ericvanlustbader.com

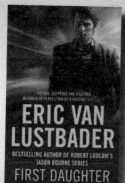

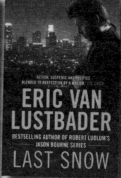

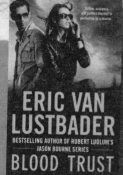

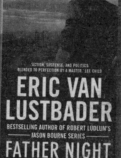

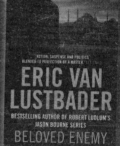

ERIC VAN LUSTBADER

JACK McCLURE

'ACTION, SUSPENSE AND POLITICS BLENDED TO PERFECTION BY A MASTER.' LEE